CITY OF DARKNESS

UNSEEN

EDITED BY ERIN KELLY AND STEWART WIECK

City of Darkness: Unseen
A White Wolf, Inc. Publication

Cover illustration by Doug Gregory.
Cover Design by Michelle Prahler

Printed in Canada

CONTENTS

ASSAULT ON
TREASURE ISLAND

BILL CRIDER

I.

It was raining again, and Lowell and I were looking for a place to hide. Hiding is a good idea when you've just tried — and failed — to kill the head of the Technocracy's Secret Police in San Francisco.

Kane was his name, and we might have gotten him if we hadn't been betrayed by another member of our conspiracy, but that was all behind us now. The thing that mattered most was keeping out of the Technocracy's clutches until we could decide what to do next.

Lowell drove my old minibus through the sheeting rain, cursing the dim headlights and the jerky wiper blades. We couldn't go back to his place. Kane's men had gotten there first. They'd killed a few

of Lowell's friends, and we'd been lucky to get away with
our own skins intact.

"You have a place in mind?" I asked, as Lowell
hydroplaned through a puddle almost as wide as the street.

"Yeah. It's not much, but nobody will be expecting us to
turn up there. I hope."

His voice didn't sound as if he really hoped anything.
Lowell is a Hollow One. He isn't big on hope.

"You mind telling me where?"

"Down in the Haight, Smith. You'll like it there. Some
of the people dress funny."

My name is John Killdeer Smith, and while I'm not from
San Francisco, I knew about the Haight-Ashbury district.
I'd been hoping for something outside the city. We
Dreamspeakers prefer to have dirt under our moccasins.

The neon lights reflected on the wet pavement as Lowell
drove. Sleepers under umbrellas walked along, intent only
on staying dry, going home to a hot meal, or eyeing the items
in shop windows. They were completely unaware of the
Ascension war that raged around them every day, a war that
I was part of whether I wanted to be or not.

We turned down a side street. "This is it," Lowell said.

In the middle of the block, I saw something that looked
like a bombed-out warehouse. On one of the half-collapsed
walls someone had painted a peace symbol years ago. It was
faded now, and part of one side was missing entirely. There
was a faded flower beside it.

"We're staying here?" I said. "You must be kidding."

"Nope," he said, and I should have known he wasn't.
Hollow Ones aren't exactly big kidders.

Lowell pulled the minibus into the wrecked warehouse,
past the crumbling front walls and along a dark, narrow
passageway filled with fragments of concrete and billows of
dust. Suddenly we started down a sharp slope. The opening
had looked like just another shadow to me, and I grabbed
the dashboard to steady myself.

"Basement parking," Lowell said.

"Does anyone live here?"

He glanced at me and brushed his long hair out of his face with one hand. "Who'd want to live in a dump like this?"

"That's what I was afraid you'd say."

We went down two levels, each one darker than the one before.

"This is it," Lowell said, pulling the minibus to a stop beside a concrete support beam that was zigzagged with gaping cracks. "I used to sit in with a band that practiced down here. We were so loud that people could hear us on the street."

I was surprised that the noise hadn't brought what was left of the building down on top of them.

"What instrument did you play?"

"Drums," Lowell said.

That was nice. I'd done some drumming myself, though not on the kind of drums that Lowell had used.

"So this place is safe?" I said.

"You mean from Kane? No place is safe from the Technocracy."

I looked out at the cracked beam. "I was thinking more about earthquakes."

"I wouldn't worry about that," Lowell said, getting out of the bus. "Earthquakes won't be a problem. Light, now that could be a problem unless the electricity is still on. One of the band members had rigged it to work somehow."

In the glow from the minibus' headlights he walked over to a wall and shoved aside a ragged piece of plywood. There was a switchbox behind it. He opened it and threw a breaker. A couple of dim bulbs lit up the darkness off to our right.

"So we have light," I said. "I hope we're as lucky with the earthquakes."

"We will be," Lowell said. "You worry too much."

He may have been right about my worrying, but he was

wrong about the earthquake. It came only a few hours later, while we were eating a couple of McDonald's cheeseburgers that Lowell had sneaked out for.

There was a slight quiver at first, and Lowell and I glanced at one another with alarm. When the floor started rolling beneath us, we made a dive for the minibus and rolled under it just before the building shook down around us like shattered sugar cubes. The ground shuddered, and a small crack opened in the floor beneath me. I could hear rubble bonging off the bus, which bounced crazily over my head.

I lay in an oil stain and waited for the world to end. It didn't, however, and after what seemed like a very long time, though it was probably no more than a few seconds, a suffocating quiet descended. Dust filled my mouth, nose, and eyes.

I was coughing and spitting dust when Lowell said, "Don't try to crawl out from under here. There might be an aftershock."

He was right, but when it came the aftershock was mild compared to what had gone before.

When things had stopped falling, I said, "Can we try getting out from under here now?"

"You can try," Lowell said. "That doesn't mean you can make it."

Typical Hollow One philosophy. I could hear a scraping noise as he pushed something out of his way.

"Can you see anything?" I asked. I was afraid we'd been buried under tons of masonry fragments. I began pushing at the fragments of debris that I could reach.

"We're okay," Lowell said after a while, relief plain in his voice. "I'm out. I don't think we're ever going to drive the bus out of here, though."

It took me a bit longer, but with Lowell's help I was finally able to clear a place big enough for me to squirm out from under the bus and stand up. I could see what he meant about the bus. The building had collapsed downward, leaving a clear shaft above us. We even had some space to move around. All we had to do was climb up the concrete fragments to street level and we'd be fine, but there was no way to drive anything out.

I looked at the minibus. It didn't look as if it would ever run again, even if we could have gotten it to the street. But we could get inside it through the broken windows, and that was good. My bow was in there.

Lowell looked even more haggard than usual, his hair full of gray concrete dust, his face streaked and bleeding from a small stone cut.

"You know," he said with uncharacteristic optimism, "this might turn out all right."

I told him that I didn't see how. To a Dreamspeaker, earthquakes are more than just a shifting of tectonic plates. A disturbance in the Earth can presage more serious disturbances in the fabric of the universe.

Lowell didn't think like that. "The quake might have hit Treasure Island. And the walls might have come tumbling down."

I got his meaning then. Kane had built himself a virtually impregnable fortress on Treasure Island, just off the Bay Bridge. But in the natural confusion that occurs after an earthquake, someone might be able to get inside, especially if the quake had breached his perimeter or interfered with his security.

There was a catch, however. The sound of sirens was already beginning to cut through the dusty air, and I knew that just getting to the island would be virtually impossible in the chaos resulting from the quake.

"I didn't mean right now," Lowell said. "You're too impatient."

He was right. I sat down and leaned back against the minibus.

"I wonder if there's anything left of those hamburgers," Lowell said.

II.

It was a week before we could get anywhere near Treasure Island. We scratched out a living space at the bottom of the shaft, and I spent the time reading all I could about the island in a couple of travel books that Lowell brought me from somewhere, while Lowell made occasional climbs up to the street for food and to see if he could recruit some expert help.

Treasure Island was, as you might suspect, named for the Stevenson novel, and I discovered with some uneasiness that it wasn't a natural formation; it was manmade. It covered between four and five hundred acres and had been created to house the 1939 World's Fair celebrating the opening of the Golden Gate Bridge and the Bay Bridge. There had even been a movie filmed there: *Charlie Chan on Treasure Island.* I wished that Charlie were around to give us some advice.

Charlie wasn't, of course, and neither were his sons. The best substitute Lowell could find was a man named Tommy Blinn, a Hollow One whose best friend had been killed when Kane's men had attacked Lowell's former residence. Blinn was even more bitter than Lowell about what had happened.

"Sure," he said when I asked him if Lowell had told him what we were going to try.

I looked at Lowell, who said, "I had to tell him. We need him."

"It's dangerous," I said.

Blinn didn't care. "They killed Gary Crane. I'll do what I can to keep them from killing anyone else."

In addition to being a bit more headstrong than most Hollow Ones I had known, which was an admittedly small number, Blinn didn't look like anyone's idea of one of that following. He dressed in black, true, but he was tall and broad-shouldered, with legs like redwoods.

"He knows how to shoot, too," Lowell said. "He pulled

a hitch in the Army when he was a Sleeper. He even knows a little about tactics."

"All right," I said. "Do you have anyone else in mind?"

Lowell hesitated and gave Blinn a look out of the side of his eyes.

"Well?" I said, knowing I wasn't going to like whatever it was he had to say.

"Jelly Ann," Lowell said. "We could use Jelly Ann."

"Who's Jelly Ann?"

"She used to be a burglar. She was good, too. Never got caught. That's how she got her name — because she was so slick."

"A woman?"

"What does it matter? Don't be sexist, Smith. Say we do get on the island. Say we even get inside the perimeter. What then? We need someone like Jelly Ann."

What could I say? We couldn't get Charlie Chan.

"Bring her on down," I said.

■

Jelly Ann was short and thin, with short black hair and black eyes that looked right through you. She had on dirty camos with the tops of the pants legs stuck in scuffed combat boots. She took charge right away.

"You got a map?" was the first thing she said.

"Pleased to meet you, too," I answered.

"Screw that. You got a map or not?"

Lowell, standing behind her, shrugged. Blinn was grinning, but he kept his mouth shut.

"Just one that came in a tourist guide," I said.

"Better than nothing, maybe. Lemme see."

She stuck out her hand. I got the map out of the minibus glove box and handed it to her. It was small and really showed nothing more than the rough outline of the island as it had been before Kane took it over.

She barely glanced at it before shoving it back at me. "What a piece of shit. This the best you got?"

"That's it. If you don't like it—"

"I'll let you know what I like and what I don't like, Smith. Gary Crane was my friend, too."

The way she said it made me realize that Crane had been more than just a friend, but I didn't inquire into the relationship. Jelly Ann didn't seem to be the kind of person who liked inquiries.

"So you don't really need a map?" I said.

"I don't need a damn thing. There's no place I couldn't get into if I really want in, not even Kane's. But a map would help. When do we leave?"

"You're the expert."

"Right. Give me a day. I need to talk to some people."

She sounded so confident that it never occurred to me to ask her if it might be a good idea to give some thought to one other little matter: Supposing we did get in. How were we going to get out?

III.

We went in at night. No moon. Just dark sky above and dark water all around.

We were in a little rubber raft that Lowell found at a surplus store. Lowell and Blinn were armed with AK-47 assault rifles. I didn't ask where the weapons had come from, but I was betting it wasn't the surplus store. I had my bow and arrows. When it came to killing, I trusted wood.

Jelly Ann refused to carry a weapon. "If you're any good, no one will spot you. So what the hell do you need a gun for? Or a toy bow?"

I ignored the insult. "Are you sure you know what's going on?" I asked.

"I know, all right, and I don't care what you do when we get to the island. I'll get you in, but I won't kill anybody, no matter what they did. Not even if they killed a friend of mine."

That was all right with me. Maybe she was going to use some magick that she didn't want to talk about, but I knew from experience that magick didn't always work against the creatures of the Technocracy. Sometimes you needed a bullet. Or a wooden arrow.

At least we had a plan now, thanks to Jelly Ann. She'd come back the next day with a map of the island, drawn to scale and marked with X s.

"Where did you get that?" I asked.

"I still have a few friends from the old days." She looked at me scornfully. "Professionals. I called in a few favors."

She spread the map on a more-or-less-flat piece of rubble and smoothed it out.

"Here's the front gate," she said, stabbing a finger at the map. "It's on the road from the Bay Bridge. No use trying to get in through the gate, though. Because of the road, it's the most heavily guarded place on the island."

I put my finger on an X. "What does this mean?"

"Guards, with automatic rifles. There's a chainlink fence all around the perimeter of the island, and there are guards every fifty yards. The fence is twelve feet high, and there's razor wire on top."

"We'll never get in," I said, looking up from the map and meeting Lowell's eyes. "We might as well give up."

"Don't be such a wuss," Jelly Ann said.

"Look," I said, "if there's no way in—"

"Who said that?" She looked around at the three of us. "Did I say that?"

No one answered her, and she put her finger on the map.

"The earthquake hit the island pretty hard. Kane's got everything up and running again, but the fence wasn't a high priority. He's got those half-man/half-machine things with rifles running around, and he probably figures the fence can wait. Who's gonna try coming through from the bay with those things on guard?"

"We are, I guess," Blinn said. "Aren't we?"

"Maybe," I said. "How do you know all this, Jelly Ann?"

"I told you. I got friends in the business. Pros. The information's good. You can count on it."

She sounded confident, as usual, so I said, "Then we're going in."

■

The water lapped gently at the sides of the rubber boat, making me a little nervous. Dreamspeakers are always more at home when our feet are on solid earth, which is the source of our power. Break the connection, and we naturally tend to get a little ill at ease.

Our aim was to land on the northeast side of the island. That's where one of the breaks in the fence was, or so Jelly Ann promised us. We knew the guards would be watching it closely, but there was always a chance we could catch them unaware. A small chance, admittedly, but a chance.

Assuming that we got beyond the fence, there was a thick stand of eucalyptus trees between us and Kane's fortress-like main building. Jelly Ann even had a rough plan of the building. Her friends again.

Kane had installed a generating plant behind the building just for emergencies such as the earthquake. Jelly Ann's idea was that we could get into the generating plant more easily than the main building. After that, we'd enter the building through an underground utility tunnel that her friends assured her was there.

If we got that far, which I wasn't betting on, things still wouldn't be easy. Jelly Ann didn't have a map of the interior of the house. Her friends weren't *that* good.

"We'll just have to hope he's in there and that we can find him," she told us. "Nobody ever said this would be easy."

So far it had been, however. As far as we could tell, no one had spotted the little boat that we'd launched from the shore near the eastern foot of the Bay Bridge. The dark outline of the island loomed before us out of the night, and the boat landed on the beach with hardly a sound.

No one said anything. We got out of the boat and pulled it up behind a rock. Wearing black, with black greasepaint on our faces, we were like a part of the night. There was a faint smell of eucalyptus in the air from the grove of trees.

I'd had a bad feeling about things ever since we'd considered trying for Kane on the island, but it was only when I'd walked for a few steps on the beach that I began to realize that we'd made an even bigger mistake than I'd thought. And it was my fault. I should have known.

Treasure Island is *manmade*. It is built of earth, but it isn't a part of the earth. There is no power in it, at least not for me. My magick would be feeble here if it worked at all, while the Technocracy's machines would continue to function as well and as relentlessly as ever.

I reached under my sweatshirt and my fingers brushed the smooth leather of my medicine pouch. There was no tingle of potency, no thrill to the touch.

But it was too late to turn back now. Jelly Ann was motioning us forward.

We walked about twenty-five yards before we came to the fence. It appeared to be perfectly intact.

Lowell said, "Looks like we got some bad info."

Jelly Ann ignored him. She motioned to the left and we followed her along the fence. In less than a minute we came to a place where there was a gash in the wire. The gash was very narrow, no more than a couple of inches wide, and it ran up the fence for about four feet.

There were no guards in sight.

"What the hell?" Lowell whispered. "Can we just pull the wire back and walk in?"

"There must be an alarm system," Blinn said, his voice husky and low.

"With those half-human guards around, they don't need an alarm system," Jelly Ann said. "Besides, if they have one, it's been turned off. The fence is breached, and the alarm won't function until the fence is repaired."

I was liking the whole thing less and less, but Jelly Ann didn't seem bothered.

"Hell, it's only been a few days since the earthquake," she said. "They're not expecting anyone. No one's ever tried for this place before, and they've gotten slack. Come on."

She didn't wait for us. She reached down and pulled at the fence. The bottom came out of the ground, and the links clinked under her fingers. I expected a burst of rifle fire to tear her apart.

Nothing like that happened. She pulled up and back, and in seconds there was a hole big enough for her to walk through if she stooped over.

I looked at Lowell. He shrugged, and we enlarged the hole a bit. Then we followed Jelly Ann into the eucalyptus trees.

IV.

We'd talked about our approach before leaving, and Jelly Ann had suggested that we split into two groups.

"That way, if two of us are stopped, the others can carry on," she explained. "If all four of us make it to the generating plant, so much the better."

It had sounded all right to me, and that's what we did. About ten yards into the trees, Lowell and I angled to the left, while Jelly Ann and Blinn headed off to the right. Each pair would makesort of half circle, getting as far from the other pair as possible to split up any pursuit.

The funny thing was that there wasn't any pursuit. I could hear the wind in the leaves, and there was a humming in the distance that might have come from the generating plant. Nothing else.

Where were the armed guards? It didn't seem right that Kane, who was after all the head of a secret police force, would be sitting at home unprotected, waiting for us to come and kill him.

And he wasn't. I heard it before Lowell, a sound that was a kind of swift sighing, almost like the wind but swifter and more deadly.

Dogs. Dobermans, blacker than the night and completely silent. Kane must have had their larynxes removed.

They were on us almost before I could react. I got my bow up as the leading dog made a leap for me, and he clamped down on the bow rather than my arm. I could hear his teeth crunch on the wood, and then I rolled backward, throwing both the dog and the bow over my head as hard as I could.

The dog's skull made a dull cracking noise when he hit a tree behind me, and I turned to see how Lowell was faring. The other Doberman had him down. Lowell's feet were kicking the air, and I think he was trying to scream, but nothing was coming from his throat except for a strangled croaking noise.

I ran over and straddled the dog, getting an arm around his throat and a hand clamped on his head. I pulled him back and up, his hard body straining against me as if it were solid muscle. His teeth were still clamped in Lowell's sweatshirt, which stretched out until it finally shredded apart. I wrestled the dog to the ground and lay on him until he stopped kicking and was still.

He'd come around eventually. I'd cut off his oxygen only long enough to render him unconscious, not kill him, or so I hoped. I didn't have anything against the dog. I was after his master.

I retrieved my bow, which would need sanding to remove

the tooth marks, and checked on the other dog. He'd have a severe headache later, but he too would be all right.

So would Lowell, who was sitting up and rubbing his throat, which was bleeding only slightly. The dogs were well-trained, probably meant to hold us until the reinforcements arrived rather than kill us.

And reinforcements would be arriving soon. I was sure of that. The whole set-up had been too easy from the start, but only because Kane had wanted it that way. He'd let us get onto the island and into the grove because now he had us right where he wanted us.

I knelt down beside Lowell. "We have to get out of here," I said.

Lowell looked over my shoulder. "Too late," he rasped.

I turned and saw that he was right. Four of Kane's guards were standing there looking at us, weapons in hand.

I started to say something, but the one in front shot me. There was a sharp, stinging pain in my chest, and then fire spread through every vein in my body.

After that, my legs and arms melted. I was out before I hit the ground.

◼

When I came to, I was sitting in a wooden chair.

Sort of. It was more like I was *strapped* in the chair. My head felt the size of a Buick, my mouth was as dry as Arizona, and my tongue was thick and swollen. Other than that I seemed fine. I wriggled my fingers and toes. Everything seemed to work.

I opened my eyes and blinked in the light. I was sitting in a white room — white floor, white walls, white ceiling. Lowell was in a chair to my right, but he was still out. I wondered what kind of drug they'd shot us with.

A door opened and closed quietly behind me. I started to turn my head, but after I'd moved it a millimeter or so I changed my mind. I was afraid it might fall off. So I just sat and waited.

A man walked past me. He was short and pudgy, with closely cropped iron gray hair. When he turned to face me, I could see that his eyes were black and shiny as polished basalt. His nose was slightly hooked and looked as if it might have been broken at some time in the past. His lips were full and a little too red, or maybe it was just that the rest of his face was too white.

"Hello, Mr. Smith," he said. "I'm Kane."

He looked like photos I'd seen, yet he wasn't exactly what I'd been expecting. I'd thought he'd be bigger, more muscular, more — I don't know. He looked like a pornographic filmmaker rather than the head of the Technocracy's secret police.

"How do you know me?" I asked, or tried to. My swollen tongue wasn't working very well.

He seemed to understand me, however. "I know everyone in San Francisco, especially the recent arrivals who are trying to kill me."

I was sure he did. He'd known I was there from the beginning, thanks to the one who'd betrayed me and Lowell's friends a few days earlier, though I didn't have to worry about him any longer. Where he was, he wouldn't be bothering anyone.

"I don't suppose it would do any good to deny that I wanted to kill you," I said.

Kane smiled. His full lips drew back and revealed very white, though not very even, teeth.

"No good at all."

"I didn't think so."

"No, you're too smart for that. What I don't understand, Mr. Smith, is just exactly *why* you want to kill me. Would you mind telling me that?"

He sounded genuinely puzzled, which was hard for me

to understand. I would have thought that Kane, of all people, would have known why I wanted to kill him.

But then when I thought about it a little longer, I wasn't so sure that I knew the answer to his question myself.

"I was told to kill you," I said.

He shook his head impatiently. "I know that. You and your friend there," he gestured toward Lowell, who was still unconscious, "and Frankie Lee. A Dreamspeaker, a Hollow One, and a member of the Akashic Brotherhood." He paused. "Whatever happened to Frankie, by the way?"

"I don't know."

"Of course you do. But never mind. It doesn't matter." He spread his hands. "But back to my original question. You were told to kill me, so you agreed to do so. Why?"

There wasn't a simple answer to that question, but I thought I might as well give it a try.

"Because I believe that your ideas of Ascension are wrong. You don't believe in freedom; you believe in controlling man and the Earth. You put your faith in the rational, in your technology, your machines. You use the Earth's resources and you don't replace them. You change people into *things*. I don't believe in any of that."

"What do you believe, then?"

He seemed as if he might be really interested, so I said, "I believe in freedom. I believe that there's something beyond the rational, a place you can't reach with the power of reason alone. And I believe that man belongs to the Earth; the Earth does not belong to man."

He smiled again, a fatherly smile, not at all unpleasant. "Thank you, Chief Seattle. And what do you think of my little island, then?"

I should have known that he would have considered the effect of the manmade island on magick. That was undoubtedly why he'd chosen it as his refuge in the first place.

"It's not a bad idea from your point of view," I said. "But I wouldn't want to live here. Now let me ask *you* something."

"Please do."

"Why did you have Lowell's friends killed? They didn't have anything to do with me or him."

Kane's smile disappeared. "So I've been told. The truth is, Mr. Smith, that I don't always have control of the people I send out on certain missions. I was genuinely sorry to hear that those people had been killed. I assure you I had nothing to do with it. The people responsible have been punished, if that matters."

He sounded very convincing, and I found myself believing every word. Could it be true that I was wrong and he was right? It went against everything I'd ever heard or been taught, but I found myself being persuaded by everything he said.

"What do you want from me?" I asked. "If you're such a nice guy, why did you have me drugged and brought here?"

"Frankly, I hoped to persuade you to stay here as my guest for a few days. I hoped that you might begin to see my side of things a little more clearly. That way you might be able to tell my side to others you know. They might not be so eager to kill me if they could hear that I'm not the monster they seem to believe I am."

He was extremely convincing. I sensed my feelings for him changing. He was not evil, not at all. How could I have been so wrong?

"One other thing," he said.

"What?"

"About the others who came onto the island with you. I haven't been able to locate them. Do you have any idea where they might be?"

"No," I said, and it was the truth until an instant after the word was out of my mouth.

That was when I looked up at the air-conditioner vent on the other side of the room, high above Kane's head.

There was a face peering back at me through the grille that covered the vent, a face belonging to Jelly Ann.

V.

It was a lucky thing for Jelly Ann that I didn't see her until after I'd spoken, for I realized suddenly that had I known her whereabouts, I would have betrayed her in a heartbeat.

And in some dim region of my mind I realized something else. The drug that Kane had used to knock me out also had another effect, one that had allowed Kane to cloud my mind, to convince me of things that I otherwise would not have given a second's credence.

With the latter realization came the power to free myself from Kane's influence. Even now I am not sure where that power came from.

I've always thought it came from the chair, as strange as that might sound.

The chair was made of wood, and there is power in wood, power that a man can preserve if he cuts the wood himself and shapes it by hand, with a proper regard for its properties and the spirit which dwells within it. I had shaped my bow and every one of my arrows with that regard.

Even the Technocracy can't remove the power of wood completely, not even by cutting and shaping it with machines.

Or maybe the power didn't come from the chair at all; maybe it came from somewhere else entirely. Maybe from my medicine bag, which could have retained something of its potency even on a manmade island.

But wherever it came from, the power *did* come, and I threw off Kane's influence and saw him for what he was. Or for what I had always believed he was.

All these things happened internally and in microseconds. Then the grille crashed down from the vent and Jelly Ann dropped into the room. She was unarmed; but Blinn was right behind her, surprisingly agile for such a big man, and he leveled his assault rifle at Kane.

The door behind me crashed open almost simultaneously with the falling of the vent, but I couldn't see what was going on back there. I could only guess by the furious expression on Kane's face that his men had been a fraction of a second too late.

"Cut Smith loose, Jelly Ann," Blinn said. "Then do Lowell."

Jelly Ann reached into her pocket and her hand came out holding a switchblade with a black plastic handle. The blade snicked open and caught the light. I don't know where she got it, but it was an impressive knife.

Also sharp. It sliced through the leather straps holding me to the chair as if they were cheap cotton thread.

I stood up and my head didn't fall off. After a second or two, my balance returned more or less to normal. By that time, Lowell was also standing, but he hadn't recovered quite as much as I had. He was leaning heavily on Jelly Ann, who still held the knife in her right hand.

I took a step toward them because I could see that he was too heavy for her, but he fell before I could get to them.

That's when the shooting began.

■

Blinn had the rifle, so they went after him first.

Bullets stitched him from groin to shoulder, splattering the white wall behind him with his blood. His finger was clamped down on the trigger of the AK-47 and its clip emptied as he fell, but the bullets went harmlessly into the walls and ceiling.

Kane tried to sprint past me and get out of the line of fire. I made a dive for him and knocked him to the floor. He kicked at my face. I turned away and the heel of his shoe caught a glancing blow on the side of my head. My nausea returned, and I thought for a second that I might vomit. I bit back the bile that flooded my mouth and swallowed hard.

I heard Jelly Ann screaming, but I couldn't make out the words. I grabbed at Kane's foot and dragged him toward me just as an explosion rocked the room. Something hit me hard on the forehead, and I lost my grip on Kane as the concussion from the blast drove me backward and away from him.

Someone else was screaming, a man this time, and then Jelly Ann was holding my arm, trying to pull me off the floor.

"Get up, Smith!" she yelled. "We gotta get out of here!"

The room was full of dust and smoke. I coughed and tried to clear my eyes.

"Kane," I said — or coughed. "Where's Kane?"

"Don't worry about him. You'll never find him in all this smoke, and if we don't get out of here, we're dead meat. Are you coming or not?"

I stood up. I still couldn't see anything more than three feet away because of the smoke.

"What about Lowell?" I asked. I didn't have to ask about Blinn.

"Lowell's over there on the floor. I think he's still alive. Let's move it."

She led me across the room to where Lowell lay. He was breathing, but that was about all.

"Can you carry him?" Jelly Ann asked.

I bent over and picked Lowell up. It wasn't easy, but I got him over my shoulders in a fireman's carry.

"Let's go," Jelly Ann said.

The smoke was clearing, and I followed her toward the wall where the door had been. There was a huge hole there now. We walked past the bodies of Kane's gunmen.

"What the hell happened?" I asked.

"I had a grenade," Jelly Ann said. "In case of emergency."

"Your friends, no doubt."

She didn't answer.

"I thought you didn't like killing," I said.

She didn't have anything to say about that, either. I followed her along a hallway and toward a staircase. An alarm was whooping now, and I thought I could hear someone running above us.

"Where are we?" I asked.

"First floor. We have to get to the basement. Then we can get in one of the tunnels and get away from here."

She still sounded confident, a lot more confident than I was, but I started down the stairway behind her. At the bottom a man appeared in front of us. He started to raise a rifle, but Jelly Ann kicked him in the balls and he fell to the floor with a scream.

"Over there," she said, stepping over him as he writhed on the floor.

I saw the tunnel entrance, and then we were through it and gone.

■

Lowell came out of it about halfway down the tunnel and I was able to put him down and let him walk for himself. When we got to the generating plant, some of Kane's goons were waiting for us, but Jelly Ann had another grenade. They weren't expecting that, and she wiped them out without a fight.

She also wiped out the generator and nearly wiped out me and Lowell, but we were able to duck back inside the tunnel and escape the worst of the blast.

We got to the trees without seeing anyone else. I wasn't surprised. They were probably trying to deal with all the confusion at the main building and at the generator, or what had been the generator until Jelly Ann got through with it.

The dogs were gone, too, and they didn't reappear, but my bow was lying by a tree along with my quiver of arrows, which must have been tossed there when Lowell and I were taken. I was glad to see the bow. Making a new one would have been a long and laborious process.

The boat was still where we'd left it. They hadn't bothered to look for it. They hadn't expected we'd be leaving. We shoved it off into the water and climbed in. For once, I was glad to be on water. Even water was better than the manmade island. I could feel some semblance of power flowing back into me. Kane wouldn't be able to get us now, even if he tried. I could summon magick if I had to.

But he didn't try. Within an hour we were back on land, and an hour after that we were back in the collapsed warehouse. My head was bandaged where I'd been struck by flying debris, and Lowell had cuts all over his arms and chest because his shredded sweatshirt hadn't been much protection.

Jelly Ann, on the other hand, was just fine.

"You should have told us about the grenades," I said, leaning on the minibus and eating a cheeseburger. Lowell had insisted we stop for them, even if Kane was pursuing us, though as far as we could tell he wasn't.

"I was afraid you wouldn't like the idea," Jelly Ann said. "You trust that bow too much."

"It didn't do me much good back there," I said. "It looks like we messed things up again."

"What do you mean 'again'?" Lowell asked. He was working on his second cheeseburger. "We didn't mess up the first time, remember?"

I remembered. Lowell's idea was that even if we hadn't destroyed Kane, we had changed the balance of power for the better. Every time we dealt Kane even a minor setback, we shifted the power to others in some infinitesimal degree. And any shift away from the Technocracy was a gain for everyone else.

Maybe Lowell was right. I hoped so. I'd hate to think that Blinn had died for nothing.

"He didn't," Lowell said when I said something about it. "Don't worry. There's one thing that bothers me, though."

"Just one?" Jelly Ann said.

Her sarcasm didn't bother Lowell at all. He chewed for a second and then said, "The thing is, from what you tell me it's hard to say who shot first back there."

"I don't know who did," I said.

And I didn't. That's what bothered me, too.

I had thought at first that when Lowell had begun to fall, Kane's men had opened fire. But maybe they hadn't. The Technocracy was responsible for the deaths of Blinn's friends, or that's what we'd all believed. So maybe when Lowell began to fall, Blinn had opened up, anticipating that Kane's bodyguards would begin firing.

And if he had shot first, then...

"Do you think Kane might have been telling the truth?" I asked. I put down my cheeseburger, which suddenly tasted like ashes.

"If he was telling the truth, a lot of people have died for nothing," Lowell said. He folded the wrapper from his cheeseburger and put it in the sack. "I wouldn't like to think that."

"Neither would I," Jelly Ann said, looking down at her feet. "I'm the one who threw the grenade."

"By that time, you had to," I told her.

"Maybe."

"And if Kane was telling the truth," Lowell said, "what does that mean about... about *everything*?"

I couldn't answer that, so I didn't try.

"Even if he was telling the truth, he won't be so happy with us," Jelly Ann said. "Look what we did to his sanctuary."

"You think he's pissed?" Lowell said.

"You're kidding, right?" Jelly Ann said.

"Yeah, I guess," Lowell said, and maybe this time he really was. He looked at me. "He'll be coming after us, won't he?"

I sighed and leaned back against the minibus. The dark

sky high above looked thick and impenetrable. I was a long way from home, trapped in a city of steel and stone.

"I'm sure he will," I said. I wondered when I'd ever see the stars again.

EYE OF
THE BEHOLDER

LAWRENCE WATT-EVANS

Bethany felt the warm blood welling up and filling her mouth, felt the hot frenzy of the Hunger — but she wasn't seeing the hapless drunkard she had settled on for her latest meal.

She saw Anton.

Anton Prihar, dangling there in his studio, the thick, ugly noose tight around his throat. Anton Prihar, who had died rather than let her Embrace him and turn him into one of the Kindred. Anton, who had loved the sun's light so much that he had refused an offer of eternal life, because it meant giving up the day.

She closed her eyes, and she still saw him, hanging surrounded by his paintings, twisting slowly, his face congested and swollen.

How could he *do* that?

How could he do that to *her*?

She swallowed mechanically and let the blood fill her, strengthen her.

She would need her strength if she truly meant to do what she had promised herself she would do. She just hoped that the strength of the blood would be enough.

Sated at last, she rose from her kill, the image of Anton faded for the moment. Flush with power, she saw the world around her in awesome clarity, in sharp-edged precision. The brick wall beside her was rich with textures, the air of the alley thick with scents, the sky above her awash in subtle color. For once, there was no morning fog.

A man at the mouth of the alley was looking at her — she could see him, smell him, hear his heartbeat and his shallow breath. He didn't seem to have noticed her victim, or if he had, he hadn't understood what was happening. Bethany smiled disarmingly at him, and took a step nearer, to where she could see that one of his eyes, the left, was so bloodshot as to appear almost solid red.

Then the man turned and walked away, as if nothing had happened.

Bethany frowned as she realized that the man had seen her, been aware of her, and hadn't cared. He had dismissed her as unimportant, irrelevant — but how could he? She was one of the Kindred and a Toreador, at the height of her power; he should have been fascinated by her.

It didn't matter, though. Ordinarily she might have pursued him, made sure that he wouldn't do anything to damage the Masquerade, but not tonight. Tonight she had other concerns.

The sky above her was beginning to lighten; the time was coming. She leapt up and caught the lowest rung of the fire escape above her, then pulled herself quickly upward.

A moment later she was on the roof, staring eastward, out across the bay to where the sky above the Oakland hills was turning pale and pink.

To her heightened senses the colors were magnificent.

Was this what Anton had seen that had so captivated him?

But mere kine couldn't see as clearly as she did, she knew that. Anton had had a true artist's perceptions, but he had been merely human, after all; he could not have seen with a vampire's eye.

Was there perhaps something Anton had seen in the sunlight that a vampire could not?

Bethany had been human once, forty years earlier; she tried to remember what it was like, whether there was something that she had lost in the Embrace, when she had gained so much. There had been certain immature feelings that she had shed, a foolish warmth and naive compassion that she had cast aside, but she could not recall any lessening of any kind in her experience of the physical world.

No, whatever Anton had seen in the sunlight was not a matter of his eye seeing more than hers could.

But he had seen *something*.

The first rays of dawn burst upward, painting gold across the sky, and she stared.

It was beautiful, there was no question of that, it was intensely beautiful... but she could feel the sun's heat on her face, even though the air was still cool. It stung her skin, it almost burned — and the sun's disk had yet to actually cross the horizon.

It was painful, yes, but she had survived plenty of pain in her life. Mere physical pain was far easier to bear than much of what had happened to her, back when she was young, both before and after the Embrace.

There were many among the Kindred who would say she was still young, young and foolish, but she knew she had learned much. She had learned to endure through pain. She had even learned to appreciate the beauty of the pain itself.

Golden light flared as the sun itself appeared, and the light cut at her like knives; she remembered Anton's painting where knife-edged sunlight had cut down the city streets. Had he somehow felt this the way she did?

She could feel her skin burning and reddening, but she stared in fascination as the sunlight transformed the sky and the landscape. The colors were so *different*, so *vivid* — she had forgotten, after forty years of darkness, how bright the sun was. The rich blue and shining gold of the sky seemed to burn into her....

And she knew that they *were* burning her; the pain was exquisite.

At last the pain grew unbearable and irresistible, overwhelming the fascination, and she knew that if she stayed any longer she would be risking her very existence. She forced herself to move, to grab the railing with blistered hands and climb down the fire escape on throbbing feet, her eyes almost blind in the shadows after looking into the glory of the sunrise. Wounded, limping, she made her way to the shelter she had prepared.

Oddly, she thought as she climbed, it had taken a greater force of will to tear herself away from the light and pain than it had taken to confront it in the first place.

And as she went, she remembered the transcendent beauty of the dawn — the beauty that she shared with Anton, the beauty the rest of the Kindred had forsaken.

That was worth any pain.

■

"She has no protector," Allanyan Serata said, as she toyed with the medallion she wore. "Her Sire is gone, her grandSire will not risk his studied neutrality on her behalf, and the Prince owes her no special favor."

"I am aware of that," Stefan said dryly. He was not so much standing before Serata's throne as slouching there, with the casual insouciance he had made a part of himself.

"And you didn't see fit to tell me?" Serata demanded.

"You didn't see fit to ask me," Stefan retorted.

Serata stared coldly at him, and Stefan realized he had

overstepped. He straightened and bowed slightly; a chain jingled. "My apologies," he said. "I had not realized you were so concerned."

"I am the Primogen of the clan for this city," Serata replied. "This upstart Artiste has cost me a precious resource; am I to simply tolerate that? If I allow this once, will I be able to prevent other, similar discourtesies in the future? No, any sort of defiance of my will must be punished, swiftly and forcefully."

"I see that," Stefan conceded.

"And as my faithful servant — and you *are* my faithful servant, are you not, dear Stefan? As my faithful servant, was it not your place to anticipate my desire to punish this Bethany? Was it not your duty to discover for me whatever difficulties there might be in administering this punishment, and to inform me of those difficulties — or of their absence? Was it wise to leave it to me, acting on my own, to determine that this neonate is defenseless?"

Stefan bowed his head again. "I rely on *your* wisdom, madame, for clearly my own is lacking."

Serata's lips twisted sardonically. "And what of your ingenuity, Stefan? Is that in any better condition?"

Stefan smiled back. "I would like to think that it is, madame, but I have had little cause to put it to the test of late."

"Well, then, little one, here's your opportunity. I do not wish this Bethany destroyed outright — allowing a human artist's suicide would not justify so extreme a response, even in this case, and I do not care to excessively alienate others of her faction, as many of the Artistes have the Prince's ear. Rather, I'd have *you* devise a suitable penalty for her. Consider this to be your penance for your own part in allowing Anton Prihar to slip through our fingers — that you shall arrange and carry out an appropriate vengeance against Bethany. Do you think you can come up with some artistic response to her affront?"

"Of course," Stefan replied, trying not to show any discomfort. "It should be a delightful challenge."

"Good," Serata said, sitting back on her velvet throne. "See to it, then."

⬛

The first step, of course, was to locate Bethany.

Vampires survive through invisibility, through going unseen even in the midst of the cities built by their prey. The Kindred's senses are far greater than those of kine, and a vampire's knowledge of vampiric ways is necessarily far greater, but still, finding a single specific vampire who does not wish to be found is not always an easy task, even for one of the Kindred.

Stefan had to admit to himself that he was not particularly enthusiastic about finding Bethany; she hated him for his part in that artist's death, and he did not enjoy being hated for something he had not meant to do. Still, he had been ordered to do so, and he had to at least make an effort.

And it would be best to find her quickly and get it over with.

He began his search at the Vampire Club, the gathering place and neutral ground for their kind. He moved from one airless underground room to the next, greeting those he recognized among the patrons, asking those he knew well whether they had seen Bethany of late. No one admitted having encountered her recently.

He did no better in the above-ground Alexandrian Club.

Stefan began to worry at that; what if Bethany had fled the city? Serata might insist he go after her. He did not relish the prospect of pursuing her to the ends of the earth; such a hunt could take years and might take him to places where the local powers would frown on any sort of artistic revenge.

Another possibility was that Bethany had been destroyed.

That might be even worse; how would Serata take being
cheated of her vengeance? She might simply accept it as the
workings of Fate, but she might equally well decide to take
out her frustration on Stefan.

He wished he had not tied his own prospects quite so
closely to Serata' s.

Stefan remained in the Alexandrian Club for hours,
watching Kindred and kine pass in and out, hoping to spot
Bethany, or to find someone who knew of her whereabouts.

His hopes waned steadily as the night wore on, but at
last, as he was about to leave, he tried one final question of
a new arrival.

"I haven't seen her lately," the vampire replied. "I heard
that she's been hunting the area between the Embarcadero
and Telegraph Hill, though."

That was more than Stefan had gotten elsewhere, and
at least she was still in the city. He thanked the man and
hurried out the door.

Once outside, though, he saw that the eastern sky was
beginning to go pale; there wasn't time to track her down
before dawn.

The following night Stefan set out patrolling the streets,
block by block.

It wasn't until three nights later, not long before dawn,
that he spotted a thin woman in black climbing a fire escape.
He could see no details at such a distance, but it certainly
could have been Bethany.

A fire escape — what would she be doing there? Had
Bethany resorted to breaking into apartments at random?
That hardly seemed likely; she had never had any difficulty
in finding her prey through more traditional, more
entertaining methods. She had been a lovely young woman
when Embraced, and forty years later her beauty was
untouched — if anything, it had been heightened by her
vampiric pallor and grace. Stefan could not imagine that she
would ever have any difficulty in finding men who would

accompany her to private places.

He turned down the alley and almost tripped over the corpse she had left.

A glance and the smell told him immediately that yes, this was a vampire's kill. Unforgivably sloppy, he thought, to leave it here like this! He looked up. The woman in black had reached the top of the fire escape and was climbing onto the roof.

That was interesting; then she wasn't breaking in windows. But what *did* she want up there?

Was it really Bethany?

He jumped and caught the fire escape and began climbing. On the final ladder, his head still a foot or so below the coaming, he hesitated — what if this was some sort of trap? What if he was walking into a diabolist's lair?

"Bethany?" he called.

No one answered.

"Bethany?" he called again, more loudly.

"Anton?"

The answer was unexpected, but it was Bethany's voice. Stefan heaved himself upward, onto the roof.

"No," he said, "it's I, Stefan."

She was sitting cross-legged in the center of the roof, staring east, away from him.

"Go away, Stefan," she said, without looking at him.

Though the words were unwelcoming, the voice was not as hate-filled as he had expected; she sounded almost resigned. He took a wary step toward her. He had been so concerned with finding her, he realized, that he had given no thought to just what sort of suitably artistic revenge he might take on her. Her asking if he was Anton, though — that might provide possibilities. Did she think someone had found a way to revive Anton Prihar? She should know better. Was there another Anton, perhaps? He regretted giving his correct name; he should have claimed to have been Anton, he thought.

"Bethany?" he said. "What are you doing here? I've been looking all over the city for you."

"Whatever for?" She still didn't turn to face him; she was staring fixedly at the Oakland hills, across the bay.

She clearly didn't want to talk to him — but on the other hand, she wasn't afraid of him, either, or she would be watching him. Perhaps, he thought, if he could gain her confidence, he could lure her into some sort of public humiliation.

"I wanted to apologize for... well, for Anton," he said. "For driving him to commit suicide."

For a moment she didn't answer, and he stood there, feeling foolish for attempting so transparent a lie.

"Thank you," she said. "I accept your apology."

He blinked in surprise and took another step toward her. He hadn't expected *that*. He had expected anger, hatred, mistrust — not a quiet acceptance. What had happened to her since their last meeting?

"Are you all right?" he asked. To his own surprise, the concern in his question was sincere.

"I'm fine," she said. "Thank you for your apology, but please go now."

"Why? I mean... what are you doing up here? Why are you sitting like that? Why don't you look at me?"

He could almost hear her smile as she said, "Poor little Stefan! Are you confused? Still caught up in your poses and your intrigues and your feuds? Still obsessed with power? Always afraid someone might be planning to harm you? Well, I'm not planning to harm you, Stefan; I'm not plotting against you, or Serata, or anyone else. Is that why you came? Has my recent absence had you worried?"

"Not about *me*," Stefan said hastily. "We were worried about you, Bethany!"

"You needn't be. I'm fine. Go away, Stefan."

"Not until you tell me what you're doing up here."

Bethany sighed, and turned her head to look at him.

"I'm watching the sunrise," she said. "I've been doing it often, of late. Would you care to join me?"

Stefan looked at her, saw her face clearly in the faint fog-reflected glow of approaching dawn; then he turned and fled without another word, almost tumbling down the ladder as he went.

■

"And did you find little Bethany, then?" Serata asked.

"Yes," Stefan said, uneasily.

"And did you take an appropriately picturesque vengeance on the little meddler?"

Stefan remembered the sight of Bethany's face, the skin blackened and blistered, here and there the flesh burned completely from the bone.

"Vengeance has been done," he said.

He saw no need to say that Bethany had done it herself.

■

On her rooftop, Bethany watched the sunlight spilling across the sky in billows of color.

Let Stefan and the rest live in the darkness, she told herself, and play their intricate games of power and dominion; she had found something better.

She had found beauty.

She knew that sooner or later the fascination of it might hold her too long, might destroy her; that if she continued her morning vigils she might one day be immolated by the sun's rays.

She didn't mind. If that happened, it happened. She would accept it.

Anton had thought the sun's beauty was worth his life.

Bethany had come to agree with him.

PERSISTENCE
OF VISION

JAMES LOWDER

Miranda Peake examined the ragged paper streamers, all that remained of a *Dracula* one-sheet from 1931. This particular style of poster was especially rare. On the collectors market it might bring over one-hundred-thousand dollars, almost a quarter of the original film's shooting cost. Now it was scrap. Lugosi's face had been bisected cleanly by the slash of a blade. A prolonged burst of automatic gunfire had reduced the rest of the one-sheet to singed tatters.

"Perhaps it was Van Helsing," said a figure lurking in the shadowy doorway to the projection room. His English was tainted by a thick Hungarian accent, but his sonorous voice lent the words a seductive smoothness. "For one who has not lived even a single lifetime, he is a very dangerous man." After a suitably dramatic pause, the man added bitterly,

"Or perhaps Karloff did it — that limey cocksucker."

"It was the two I left on guard duty. They've switched sides."

The cloaked man in the doorway sank a little deeper into the darkened hallway. "At least they didn't get to the projector. Perhaps you can repair the damage to your belongings. Your sorcery is strong—"

"I haven't the Quintessence to spare on sentiment," Miranda interrupted. "I've got to focus all my magick on keeping the projector safe from Summerlee's thugs."

The remnants of the *Dracula* poster slipped from Miranda's fingers. It fluttered down to the carpet of shredded lobby cards and torn scripts spread across the floor. Lugosi's twisted, disembodied face stared up from the sea of paper and spent shell casings. Around it, coils of spilled celluloid arched up like the backs of sea serpents in a cheap lost-world flick.

"At least show it more respect." The shadowy figure gestured with his cane to the poster fragment. But Miranda didn't seem to hear. She stood unmoving, her gaze fixed on something over the door.

Cursing in Hungarian, the man shuffled forward. The concealing shadows receded like a night tide and deposited him, driftwood, in the small, harshly lit room. He was gnarled and old, leaning unsteadily on a silver-topped cane. His scowl was a black gash beneath his prominent nose. Eyes that had once driven women to swoon now offered only an addict's watery stare. The folds of a moth-eaten black cape softened his frail, bony form.

He grimaced at the slashed *Dracula* poster. It was like looking into a mirror, one fractured and unstuck in time. The face on the floor had been the cloaked man's face once upon a time, before age and misuse had ravaged him. A hint of a smile flickered in Bela Lugosi's dark eyes. His expression was both wistful and pained as he used his cane to smooth the torn image of his youth.

"You must value your past," he said. "That's what's wrong with the idiots who run the studios now. They have no memory. They're trapped in the present."

Miranda didn't reply, only continued to stare at something above the door. Impatient, Lugosi raised his cane to rap her on the shoulder. The stick had barely reached its zenith when she clamped a strong hand around his wrist. "I am fond of you, Bela," Miranda said coldly. "But you are my servant. Don't forget that."

"Forget?" Lugosi spat. "I feel the pull of the void every moment I spend on this side of the screen. Only your projector keeps me from the ghost realm. Only your projector gives me substance. I am *always* aware of the power you wield — and of that power's focus." He narrowed his eyes to slits. "Your sorcery can conceal the projector, but the machine calls to any of us who have felt its caress."

He turned slowly, head tilted like a wolf testing the air for some trace of its pack. Lugosi raised one age-spotted hand in an overly theatrical gesture. "There. Floating just off the floor."

Miranda dispelled the cloak of invisibility she had set, revealing an ancient film projector. The humming, clattering contraption hung, suspended by magick, in the room's far corner. Glowing radio tubes and thick black wires protruded from the chassis. An arcing Jacob's ladder rose from the rear. Dials and meters both scientific and arcane lined the base. That was all Miranda's doing, along with more subtle alterations to the machine's guts that gave it the ability to open a gate between the mundane world and a dream realm inhabited by cinematic specters like Lugosi.

Until Halloween night, only one month past, Miranda had hoped to use those familiar phantoms to enlighten the mass of humanity as yet untouched by magick. She had been a disciple of the Sons of Ether then, and blind in her own way to the universe's true nature. But the dream realm's darker spirits, the specters born of slasher flicks and hardcore porn, had torn away her veil of innocence. Miranda's cheerfully narrow vision of the realm she called Filmland hadn't included such monstrosities, but they could not be denied. Neither could their message.

Existence was nothing more than the crass, violent dance of predator and prey. Miranda understood that now, just as she understood why Professor Summerlee and the rest of the Sons sought to destroy her and her work. Fear. It was the music to which the dancers kept time.

She could almost hear the lingering chords of fear in the projection booth now. The Sons had failed again, and they were beginning to panic. The room's destruction manifested their desperation. Their agent had turned Miranda's guards, but hadn't been able to break the wards set on the projector, not even the invisibility cloak. In their defeat, they'd rioted like frustrated children.

Miranda moved closer to the etheric projector and the unseen field of magick surrounding it. A triumphant smile crossed her lips as she saw the melted celluloid pooled beneath it. The wards had done more than frustrate the saboteurs.

"An arm, perhaps," Miranda said, prodding the ooze with the toe of one worn boot. "Almost up to the shoulder."

Lugosi craned his neck to get a better look, but remained cautiously at the room's center. "Ah, it bleeds film stock. So your enemy is one of us."

"From the looks of things, she was testing the wards when the disrupter field got hold of her arm. Our former guard dogs must have rescued her." Miranda scraped her boot clean on the latest issue of *Variety*. "They were fast, but not fast enough. It'll take her at least a few hours on the other side of the screen to recuperate enough for another try."

"'Her'?" Lugosi repeated. "You know who they've sent against you?"

"I've suspected for a while, but that proves it."

Miranda pointed, directing Lugosi's gaze to a poster

hanging over the door. Of all the movie memorabilia in the room, the vandals had left only this lurid one-sheet intact. *Bride of the Chainsaw* it screamed in dripping, blood-red letters. Below the banner, a scantily clad woman fled a maniac whose scarred face was split unpleasantly by a toothy leer. He toted his bloody chainsaw at waist-level, an insultingly obvious phallic symbol. The amateurish artwork was matched by the awkward sell copy: *More nightmarish than* **Night of the Living Dead**! *More evil than* **Evil Dead 2**!

"I don't understand," Lugosi admitted after studying the poster for a moment.

Miranda slid open the small window overlooking the theater. "You will," she said, then turned up the house lights.

Row after row of empty seats spread in orderly array before a small stage and a two-story-high screen. At one end of the stage stood a ruggedly handsome Japanese man dressed in the loose-fitting garb of a samurai — Sanjuro, a *ronin* unrivaled in strength and swordsmanship. The fashionably attired Chinese hitman at the opposite end of the stage was equally dangerous. As if to remind Miranda of that, he slowly raised his arms and crossed them over his chest. The twin pistols in his hands gleamed ominously in the theater's dim light.

Miranda cursed softly. These two film specters had been her guards. Now they guarded the gateway to Filmland.

She'd chosen them — Toshiro Mifune's avenging samurai from *Yojimbo*, and Chow Yun-Fat's peerless assassin from *The Killer* — because of their skill. She'd never considered the soft, sentimental hearts that beat beneath their callous facades. The Sons' agent had won them over easily.

"Where is she?" Miranda asked in Japanese.

One of the samurai's hands vanished into his sleeve, only to reappear from the robe's open front. "You would be wise to surrender now," he said and scratched his unshaven jaw. "A long life eating mush is better than the brief one you are pursuing."

Miranda frowned. "Innocence does not equal virtue. She's lured you to the wrong side of this war."

"Hardly a war," came a cheerful voice from the screen itself. "More like an internal debate gone wrong."

"That voice," Lugosi hissed. "It's—"

"Mine," Miranda interrupted. She silenced her minion with a glare, then turned back to the stage. An incomplete human form had appeared at the screen's center, pale gray against the silver-white background. Its right arm was missing, all the way up to its ragged shoulder. Even so, Miranda recognized the form as her own — a few pounds lighter, to be certain, but then she'd been a poor graduate student when she accepted the part in *Bride of the Chainsaw*.

"You've tipped your hand too early," Miranda said to the shape on the screen, aware of the cruel pun but finding no humor in it. "Now that I'm certain it's you, I'll find a way to end your interference."

Laughter filled the Oasis Theater, pouring from the screen and echoing from the speaker system. It was a hopeful, indomitable sound — and utterly chilling to Miranda. She felt as if she were listening to herself on some old tape, like the ones she'd made with her friends in grade school. Her doppelganger's mirth seemed that innocent, that distant.

Miranda slammed the window closed. "I've got to leave the theater for a while," she said brusquely. Lugosi took a step back, stammering the beginning of a reply. The mage didn't wait to hear it. "I can't spend the energy to keep you on this side of the screen, so cross over as soon as they leave the theater. The wards will keep things safe in here."

The unsettling sound of her own laughter followed Miranda all the way to the street.

■

The sidewalk outside the Cult of Ecstasy's pleasuredome

vibrated in time with Lenny Kravitz's "Are You Gonna Go My Way." In some other locale, the neighbors might have complained about the noise, or the establishment's strange clientele, or the haze of decadence that hung over the place. But this was Berkeley, and so long as no one flaunted the law too blatantly and no one got hurt, the locals didn't much care what went on inside the odd club with the overactive sound system and the psychedelic facade.

Miranda took the half-dozen stairs leading up to the pleasuredome's entrance in two bounds. She was greeted by double doors completely awash in a flowing George Dunning mural, painted in the surrealist style he'd used in animating *Yellow Submarine*. Against a background of blossoming peace signs and towering musical notes, ultra-cool caricatures of Jimi Hendrix and Billie Holliday jammed with Sergeant Pepper's Lonely Hearts Club Band.

As Miranda reached for the ankh-shaped door handle, a Blue Meanie near the mural's center turned its round eyes to her. "You dis' the Cult here, you get dissed yourself." It opened one cupped hand to reveal an ancient glyph inscribed in its puffy blue palm.

Miranda understood the obscure threat promised by that glyph, but she paid it little heed. She pushed through the doors and strolled up to the slim, dreadlocked man posted just inside. The bouncer's casual attitude didn't surprise her; the door, or some other magickal sentry, had trumpeted her arrival and her status as a Rogue mage long before she'd crossed the threshold.

"R. D. Mikels?"

The bouncer pointed to the bar at the room's far end. "In conference," he said in a voice that was somehow both dispassionately restrained and loud enough to be heard over the blaring music.

Martial artist, Miranda decided as she turned away. Perhaps one of the Akashic Brotherhood. Or maybe just a chop-socky freak.

The pleasuredome was under constant renovation, its interior changing as frequently as the musical and cultural interests of the mages who'd established it. At the moment, the cavernous room was an odd mix of retro-Woodstock and industrial. Autographed tour posters from Nine Inch Nails hung in macramaed frames. Tie-dyed banners and curtains of beads dripped from thrumming metal ducts. The patrons lounged in beanbags or sat rigid in chairs wrought of discarded oil drums.

Behind the long glass-and-steel bar, a massive bank of monitors displayed the final seconds of the Lenny Kravitz video. The song hadn't stopped humming in the speakers before the Warner Brothers logo filled the screens and the raucous Looney Tunes theme started. By the time Miranda crossed the room, a fat stage magician with a drooping, pencil-thin mustache had smashed a blackberry pie in Bugs Bunny's face.

Mikels was slouched against the bar, one hand cradling a drink, the other working its way up the bare thigh of the blond woman next to him. She was giggling vapidly, but Miranda could see it was only an act. There was a calculating quality to the starlet's eyes — one blue, the other oddly bloodshot — that belied her brainless act.

"I need to speak with you, Ray," said Miranda by way of a greeting.

The sometimes-agent, sometimes-director, full-time acolyte of the Cult of Ecstasy let his smoked granny glasses slip partway down the bridge of his nose. "Oh, oh," he slurred in mock surprise. "It's Charlie, and she's got a message from the Sour Grapes Bunch."

Mikels laughed brayingly at his own joke. Miranda nodded curtly, her mouth a grim line.

"I don't get it," the blonde said.

"It's from TV, baby. *The Banana Splits.*" Mikels let his gaze wander drunkenly from her legs to her face. "And I'm afraid that's what you're gonna have to do for me — split."

He slipped a dram vile of coke into her hand. "Why don't you go powder your nose or something. By the time you get back, Sour Grapes here will be gone."

"I want to appear in whatever picture you're making," Miranda said once the starlet had sauntered off.

"It's possible," Mikels said without looking at her. He signaled the bartender to refill his glass. "Why the sudden interest in rekindling your film career?"

"I need to put some polish on my resume. The old accomplishments just don't shine the way they used to."

"That's funny. You've never referred to *Bride of the Chainsaw* as an accomplishment before."

Miranda leaned close, one leather-gloved hand coming to rest menacingly on the acolyte's shoulder. This close, he reeked of vodka and cigar smoke. "I did that film as a favor to you. Now I want the favor returned. It's important."

Like the viper with which he'd been so often equated, Mikels slithered backward in his chair, out of Miranda's grasp. "I know what this is about." He pushed his dark glasses up to conceal his eyes. "Since you broke with the Sons of Ether, you're considered a wild card, a real loose cannon. Everyone here heard about your ham-fisted attempt to bump off Summerlee. The old prof himself told me how you directed your film phantoms to attack him—"

"You've spoken with Summerlee?" She spat the name as if it were poison on her tongue.

"When he bought a print of *Chainsaw* from me."

To fill the uncomfortable silence that followed this revelation, Mikels took a long, thoughtful sip of his Skye and tonic. "Is Summerlee using the print for some kind of Sons techno-voodoo?"

"Something like that," Miranda admitted. "I need to appear in another film as quickly as possible to counter his work."

Mikels shook his head slowly. "You're a good kid, at least you used to be. But I've got too many contacts and clients

in the Traditions — the Cult, the Sons, even the Virtual
Adepts — to help you directly. The best I can do is hook
you up with somebody else. I know this guy who does
hardcore loops...."

"Porn?" Miranda looked away, her mind reeling with
disgust and confusion. Her eye fixed sightlessly on the
cartoon battle flashing across the monitors as she turned her
predicament over in her thoughts.

The film specter Summerlee had contacted through the
print of *Bride of the Chainsaw* was a manifestation of Miranda
as she'd been in the movie. Its appearance mirrored the role
she'd played, but its consciousness was shaped by the beliefs
she'd held then — her optimism, her trust in the Traditions,
her loyalty to the Sons of Ether. Each performer created only
one phantom, no matter how many roles she played, so
Miranda could instantly enlighten hers, update it, by
appearing in another film. If her only option was a hardcore
sex loop—

The screens above the bar began to flicker unevenly,
drawing Miranda's attention back to the noisy pleasuredome.
She blinked and shook her head. Only then did she realize
that Mikels had been waving his hand before her staring eye.

"I was beginning to think you'd put the patch over the
wrong eye. Or maybe my hand had gone invisible." Mikels
waved his gold-ringed fingers before his own face. "Nope.
Solid as ever."

He paused, then resumed fluttering his hand before his
vodka-fuzzed eyes. All the while he stared intently at the
Bugs Bunny cartoon. "Funny, doing this makes the video
look like one of those old nickelodeon thingies. The
flickering, I mean." He snorted. "The cartoon still makes
sense, though. I must not be drunk enough."

"Persistence of vision," Miranda offered absently. "Your
mind fills in the gaps so you don't notice the moment of
darkness—"

Mikels wasn't listening. He'd retrieved one of his gilt-

lettered business cards and was scribbling the loop director's
name on the back. But when he turned to hand the card to
Miranda, he found her chair empty. She was already halfway
to the door.

███

Miranda didn't realize how much she'd welcomed her
brief escape from the Oasis Theater until she returned to
its depressingly familiar confines. Once, she had considered
the theater her cocoon. No longer.

The assaults Summerlee orchestrated kept her anchored
to the place for all but emergencies. When she did leave,
the elaborate web of wards and alarms she erected often left
her exhausted. She had no visitors, no customers. The police
had closed the Oasis's doors to the public after rumors of
disappearances started to circulate. The whispered stories
were true; the more dangerous phantoms sometimes slipped
through the screen to prey upon stragglers after midnight
shows. One amorous corpse from *Nekromantik* had even
pursued two women into the lobby.

In a way, she'd been relieved to close up. The grim films
the theater offered — like the Ed Gein double bill for
Thanksgiving, *Deranged* and *Three on a Meathook* — made
the place all the more oppressive.

Miranda murmured something derisive about the masses
and their infinite hunger for sleaze as she leaned over the
open guts of her etheric projector. She finished her
adjustments, closed the chassis, and loaded her print of *Bride
of the Chainsaw*. As the leader count flashed onto the screen,
she hurried from the projection booth to the balcony. The
theater lay empty before her.

The slasher flick opened with a predictable voyeur's
point-of-view shot through the bedroom window of a girls'
dormitory. Miranda winced as she watched herself stroll into
the scene, the stern housemother come to tell the negligeed

coeds it was time for lights out. She consoled herself briefly with the thought that she hadn't been required to strip before her ludicrous death scene at the hands of the chainsaw maniac.

The summoning she used next wasn't so much an incantation as a silent demand. Miranda had learned that figures on the screen could not resist the summons, and her doppelganger was no exception.

Bride of the Chainsaw vanished as the phantasmal Miranda stepped off the silver-white sheet. She was still clad in her harsh blazer and skirt, long auburn hair trapped in a tight bun. Her right arm remained ghostly even after she'd crossed into the theater. She positioned herself so the injured limb kept contact with the screen, her hand buried to the wrist. Even so, the expression on her face was knowing, defiant.

Miranda felt herself cringe beneath her younger self's confident gaze. How she must look from that vantage — her long hair cut short and dyed raven's wing black. Her face haggard from lack of sleep, her fingers bruised from her hurried modifications to the etheric projector. There was a knife secreted in her black leather boots. There were worse things secreted in her heart.

Of course Professor Summerlee and the others at the Sons of Ether chapter had recruited the doppelganger for just that effect. Not only was she the person best-suited to unravel any magickal wards Miranda might concoct, she would also force the apostate mage to turn her crippled gaze inward.

"With that eyepatch you look like mad old Dr. Serizawa," the specter noted glibly. "You remember him — the Japanese scientist whose Oxygen Destroyer wiped out that radioactive mutant dinosaur in Tokyo."

"Serizawa is a character from *Godzilla*," Miranda replied coldly.

The specter shrugged. "So? Film figment or flesh and

bone — there's not much difference around here."

"There most certainly is." Miranda cocked an ear toward the projection booth. The hum of the etheric projector had become a chatter. Right on schedule.

"Don't think I came here unprepared," the doppelganger called from the stage. She withdrew her right hand from the screen, guiding a second specter into the theater. It was Lugosi, looking old and miserable in his *Dracula* cape. "I've used magick to link Bela to me, Mira dear. Anything you do to me will harm him, too."

A ball of blue-white electricity appeared suddenly over the stage. It plummeted toward Lugosi but rebounded harmlessly off an invisible shield just above his head. The sizzling energy hung motionless for an instant before it dissipated.

"Wasted Quintessence," the doppelganger said.

"She's not about to let you melt me so I can re-form on the other side of the screen," Lugosi said bitterly. "She knows that will leave her exposed to more... *permanent* annihilation."

A triumphant smile crossed the unreal Miranda's lips. "Face it, this is a stalemate. Let's be more constructive, then, and talk about a cease-fire between you and the Sons. They want you back, Mira. Professor Summerlee is even willing to settle your dispute before the Assembly at the Great Hall. That's quite a—"

The rest of the doppelganger's sentence was lost as she and Lugosi vanished. For an instant, darkness covered the stage. Then the two specters reappeared.

"Wait," the doppelganger cried. "What's happening? What are you—"

Darkness descended again, underscored by the slowing clatter of the etheric projector. When the specters appeared once more, a horrible comprehension was clear on the doppelganger's face. She realized that the projector had been modified to run the film out of synch, making her stutter out of existence.

"But Bela?" the doppelganger cried before she vanished again.

"There's always a cost," Miranda replied to the empty stage. "And you've got to be ready to pay it. Too bad you hadn't learned that yet."

As the clatter of the etheric projector became a death rattle, and the specters manifested for the last time before slipping into the lightless void between the film's frames, Miranda caught a glimpse of Lugosi's face. He was young again, the handsome Hungarian who had played everyone from Romeo to Christ. He'd wrapped one arm protectively around his spectral companion's shoulder. Chin held high, he regarded the woman in the balcony not with anger, but pity and disdain. Then the two were gone.

Miranda stared at the darkened screen for a time before turning toward the exit. This victory would grant her a respite from the Oasis, at least until Summerlee realized what had happened. She'd need time away, too. Once word of Lugosi's demise spread among the phantoms on the other side of the screen, she might have to put down a revolt or two. There were throngs of rabble-rousers in Filmland waiting for just such a cause. The cast of *Spartacus* alone could keep her occupied for months....

As she reached the glass doors leading to the street, Miranda paused. A woman with a camcorder was making a study of the local architecture. If she caught Miranda on tape, a new film phantom of the mage might be born, or the old one might be released from its prison.

A news truck passed by, and the mage shrank back farther into the dimly lit lobby. She huddled there in the shadows for a time, until the reality of what she'd done to herself came suddenly, terribly clear.

She would never leave the Oasis Theater again.

Her past had been spread behind her like the carefully ordered images on a strip of film. And when she'd jarred one frame into the darkness, all the lock-stepped frames that followed — including her own — had slipped into the darkness along with it.

SELF-PORTRAIT
IN NIGHTMARES

THOMAS S. ROCHE

Christa gave the guy a dirty look as he entered the coffeeshop. "I'm about to close," she told him. "All I can give you is coffee. In a cardboard cup."

"That's not a problem," said the man. He had a slight accent. "A small."

"All I've got are large cups," said the woman testily. "I'll charge you for a small. You need room for cream?"

"Ah… yes. Please. Do you mind if I stay till closing?"

Christa shrugged. "No problem," she said. "But I've gotta hightail it out of here at midnight. Got places to be."

The man took his coffee, paid Christa and nodded. He didn't add cream.

Freak, thought Christa sourly as she gave him his change.

The man wore a white shirt and thin black tie under a ragged, black wool overcoat. His hair was long and black and pulled into a slick ponytail. He would draw stares in most cities, but here in the Mission he wasn't much out of the ordinary. He still seemed like a freak to Christa, though. Christa plucked irritably at the ring in her lower lip. The guy still seemed pretty harmless, just kind of weird. Christa started to count out the register drawer.

The guy walked to the back of the café, where paintings lined the walls. Christa looked up curiously as the guy inspected the paintings closely. He leaned very close as if to inspect the brush strokes, the texture of the paint, the grain of the canvas. Christa watched nervously. She went back to counting the drawer, but her mind kept wandering to the visitor. There were six paintings on display, and Christa watched absently as the guy went to each one, spending several minutes studying each. She kept losing count.

Finally, the guy paused in front of the piece titled *SELF-PORTRAIT IN NIGHTMARES*. He stood there, motionless, inspecting the painting with his eyes less than a foot from the canvas.

Christa finished counting out the drawer. It was almost ten minutes past midnight.

"She's really fabulous," Christa blurted. "She's a really incredible artist. Definitely one of the best in the city."

The guy was still studying the portrait of the girl.

"It's incredible work," he said emphatically. "She is a remarkable woman."

"Yeah, she used to be a friend of mine," said Christa cautiously. "You think you might want to buy something of hers?"

"Yes," he said. "I would like that very much. Do you think she might be willing to sell?"

Christa said nervously: "Get it straight, she's not my friend anymore, I don't even know where she is. She vanished a while ago. I think she went in the nuthouse, she was always pretty unstable, you know? I haven't heard from her since, but I heard a rumor that she's off in Europe or something. Like she's on the run, OK? I hear her parents are real freaks, like some born-again weirdos or something, tried to have her deprogrammed. Anyway, I don't know her anymore. I don't even know her real name. OK? But like maybe I could talk to her agent or her ex-boyfriend or call up some people, OK? You really interested in buying?"

The guy turned suddenly and fixed Christa with his gaze. His eyes were jet black. Christa found that she couldn't look away. She drew a sharp breath, looking at the guy.

His pale face softened, and he nodded. "I'm interested in purchasing the self-portrait. My name is Felix," he told Christa. Smoothly, he extended his hand. Christa took the card he offered. *Felix Bataille, MD, Art Collector. 44 Weiburgstraße, Vienna.* There were an awful lot of digits in the phone and fax numbers.

Christa noticed that the guy hadn't sipped his coffee.

"MD?"

"I'm semi-retired."

Christa looked at him for a minute. The guy didn't seem old enough to be any sort of retired, but what the hell. "I'm Christa," she said. "Nice to meet you. Maybe I can talk to some people about the painting."

"I'm staying with friends," said Felix politely. "They don't wish me to distribute their phone number. Would it be possible for me to return, perhaps tomorrow night?"

"Fine," said Christa. She relaxed a little, shrugged. "I'll see what I can do. But try to come a little earlier, will you?"

The guy turned and left, leaving his coffee untouched on the counter. "G'night," she said half-cheerfully as he left. Christa locked the door behind him, poured the coffee down the sink and tossed the cup in the garbage. Slowly, she rounded the counter and walked up to *SELF-PORTRAIT IN NIGHTMARES.*

Christa looked at the painting for a long time, until tears began to shimmer in her eyes. She licked her lips, remembering the taste of the girl's tears.

"Fuck you, anyway, Candle," she said flatly. "Who fucking needs you?"

The eyes seemed to follow Christa as she left the coffeeshop and locked the door behind her.

■

The hunger had become a sharp terror that migrated throughout his body. Felix sat in the dark hotel room contemplating the prospect of another feeding. The agony of hunger was mixed with an equal dosage of shame.

He rose like a spectre. It would soon be over — for better or for worse. And he, Felix the Cruel, would have taken another life.

The black eyes flickered over the unconscious form on the bed. He had not intended to take one so young, but they were sometimes easier to come by. The woman was bound and sedated, which was how Felix preferred his victims. In the faint moonlight from the window, she looked angelic, peaceful. Felix knew she wouldn't have time to scream, but he had gagged her anyway, using a ball gag purchased from a porno shop. Felix crossed himself and began to weep.

"Forgive me, child." He came down onto the bed, and his lips pulled back in a grimace of ravenous need. He was about to take her when the woman began to stir. Felix cursed. He must have miscalculated the dosage. She was awakening. She was about to scream. Felix hesitated, frozen in a moment when the terror and hunger came over him, the need for the girl's blood, the agony of taking another life. He couldn't do it.

"Jesus, Mary and Joseph," he whispered, crossing himself.

The girl's eyes went wide as she saw Felix's face hovering over her. His fangs shone in the moonlight, and the sight struck fear to the girl's very soul. Behind the gag, she screamed. It came out as a muffled sound inside her throat. The woman's face turned bright red and she broke a blood vessel in her eye. Her tongue lolled out in terror as she fainted.

Inwardly, Felix cursed his conscience and in that moment granted the woman the pleasure of death.

Like an avenging angel, Felix descended with a shriek of agony. She came to again and her back arched as the fangs pierced her — and then there was only surrender as Felix's tears mingled with hers. The youthful body twitched and squirmed underneath him, until the wrist bones had cracked and the tendons ripped. Finally the strength went out of her as Felix drank deep. The girl uttered a final, choking sob. Felix rested fully upon the body, caressing the stringy, dyed-black hair, stroking the many rings in her ears. Her name had been Valery. She was fourteen and a runaway. She was dead now.

Felix pried open the girl's mouth, saw the track marks under her tongue. That explained why she had come to her senses even at that high a dosage. She was a junkie. She shot under her tongue so the cops wouldn't nail her for possession and her johns wouldn't think she had AIDS. Felix, like a second-rate quack, which was what he'd always been, had missed the signs Valery had wanted him to miss. He felt like a fucking amateur.

His eyes filled with tears. Felix bent and kissed Valery's still lips. He left a smear of blood across her chin.

Felix wept late into the night, his body curled with Valery's on the hotel room bed. Felix was tempted to remain in the window when the sun cracked the horizon. He could not. Cursing himself for being a coward, he disposed of the body and returned to the hotel room just in time to close the lid of the velvet-lined steamer trunk and lock it from the inside. The sound of his weeping remained until well after sunrise.

■

Christa looked at the clock as Felix came in. "It's almost closing again," she said, irritable.

"I apologize." Felix was stony-faced.

"You can have the painting," said Christa. "Five hundred."

"Are you sure?" said Felix. "If you don't know where the woman is..."

"Let's get something straight," said Christa bitterly. "She's on the fucking moon for all I care, OK? She went off somewhere. She's out of the picture. You can have the damn painting, but it'll cost you five hundred."

Felix sighed. "That's not a problem," he said. "But it seems like such a low price."

"Yeah, well, her art's not selling much anyway. You know, I mean it's so 1980s."

Christa looked uncomfortable, as if daring Felix to challenge her. Instead, Felix took out his wallet and counted out five crisp hundred-dollar bills. Christa stared at the money, unbelieving, mute.

"May I take the painting with me right now?"

"Yeah," said Christa, still stunned. "Here, let me help you get it down."

The two walked over to the painting, and Christa helped Felix take the piece down.

Christa looked very sad for a moment. "You know, don't get me wrong. I mean, I used to be into her stuff and all. It's fine. I mean, if you like this kind of thing. She used to get all weird when she painted, you know? Like she was in a trance or something. And she'd paint in the dark. I mean, she'd start like in the afternoon or something, but she'd just keep painting without turning the lights on. And, well, she just kept... the whole time she was doing this painting, she just kept adding... well, adding stuff to the paint. I mean, what I'm trying to say…" Christa hesitated, groping for words.

"She painted with blood," Christa said, finally. She had started to cry. "It was really weird. But it seemed kind of magical. I mean, at the time I thought it was really hot. You know?"

"I know," said Felix. "Very well."

Christa wiped her eyes on the sleeve of her DKs T-shirt. "Shit, I'm embarrassing myself. We were just real good friends, is all. And I don't know where she is. She never even wrote me from the psycho ward. Fuck her."

Felix shook his head sadly. "My vehicle is just around the corner," he said. "Thank you very much, Christa. Please don't cry too much. I'm sure your friend is all right."

"Thanks," said Christa glumly. "Enjoy your painting."

Felix carried the painting out into the night, and Christa locked the door behind him. She sat in the back of the coffeeshop crying her eyes out and looking at the blank spot on the wall where Candle's self-portrait had been. Fuck her, anyway. Five hundred bucks was five hundred bucks. At least now she could afford to see Dinosaur Jr. next week.

■

Felix placed the painting up against the sofa so that it would catch the moonlight. He sat down in a chair and looked it over.

"My dearest 'Candle,'" he said. "Is that what you still call yourself? Shall you come out and visit me, or must I come in for you?"

The painting began to shimmer in the moonlight. The Candle in the painting was around sixteen, grim, dangerous. The hair was dyed black and the skin pearly white. Slowly the hair became lighter, until it was almost blond. There was a scar above the cheekbone that hadn't been there when the portrait was painted. Slowly, Candle stepped out of the painting.

She was still wearing a long-sleeved black lace dress, just like in the painting. Felix began to chuckle.

"More beautiful than I had imagined."

Candle took a brief look around the room. Then she looked at Felix, remembering.

"I thought it would be you," she said.

Felix sighed. "Then you received my letter."

"That was years ago. How did you track me down?"

"Friends. Art collectors. Bohemian types. You must have known other people could tell what you were doing."

Candle shrugged. "I don't think I realized it myself, at first. You could tell, even in the magazine?"

Felix nodded. "The power of the blood calls out over any distance. Even through a photocopier, certain elements in the style become evident — though of course none of the powers remain. As I'm sure you know."

Candle shook her head. "I'm afraid I don't know much."

Candle had received Felix's letter when she was fifteen, a few weeks before she escaped from her parents' house. Her work had appeared in a Philadelphia goth zine called *Blood Persuasions*. In her bio, Candle remembered vaguely, she had mentioned that her fondest wish was to go to San Francisco and be a "freaky goth dyke." Felix had written the publisher, asking that he forward the letter to Candle, which he had. The letter had completely freaked Candle out, talking about blood and nightmares, damnation and death, things Candle dreamt about but never imagined would be evident through her work. Felix's letter was deeply personal for several pages, talking about his life as a physician and his artistic connection to blood. The letter finally asked Candle to come to Vienna at Felix's expense, so she could paint a portrait of him. He had included a photograph of himself to prove that he was a worthy subject.

"You never responded," said Felix. "So I came looking

for you. I thought you might have come to San Francisco and become — how did you say it? An unusual gothic lesbian."

"Yeah, right," said Candle. "That's exactly what I am. Why do you need me so badly?"

Felix sat down on the hardwood floor with his back against the wall. "I suffer from certain... needs. I can no longer feed them as often as I should without suffering incredible guilt. Oh, my dear Candle, how painful it is for the predator to know the anguish of his prey! I wish to place myself in a suspended state, where my physical body would be without need and my mind could roam. Where I would no longer be a slave to my dark desires." Felix's voice broke as he tried to go on. He smiled feebly, and Candle realized he was weeping.

Her heart went out to him. Candle moved over to where Felix sat and took him in her arms. The pain on the man's face was incredible. She couldn't see him as a stranger — not after his letter, and not after all that had happened to her in the last year.

Candle felt a chill go through her as Felix's body stiffened. His head rolled back, and his lips pulled into a grimace. His eyes had lit up with rage and hunger. A hissing sound came from him, and Candle jumped back. She saw his fangs, shimmering like pearl in the moonlight.

"Blood," she said. "How could I have been so stupid?"

Felix began to weep.

"You must paint my portrait," he said. "Save me from myself. I can no longer drink the blood of the living. Free my spirit into one of your paintings. Imprison me.... Become my jailer, Candle. Perhaps then my conscience will rest.... What is it like, being imprisoned in a blood painting?"

"Like nothing... and everything. You remain still, both your body and your mind. Your thoughts can roam, but there's a curious kind of stillness to them. It's not unpleasant at all. You sometimes become aware of things outside the painting, but mostly it's like being in one of those... in a lucid dream. And time doesn't really pass, as such."

"It sounds like heaven," whispered Felix. "To be freed from the incessant hunger... if you cannot help me, then I fear that I must face the sunrise."

"All right," said Candle. "I'll help you. But you must understand a couple of things. First. I'm being chased. There are some people who want me dead."

"I sympathize," said Felix, touching the scar on his chest. "It happens to the best of us."

"Yeah, well, I need to get out of San Francisco. Right away. I must disappear without a trace, and do it without a passport. Second. You've got to donate some blood if this painting is going to work. Your own blood."

Felix nodded, his lips curling in a smile not unlike that of an excited child. "You can have all of my blood, if you need it! You will paint my portrait? If I bring you to Vienna, to my house? You will place me in my cell forevermore, where my mind can finally be liberated from my animal needs?"

Candle put her arms around Felix again. Her warmth flowed into him, as his coldness seemed to rob her body of energy. But his lips did not pull back, nor his fangs show themselves.

"I don't see why not," said Candle. "If you take me away. Will you promise me that you don't want to drink my blood? I'm kind of short on the stuff lately."

Felix nodded. "I would have done it already," he said. "If I so wished. But... it would be a crime to rob the universe of such a talent as yours. For the blood is the life...."

Candle felt her pulse throbbing in her veins. For life is the blood, she thought....

ANTIPHON

JACKIE CASSADA

I will sing of mercy and judgment: unto thee, O Lord, will I sing.

—Psalm 101

"How are you and Johanna getting on, Michaels?" Carruthers' question startled me out of a momentary reverie, sparked by the view of San Francisco's majestic sprawl. From our vantage point on the 27th floor of the Transamerica Pyramid, the city below stretched like a protective, glittering shield against the ever-pulsing forces of destruction that rumbled beneath its surface. The previous week's earthquake had faded from the memory of most of the city's residents, who now braced themselves for the onslaught of holidays that marked the final months of the year.

Although I had already filed a report after my Halloween weekend encounter with Johanna Talbot, I had been expecting a follow-up, particularly since I had departed from the instructions given to me by the man now standing beside me. My years with the Progenitors' International Public Relations Bureau had taught me that the best way to defend questionable tactics was to take the initiative. Sebastian Carruthers had just deprived me of that vital advantage.

"I'm satisfied that any work she might have been planning for the Celestial Chorus here has been curtailed." I injected as much finality into that statement as I could, turning to face Carruthers as I spoke, hoping that eye-to-eye contact would reinforce my conviction. "Furthermore," I added before he could question my assessment, "I expect that Johanna will eventually prove willing to assist us in our efforts to promote the stability of the area."

"Are you saying you think you can turn her?" Carruthers arched an eyebrow. I detected a faintly disguised skepticism in his voice. Members of the Celestial Chorus — like Johanna Talbot — had a reputation for fanatical devotion to their magickal Tradition. Most attempts to recruit them had either failed miserably, or, where they had succeeded, had so warped the personalities involved as to render them useless as inside operatives.

"I think I can make her see our point of view," I said. "She's a very bright young woman with a passionate desire to do good. All she needs is a redefinition of terms."

Carruthers glanced out the paneled window as he fiddled absently with the expensive watch on his wrist. Most people would mistake it for a Rolex at first, and probably only, glance, but I suspected that it had its origins in the production labs of one of our fellow Technocracy Conventions — most likely the tinkers of Iteration X. Working on the assumption that he was monitoring my physical reactions as I answered his questions, I tried to keep my involuntary cues as neutral as possible.

"My recommendation to you at the time was that she be

eliminated as a possible threat," Carruthers said, and for just a moment his voice lost its practiced blandness, becoming as soothingly deadly as a cobra's mesmerizing sway. I recognized the sound of eggshells crackling under my feet when I heard it, and knew I was treading on dangerous ground.

"Developing the human resources available to us is my primary task, Dr. Carruthers," I began carefully. "In my opinion, Johanna Talbot presents a perfect opportunity for research into more effective means of pacifying the efforts of Tradition practitioners in the Bay Area." I pushed my mind away from the recurring thought that, after spending time in Johanna's company while I was supposedly on the run from the "evil" — as she saw us — Technocracy, I found myself reluctant to follow through with my orders to kill her.

Carruthers shoved both hands in his pockets and turned away from the window abruptly, motioning with his head for me to follow him through the building's concourse to the elevators which would take us to the ground level and to our respective destinations. Apparently, the interview was over — at least for now. We made the downward trip in silence, the only two passengers in a conveniently "express" car. Just before emerging onto the street, Carruthers put a fatherly hand on my shoulder.

"Are you planning on seeing Ms. Talbot today, Gideon?" His use of my given name was, I'm sure, meant to put me at ease while at the same time emphasizing the differences in our respective standings within the organization.

"As a matter of fact," I said, " I was thinking of dropping in on her sometime before her shift at the shelter this afternoon."

"Good. Then you can extend to her an invitation for both of you to join me for dinner tomorrow evening at Masa's. I'd like to conduct my own assessment of her potential. I'll be bringing along a colleague, so it will be just a friendly meal for two couples." He smiled as I gave my expected agreement.

"I'm sure Johanna will be pleased to meet you," I said, hoping that the triteness of the response would cover my doubts as to her true feelings.

"What's done is done, Gideon." Carruthers flashed a brief, predatory smile. "We accept that and adapt — and we are, if nothing else, supremely capable at adaptation. I'm sure this will all turn out for the best. Eight o'clock tomorrow evening, then?"

I watched him take his leave, not knowing whether to feel relieved or worried at the apparent superficiality of our interview. When he had gone, I made my own way through the streets of the city, using the rhythm of my footsteps as a backbeat against which I rehearsed what I would say to Johanna to encourage her to cooperate.

■

I let myself into Johanna's apartment a little after noon. That I had a key to her walk-up was one of the prerogatives I had insisted on when we began discussing the parameters of our relationship. I told Johanna it was necessary for security reasons that "we" have theoretical access to her at all times. She accepted that — as she seemed to accept everything. Sometimes I worried about her infinite capacity for acceptance, suspecting that she was concealing an inner rebellion against her agreement to cooperate with the enemies of her Tradition. Yet my own examination of her biofeedback mechanisms indicated that she was never anything but absolutely truthful with me. I had come to the conclusion that the woman was incapable of lying. And that worried me — particularly in light of what I had to ask her to do.

Her kitchen was empty, although the freshly-rinsed dishes beside the sink indicated that she had just finished washing up after lunch. I guessed that she was making last-minute preparations before leaving for her job at the Mission Street Shelter, where she volunteered her time helping the city's hordes of homeless and where the shelter manager, one of our agents, had first spotted her and brought her to our attention.

I took a seat at the kitchen table and waited for her, sure that she had heard the sound of my key in the door.

After I had waited for several minutes, I began to suspect that I had just missed her. There were no sounds indicating that anyone other than myself was inside the apartment. Finally, I decided that I had waited long enough. I made my way through her living room to her bedroom door, which was pulled shut but not fully closed. I rapped a knuckle against the door.

"Johanna?" I called softly, then waited for a reply. There was none. I called her again, pushing the door open as I did so.

She was lying on the floor, face down and fully clothed. My first thought was that she had fallen and hit her head, but realized that an accidental fall could not account for the position of her body: arms outstretched to either side, legs together. A current of dread rushed through my nervous system, and I hurried across the room to her.

"Johanna!" I reached for her neck to find a pulse, when she started and lifted her head, turning my gesture into an unintended caress. She flushed, embarrassed, then raised herself to a kneeling position. I let my hand drop from her cheek.

"You startled me," she said. "I wasn't expecting you."

"Are you all right?" I tried to force back the flow of adrenaline that was running its inevitable course through my body so that my voice would show only concern, not the sheer panic that had prompted me to action.

"I'm fine," she said. "I was meditating." I stood up and extended a hand to her, helping her to her feet. For a moment we simply stared at each other as if some unspoken barrier had just been breached, requiring a period of adjustment to its absence. I had become an inadvertent witness to a confidence.

"It's called prostration," she said, breaking the silence. "Nuns and priests do it sometimes as penance or to remind themselves of the agony of the crucifixion."

"The cross shape," I said, feeling rather stupid for my sudden comprehension of the obvious.

She nodded. "I am still a nun — sort of," she said. "At least I will be for the next ten months. After that, I don't know." Her voice trailed off. I waited, sensing that she still had more to say. "I think of it as holistic meditation," she continued. "It involves the whole body in the process, not just the knees or the hands — or the navel, for that matter. I'm sorry if it disturbed you."

"I thought you were hurt," I said. "I don't really care if you pray or meditate or whatever. I came by to talk to you about a rather delicate matter."

We moved from Johanna's bedroom to the kitchen, where she fixed tea for both of us while I recounted my earlier conversation with Carruthers, edited to exclude my original intentions toward her, and passed along his "invitation" for dinner tomorrow evening.

When I finished, she rose from the table and began clearing away the cups and saucers. Her hands trembled slightly, and I caught the hint of some inner struggle in the changing lines of her face. For an instant, I felt a wave of pity for her, remembering an earlier confrontation in this same kitchen. At that time, the lines of power had been clearly drawn — I had maneuvered her into trusting me, into admitting that she was a Tradition mage. I had constructed an elaborate scenario of pursuit by two Men in Black, actually my coconspirators, arranged my apparent capture by them, and then made my way to her apartment and waited for her to return, desolate at her failure to keep me out of the Technocracy's clutches. Her helpless outrage then at discovering how she had been led along and her later rigid compliance with the strip search I forced upon her had made it very clear that she was no longer in control of her own reality. I took deliberate advantage of her vulnerability to persuade her that her own best interests lay in cooperation with the Technocracy. Somehow I managed to convince her, despite the fact that I was asking her to go against all her training and her preconceptions about the evil technomancers I represented.

Although Johanna and I had come a long way in just a few days from our original antithetical stances, the invisible dynamics of power were still very much present. I tried not to intrude too much on her privacy or make too many demands, aware of the tenuousness of the agreement between us and of the need to steer her gradually away from the constraints of her retroactively mystical magick. Now, however, the gloves were off again, and I was demanding that she play the trick pony before a critical audience.

I watched her struggle for self-control. I wanted to say something that would comfort her, but I knew that comfort wasn't what she needed.

"So they want proof that you've tamed your Celestial Chorus mage," she said bitterly.

"I'm afraid so," I answered.

She closed her eyes and inhaled deeply, then let her breath out in a long, audible hiss that I recognized as her way of releasing bodily tension. When she opened her eyes, her face shifted into an expression of ironic amusement.

"Do you think I can pull it off?" she asked. "I'm not good at lying or mouthing platitudes. And stress-interviews are not my strongest suit."

"We have until tomorrow evening," I said. "I'll help you master the jargon. We'll work on bending the truth so you don't have to lie."

"Why don't we just go out and buy a collar and chain

for me to wear," she said, smiling quickly to soften the bitterness that still lingered in her voice. "Maybe I wouldn't be expected to say anything at all then."

"No such luck," I said, keeping up the banter I hoped would ease both of us into a more productive pattern of thought. "They won't let you — or me, for that matter — off so easily."

"Then we'd better start rehearsing my lines," she said. "Did I tell you that acting isn't my forte either?"

I met her later in the evening when she got off work at the shelter, and we worked on her presentation until early in the morning. She had the following day free, so the two of us went shopping for the appropriate "costume," as she called it, for elegant dining. She settled for a deep-blue dinner dress — I counseled her against wearing either black or white — and low heels. When I offered to pay for the clothing, she surprised me by accepting. "Nuns usually don't have funds for luxuries," she said.

All too soon it was time for our rendezvous with Carruthers and his "dinner partner."

Although Johanna and I tried our best to arrive at Masa's a few minutes early, hoping to be seated when our hosts arrived, Carruthers was already waiting for us. Along with him was a tall, sleek brunette whom he introduced as Dr. Mariel Blanchard. The four of us followed the maître d' to a small table conveniently located in a secluded corner of the restaurant. Carruthers ordered champagne for all of us, then turned to Johanna.

"I'm so pleased you could join us on such short notice, Miss Talbot," he said. "I particularly wanted a chance for you to meet Dr. Blanchard. She is one of our foremost consultants in the field of social demographics. Your work with the homeless of the city has some interest for her."

"Your interest in me and my work is flattering," Johanna said, speaking carefully to both Carruthers and Blanchard. "I only hope that my limited experience at the shelter is of some small worth to you."

Mariel began a desultory conversation with Johanna about the particulars of the shelter, the number of clients it served, the reaction of the local community to the existence of a transients' house in their midst, and other details. The arrival of the wine and a brief discussion of appetizers interrupted the table talk for several minutes. When it resumed, Carruthers turned to me and began a discussion of the comparative qualities of domestic and imported wines, a conversation I immediately recognized as a ploy designed to keep me from running interference for Mariel's thinly camouflaged interrogation of Johanna.

The appetizers came, and conversation stopped once more while we ordered our meals. Johanna pleaded ignorance regarding haute cuisine and suggested that Carruthers order for her, which he did with a flourish and only a moderately bad accent. During the wait for the entrees to arrive, Carruthers turned to Johanna.

"I've behaved abominably by ignoring you, Miss Talbot — may I call you Johanna?" "Please," Johanna murmured as Carruthers continued to speak. "I'm interested in your impressions of San Francisco. As a relative newcomer, you must have some insights which could be illuminating to us long-time residents." At the same time Mariel, as if on cue, engaged my attention by asking me about my European experiences.

Again, I tried to keep one ear cocked toward Johanna's conversation, but aside from catching an occasional phrase we had practiced the night before, I was unable to concentrate on the substance of her comments. As the evening wore on, however, I began to hear an occasional laugh from Johanna in response to something Carruthers had said, and now and again an amused chuckle coming from him. Halfway through the entrees, I was able to relax and savor my meal. I caught an approving nod from Carruthers as the dishes were being cleared off, and realized that

Johanna's behavior had apparently satisfied him.

When the waiter had poured the last of the champagne in our glasses, Carruthers lifted his glass toward the center of the table. "A toast," he said expansively, "to progress and good fellowship." One of us seemed to join in a bit too enthusiastically, however, for along with the clinking of glasses came the shattering sound of burst crystal. Johanna caught her breath with a small cry of pain as the glass in her hand exploded, covering the tablecloth in champagne and slicing her hand in several places. I left my seat to assist Johanna, but Mariel was already at her side.

"Let me take her to the ladies' room and get the bleeding stopped," she said, and took Johanna gingerly by the wrist before anyone else had a chance to reply. A waiter appeared to clean up the broken glass and sop up the spilled liquid, muttering both an apology and an excuse about an obvious weak spot in the crystal.

A few moments later, Johanna and Mariel returned to the table. Johanna's hand was wrapped in two places with what looked like gauze. She looked faintly embarrassed.

"Will you need stitches, do you think?" Carruthers asked, his tone belying the concern in his words.

"I don't think so," Johanna replied.

"The cuts were superficial," Mariel said. "A lot of blood but no really deep incisions. I made sure we flushed out all the slivers."

"Nice bandages," I remarked, as Johanna held out her hand to me to inspect. "Medical gauze?"

"I carry a first aid kit with me as a matter of course," said Mariel. "Antihistamines for bee stings and allergies, antibiotic ointment, tweezers for splinters…" she patted her purse as she listed a half-dozen other precautionary items and medications. "You never know what will happen."

We passed on dessert in favor of after-dinner coffee and small talk while Carruthers settled the bill.

I drove Johanna back to her apartment and escorted her

to her door.

"Well?" she asked.

"I think you passed," I said, taking my cue from the convivial atmosphere surrounding the end of the meal.

"Both of them were actually quite pleasant," she remarked. "And Mariel was downright solicitous when she cleaned up my hand. She has quite a medical arsenal in her purse — including plastic bags to hold the pressure patches she used to stop the bleeding. Though why she didn't just throw them away made no sense to me." Johanna held her bandaged palm out in front of me. "It's healing already," she said conspiratorially. "By morning, the marks should be nearly gone."

"I'd continue to wear the bandages for a day or so," I cautioned her. "Just in case."

"I will," she promised. "I'm not an utter fool."

My sleep that night was full of strange dreams, and I woke with a vague sense of urgency. Halfway through my morning shower, as I was reviewing last night's dinner in my mind, the pieces fell into place. It was only with the greatest effort that I managed to complete my morning routine without panicking.

Johanna wasn't the utter fool. I was. I had believed Carruthers when he said that he wanted to interview Johanna. I had dismissed Mariel as window dressing to put Johanna at ease so that Carruthers could step in and conduct his own interrogation.

It wasn't her personality they wanted to pass judgment on, it was her blood they needed. Carruthers was planning on creating a clone.

My first thought was to warn Johanna. Then I realized that a warning was useless unless I could follow it up with some sort of plan. For that, I needed confirmation of my suspicions — and there was only one way to achieve that end. I hadn't survived this long by being cautious. I decided to pay a visit to Carruthers in his laboratory.

■

I rarely visited the Progenitor Experimentation Station to which I was technically assigned. As a field agent, my duties lie less with research and development — although over the years I've garnered a string of credentials in those areas — than with recruitment and counterespionage. Nevertheless, I had no trouble gaining access to the facility. Once past the glass doors of the nondescript eight-story building sandwiched between a pair of pretentious high rises in downtown San Francisco, I located the "express-only" lift, inserted my access card in the designated slot, and waited. For the normal executives who worked in this building, the insertion of a card in the slot would result in a nonstop trip to their elegant offices on the eighth floor. My card was different, triggering the car to "sideways" into a Horizon Realm, a pocket of otherspace where the laws that governed reality were not quite so fixed and where we could conduct our boldest experiments in bioengineering without fear of violating those laws.

Almost anything imaginable was possible in this extradimensional laboratory, one of several Progenitor enclaves in San Francisco. The cloning of human individuals from a few samples of tissue or blood was only one of the many operations that took place here. For now, though, it was the only one which interested me.

The lift door opened, and I stepped out into a lobby — actually a screening room for those rare occasions when someone unauthorized managed to gain access, often by happenstance. I passed through security and hurried down the main corridor of the laboratory complex until I located the cloning tanks, which were still where I remembered them. The technician on duty gave me a questioning look when I entered her sanctum and began prowling through the rows of suspended clone chambers, but offered no direct challenge. I expected that the most she would do would be to summon someone further up in the hierarchy to confirm my legitimacy.

Halfway down the second aisle, I found what I was looking for. The identification code slotted into the tank's face meant nothing to me, but the growing mass of amorphous flesh that swam in a liquid nutrient bath was already beginning to take on the appearance and form of Johanna. I felt something wither and die inside me.

"Accelerated growth," a familiar voice behind me said. "She should be ready for insertion in just a few days."

I turned to face Carruthers, trusting in my years of training to keep my face from betraying the anger that smoldered dangerously close to the surface.

"Why this?" I asked. "Are you afraid I can't deliver what I promised?" I looked closely at the face of Sebastian Carruthers, searching for some clue as to his motivations, using my own grasp of entropic systems and biophysical indicators to direct my perceptions. "Or are you afraid that I can?"

Carruthers turned his back on me abruptly, as much as telling me that I had scored. "Let's talk in my office, where we can have some privacy."

I followed him to his private cubicle, an austere room devoid of the personal touches that usually indicate a place where someone "lives" as well as works. Carruthers seated himself behind his desk, a stainless steel and plastic workspace on which rested a slim file folder. I took the other available chair, opposite the desk and facing Carruthers.

"You have quite an impressive list of credentials, Dr. Michaels," Carruthers began. His hand strayed to the folder on his desk — a hard copy of my personal file, I assumed. I waited for him to continue, unwilling to go on the defensive so early in the game. Carruthers flipped open the folder and absently began to page through the contents.

"Harvard University, Oxford, University of Heidelberg, field assignments in Geneva, Belfast, Chicago, Mexico City, and now San Francisco. You don't look old enough to have so many years of experience behind you."

"My chronological and physiological ages are slightly out of sync," I offered, not intending to elaborate unless it became necessary to do so.

"Have you ever been cloned, Dr. Michaels?" Coming from Carruthers, the question, a fairly normal one in Progenitor circles where cloning is seen as a ticket to immortality, sounded like a thinly veiled threat.

"Not successfully," I said, "and not recently." When I had opted out of research in favor of assignments that would allow me to exercise the interpersonal skills which were my strongest assets, I had altered my own genetic pattern to ensure that any clone taken from me unknowingly would not survive more than a few hours inside the tanks. That I was willing to undertake potentially hazardous field operations without the security of a clone backup was deemed by my superiors as an acceptable risk. To me, any other would have been unacceptable. We settled on rejuvenation drugs to delay the effects of aging and increase my probable length of service.

"It's highly unusual for an operative of your caliber to operate without the usual…" his hesitation indicated that he was searching for a polite way of indicating that I was, in some fashion, a free agent. I decided to deprive him of the delicacy.

"Controls?" I interrupted him, smiling as I supplied the word.

"Contingent backup material," he finished. "Frankly, I don't put as much faith in you as some of your colleagues."

Another piece seemed to fall into place. "So you want

to use the threat of replacing Johanna with a clone as a guarantee that I'll be able to turn her?" I began to relax in the face of a less-imminent threat.

"Oh, no, not at all," Carruthers said. "In fact, I will expect you to perform the actual clone insertion. It is my understanding that you have Johanna Talbot's mental pattern?"

I nodded, unable to speak for the moment. One of the first things I had done upon meeting Johanna was take a mental reading of her so that I could be certain of finding her again if necessary. I had taken great pains to include that in my initial report to Carruthers.

"The clone will be ready for you to pick up in five days, Dr. Michaels. Consider this a test of your convictions — your loyalty." Carruthers stood up and closed the folder, ending our conference.

I left the building as quickly as I could. I was anxious to feel the concrete sidewalk under my feet rather than the sterile laboratory tiling, to surround myself with masses of people whose only concerns were simple ones involving their small hopes and dreams, to distance myself from the strangling, paranoid bureaucracy that exemplified the worst aspects of Progenitor methodology. If it were not for my firm belief that our scientific vision held the best hope for humanity's ultimate perfection, the constant infighting would have driven me from the fold long ago.

Most of all, I realized, I hungered for Johanna's presence, especially since it now seemed that my time with her — with the real Johanna — was at a premium.

■

I spent as much time as possible with Johanna, trying to reconcile myself to what I had to do while at the same time trying to capture as much of her as possible. I knew enough about standard cloning procedures to know that the clone they were making for Johanna would be a reasonable facsimile of her — both genetically and physiologically, but it would not be the superior class of clone reserved for those Progenitors thought deserving of serial immortality. It would be up to me to transfer Johanna's mind pattern onto the clone, but even if the process were perfect, there would still be differences. Furthermore, I knew there would be some initial programming inserted into the clone so that its loyalties would be directed toward the Technocracy. That alone would forever prevent it from becoming Johanna Talbot, mage of the Celestial Chorus.

Johanna seemed pleased when I showed up at the shelter to volunteer my services working alongside her at the soup kitchen. It was the day after my meeting with Carruthers, and the clamor and constant press of the city's street people as they filed past us for what might very well be their only source of food helped to numb the thoughts that were forming unfathomable patterns inside my mind. I spoke with Clarence Dawson, the shelter manager and one of my own agents, and arranged for Johanna to take the week off. She seemed hesitant to leave her responsibilities, but in the end, acceded to my insistence.

For the next four days, I had her to myself. We roamed the city like a couple of tourists, picnicking in the Japanese Tea Garden, riding the trolleys, eating our way through the sidewalk dim sum restaurants in Chinatown, gawking at the old Victorian houses of the Haight and on one particularly glorious day — for November — walking the length of the Golden Gate Bridge. Halfway across, we stopped for a moment to catch our breath and stare out at the waters of the bay. A brisk wind was blowing up from the water, and Johanna laughed as she brushed aside a stray strand of hair that had caught in the corner of her eye.

"You're growing your hair," I said.

"I'm surprised you noticed," Johanna replied. "Last week, when she was fixing my hand, Mariel — Dr. Blanchard —

remarked that I'd look better with longer hair. I'd never given it much thought before."

The cold wind that blew through me had no relation to the wind from the bay. Johanna's clone would naturally have longer hair than the short cut Johanna customarily wore.

"Cut it," I snapped.

Johanna flinched as if I'd struck her.

"Please, as a favor to me," I said more gently.

"Fine," she said, and I couldn't even begin to analyze the undertones in her voice. "As soon as we get off the bridge, we'll look for a hairdresser's."

"Thank you," I offered by way of apology.

"It may take awhile, if I'm a walk-in," she said as we started back toward the city.

"I'll wait."

As it turned out, the hairdresser we found conveniently had a sudden cancellation and took Johanna right away. I sat in the waiting room, leafing through issues of *Redbook*, *Vogue*, and *National Geographic* until Johanna returned, shorn of the excess hair and looking very much like she had when I first met her.

"We still have time to shop for a turkey," she said, pulling me down the street toward the lot where I had parked my car.

"A turkey?" Then I remembered. "Thanksgiving's the day after tomorrow," I said.

"I don't have room at home for a frozen turkey, so I thought I'd get a fresh one today and spend tomorrow getting it ready for Thursday. I thought you might want to share it with me."

"I don't know if that's possible," I said. I had an appointment with Carruthers tomorrow morning. When I left him, I would have Johanna's clone along with me.

"Why not?" Johanna asked, sounding both puzzled and hurt. "Are you going away or something?"

"No," I said quickly. "I'm not going anywhere." I took

Johanna by the arm and steered her to my car. "Let's find someplace private — like a cemetery or a church," I said, knowing suddenly that I couldn't allow her to remain ignorant of what her future held — and just how short that future was. "There's something I need to tell you."

Johanna took me to a small Catholic church on Valencia Street. "They still say the Latin mass here," she informed me as we settled into one of the rear pews. The faint aroma of incense from the morning's services still hung in the air. Light penetrated obliquely through faded stained-glass windows, and near the front a few votive candles flickered before a statue of Mary. I sat quietly while Johanna knelt beside me and prayed. When she finished, she reached for the small golden sun medallion she wore on a chain underneath her blouse. She lifted it to her lips in a gesture I had seen many times, murmuring something faintly as she kissed the symbol of her magickal Tradition, then replacing it once more next to her heart. She rose from her knees and joined me on the bench.

"Tell me what you have to say," she said, simply. And, as simply as I could, I told her everything. When I was done, she looked at me for one long moment before finally lowering her gaze to her hands, knotted together in a white-knuckled grip. "Thank you," she said.

I nodded. "You had to know. What are you going to do?" I asked, hoping that I would hear her say she would make plans to leave town tonight, return to her convent and conveniently disappear behind the walls that would hold her safe — at least for a while.

"I'm going home," she said. "And I'm going to meditate until I know what I need to do. What about you?"

I looked away, unable to face her. "I'll do what I have to do," I said.

After I left Johanna at her apartment, I spent the rest of the afternoon and evening calling in every favor I had ever acquired over the years.

■

Carruthers was waiting for me the next morning outside the building that housed his laboratory.

"I'll have to take you inside," he said. "We've had to make some minor changes in our security and there hasn't been time to brief you on the protocol."

"I understand," I said, hoping that the tone of my voice would let him know just how well I understood.

"You know the procedures for clone insertion?" he asked as we made our way toward a small room to one side of the clone tanks.

"I know the drill," I said.

"And you've made arrangements to dispose of the alpha body, I assume." Already in his mind, the original Johanna Talbot was a thing of the past, superseded by her clone — the beta-Johanna.

"I've made all the necessary arrangements," I said, although I was certain Carruthers was unaware of the nature of those arrangements.

Carruthers stopped in front of the door, one hand poised on the handle. "Gideon," he said, "I realize this is difficult for you. If you think it's too difficult, there's still an out. I can always use a good research technician here in the lab. The combination of your obvious scientific abilities and my direction should prove extremely productive."

I shook my head. "Thanks, but no," I said. "Regardless of whether or not I participate in this operation, you intend to replace Johanna with what's behind that door."

"You've given us too good an opportunity to pass up," Carruthers said. "We need more information about the Celestial Chorus, information that can only be supplied from within."

"Then I will do what I have to do," I said.

"Good," Carruthers said, opening the door.

■

My first thought when I saw the woman standing before me in the tiny waiting room was "They've brought Johanna here to make the switch!" Then I saw her eyes, the same pale blue as Johanna's, but lacking the fiery intensity that made them hard to look at for more than a few seconds.

From the doorway behind me, Carruthers said, "She has been brought to a minimal level of self-awareness, but aside from some preliminary programming, her mind is an empty template. The pattern transference, when it's made, should be nearly perfect."

The clone and I regarded one another for a few awkward seconds before Carruthers spoke again.

"I'll leave the two of you alone for a few minutes," he said. "Say hello to Gideon, Johanna." The door shut softly behind me.

"Hello, Gideon," a voice very like Johanna's greeted me.

"You're going to come with me," I said, trying to keep the disgust I felt out of my voice. I held out my hand, anxious to get the whole affair done with.

She came into my arms instead, pressing her body against mine with an artless sensuality that could only come from someone devoid of ego. I had felt Johanna's body only once before, on the night of our first meeting, and then it had been rigid with humiliation. Although I have since regretted the necessity of the strip search, I have never forgotten the feel of her flesh under my probing hands. This was not Johanna, I knew, and would never be. I extricated myself from her as gently as I could.

"No?" she asked.

"No," I responded. "Not now." Not ever, I thought. I knocked on the door to let Carruthers know that I — that we — were ready to leave.

Outside the lift that would take me and the clone to the street level, Carruthers gave me a conspiratorial look. "I requested a few instinctual enhancements for her," he said. "I thought you'd appreciate them."

"Oh, I do," I said noncommittally. Before I left, a technician approached us, a worried look on his face. "Dr. Carruthers," he said, "you're wanted in the seminar room. Something's come up."

I smiled as the door to the lift opened and the Johanna-clone and I stepped inside.

■

Johanna was waiting for us in her living room. "My God," she said when she saw her double standing beside me. Her face grew very pale, and one hand went to her neck, where the chain of her focus medallion was just visible over the collar of her blouse. This time, the gesture seemed a preparation for some magickal effect, rather than a harmlessly superstitious habit, but I felt disinclined to stop her. Let her defend herself from what I had come here to do, if she could.

She lowered her hand, and for the first time I noticed that her eyes were wet.

"Forgive me for being less than the perfect hostess," she said, managing a small smile that wavered at the corners of her mouth before disappearing. "I'm afraid I don't know what the proper courtesies are at a time like this."

I resisted the impulse to go to her. "I rather hoped you'd be gone," I said to Johanna. "I have to go through with this, one way or another."

"I thought about it," she said. "I couldn't do it. You need me here to make the mind transfer, don't you? Otherwise they'll know she's not me."

As we talked, the clone's head turned to face Johanna, then me, then back again to Johanna in the manner of a person trying vainly to follow a conversation in an unknown tongue.

Johanna noticed the motion and said, "Poor thing. She's innocent of all this."

"She's not innocent," I said. "Her mind's a blank. Look for yourself, Johanna." I urged. "Look inside her and try to find someone present."

Johanna looked, focusing all her concentration on the body of the clone, searching for the spark of individuality that would indicate an active, processing mind — what Johanna would call a soul.

I knew that if I were going to go through with the operation as planned, now would be the time, while Johanna's attention was occupied. All my training had taught me to take advantage of the opportune moment. My own sense of fairness told me that death without warning was often kinder than prolonged anticipation. I reached in my pocket for the portable device that would allow me to make the mind transfer from Johanna to the clone — killing Johanna in the process. I waited too long.

"You're right," Johanna said, her voice soft with awe. "There's nothing there but a sequence of instructions — and... desires." Her voice trailed off, and she looked at me as if seeing me for the first time. "I'm sorry I can't be that to you," she said.

"Neither can she," I said, and knew then that if one of the two had to die, it would not be Johanna. "Go into your room, Johanna," I ordered. "Shut the door and stay there until I tell you otherwise."

For a moment, Johanna looked puzzled. Then comprehension filled her face. She turned and began to walk toward her bedroom.

I pulled out the transference device and adjusted a few settings, then approached the clone. She stood motionless, expressionless, as I prepared to deliver a lethal neural charge to her system.

"Now?" she asked, a sort of expectation filling her eyes. Once again, I hesitated, feeling the killer instinct wither inside me. She looked too much like Johanna.

"Damn you, Johanna," I whispered. "I can't do it."

"I can," I heard Johanna's voice behind me, belatedly recalling that I had not heard her shut the door to her bedroom. Johanna walked past me, reciting something in Latin. A faint glow surrounded her, and I backed away involuntarily. She laid a hand on the clone's forehead, as if in benediction. When she stepped away, she was trembling, and the light had left her to engulf the clone. I shut my eyes against the sudden glare that filled the room. When I opened them, Johanna and I were standing almost side by side. Where the clone had been was a small pile — a few milligrams — of fine, dusty powder.

Johanna turned to me, tears streaming down her face. "Hold me," she said. I locked my arms around her and held her until she stopped crying. Then we disposed of the clone's remains.

"What did you do?" I asked, when I sensed that Johanna could speak without breaking down again.

"She — it — had no Avatar, no immortal spirit inside it — not even a sleeping one," Johanna said, her voice strained but under control. "If that was the case, then all that was there was an overgrown piece of my own tissue — my blood from the restaurant. I disempowered it," she said. Her face told me that she could give me no better explanation.

"They were right, after all," I said. "You are dangerous."

Johanna shook her head violently. "Not to you," she protested. "And not to anything that has even a shred of a soul."

"I believe you," I said, taking her by the hand and leading her into the kitchen. I made tea for both of us, careful not to let her see that in some ways I was as shaken as she. For the next hour we talked, or rather Johanna talked while I listened. I knew I was passing up the perfect opportunity to gain an unprecedented insight into the workings of the Celestial Chorus. In her frame of mind, she would have told me anything I wanted to know about her Tradition of magick. Instead, I let her tell me little things — about herself, her past, and the vision of serving others that led her to the convent and, through her faith, to magick.

When I judged that she had come to some sort of peace with herself, I rose from the table.

"I have to go now," I said. "They'll be expecting me to report to them."

"What will you tell them?" she asked. "Won't you be in danger from them now?"

"I'll tell them the clone was defective," I said.

"Won't they just try again?" She shuddered as she voiced the question, and I could see her contemplating the thought of an infinite series of replays.

"Not if I played my cards right," I said.

■

After leaving Johanna's apartment, I returned to the laboratory and reported a catastrophic failure during the transference procedure, resulting in the complete dissolution of the clone. I theorized that there had been a fault in the original tissue extraction process that produced spontaneous decomposition when catalyzed by contact with the tissue donor — Johanna. I further speculated that Johanna's "pitiful" efforts at self-defense had perhaps provided the electro-neural stimulus that initiated the retroactive behavior of the clone.

I concluded my report with a strong advisory against further attempts at clone insertion with this particular subject.

Fortunately for me, the new head of the laboratory, a Dr. Carmen Mendez-Holmes, indicated her concurrence with my recommendation that Johanna be regarded as a field experiment with myself as primary liaison.

Johanna and I spent Thanksgiving Day at the shelter,

sharing a turkey dinner with nearly a hundred of the facility's regular clientele, a few of whom I was beginning to recognize. In the evening, I took her to The Lost Chord, a club near Union Square that Johanna sometimes visited because she liked the music. There, in the relative privacy created by noise and conversations, I told her what she needed to know.

"What happened to Dr. Carruthers?" she asked.

"Both Carruthers and Blanchard were reassigned to less volatile population centers," I said. "It seems that some of their policies conflicted with the work of other, more vital Progenitor concerns here in San Francisco, so they were transferred."

"So there won't be any more trouble for you?" The genuine concern I saw on her face and heard in her voice prompted me to hesitate, feeling she deserved more than a facile answer.

"I will probably have to be a little more circumspect in my activities from now on," I said. "They believed me this time, largely because I was telling them the truth as I saw it. I was lucky. That may not always be the case."

Johanna pondered my answer for a few moments as we sat in companionable silence, listening to the hypnotic dance music coming from the stage. Johanna toyed with the froth on her cappuccino.

"Was it murder?" she asked finally.

"Technically or theologically?" I countered.

"I've been trying to reason it out for myself," she said. "I would never have thought myself capable of taking another human life — not even in defense of my own."

"But you did," I pointed out.

"She had no soul," Johanna said. "She was not human, not even animal. Her existence mocked the act of creation." She stopped abruptly, aware that her voice had risen above the general background drone. "At least, that's what I tell myself," she said ruefully.

"It wasn't murder in the legal sense," I said. "The clone had no legally verifiable existence — no identification documents, no birth records, nothing to prove that she ever lived."

"That's not the answer I was looking for," Johanna said.

"I know. You may never find it."

Johanna nodded solemnly, and I found myself thinking that whatever Johanna had been before, she was now both more and less. I could not help but hope that she would begin to realize that the answers provided by the Celestial Chorus were outmoded in today's scientifically oriented world, that she would eventually come to embrace the vision of humanity's perfection through its own efforts rather than through the direction of some divine spiritual guide. Her action the night before had cost her. Her innocent idealism, many of her principles, had died along with her clone.

What I did not tell Johanna, what she did not need to know, was the price I paid to keep Johanna safe — and to keep myself from official censure. I had not only exhausted every favor owed me in removing the danger posed by Carruthers and his flunky, I had sold myself so thoroughly that it would take more than one lifetime to repay my debts.

Fortunately, I would have more than one lifetime. The real price I had paid rested in the small, rapidly healing incision on the inside of my left arm. I had finally agreed to donate a sample of my own flesh and blood to Dr. Mendez-Holmes' clone bank. I am not as free as I used to be. Both Johanna and I will have to live with the consequences of the choices we have made.

THE DARK

OF THE YEAR

KEVIN ANDREW MURPHY

Some days you wanna rip your fuckin'
eyes out.

I hate seein' things. It sucks. Sucks real
hard. I'm here, trying to hang out, have a
nice afternoon, pass the time of day, all
that shit, and there's three ghosts in the
place, a giant spider in the rafters,
Neville's around, and he ain't got a fuckin'
soul (leastways not one he keeps in his
body), and here comes Penny, who's
usually bright and happy and cheerful and
one of the few people who actually makes
me glad I'm still alive (if you call this
livin'), and she's got this black cat perched
on her shoulder, lookin' 'round as if it
owned the place, an' for all I know it does,
'cause whatever it is, it ain't a cat.

An' there she is, smiling for all the
world like it's Show-and-Tell Day and she's
brought her new pet in for the class to see,

an' she comes right up to me, an' I don't think she knows what the fuck she's got on her shoulder.

I look at it, and it looks back at me, and its eyes are as bright as a couple of emeralds, and just about as old. I lick my lips. "That ain't a fuckin' cat."

The cat that ain't a cat looks at me and cocks its head like a real cat would, then turns to Penny and says, "Is he usually this rude?"

Penny rolls her eyes and takes the ain't-a-fuckin'-cat down off her shoulders and cuddles it like a baby an' says, "Worse." She looks up at me and makes a face. "Really, Peter, do you have to be such an Eeyore? What's your problem?"

Eeyore. Yeah, right. She's calling me a fucking donkey, while she's there cuddling a bunch of black fur that's older than the pyramids. But all I say is, "You'd have a problem too if someone stuck a rusty thumbtack in your ass."

I stomp off while Neville's saying something calm and logical to Penny like you'd expect from someone who ain't got a fuckin' soul, an' then I suddenly have to deal with a soul that ain't got a fuckin' body, not that Thaddeus ever shows much more feeling than Neville.

He tilts his hand, hardly a motion, an' catches my arm with the hook of his cane. "Hold a moment, Peter," he says — as if I could do anything else, with a ghost ivory dragon's head snagged on my elbow, ready to poke its fangs into my soul if I so much as move an inch.

Thaddeus reels me in like a fish, then unhooks his cane and takes off his spectacles on their little ribbon an' starts polishin' them like he always does when he's about to say somethin' he thinks is real wise and pithy an' somethin' he thinks I haven't heard a dozen times over, even if I haven't been around since before Queen Victoria kicked off like he has. "I believe you owe the young lady an apology."

"What the fuck are you talking about, you ghost bastard?"

Thaddeus inspects his spectacles for dirt. "In my day," he says, like he usually starts his lectures, "a young man would never take his leave of a lady without at least begging her pardon and excusing himself. To say nothing of refraining from vulgar comments regarding thumbtacks and one's nether regions."

"She called me a jackass."

"No, she made a literary allusion which implied that you were being a depressing little donkey. Hardly the same thing." He sticks his ghost spectacles back on his ghost nose and smiles. "Why were you so rude, anyway?"

I stand my ground. "That ain't a fuckin' cat."

"Not an ordinary one, at least." Thaddeus inclines his head and sneaks a glance. "I believe Penny has gained the services of a witch's familiar, and from that we may surmise that Penny is quite a bewitching young woman — a fact with which I know you are already well acquainted."

I don't need some fuckin' Victorian-Age Robber Baron dirty-old-ghost lawyer telling me when I've got a hard-on. I walk the fuck out of the Waydown an' let him trail after me, swaggering his cane, heel-and-toe, heel-and-toe, ever-so-fuckin'-proper, Mr. High-and-Mighty, better-educated-than-you'll-ever-be ghost.

And you wonder why I wanna rip my eyes out sometimes?

There are dead leaves everywhere, skeleton leaves, and cobwebs and broken stone, and the light's dyin' early, four days after Thanksgiving, and what the fuck is there to be thankful for? An alcoholic father? A dying grandfather? A bunch of old aunts who think they know everything, when all they know is recipes and gossip and old lady shit like that, and not the weird-assed evil shit that goes down in the world every day, like ghosts and spiders and Neville not having a fuckin' soul and Penny getting a witch's cat to play baby with?

Fuck.

I sit down hard, between the headless deer and the headless lamb that sit at the feet of the Marie Antoinette St. Francis statue that stands outside the old church, and it's cold and hard and just the way I wish I felt inside, but I don't and I can't and I can't even talk about the things I see 'cept around people like Neville an' Penny an' her cat, 'cause then they think you're crazy an' they come for you an' take you to the nuthouse. An' if you think the world outside is cold and evil, you ain't seen what it's like inside one of those places.

They've got demons there, and imps, and little things that crawl on your shoulder and whisper bad things in your ear. "Kill! Kill! Fuck your mother!" All that shit. And then there's the men in the white coats and the men in the black coats, and the ones who don't have demons in them don't have any souls either, and they look at you with their empty eyes and show you their little cards and ask you what does this look like to you, and what does that look like to you, and what do you think when they say that and when they say this, and fuck, they ain't got any souls, an' not like Neville either, 'cause they seem glad they lost theirs, which ain't like Neville, 'cause he just acts like, whether or not he's got a soul and what he's done with it, is his business, not yours, and he ain't about to go askin' for anyone else's or tellin' you what you should do with yours.

Which ain't a thing like the nuthouse, 'cause when you go in there, they want you to show them your soul so they can suck it out, or stick one of their little imps in it, or do some other fuckin' evil shit. But don't you let them. Tell 'em what they want to hear. Tell 'em you don't see anythin'. Not the demons, not the ghosts, not the little imps crawlin' into people's ears. None of that shit. Just tell 'em you dropped some bad acid, but you're fine now, and you won't ever do it again and they'll let you go, 'cause then you're as boring as the rest of the world and your soul won't be very tasty.

It's happened to me before, and that's the way I got out with my soul intact, and my skin too. If, like I said, you can call this living.

Thaddeus is there, smiling, and one thing being in the nuthouse taught me is you don't talk to ghosts, leastways not if you don't want to go back in. But Thad isn't like most ghosts. If he wants an answer, it's usually just a yes or a no, not something more, and like a lot of living people, he likes the sound of his own voice, 'least when there are people to hear it.

"Really, Peter," he says, "are my lessons on propriety and decorum for naught? I've told you again and again, speak politely, nod, answer when you are spoken to and not before, always be gracious, especially in the presence of a lady, and whatever you do, do not voice facts about others that they do not wish to be reminded of or made public. One's illusions about oneself are sacrosanct, and people resent having them shattered. And the only thing they resent more is being told unpleasant truths of which they are already painfully aware."

"You're dead. Fuck you. Go away."

Thaddeus clucks his tongue, but I'm the only one who can hear it, even if I weren't the only one outside. "Really, Peter. What have I just been telling you?"

Like I said, Thad likes the sound of his own voice, and most of his questions don't need any answers. He's already got them all himself.

There's weird shit in the air. You can smell it going down. Omens. Dead leaves and cobwebs. All that shit. Like having a finger on a spiderweb. You can feel the spider move her feet if you're sensitive enough, and I am.

Always have been, even before Thad and the rest of the rotten ghost bastards nearly got me killed. That just made me more sensitive. Like bee stings. A little poison, a little death, makes you know it when it comes around again. You can feel the buzz. Wings caught in webs. One prick and it's death, or sensitivity and pain.

Bet you can guess which I got.

And it's twilight and a car pulls up in front of the Waydown, black as pitch and twice as shiny, with silver

mirrored windows that you can't get legally, and the door
opens up and a man gets out an' comes 'round the back, his
coat as black as the car but dead as night where the doors
are shiny, and it's one of the bastards without any souls, I
know it, even though I can't look in his eyes to tell for sure
'cause he's got mirrorshades on, shiny like the windows,
reflecting everything but the soul he ain't got.

But he ain't payin' any attention to me. He goes to the
rear door and opens it, holdin' it open for this huge Japanese
guy, like a giant sumo wrestler with a crewcut, if sumo
wrestlers wore twelve-hundred-dollar gray pinstripe suits
instead of giant white diapers and sweat. An' the sumo guy
gestures to him like he was just some normal chauffeur, 'cept
I can tell the sumo guy knows he ain't (Don't ask how I
know. I just know these things, okay?), and he says, "Bring
the car back around midnight."

The man in black just nods and goes and gets back in
the car and it drives off, as silently as it appeared, and here
it is, still twilight, and the sumo guy is walkin' over to me
and I can feel the buzz in the air like a bee caught in a web.

"Now this," Thaddeus says, "is a gentleman. Observe
him, Peter, and you may learn something."

Observe him. Yeah, right.

The sumo guy hasn't noticed Thad, but Thad's smiling
like he knows when he sees a kindred spirit, 'cause the big
Japanese guy is smilin' the exact same, ever-so-proper
diplomat's smile, and I know if he had a cane or a cigarette
he'd be playin' with it or lightin' up to give him another
minute to stand there and pose and look polite, except he
ain't the type who smokes, and he'd break a cane if he used
one, so he just folds his hands and nods and makes this funny
little half-bow to show that he's noticed me and considers
himself above me, but he's still being polite 'cause he wants
to ask me a question and he doesn't usually come to
neighborhoods like this one and wants to make sure that I
know that he doesn't.

So what's to observe? I got his number, it's the same one
Thaddeus uses, and the only thing I don't know is why a
flash dude like him is in a place like this an' what he wants
and why he's so important that he's making my sixth sense
jangle like a key ring in the hand of an epileptic.

"Excuse me," he says, "is this the place known as the
Waydown?"

Talks just like Thaddeus. "This is the place known as the
Old St. Francis." I jerk my thumb back at the headless statue.
"This is St. Francis. He's seen better days." I wait a beat.
"So's the church."

Mr. Sumo looks around, taking in the leaves and the
cobwebs and the burnt-out hulk of the church we Hollowers
use as a crash pad sometimes and he nods and smiles. "I —
I was given to understand it was a nightclub."

"You were given to understand wrong." I lean back
against the deer and kick my boots up over the lamb's back.
"Does it look like a nightclub?"

Mr. Sumo has to admit that it does not, and the
Waydown hasn't been held at the St. Francis since
Halloween, or All Hollow's Eve like Penny and Blackrose
like to call it when they get silly and start makin' up stupid
Goth names for everything. Samhain isn't anything to joke
about, 'specially not this past one.

Even if the Waydown were open more often, though, it
wouldn't be open tonight. Mondays are for Death Guild over
at the Trocadero, and if the Waydown were going down
tonight, it would be going down there.

Mr. Sumo smiles again and says, "Actually, I am not
really looking for a nightclub," but Thaddeus smiles and
holds his finger to his lips so I don't say "No shit" like I
want to. But the lawyer ghost's got good instincts, 'cause
one of the things he's taught me is that if you hold your trap
shut, people tend to blab on and tell you things they usually
wouldn't.

The Japanese guy bobs his head again, realizing he's not

going to get a response, and says, "Dr. Ken Himiitsu, U.C. Medical Center" and holds out a hand that looks like a slab of bacon, 'cept that slabs of bacon don't usually have diamond pinkie rings.

"It is customary," Thaddeus says dryly, "to shake a hand that is offered in greeting, and to give one's own name in exchange." I ignore him too, and he says, "If, on the other hand, one intends to give insult by not accepting such a gesture — as I assume you wish to refrain from giving him your name — then it is particularly effective to make some meaningless pleasantry and observation so as to defuse the situation."

Like I said, the lawyer's got good instincts. "Nice pinkie ring," I say, and Dr. Sumo looks flustered and plays with it and gives a "Yes, I'm flustered, and I hate you 'cause you've snubbed me, but I can't actually hit you 'cause you've complimented me on my pinkie ring which I actually am fond of" look, then squares his shoulders, which are about as wide as he's tall, and says, "We appear to have gotten off to a bad start here. I am one of the Progenitors. You have heard of our organization?"

"No." I shrug. "Was I supposed to?"

Dr. Ken Himiitsu, Mr. Sumo Progenitor, gives a "Well of course you weren't supposed to hear about our secret organization, but..." look, and plays with his pinkie ring some more, then says, "You have no idea who the Progenitors are?"

I wobble my boots back and forth, kicking back. "Some wacky fringe group of Operation Rescue?"

"No." He puts his hands down and squares his shoulders. "Let us not play games. The Progenitors are a Convention of the Technocracy, and you, I am certain, are an Awakened mage. You are one of the ones who call themselves the Hollow Heads?"

Thaddeus laughs, and I chuckle a little bit inside at the same time as I feel the anger start to build up behind my eyes. Someone had fed this bastard a line of bull, 'cause we Hollow Ones don't take kindly to the fancy-pants bastards in the Technocracy. Hollow Heads. Heh, that's a good one, and it's all the information the Technos deserve. But it's more than one of us Hollowers would say unless one of the Technos stuck a gun in his face, and a pretty big gun too.

But I take Thad's "If you can't say something nice, don't say anything at all" shtick and wait and see what Dr. Progenitor is going to say next.

"I know you might have reason to distrust me, but please, be assured that I have everyone's best interests at heart— "

"Glad to hear it."

"—but—" He pauses, flustered, then starts over. "Young man. I truly do not wish to trouble you or any of your fellow Hollow Heads, but I was wondering if perhaps you had seen a spider lately."

I point to one of the cracks in St. Francis's robe. "Yeah, right there. Spiders all over the place."

Dr. Himiitsu smiles. "I meant a larger spider. Much larger."

"You been droppin' acid, mister?"

"No." He smiles graciously, though I'm pushing him to the breaking point. "I was referring to a pattern spider. A very large pattern spider. Her name is Weaver, and I had a hand in her creation."

I kick my feet off the headless lamb and come up quick, but Thaddeus has his cane barring my way. "Steady, Peter. Steady."

The anger's buildin' up behind my eyes, and the pain, and some of it's startin' to bleed through, and fuck, it hurts. Hurts like it always does, and everythin's turnin' red. "You pig," I say. "You're the pig who turned Norna into that thing."

"Ah, so she is here!" Dr. Himiitsu beams, and fuck, the only thing that's keepin' me from jumpin' him is Thad's cane in my throat and the fact that the pig weighs about three times as much as me and not all of it's fat. Well-marbled bacon.

And fast, greasy bacon too, 'cause the next thing I know, Dr. Pig's hand is pushin' me flat against St. Francis. "Please, young man," he says. "I have no wish to harm you, as I had no wish to harm Norna. It was simply necessary for the safety of the city that she become a pattern spider and reweave the broken threads of the tapestry. Regrettable, but necessary. I have already died once in this business, and while unpleasant, it was hardly permanent, so please, do not take any rash ideas into your head as to taking my life, as I must assure you, that will not only be difficult, but impermanent. Which would not be the case if I were forced to take yours, for you do not have the luxury of having clones on file, as do I." He smiles. "I am a doctor, and I prefer to preserve life when possible. I only wish to collect Weaver and leave."

"You're a fucking pig, that's what you are," I say, and fuck, the pain's burnin' behind my eyes, and it hurts. Hurts like a motherfucker, an' everywhere I look everythin's gone red as blood. "I don't care how many vats you crawl out of, or how many times you come back, you're a pig and you always will be. A filthy pig! You know what? Just before you came back last time someone tossed a bag of pork rinds in the tank, 'cause they couldn't tell the difference. Pig skin on the inside, pig skin on the outside. You're nothing but a pig, through and through, and no matter how many times you come back, that's all you'll ever be. Pig! You're nothin' but a fuckin' pig!"

There's this story I read when I was a kid, 'bout a girl who had a magic finger, an' when she got mad, it zapped out and turned her teacher into a cat, and some kids into ducks, and it happened whether she wanted it to or not. Just when she got mad.

My magic ain't in my fingers, but you don't want to get me mad either. An' if you do, don't look me in the eye.

There's a lot said 'bout the evil eye, but the main thing is that you don't want it, and don't want to get whammied by it.

Dr. Pig stares at me, gettin' even redder in the face, or really pinker, and his eyes get all squinty and his nose gets more piggy and his canines start stickin' out of his lower lip. But he ain't noticin' until his pinkie ring starts cuttin' into his ham hand and he pulls it back and stares at the blood pourin' down it as it starts turnin' into a pig's trotter with a diamond ring stuck in the side.

I jump up on the base of the statue and point my own magic finger at him and shout, "Pig! You're nothin' but a fuckin' pig, and that's all you'll ever be!" and Dr. Himiitsu squeals and drops to all fours and his suit pops open as he gets even bigger and fatter an' then there's this giant fuckin' razorback hog starin' right up at me and St. Francis.

It screams an' goes after me, but then it realizes that pigs can't climb fuckin' statues and it glares at me with its evil little eyes and turns and starts rootin' through its clothes, but not like a pig would, but like it's lookin' for somethin', an' then it rips open a pocket an' out pops a prescription bottle that goes skitterin' across the cobblestones in front of the church. An' Dr. Pig goes trottin' happily after it, like he knows what's in it, but then Thaddeus says, "Allow me, Peter," an' jogs over to where the pig's about to get the prescription bottle an' whacks it with his cane — the bottle, not the pig — an' the bottle goes skitterin' out into the middle of the street, an' the pig looks at it, then looks at me an' does a double-take, 'cause Thad's a ghost an' it can't see him, then it goes after the bottle as Thad's skippin' along, laughin', gettin' ready to use his cane as a nine-iron again.

"'Thou elvish-marked, abortive, rooting hog,'" Thaddeus says an' gives the bottle another whack just as Dr. Pig is about to get to it, an' fuck, I don't know what he's talkin' about, but it's a cool-sounding curse, then Thad waits until the pig is just about to get to the bottle one more time an' he whacks it right down the storm drain like you'd shoot the ball into the little castle at the miniature golf course.

An' the pig screams an' Thad just takes out his pocket watch an' smiles an' looks at it an' says, "Just on time," an' steps back, an' fuck, I can feel the web jangling like the spider's dancing a rhumba on it, an' the next second the pig screams an' the brakes scream an' a *San Francisco Examiner* truck plows right into the razorback an' skids out an' smashes it into a fire hydrant an' blood an' water fountain everywhere.

Thaddeus stands there and smiles an' says, "Even timely news is seldom pleasant," an' I see Dr. Himiitsu's soul come out of the pig's body an' fuck, it's one of those moments when I ain't the one pullin' my strings, 'cause the next thing I know I'm pointin' and sayin', "You are a pig, you were a pig, and you always will be a pig!" an' the web snaps and thunder claps and Thaddeus stamps his cane three times on the ground and says, "It has been witnessed!" an' fuck, Dr. Himiitsu's soul winks out of there, off to the vat in his lab where he'll become a pig all over again. I just know it, okay?

Then it's all normal again, or at least as normal as it can be, with a fire hydrant gushin' water and pig's blood all over a newspaper truck, and the driver comin' out and wonderin' what the fuck's happened, an' whether he should call the police or animal control, an' one of the driver's eyes is blood red an' fuck if I know what *that*'s supposed to mean, an' Thaddeus is there grinnin' like he planned the whole thing, or at least knew it was goin' to come down, an' I think he did, and then there's Neville an' Blackrose an' Penny an' her cat comin' out of the church to see what all the commotion is about, an' fuck if I know how I'm going to tell them.

"Rather vulgar but effective nonetheless," Neville says, cold as ice, as if a man hadn't just been turned into a pig and butchered all in a minute's time. "I'm surprised you're not reeling from the Paradox, Peter."

"Ain't my problem, ain't my fault, ain't my Paradox," says I. "Bastard turned Norna into spider, an' if I guilt-tripped him into turnin' himself into a pig, well, that's his problem an' his Paradox, not mine. Karmic scales balancin', Threefold Law, all the rest of that shit."

Blackrose's lightin' up one of those clove cigarettes that I know's goin' to be the death of her, an' she takes a drag and looks at the pig an' the fountain an' the newspaper truck an' says, "I thought it was rather like the Witch Queen's spell in *Willow*. Or what Evil did to the dwarf in *Time Bandits*."

Penny rolls her eyes, sayin', "Remember the Duchess's baby? Lewis Carroll beat them both to it," an' she pets her cat an' it purrs like a normal cat would, but under the purrin' I hear it say, "A very ancient curse. Nicely done, young master," an' fuck, I can't take it anymore.

I turn to Neville. "A guy without a soul's goin' to be back here 'round midnight. I'd get myself lost if I were you." An' I turn aroun' an' walk back 'round the church to where I parked my car, 'cause I don't want to deal with the guy in the black trench coat when he comes back to pick up Dr. Himiitsu an' all he finds is a ripped suit an' a butchered hog.

An' Thaddeus is taggin' along like he's been doin' for the past month, but he's not sayin' anythin', an' neither am I, 'cause if you stopped to tell off every ghost you saw, you'd never get anywhere. Leastways I wouldn't.

An' the trees aroun' the back of the church are hung with spiderwebs an' skeleton leaves an' dewdrops the size of pearls like in one of those old fairy-tale book pictures like Penny likes, an' fuck, it's all gettin' weird again, 'cause instead of the back of the church an' the street where I parked my car, there's a forest grove with trees with cobwebs and diamonds and skeleton leaves, an' I step into the grove an' a star comes down from the constellations overhead, 'cept it ain't a star, it's a giant silver spider, an' the constellations have lines in them like they do in picture books, an' the spider's turnin', turnin', faster and faster like one of those crystal window danglies they sell down on Haight, goin' into a sparklin' silver blur.

Then it slows down, an' instead of spider legs, I see silver cords, woven together into one of those hammock chairs like they sell at Ren Faire, an' in the chair is Norna, like I remember her, 'cept that she's dressed in cobweb lace that's made out of real cobwebs, silver an' gray, an' she's got a spiderweb tattooed across her cheek, an' silver chains going from the rings in her eyebrows to the cords in the chair, an' her eyes are blue as sapphires with pupils in the shape of black widows.

"Nice contacts," I say, but fuck, they ain't contacts, they're the way she really is, though it looks fuck-all better than the giant spider I've seen runnin' around the vault of the Waydown. "Long time no see, Norna."

"Norna," she says. "A Norn. Weaver. Fatespinner. All are me. I am Three."

"You're fucked in the head, that's what you are," I say, an' Norna laughs, a tinklin' sound like bells and crystals, but whatever it is, it ain't human, an' she says, "Urth. Clotho. Aglaia. Call me what you will. This is my Destiny and Dr. Himiitsu was but its agent." She pauses an' laughs again an' I see a glimmer of the old Norna. "Dr. Himiitsu has met his Destiny, and you were but my agent. Thank you, Peter."

Then she kicks back in the chair and it starts spinnin' again, an' she chants more names: "Skuld. Atropos. Thalia. Grandmother Spider, there is need!" an' she spins in a blur of silver and crystal, but instead of slowin' down to a stop like before there's this sudden *Snap!* an' the hammock drops to the ground an' there's this old bag lady gypsy-witch fortuneteller with a pair of big iron scissors over her head like she was a flamenco dancer an' they was castanets or somethin' an' the thread Norna was hangin' from is snapped in two an' Norna's gone.

"Shuttle and Loom. Destiny. Doom. Free Will or Fate?

Which will it be, young man?" an' fuck, I know this old biddy, she told my fortune just before the ghosts nearly killed me the last time, an' she smiles an' says, "Ah yes, you will remember Madame Cleo Verthank, won't you, young Peter? Here, see, I will remember you too," an' she reaches into her sleeve an' pulls out a snag about as thin as a piece of spiderweb an' as long as your arm an' she says, "Ah yes, here will be your thread. Try to cut it, we do, but see, it will be stubborn," an' she takes the big iron shears an' goes *Snap!* right on the thread. *Snap! Snap!* But it ain't broken, an' she shakes her head an' says, "Stubborn, stubborn, stubborn. There will be Destiny spun into it. Frayed it, we have, but it won't be broken. Not till we get sharper shears."

She looks up and smiles an' her teeth are all snaggled an' rotten. "But we will have sharper shears now. See, young Peter?" an' she holds up her scissors an' they're glistenin' silver like they came brand-spankin' new from Ginsu, an' fuck, I know they can cut me faster than they can cut a tomato, an' she holds the scissors close to the thread and moves them gently back and forth — *snip! snip!* — but she ain't cut my thread yet, an' she says, "It is such a strong thread, though. It will be a pity to cut it short, even if Destiny will be all that holds it together. But perhaps it will find a useful place in the tapestry and we will not have to cut it just yet. Yes?"

She smiles like a housewife on TV an' looks at her new shears an' says, "Such pretty scissors. We will enjoy them very much," an' then she tosses them in the air, open, an' they get bigger an' bigger and they come down toward me an' Thad says, "Do not move, Peter," an' the next thing I know the blades are bigger than Christmas and twice as bright an' they come down on either side of me an' I'm there right between the blades.

Then everythin' shimmers an' I'm there on the street corner, with rain on the street on either side of me, shinin' in the moonlight like the old witch's scissors.

"What the fuck was that?"

"That was an omen," Thaddeus says, an' stands there, polishin' his glasses. "The Fates have informed you that you will shortly come to a crossroads in you life, and how you decide in that matter will determine whether you live or die."

Fuck, I already figured that out myself. Like I said, Thad likes statin' the obvious, an' there's only one thing I haven't figured out yet. "What's it to you?"

"To me?" Thaddeus is taken aback, then takes another second to polish his glasses and put them back and flick the ghost dust from his suit. "I was wondering when you'd get around to asking. I am your spirit guide, young necromancer, duly bonded and deputized by the Fates."

"I didn't ask for a fuckin' spirit guide."

"You get one, nonetheless." Thaddeus stands there, gray-gloved hands on top of his dragon's-head cane, top hat tilted to one side. "I meddled in your Destiny one too many times, I'm afraid, and one does not toy with Fortune's Favorites unless one is willing to pay Her price. Thankfully for me, the Fates recognized my talents, and the position is one to which I am well suited."

Thaddeus is a lying bastard when it suits him, but what he's sayin' right now has the ring of truth, and I don't like it. Don't like it one bit. "So you get to play Jiminy Cricket for me?"

He adjusts his gloves. "Hardly, Peter. You already have sufficient conscience, and certainly more than I possess." He taps his hat with his cane and smiles. "I believe my job in death is rather the same as it was in life: counselor, advisor, occasional agent and go-between. You need tutoring in diplomacy and tact, wisdom and manners, things that I can provide, if you are ever to become a creditable mage."

"I ain't a mage; I'm just a kid who nearly got killed and has had weird shit happen to him ever since."

Thad gestures with his cane. "If that isn't an admirable

definition of a journeyman spiritualist, I don't know what is. You talk to wraiths, you see omens in the everyday, and you associate with two young witches — one of whom has a very potent familiar, I might add — as well as a wizard who has succeeded in the ancient magic of removing his soul from his body and placing it elsewhere for safekeeping. And you just cursed an enemy sorcerer such that he turned into a pig. Tell me, if presented with such a case, wouldn't you define the person in question as a magician?"

"Fuckin' lawyer," I say, but he's got a point, an' I shiver as I feel the spiderwebs around me. "What do the Fates want me to do?"

"That, unfortunately, I cannot say," Thad says, an' I look at him an' he quickly puts up his hands, fingers spread, cane held in one thumb. "Not, mind you, because I cannot, but because I honestly don't know. The Fates, if I may be so bold, are rather like politicians: They are deliberately vague, such that they cannot be held to any one thing in particular. What is before you is a matter of free will, and they will decide whether or not to cut your thread based upon your decision. To tell you exactly what the crossroad is, however, would be to affect that decision, and thereby impinge on free will. Q.E.D. I am therefore as much in the dark as you."

Shit. Fuckin' lawyers everywhere. "All right then, Thad. You're my spiritual advisor. Advise me."

He doesn't look as flustered as I'd hoped, but then he's a fuckin' lawyer an' he's used to being put on the spot. He reaches into the pocket of his waistcoat an' checks his watch. "I would advise, Peter, that we leave this place posthaste. Time flows rather quickly around Madame Cleo, as would befit the Muse of History, and it is currently a quarter to midnight. And as I would suspect the gentleman in black is highly punctual, that gives us only fifteen minutes to get ourselves away from this place."

Good advice, I'll admit, an' I get in my car an' start 'er up an' pause just a moment to let Thad in, 'cause ghosts can't open doors unless they get real pissed, an' even if they do, they tend to slam 'em somethin' fierce. So we just get the hell away from the Waydown and go off to Death Guild.

Death Guild, like I said, is on Mondays, at the Trocadero on Fourth, an' it's a lot like the other Goth clubs, but more low-key than Usher an' less kindergoth than Temple. I find parkin' on the street, an' that tells you how dead it is, an' Thad an' I make our way down as he keeps up this lecture on respectability and propriety and decorum and how to be a stuffy, pompous wizard and fuck-all who knows what else, an' then I see her an' whoa-mama an' holy shit.

There's a lot of weird stuff goin' down tonight, that's all I can say, 'cause there, hangin' out in front of the club like she's waitin' for me, is the most righteous Goth chick you ever seen, with black leather an' black lace an' thigh-high bitch-boots with buckles all over the place an' jet black hair down to her waist, and it ain't none of it dyed 'cept the lace an' leather.

That's what you see at first glance. But when you blink you see the same outfit — bitch-boots, leather, lace, ankh, all the rest of that shit — but the woman in it is so old she makes Madame Cleo look like a prom queen, and the fortuneteller witch is so bagged-out she makes a sack of rotten potatoes look good. The woman here is shriveled up in her skin, which'd be dried up like a mummy's if it weren't so wrinkled, and her head's bald 'cept for some long wisps of white hair, so fine they look like spiderwebs, an' the only thing that looks young about her at all is her left eye, which is bright as an agate an' lookin' at everythin', an' I mean *everythin'*, but I don't mean it's precisely young either, just that it's not covered with cataracts like the other one, 'cause the look in that eye is twice as old as Penny's cat an' a lot hungrier.

An' then I blink an' I see the righteous Goth chick again an' she's smilin' an' laughin' an' whoa-mama, is she a kick in the crotch, but when I look in the reflections in the windows of the shops next door, all I can see is the old bat strapped into the young chick's clothes.

At least that's what I see, 'cause everyone else is smilin' an' laughin', or not as takes their fancy, but no one is takin' any notice of the righteous Goth chick 'cept as one hot babe who's too cool to touch.

I pause at the end of the line an' nudge my spirit guide. "Thad, check 'er out. Watcha see?"

"See?" Thad echoes. "I can only assume you're referring to the woman standing next to the door. I see a woman divided; the left side of her is young and beautiful, but strangely repellent, while the right is ancient to the point of death, though much more natural. Strange. I can only assume that she suffers from a divided fate as do you, Peter. Also, take note of the intriguing tattoo on her forehead; a signet of some form, but I must admit that I find it singularly disturbing, though I've never seen its like."

I usually don't like lookin' any harder than I do already, but Thad's piqued my curiosity, an' I give her the hairy eyeball, an' holy shit, Thad's right, right there on her forehead are a couple circles filled with funny letters an' squiggly lines, an' I know what it is, though only place I ever seen one before is in a book, an' I hope I never see one again.

Let me tell you somethin'. You know how kids like stickin' little tags in their books that say *Ex Libris* or *This Books Belongs To* an' have a little picture with all sorts of flowery shit like hearts an' unicorns an' teddy bears, along with their signature an' address so if the book gets lost, someone can send it back to them? Well, kids ain't the only ones who do shit like that. Demons do it too, an' they each got their own special sigil like cattle ranchers got their brands, an' when they get a soul, they burn it with their own special mark so the other demons won't go poachin' on the souls that belong to them.

I saw a book once that had a whole bunch of demon sigils in it, an' I didn't want to look at it very long so I don't know which demon's bookplate this lady had stuck on her forehead, but shit, I was scared, 'cause if you know anythin' about demons, the ones that got bookplates are the high-class mucky-muck types an' not the little shit imps like the ones in the nuthouse who go around sittin' on your shoulder goin' "Kill! Kill! Fuck your mother!"

But a couple girls had slipped into line behind me when I was lookin' at the hag chick's forehead, an' I'm standin' there, an' I can't just go back to the car 'cause then the bat chick would notice that I'd noticed, an' like Thad told me earlier, people don't take too kindly to you noticin' nasty facts about them that they're tryin' to hide, an' fuck, if *I* were four hundred years old an' had a demon's bookplate stuck to my forehead, I wouldn't want to go advertisin' either.

So I just get my money an' my I.D. out, an' I can see the hag chick checkin' out my driver's license as I check in, an' fuck, she's already got her hand stamped, an' she cruises in after me, an' the deejay has Kill Sister Kill on an' I just wander on up an' through an' over to the upstairs bar, Thad close behind me, an' fuck, I've never been so glad to be around a ghost before, 'cause he's one more person between me an' the bat chick with the demon's bookplate on her forehead.

I get a seat at the bar, an' Thad takes the empty one next to me, an' I get a beer, an' he gets nothin', an' fuck, I knew it was goin' to happen, my warnin' bell's goin' off like a fire alarm, an' the next thing the bat chick is next to me an' she's sayin', "Is this seat taken?"

I try to play it cool. "Do you see anyone sittin' there?"

She looks at Thad, or really right through him, an' smiles an' says, "No," an' she sits down, but Thad's a ghost an' he's used to people nearly sittin' on him so he's out of there, but fuck, I swear it, the dragon's head on his cane comes to life for a second an' hisses at her, an' that's a real trick, 'cause the cane's as dead an' buried as Thaddeus is, an' twice as old.

But the woman next to me looks like she could beat them both by a long shot even if you added both their ages together, but then I blink an' she's beautiful again, 'cept for the demon's sigil on her forehead, an' she leans over an' smiles an' breathes out through perfectly made-up black lips, "Buy a lady a drink?"

I take a swig of my beer, wishin' it was somethin' a lot stronger, but I shrug an' say, "Sorry. I'm broke. This is about all I can afford." I slosh my beer an' she smiles, an' it's the most beautiful smile I've ever seen, an' I'm not lookin' at the demon sigil. Not lookin' at it no way.

Then I blink an' the old hag is leerin' at me, an' she reaches out one withered hand an' puts it on mine an' says, "Let me buy you one, then," an' I flinch back, blinkin', an then she's drop-dead gorgeous again an' leanin' over to the bartender, who's givin' her this look of jealousy an' lust, equal parts mixed, an' the Goth chick is sayin', "Bartender, something special. Goldwasser and Aquavit. Two, please."

Then I see the hag again, but the bartender is still givin' her the lust-envy look, an' she's sayin', "I'm sorry, but we don't have any—"

"Oh, I'm sure you do. I can see them from here, those two bottles in the back." An' the bartender gets down on her knees an' reaches to the back of the liquor cabinet an' pulls out these two bottles, all fancy, an' one of them has flecks of gold floatin' 'round in it, but I been to Death Guild before an' they didn't have no Goldwasser then, an' none of that other stuff either, but the bartender is fixin' up glasses of them next, neat, an' I don't recall the bar havin' glasses anywhere near that nice either, but they do now, an' the bartender sets the drinks in front of us an' the old hag hands her a fifty an' says, "Keep the change," an' fuck, I blink an'

next thing she's the knockout Goth chick an' she's raisin'
her glass an' says, "To pleasure," an' tosses it back.

I grab mine, but I stop myself before I slug it back, no
matter how much I want to, 'cause fuck, you don't take
candy from strangers, an' you don't take drinks from women
with demon brands on their souls. An' I wince an' blink one
eye an' not the other, an' fuck, I'm seein' 'em both, the Goth
chick an' the old bat, one over the other like a double-
exposure.

"My name's Jodi," she says, then looks down at my drink,
"Go ahead, try it. You'll like it," an' there's little specks of
gold floatin' around in it, blue and gold, an' I set it down
'cause I don't want to trance out, not lookin' at somethin'
like that, 'specially not somethin' that's been given to me
by a woman who can't make up her mind whether she's
young or old an' has a demon's bookplate stuck on her
forehead.

"Ain't finished my beer yet," I say, an' I take a pull from
it, an' she just smiles an' takes a sip of her own drink, gold
an' blue, but fuck, just the smell of it is a turn-on, an' if it
weren't for seein' the old hag an' the demon's brand on her
soul, my cock would be thumpin' the underside of the bar.

"You're Peter," she says, an' puts her hand on my knee,
an' fuck, my cock does jump at that, 'cause it can't see the
wrinkles or demon's sigil, an' in four hundred years, she's
learned how to turn a trick or two, that's all I can say. But
she says, "I saw your I.D, and I know your friend Penny.
Haunted Peter, Spooky Pete, that's what they call you."

"You where she got her cat?" I say, an' her hand stiffens
on my leg then, like a claw, an' that sure ain't sexy, but then
she relaxes an' says, "Why, yes. My cat, her cat, who can
really say? Who can ever claim ownership of a cat?" an' she
laughs, long and light, but it sounds real fake an' strained.
"I'm sure Grimalkin will come back when he tires of her,"
but she doesn't sound so sure, an' I decide that what gave

me the creeps about the cat wasn't how old it was, but that it had spent that much time with her.

An' I want to get out of there real bad, but I don't want to piss the bitch off, so I lock eyes with Thad an' he smiles an' nods an' says, "Perhaps a trip to the ladies room would be in order," an' whacks Jodi's glass toward her.

But shit, the only thing I ever saw move that fast was a vampire, 'cause Jodi catches it before it spills even one drop. "*Clumsy—*" she says, then stops, 'cause the bartender is at the other end of the bar, then she looks around. "Strange. Do you think there might be ghosts here, Peter?"

I don't see any reason to hide it. "Sure. There's ghosts everywhere. Just don't get 'em mad."

An' she looks around an' I think she's got a little spooked, 'cause I'm thinkin', if this bitch is into demons, then I'll bet even money she's killed more than one person, an' if she fucked up even once an' didn't get a demon (if you can call that fuckin' up), then a demon weren't there to eat the person's soul an' she's gonna have at least one real pissed dead person out there, an' I wouldn't want to trade places with someone who did somethin' like that.

Then she cocks her head at me, an' I'm seein' the hag an' the knockout at the same time, an' she says, "You don't trust me, do you, Peter?" An' fuck no, I don't trust her, but all I say is, "Sorry. Don't trust anyone."

Then she picks up her drink an' swirls it aroun', gold dancin' in the blue, an' she says, "Poor Peter. So much pain. Let me take the pain away…" An' she takes a sip, and then fuck, I told you how fast that bitch can move, she grabs me by the back of the head an' she pulls me close an' sticks her tongue between my lips, an' I don't want to let her in, but I do, an' the next thing I know I taste this sweet taste like lemons and cloves, an' shit, it's the drink she wanted me to take a sip of, an' then I just melt an' black out an' I'm scared 'cause it feels so good and so dark and warm all around, like dyin' did, like falling asleep in the snow.

An' then I wake up, or at least I think I do, 'cause it's warm an' there isn't any pain an' I hear people laughin' in the background, but it's nice laughter, not mean, an' there's a smell like apples an' smoke an' I open my eyes an' I'm lyin' on a couch, crushed green velvet, made for lyin' down on like those psychiatrists got in the old pictures, not like the real ones, 'cause I been in those places an' the couches the shrinks have are made of orange vinyl with scratches on them from where people have chewed them.

But this one's nice, like I said, an' instead of wearin' my own clothes, I've got a tux on, old-fashioned black velvet, an' the apple smell's comin' from the fireplace next to me, an' the flames are jumpin' an' cracklin', but it's not a real fire, I can tell, 'cause if it were a real fire I'd be trancin' out an' seein' little pictures, or salamanders dancin' in the flames, but it's not, 'cause all there is is a fireplace with a fire in it, nothin' else.

An' opposite me, on another fancy, old-fashioned shrink's couch, is Jodi, but she don't look like the old hag no more, an' I don't see the demon sigil on her forehead neither, an' all of the Goth chick stuff is gone too 'cept for the long black hair, an' she's wearin' this red velvet dress, but it's real nice, not slutty, like somethin' your sister would buy for a Christmas party, with poufy sleeves an' lace an' a little heart-shaped silver locket in place of the ankh 'round her neck, an' fuck, no matter how hard I look, I can't see nothing wrong with her, an' with nothing else, neither.

Then this Mexican girl comes up, dressed in another Christmas dress, but this one's blue, an' she's got a tray with a pitcher an' a couple of mugs an' I can smell the cinnamon comin' from it, an' the chocolate, an' Jodi says, "Thank you, Consuela. No, I'll manage," an' she takes the tray from her an' sets it on the little table between us an' starts pourin' cups of Mexican chocolate.

"Where the fuck am I?" I say, an' she starts to try an'

give me a cup of chocolate, but then when I won't take it, sets it down an' says, "The Hellfire Club."

I don't know whether she's makin' a bad joke, or the demons are, but I say, "The Hellfire Club's a place in the X-Men comic books. And you sure as hell don't look like Miss Frost, so I guess that makes you Selene."

"Selene?" she says an' laughs like at some private joke, an' I don't know what's so funny, 'less she knows that Selene's this mutant vampire demon huntress witch who goes around suckin' people dry for their youth an' power, an' that's how she gets her jollies too. "No, I've never gone by that name, I'm afraid. I'm Jodi. And the Hellfire Club is much more ancient than... what was that comic book you mentioned?"

"The X-Men."

"Yes, yes, the X-Men. No, I'm afraid that the Hellfire Club goes back quite a bit further, publicly to at least the eighteenth century. A meeting place for philosophers, revolutionaries, freethinkers. Why, Benjamin Franklin was even a member."

She gets this dreamy look in her eyes an' sips her chocolate an' I don't care, I know she's a witch, an' she knows I know, an' she knows I got power, so I say, "How was old Ben in the sack?"

"Quite amusing," she says, then looks at me, realizin' what she said, then shrugs it off an' leans back an' sips her chocolate. "He wrote an essay on why you should have sex with an older woman, you know. I was the inspiration."

"'Koo-koo-kachoo, Mrs. Robinson,'" I say, but I ain't The Lemonheads, like to think I got more sense than that, an' this Hellfire Club just looks like some nice holiday party at some fancy place 'round Nob Hill, 'cause out the window I can see the city an' the bay, an' it looks so fuckin' nice 'cause I can't see anythin' but what's in front of me, not people dyin', not scars on people's souls, not love an' fear an' hate an' death an' ghosts an' demons an' all the rest of that crazy shit, none of it, 'cause it's all just nice an' normal, like a holiday party, an' I want to just sink right back an' relax an' enjoy it 'cause it's nice an' I don't feel or see anythin' wrong, but that's what it's like when you fall asleep in the snow, that's what it's like dyin', an' I want to believe in it but I can't, 'cause if you do, then you fall into darkness just like the Little Match Girl, an' the next day they find your frozen body, an' it may look like Heaven, but it ain't, 'cause Jodi said it was the Hellfire Club, an' she's got a demon's bookplate on her soul so she knows what she's talkin' about.

"Poor Peter," Jodi says, "you're still so very troubled. I thought if I took away the pain, you'd be willing to hear me out. But I see so much of the pain is inside." An' she leans back an' holds her little heart-shaped locket an' takes a sip of her cocoa an' says, "I was so hoping you could help me."

She looks real pretty, real sweet, just the sort of babe you'd want to hold and stroke her hair an' tell her it's all right, but I know stuff about magic, an' demons, an' shit like that, an' if you say you can help her, she can hold you to it, an' I don't know what sort of help she wants so I hold my trap shut like Thad taught me an' wait for her to say something.

She finally figures out that just smilin' an' lookin' pretty ain't gonna be enough, so she goes, "I'm very old, Peter. Much older than I look. You probably couldn't guess how old I am," an' I think, *Fuck I couldn't*, cause I saw the way she looked before she slipped me some of that drink on her tongue, but Thad told me to keep my trap shut, an' you don't talk about a woman's age, so I just let her rattle on. "My time is very near done on this earth. Oh, there are things I could do to extend it — potions, rituals, great secrets and mysteries — and I'll admit that I've done some of them, but it hasn't been enough. Not enough to extend these last few haggard years. And you see, I fear death, not because I fear dying, but because I have made a pact with one of the Dark Masters, Charnas, and after my death he will have my soul. Not for eternity, but for a long, long time."

She stops and pours herself another cup of chocolate, lookin' for a second at mine, 'cause I haven't touched it an' I'm not gonna, then takes a sip an' smiles an' goes on: "I will not complain of my treatment from Charnas. He has honored his side of the bargain, and I have received for my trouble great power and pleasure, and a long and satisfying life. Almost all on credit. However, the bill is coming due, and he will extend credit no further, and my attempts to extend my life by other means have met with some... frustration.

"And so I though it might be possible to renegotiate my contract. I will not sell myself short — I have a powerful soul, a fine mind, certain talents, and a place in the order of things. But you, Peter, I must envy, for yours is one of the most powerful spirits I have encountered, and you are marked by Destiny for great things... provided you live long enough." She takes a sip of her cocoa and her eyes are sparklin' above the cup, pale green and witchy. "I know what you fear, Peter. Your lifeline is at a crossroads, and if you make a false turn, your Destiny will be at an end. I saw it when I glanced at your palm, when I saw your name.

"But it needn't be that way. If you were to take my place on my contract, Charnas would surely approve the deal, leaving me free, and giving you many powers and gifts in the bargain. Even freedom from death, Peter. Charnas gave me a greatly extended lifespan and protection from all manner of petty deaths and troubles, and that merely for a promise of servitude for a span of years. For a greater commitment, you might have eternal youth and beauty, as well as freeing me. And in exchange for this boon, Peter, I would willingly serve you as I would have served Charnas for that same period, be your lover, your plaything, your wife, whatever it is you might want."

I've got a hard-on like you won't believe, an' she starts suckin' on her chocolate an' it feels like she's suckin' on my cock, an' holy shit, I've heard of sympathetic magic an' suggestion, but I never heard of anything like this, an' she's suckin' on the chocolate an' whoa-mama!

I'm just lyin' there, gaspin' an' pantin', an' then I look up from the shrink's couch an' she smiles over the top of her cup an' licks the cream off her upper lip. "Just a sample of what I can do," she says. "Would you like some more chocolate, or should I finish the rest?"

I just lie there, panting, an' she smiles, then takes the pitcher an' pours herself another cup, all the way to the brim, an' I feel my cock get hard all over, an' she lifts the cup, not spillin' a drop, an' touches it to her lips, then takes it down an' says, "Are you sure you wouldn't like some chocolate, Peter?" an' fuck, my cock is feelin' like it's gonna burst, an' her long red nails are strokin' the sides of the cup, an' she's lickin' her lips but not tastin' it, an' I can't take it anymore.

"Finish it," I gasp.

She smiles and lets her fingernails stroke the cup. "If you insist," she says, an' smiles, an' leans over the cup, just kissin' the surface, then slides her tongue across it, tastin' it, an' I ache an' moan on the couch, an' then she opens her lips an' tilts back her head an' chugs the whole thing all in one gulp an' whoa!

My eyes are squeezed tight with tears, an' I'm lyin' there, gaspin', an' I finally I open them up an' see Jodi smilin' an' settin' the cup back on the tray, an' then Consuela comes over an' says, "More chocolate, Miss Blake?"

"No!" I shout, an' there's a pause in the laughter in the room, but then there's a lot more of it an' the sound of clinkin' glasses. Jodi smiles an' bounces her eyebrows. "No, thank you, Consuela. But perhaps later we'll have a dessert wine."

Consuela leaves, an' Jodi's leanin' on the couch opposite

me, her head at the same level, an' she says, "That is but the least of the tricks Charnas taught me. Think, Peter. That and more could be yours tonight and every night."

Fuck! The bitch wants me to sell my soul for a blow job, but the way I'm feelin' right now, I'm ready to do it. But a little voice in the back of my head makes me say, "Evil…"

"Oh please, Peter," Jodi says. "This is the Hellfire Club, we're freethinkers here. Evil? What is evil? What, for that matter, is good? Evil is everything that makes us feel good. Lust, hunger, anger, all the passions, all of them are defined as evil, and yet when we satisfy that evil, we feel good. Didn't you enjoy the chocolate? I know that I did. I satisfied my hunger, and that felt good. And I know you felt the same. Don't deny it. You want more." She licks her lips, an' I feel her tongue across my cock. "Maybe not now, but later."

She rolls on her back on the couch an' hangs her arms over the back, hugging the pad an' closin' her eyes an' smiling. "The Dark Masters are merely the spirits that guide our darker passions, nothing more, nothing less. Don't dismiss them as 'Evil' without knowing what that means. They are our primal urges, the things that give our life its flavor and savor. Without them there would be no art, no beauty, nothing of any meaning in this world of flesh."

"Then why are you so fuckin' afraid to go with them?" I just manage to gasp it out, but it's somethin' I wanna know.

Jodi rolls over an' opens her eyes, her hair hangin' down over the back of the couch beside her. "Because I'm afraid it will be too much for me. Oh, I know it may sound silly, but no matter how long I've lived, I'm not yet jaded with this pretty world, and I don't want to give myself over just yet." She smiles an' says, "But I believe you're ready. Let me introduce you to Master Charnas."

She smiles an' tugs on the locket 'round her neck an' pulls it off an' tosses it into the fireplace an' it lands there in the logs, the silver caught in the coals, right in the devil's den, an' then it lights up like a flare an' the flames crackle purple an' red an' the next thing they boil up an' roll out of the fireplace an' then there's this guy standin' there.

Remember how I said Dr. Pig was a flash dude? I mean, before he turned into a pig. Well, Dr. P. ain't got nothin' on this guy, 'cause when I say flash, I mean flash, dressed in black leather, stretched an' stressed an' with a purplish sheen, cut an' tailored to a T, an' it doesn't look like cow leather neither, somethin' else, an' he has long nails an' white teeth an' pointed ears an' black hair slicked back from his widow's peak an' he's handsome as the devil, though you'd probably expect that.

"All hail Master Charnas!" cries everyone in the room but me, an' he waves his hand like he was at Ren Faire an' calls back, "Hail and well met! The Lord of Misrule is here! The Dark of the Year is upon us, so let the merriment continue!" and there's cheers an' then he sweeps Jodi up from the couch an' she just swoons in his arms like she's on a romance novel cover, if romance novels had demons on them, an' he says, "Kiss me, Jodi, my sweet," an' he grabs her an' holds her tight in a clench an' whoa-boy! I can feel his tongue on my cock, an' I'm not gay or nothin' but that kiss was like nothin' Jodi ever gave me, an' what she gave me was like nothing I ever had before, an' I just pass out an' moan.

An' I wake up to hear him sayin', "Chocolate. You've been drinking chocolate, Jodi dearest, and here's the dear boy and we've hardly been introduced. Naughty girl." An' I open my eyes to see him give her another kiss, but real chaste, on the lips but with the mouth closed, but I still feel it on my cock.

I look at him, an' he smiles at me, an' all his teeth are pointed, but then he looks at Jodi an' says, "Very naughty girl. You've put a spell on him. How do you expect me to enter into a compact if his senses are deceived? Remove the scales from his eyes."

"But Master," says Jodi, "he could not bear to see you in

your full glory!" an' I don't know jack about scales, but the line sounds fake to me, an' then Charnas says, "Jodi..." an' she blows two kisses toward me, an' holy fuck, I can see again, see the way I usually do, an' Jodi's an old hag with blood runnin' down her face from where his tongue cut her, an' the fireplace has little imps dancin' around in it fuckin' like weasels, an' Charnas...

Holy fuck, I don't know what to say. Charnas, he... Like when he kissed me, but... Oh God, an' I don't say that lightly. You know I don't. I'm lookin' in the face of a god, 'cause he ain't like the usual run of demon, nosiree, he ain't. An' I ain't gettin' a straight look at 'im neither, cause I'm lookin' at the floor, an', oh shit, the sight's still burnin' me, an' I squeeze my eyes shut an' I scream, 'cause I don't ever wanna look at that again, but a part of me wants to look at him straight on an' burn right up, an', oh fuck, it hurts, it hurts so bad I don't ever want it to stop.

An' then I hear his voice, an' it's all aroun' me, an' it feels like blood's pourin' out my ears, it feels so good, an' he says, "ALLOW ME TO APPEAR IN A MORE HUMBLE SEMBLANCE."

"Yeah! Sure! Please! Anything!" An' then I feel nails on my face, an' two kisses on my eyelids, an' I open them an' I look up, an' it's Charnas again, but the way he looked before, just flash an' handsome an' not so great you can't take it, an' his tongue slides out, long an' thin, an' touches my ears, an' I moan, an' I can hear again, but then I look aroun' an' he's the only thing that's changed, 'cause Jodi still looks like an old bat an' the imps are still goin' at it in the fireplace an' aroun' the room are people with demon bookplates stuck on their foreheads, some Charnas's, some not, an' ladies without souls, an' guys with demons in them, but I mean regular demons, not high mucky-muck types like Charnas with the bookplates an' all that.

Charnas smiles an' lets his nails trail down my face, an' it's the biggest turn-on I've ever felt, an' I don't want him to move away, but I do, an' he ends up movin' down my arm an' holdin' one of my hands in his own as he's kneelin' next to me an' he raises it to his lips an' kisses it, then he pauses an' his tongue slides out again, long an' thin, an' licks me aroun' the wrist an' I just about pass out, but he holds my arm so I don't fall back off the couch. "Pardon me, dear Peter. That was so forward of me earlier, we'd hardly been introduced, but Jodi can be so careless with her charms." He smiles an' licks his lips, an' I feel just a whisper of it lick along me, but that's enough to make me moan, an' Charnas smiles. "Jodi tells me you might be interested in taking over her contract. And while I would deeply regret losing the services of so sweet and accommodating a soul as Jodi, I must admit she told the truth, you are a prize worth fighting for. And so," he says, "what would you like in your contract?"

There's a pen on the table then, an old-fashioned fountain pen, and an inkwell and a piece of parchment and a little knife. But the inkwell's empty, but I know what's supposed to go in it, an' fuck, the threads are janglin' around me and it's now or never, live or die, but I don't want it now, but it's gonna go down anyway, an' I say, "I want my fuckin' lawyer."

Charnas pauses an' lets go of me an' I nearly fall off the couch, but I grab it an' the headrush helps me come to. "Dear me. You children of the modern age. So distrustful..." but I'm lookin' around, but I don't see Thaddeus, an' shit, I'm seein' everythin' else too, so I should see ghosts unless they're not here, an' I look aroun' an' scream, "Thad! Where the fuck are you?"

"Goodness, Peter. I was wondering when you would have the sense to call," Thad says, an' he's there, standin' right next to me, then he looks around an' sees Charnas an' Jodi an' the whole bunch of people without souls or with demons or bookplates or fuck-all who knows what evil shit wrong with their souls. "My, it appears you've gotten us into a rather difficult situation."

"I am Charnas, the Lord of Misrule," says Jodi's high mucky-muck demon lover and he grinds his pointed teeth at Thaddeus. "Who are you and what business have you here, shade?"

Thad's in his element all of a sudden, 'cause he's doffin' his hat in a long flourish an' makin' a fancy bow, then coming back up. "Thaddeus Anthony Winters, attorney at law, Advocate for the Loyalists, Herald to the Hierarchy, and duly bonded and appointed spirit guide to Peter Cameron, my client, by the authority of the Fates. My card, sir," he says an' hands Charnas this piece of ghost paper, then as the demon's lookin' at it, puts his hat back on an' taps it into place an' the head of his cane is hissin' at Charnas as he does it an' for all I know it's swearin' in Chinese.

Charnas smiles at Thad an' says, "We shall be seeing a good bit of each other then, Guide Winters, for your Peter will soon be contracting with us for a period of service, we hope a long one."

Thaddeus adjusts his spectacles on their ribbon an' looks at me an' says, "Indeed?" an' I'm rememberin' what it felt like when Charnas touched me, an' I point to the table an' say, "I ain't signed nothin', but he's got a contract," an' Thaddeus goes an' picks it up, which I guess he can do, all cold an' proper, 'cause it's a demon contract, but Jodi's lookin' at it floatin' in the air by itself I guess, 'cause she can't see ghosts, an' then Thad turns to Charnas an' says, "Sir? A blank contract?"

An' Charnas says, "I meant to fill it in."

An' Thad says, "Indeed you will, sir. And I will be going over every last letter."

An' Charnas says, "You approve?"

An' Thad says, "It's not for me to approve or disapprove. It is for me to negotiate and find the best possible deal for my client, and advise him of the best course of action, and currently that is to not sign anything until I have inspected every last letter. Moreover, I object to my client being drugged and spirited away, and I might add that it reflects very badly on you, Lord Charnas, to use such tactics. Very badly indeed."

Charnas looks real upset, then he takes his long nails an' grabs Jodi by the chin, an' she's still bleedin' from where he kissed her, an' says, "Jodi, sweet, this will not do at all. Take Peter back to where you found him, and in the meanwhile I will... negotiate... with Guide Winters." He looks to Thaddeus. "Will that be acceptable?"

Thaddeus considers. "For the time being, yes. First off we will need to work on ironclad definitions of the soul and eternity. Do you agree that that is reasonable?"

Charnas grinds his teeth. "That will take a great deal of time."

"Indeed." Thad smiles. "But you must surely admit that that is the prerequisite before any truly meaningful contract may be drawn up involving either, and I assume that you would want both."

"One would suppose so," Charnas grinds out, then looks to me. "But before you go, charming Peter, let me give you a gift. A little trifle to remind you of your time spent with us, and an apology for these unfortunate misunderstandings." He smiles an' waves his claws. "No strings attached."

"Let me also," says Thaddeus, "remind you, Peter, of the Fates and politicians. Accepting anything from anyone — no matter how innocently — may taint you in the eyes of those opposed to same," an' Charnas looks like he'd like to eat Thad's soul right now, but Thaddeus says, "It is also grounds for dismissal of any contract if it can be proven that one party has interfered with the other's legal counsel."

"Jodi!" Charnas says, an' she comes over to me an' leads me to the door, an' she's leerin' at me like she's still all sexy, but she's actually just an old bald hag with one good eye an' only one tooth. "I will always remember this evening, Peter," she says, an' licks her lips, an' I still feel her tongue across me, then she opens the door an' I get the fuck out of there, an' the next thing I know, I'm standin' outside the Trocadero, but it's closed, 'cause it's a lot later in the evenin'.

An' Jodi an' Charnas an' all the rest of their gang are gone, an' I look aroun', then get my ass down the street to where I parked my car, an' thank God, I got my leather jacket back on instead of the velvet tux Jodi dressed me in, an' I grab out my keys an' open the door an' climb inside an' slam the lock tight, an' it feels good to have the iron between me an' all the weird shit out there.

"Snip-snip," says a voice. "Snip-snip." An' I look in the rearview mirror, an' there, in my back seat, is Madame Cleo, an' my thread, an' her brand-new, shiny Ginsu scissors, an' I turn 'round an' she ain't there, but then I turn back forward an' I see her in the mirror goin' "Snip-snip, snip-snip," an' fuck, I can't take it anymore, an' I scream, "Fuck! Thaddeus, get your ass over here!" an' Thad appears in the seat next to me, his top hat gettin' scrunched into the roof, an' once he gets it off I say, "There's one of the Fates in the back seat an' she's gonna cut my fuckin' thread! I want you to sue the old biddy!"

Thaddeus looks around. "Indeed? I don't see anything, Peter," an' I look in the mirror, an' I don't see anythin' neither, no Madame Cleo, no scissors, no thread. Nothin'.

"Shit, all I want is to be able to control my own life," I say, an' fuck, it's all just too much for me to take, an' I wanna rip my eyes out, it all just hurts so much, an' all I want is darkness. "Just my own Destiny. Can you do it, Thad?"

"That is the most any man could wish for, and I doubt even Lord Charnas could deliver it." Thaddeus pauses a moment, an' all I hear is silence. Silence an' darkness, an' it's the best thing I ever had. "If it's any consolation, I believe you comported yourself quite well this evening, all things considered."

"I fucked up."

"No, you're being unnecessarily harsh on yourself. You are a pawn of Fate, and you managed to avoid being sacrificed, which is the most one can hope for when playing Fate's proscriptive game.

"When you reach the end of the path they've set you, assuming the metaphor holds true, then you will become a master of your own Destiny and a power to be reckoned with." Thad pats me on the shoulder. "Until then, however, Peter, please, call me the moment anyone mentions contracts."

He's got that fuckin' right.

Some days you wanna rip your fuckin' eyes out. You see what I mean now?

Some days you'd be happier just stayin' in the dark.

CROSSROADS

NIGEL D. FINDLEY

As above, so below. I read that somewhere.

I think I did, at least. Maybe I heard it, or even said it. It's difficult to keep track, to make sense of it all. I remember a lot from before... from *before*. But I've also lost so much. More than I realize, I'm sure. How can you tell you've lost a memory? You don't — can't — remember ever having it.

Maybe it'll come back with time, like my name did. How many days did I wander around in the gloom, not knowing who I was? Not knowing — suspecting, perhaps, but not knowing or admitting — where I was. *What* I was. That came back, didn't it? I'm John Cross (I still feel an unreasonable pride in having a firm grip on that). Born, lived — and eventually died — here in San Francisco.

I don't remember much about my actual death, and that could well be a blessing. I have this vague sense that there's *something* there, just beyond the veil of remembrance. Something terrible. When I let myself think about it, even peripherally, I can't shake the feeling that even that will come back in time, that the veil will draw back and I'll see it clearly.

And that terrifies me. It's a hell of a thing. I always thought death was the worst thing that could happen to me. I can't shake the feeling that this is worse.

With an effort, I push those thoughts away. It's neither the time nor the place for them. There's a figure coming toward me out of the misty gloom surrounding the entrance of the M.H. de Young Memorial Museum. I recognize it at once. Not the way it looks, that's very different from how I remember — and is that difference an artifact of my memory, or of changes rung by death itself? It's the way the figure moves that's so familiar, the way it carries itself: energy and drive, held in check.

I stand in the shadow of a parked tour bus and wait for my old mentor to approach. Part of me wants to run to him. He always answered my questions when both of us were alive — or, more commonly, followed the Socratic method and helped me answer my own queries. I want that wise, steady guidance again now, perhaps more than ever. There are so many more questions now...

But I don't move, I wait for him to approach me. As part of me wants to run to him, there's another part that desperately wants to run from him. That wants to turn and flee, to lose myself in the depths of the Shadowlands Golden Gate Park. I bite down, and I hold my ground.

His face is different; younger than I remember it. Smoother, less lined, less troubled. His eyes are unchanged, though; steady, sharp, eyes an eagle would kill to possess. They fix on my face, and once again I feel them probing the depth of my soul.

"Mr. Cross," Geoffrey Battersby says, the genuinely warm smile on his face belying his dry tone. "It's been some time."

For the first time, I manage to tear my gaze away from those eyes. I realize how he's dressed (or, at least, what outward appearance he's chosen for his Corpus, his "body" as a wraith). While he was alive, I had never seen him wearing anything but a conservative business suit, custom-made by the finest tailors in Saville Row. Now he's wearing a robe, or maybe "sari" is a better description: swaths of silky fabric, brilliantly and clashingly colored, wrapped loosely around him. And I see the symbol on his forehead — a complex glyph, raised and bone-white like scar tissue against his pale skin.

What am I doing here?

■

It seemed to make sense at the time. I needed something. Something to do, some course to my life, or unlife, or whatever. (Old turns of phrase die hard.) For days that felt like months, I wandered the Shadowlands of San Francisco. At first, I was searching for what I'd lost — memory, identity. Some kind of underpinning to who I was, who I'd been. I walked the streets of the city I knew so well, seeking fragments of my life, collecting them like the shards of something precious. I... well, *haunted* is as good a word as any, isn't it? I haunted places with emotional significance to me. The business district — that most of all. Nob Hill. The Grace Cathedral on Taylor, where my father's funeral had been held (and presumably my own). Housing developments I'd designed, strip malls I'd bought out and turned into money-making concerns. The marina over in Sausalito, where some buddies and I had sailed when we were up-and-comers still in business school.

I prowled just about every neighborhood of the city I'd always loved. All but the marina district, around Buchanan

Street. Why not there? Fear, that's why. That deep-down instinct in the gut, where you feel ultimate truths. There was something there, in that quiet residential area, that was dangerous to me. Potentially deadly, if that word still had any kind of meaning. I'd made my living — a very bloody good living, come to that — by trusting my gut. I trusted it now. I stayed away.

Apart from that restriction, I traveled far and wide through the city I'd always loved. I walked the streets of Russian Hill, unnoticed; strolled Market Street, watching unseen the predators who once would have scared me white. I rode, invisible to the passengers within, atop the cable cars that rumbled and clattered past Union Square down to the northern waterfront. By night, I walked the crowded sidewalks of Castro Street, watching the flow of people part around me like a river around a rock.

They couldn't see me, these living, these "Quick." I knew this, just as I'd never seen the many dead I must have passed while I was alive. They couldn't see me, but at some level they could sense me. At some atavistic, pre-conscious level, they knew *something* was there — something that didn't belong. And, for reasons they'd never be able to explain to themselves or each other, they always stepped around me or turned aside.

And there was more. Sometimes, I could fix a person with my gaze — just stare at them — and watch them become uncomfortable, sometimes even shiver and go pale. (Why only some people? Were the ones who did react like this more sensitive in some way? Or was it that they were closer to death?) What did they feel, these people, when I looked at them? Was it that strange chill that sometimes struck me without warning while I was alive, the sensation my mother used to describe as "someone walking on your grave"? When I'd felt that, had a wraith been staring at me?

It worked with cars, too, although not as reliably. Darting across a street, I'd often hear the honks of horns —

sometimes the squeal of tires, and the crash of impact — as drivers swerved for no reason they could adequately explain to their insurance companies. It was...

Well, it was intoxicating, once I'd realized what it meant. For an hour, maybe more, my dark mood flipped, inverted — shifted from one to the other pole of being, from depressed to manic. I remember laughing aloud as I ran out into the traffic on Van Ness. In my mind, I had an image of myself sprinting the length of the Golden Gate Bridge during rush hour, watching the cars slam into each other as they tried to clear out of my way.

When the car blindsided me, I think it was the surprise, more than the pain, that ripped the scream from me. Oh, the pain was there — sharp, tearing, but still somehow distant — as I was flung to sprawl on the median, but I think what I felt most in that moment was outrage. Affront that maybe I wasn't invulnerable, as I'd thought for those glorious few minutes. As I picked myself up, I watched the car that had hit me hurtle on. No brakelights, no response at all. Had the driver not sensed me? Had he been drunk, maybe? Or hadn't he had the time to react after he had sensed me? I didn't know, and couldn't think of any way of finding out.

I crouched there on the median, feeling the throbbing pain start to ebb from my body. My manic joy was gone, leaving nothing but a bitter aftertaste, and the darkness settled into my soul again.

I think I cried then. Not because of the pain. Not even because of the disappointment. No, it was another thought that cast those bleak shadows into my soul. A question.

What do you do with eternity?

What's that old joke? "It's not that life's so short, but that you're dead for so long..." I'd laughed at that one once. Now it didn't seem particularly funny. (I remember I hadn't laughed at the companion line: "He who dies with the most toys... still dies." And it still wasn't funny.)

I suppose this kind of afterlife would be the next best

thing to paradise for some people; hell, I'd gone to b-school with some of them. Luke Andrews, he'd have gotten off over being the perfect Peeping Tom, finally able to get his fill of looking at tits. And John Brown, he'd have staked out a seat in the back row of some art-film cinema and watched movies until his eyes were square.

Christ, think about it for a moment. Nothing to worry about, right? You're fucking *dead*, what else can happen to you? You don't have to eat, you don't have to crap, you don't get sick (I don't think). You don't have to buy clothes, or fill up the car. Hell, why *not* just sit back and watch the tits go by? You don't have to monitor your investments, or save for retirement, or pay the mortgage, or go to work to earn a living. More to the point, you *can't* do any of those things — whether you want to or not.

You can't do any of those things that had been important to me. The things that had given my life meaning and purpose and value. And think about that for a moment.

I mean, really think about it. Think about losing your livelihood, your self-image. About someone pointing to the things that you're good at, that you excel at, that give you "juice," and telling you, "Right, that's all, never again."

It's another joke, the kind of thing you could put on a T-shirt: "If what you do is what you are... then when you *don't* you *aren't*." Another joke, even less funny than the others. Think about it, and see if the cold wind doesn't whistle through your soul.

■

"A long time, Mr. Cross. A very long time indeed." My old mentor stops a few feet from me, looks me up and down carefully. I proffer him a hand; he takes it.

And then suddenly he steps in toward me and wraps me in a hug. The pressure of his arms around me is strong, claustrophobic.

He's shorter than I recall, I realize with a faint shock. I can look down on his balding head, pressed against my shoulder. Strange. I'd always been sure he was taller than I was.

The hug lasts for seconds. Too long. I want to pull away. I clear my throat, make a subtle movement. Battersby responds by squeezing me tighter. I feel my muscles stiffen. I don't like this, it… it scares me in some way.

Finally, when I think I'm going to have to pull away, he releases me, holds me at arm's length, looks up into my face with his raptor's eyes. "Mr. Cross," he says again, quietly. "Jonathan." There's a strange expression on his face, a complex one. Sadness — that's one of the elements. But there's pleasure there, too, plus a kind of… is *wisdom* too strong a word for it? And concern. For me? I shift uncomfortably.

"Geoffrey. How…?" I let my voice trail off. What the hell do you ask someone who's been dead for a decade longer than you? *How are you? Well*, dead, *Jonathan*…. I blink in confusion. And then I blurt out, "Was it suicide?"

I stare at him, aghast, my cheeks burning. Christ, what the hell am I thinking? How could I have…

But it doesn't seem to faze him, not at all. In fact, his expression seems to soften slightly. As if he approves of my question? What sense does that make? "I'm sorry," I say quietly, just to fill the silence.

He shakes his head — that quick, birdlike gesture of negation I've remembered all these years. "Never apologize for asking a reasonable question," he says firmly. "Didn't I teach you that? And that a reasonable question, considering the circumstances."

He pauses, and those sharp eyes unfocus for a moment. His smile fades, the sadness written more clearly across his features. "It's hard to recall," he says at last, his voice little more than a whisper. "I think not, but…" He shrugs millimetrically. "It's hard to know. When I lost control of the car? No, that wasn't intentional. But," another shrug, "would I have been driving then, under those conditions, if the thought hadn't been somewhere in the back of my mind? I think not."

I nod slowly. "We always said you'd gone out the way you lived. On your own terms, nobody dictating to you. No doctors, no one. We admired you for that." I blink again. "We never told anyone that, not even each other. But we did."

His eyebrows go up in that familiar questioning expression. "'Admired,' is it? Why? For my courage?"

I nod once more, suddenly feeling very uncomfortable. "We thought it was courageous." There's a defensive tone in my voice that surprises me.

Battersby looks away for a moment, and it's as if a cloud passes over his expression. Then his eyes fix me again. "I suppose I did too. At the time."

I wait for him to go on. There's obviously more, but he remains silent. Finally, "And now?" I prompt.

"Now?" He shakes his head again. "There was no courage in it. Weakness was more like it. I turned aside from learning — the chance to learn the most important thing I *could* learn — to avoid some pain." He sighs. "Pain passes, when you're alive, at least. Learning doesn't. It's the only thing you can really call your own."

I blink. This isn't what I expected. This isn't the Geoffrey Battersby I remember. And the discrepancy disturbs me, down on some profound level. But still I can feel the power of his intellect, of his personality. It's that power that prompts me to ask, "What learning? What did you miss out on?"

He smiles, a bittersweet expression that touches something within me, that almost wakes something I'd rather leave slumbering. "The meaning," he said simply.

I snort. "The meaning of life?"

"The meaning of *my* life." I look into his eyes again, and

I realize he's serious. This isn't any joke. And that realization sets me back. What the hell is this, Philosophy 101?

I snort again. "Do you think pancreatic cancer would have taught you that?" I ask, a touch sarcastically.

"I never gave it the chance," he says simply.

And I don't know what to say to that. The silence stretches uncomfortably. Then my old mentor lets me off the hook. "You sought me out, Jonathan," he notes quietly. "You sought me. Now you've found me. What can I do for you?"

There's still something unfamiliar in his tone, but at least the words set me at ease. This is the old Geoffrey Battersby, cutting to the bottom line. I let my face settle into its "business mask" — a smooth expression of confidence, as though it's inconceivable I won't get what I want. It's an expression that's stood me in good stead more times than I can count.

"You've got something going, Geoffrey," I tell my mentor calmly, firmly. "And I want in."

■

And so, again I walked the streets of my hometown. Bitter, I felt empty, hollow. Memories loomed up out of the murk, many of them incomplete, but all threatening in their way. Times when I'd lost control of my course through life. *Is this what eternity's going to be like?* I found myself wondering. *Centuries of wallowing in memories and emotions and doubts? Constantly questioning myself?* I had to move, I had to *do* something.

Almost spasmodically, I pushed myself away from the railing of the Golden Gate Bridge where I'd been standing. I had to *do* something. I repeated that to myself over and over again, like a mantra. And I knew that I was right. Even coming to that decision seemed to push back the darkness, push back the threatening doubts, the questions. I had something to cling to, to focus on. I was going to take charge of myself again, take back the reins of my own life... or unlife. And I thought I knew how.

For the first time, I sought out others like me. I'd seen other wraiths up to this point, of course: typically, miserable-looking creatures, sunken in despondence and misery, watching me hopelessly from doorways, or vacant lots, or — clichéd but true — from abandoned houses, or even from graveyards. Some of them had looked at me as though they'd considered approaching me, striking up a conversation. When that had happened, I'd just set my face in a firm, expressionless mask, and I'd let my gaze pass over them as if they hadn't even registered in my consciousness — the classic "neutral scan." None of the pathetic wraiths had even tried to breach the impalpable shield I'd put up around myself. (It was reassuring to know that some of the techniques I'd used to such great effect during my life still worked after it was over.)

But now I changed my approach. I sought out other wraiths, and it was I who struck up conversations with them. I hadn't lost what I'd always considered one of my greatest skills, I learned quickly. I was still a "social chameleon." I'd always prided myself on my ability to fit in with any individual, any social group. It had always seemed so simple to me that I couldn't understand how and why it was beyond so many people's grasp. It had always been a combination of perception and performance — sense what it was that people expected, what it was that they wanted, and give it to them. Put on the persona — "wear the mask" — that makes you a "kindred spirit," that makes you just like them. One of the greatest weaknesses of humankind is the desire for other people to validate your decisions, your attitudes, simply by sharing them. And it's that weakness I learned how to exploit very early in my business career. It always stood me in good stead, both on the job and off. With that simple technique, I could sway a hostile Board of Directors, ingratiate myself with trash-mouthed construction workers, or talk my way between the legs of just about any woman I wanted. Maybe some things do change when you cross the barrier between life and death, but that need for validation doesn't.

I talked to the other wraiths who up to this point I'd ignored. I "worked" them as carefully as if they were prospective investors in a project I had on the go. (And, in a way, I suppose they were.) I had to put up with much of the same mindless crap that made up most people's conversations when I was alive. I had to nod understandingly, make noises of commiseration as the wraiths told me the same sort of "victim" stories that had so sickened me while I'd lived. "Poor me, the world's too hard, I can't get ahead, everyone's putting on me, everything's so *difficult*..." And they threw up the same empty beliefs, the same false "religion" and "spirituality" that so many of the living hid behind. Sure, the trappings were different: Charon replacing God, or some fanciful Shining Lands replacing Paradise. But at their heart, the stories were just the same desperate attempts to abdicate responsibility, to pass on accountability for success and failure, life and death, to someone (or some*thing*) else. Self-defeating foolishness. But as I listened to this crap, I kept my real feelings to myself.

And, all in all, I was reassured. I knew I was on the right track. The wraiths I talked to were the losers, the know-nothings, the ciphers. I'd seen so many of them in my life.

Yet didn't that mean there were the others here, too? Those more like me? The ones who took responsibility for themselves rather than whimpering about fate, and fairness, and destiny, and all that crap — the ones who acted? Yes. It was just a matter of tracking them down.

The so-called Hierarchy was the place to start. The... well, "government" encapsulated part of the meaning, although "church" wasn't too far off-base either. A

monolithic organization that claimed — and some of whose
members actually believed — it was the heart, the soul and
the brain of wraith culture. Yes, it was a place to start.

But, like so many human organizations — living human
organizations, I mean — only a minority of its members were
the real movers and shakers I was looking for. The agents
— those who acted, rather than being acted upon. Within
the Hierarchy, there were the same losers as without: those
who believed that a title like Centurion set them apart and
made them worthwhile. There were the "wannabes," the
would-be agents who just didn't have the jam to do it right.
And there were the higher-ups who'd been promoted —
usually through simple seniority — beyond their level of
incompetence and spent their time being scared shitless that
somebody would figure it out.

Then, few and far between, there were the ones who were
carving out their own course. They were easy enough to pick
out, if you knew what to look for. I did. Iconoclastic,
innovative, constantly questioning the status quo, constantly
improving. Often unpopular within the monolith of the
Hierarchy, because they didn't buy into some of the sacred
cows, like seniority, shared responsibility, and ass-covering.
But sensitive to the dynamics, the flows of power, and ready
to take advantage of any shift in that flow.

These were the wraiths I was searching for.

I should have expected it, really, thinking back on it now.
But it came as a surprise when I encountered the first wraith
I'd known while I was alive.

■

Battersby looks at me in silence. I watch his eyes, waiting
for some cue. I'm expecting to see the steel doors slam shut
behind them, the way they always used to in negotiations,
when he'd hide his feelings and his true thoughts so deep
nobody could take advantage of them. But that's not what

happens. Instead of the cold, corporate steel I expect, I see...

Concern. Sadness. Even pity.

"What do you mean?" he asks me quietly.

A flash of anger burns in my chest. Quickly, reflexively, I suppress it. Emotions have no place in any negotiation. They cloud the mind, get in the way of a logical decision. I let my lips quirk up in what looks like a smile, but one without any emotion behind it. "You know what I mean, Geoffrey," I say, injecting confidence into my voice — confidence I'm not sure I feel anymore. "You've got something on the go."

He blinks, almost as if he's confused. On my mental tally sheet, I give him a point for his acting skill, but one point down for his tactics. He should know I'm not going to fall for this.

"Look." I take a step toward him, lean in conspiratorially. "You know what I can bring to the table, you know my skill-set, my strengths." I chuckle. "Hell, you taught them to me. Think about it: There's a place for me in your plans. And I want that place."

Battersby shakes his head slowly. The confusion's gone, and the sadness — the pity — is back. "I see," he muses. "I think I see. Yes, I really think I do. And I understand why you've reached the conclusion you have." He smiles, a bittersweet expression. "In your place, I'd conclude the same.

"But things have changed, Jonathan. More than you know."

The anger's back. Why's he playing these games with me? And this time it's harder to force it down. "Some things *never* change," I point out firmly.

He raises an eyebrow quizzically. "No?"

"No." I pause. "Look," I try again, "if you've got other partners and there's no room for me, just come out and tell me, okay? Maybe there's something I can bring to the table that they don't have, maybe there's some way to make this a win-win. But we can't get to that point if we don't lay it all out on the table. Right?"

Battersby sighs and shakes his head again. "You learned your lessons well, didn't you, Jonathan?" he asks softly. He reaches out and squeezes my upper arm with a surprisingly strong grip. "Listen to me," he says. His voice is still quiet, but there's an undertone of intensity that transfixes me. "Will you listen to me, Jonathan?"

The feel of his hand on my arm makes me uncomfortable, but I don't draw away. "Of course."

"You think I've got a deal going, don't you? You think that this," he gestures around him, to the museum that looms over his shoulder, to the whole of Golden Gate Park, "all this is some kind of business endeavor. A deal I'm putting together. A bargaining ploy to back that deal. Don't you?"

"Of course," I repeat.

Again he shakes his head. "Oh, Jonathan." His voice is a sigh. "You learned so well, every lesson I taught you. All the wrong lessons."

Wrong lessons? "I learned how to get the deal," I said firmly. "You taught me that. And I was good at it, very good. And I still am."

The pride in my voice seems to sting him. His raptor's eyes glisten in the half-light. *Tears?* "The deal," he echoes. "Always the deal. As if that's all there is to life."

Suddenly his expression hardens, his gaze pierces me to the soul. "It's meaningless, you hear me? Here and now, 'the deal' is meaningless. It doesn't matter. And, moreover, it *never* mattered. But I don't expect you to believe that."

I shake my head. "I don't understand you, Geoffrey," I tell him slowly.

"But you do," he shoots back firmly. "You understand. What does the deal matter? You and I, we're dead. Do you comprehend that? *Dead.* To the dead, the deal doesn't matter — can't matter."

"What does, then?" I almost snap at him.

"What always mattered." He's calm again, almost placid. "What always mattered when we were alive, though we didn't see it... or admit it. Questions. Answers. Understanding. Primarily, and above all, *understanding*."

I grasp at one of his words. "Questions. What questions?"

"Questions of meaning," he answers. "Arguably the only questions that ever matter." He gestures around himself again. "What is the meaning of this? Of all this?"

"Meaning again," I say disdainfully.

"Precisely."

"What meaning?" There's an edge to my voice. Something about Battersby's words is getting to me, driving deep into me. Angering me? When I continue, my voice is almost harsh. "What if there's no meaning? Did you ever think of that?"

"But there must be," he presses. "Don't you see? There must be."

"Why?" My anger is a sharp presence in my chest, but it is somehow hollow, too. As if it's a shell around something deeper. No, I won't let myself examine that idea, not now. "Why the hell does there have to be a meaning? Tell me that."

His sharp gaze drifts off my face, focuses on infinity. He's looking up, into the murky depths of the Shadowlands' sky. *What does he see there?* The thought strikes from nowhere, unsettling in its intensity. "Well?" I demand.

His eyes focus again on my face. "We don't belong here," he says, so softly I have to strain to hear him.

"What the hell do you mean?" The anger — or whatever it is — puts steel in my voice.

"We don't belong here, Jonathan," he repeats earnestly. There's a hint of something new — of pleading? — in his eyes now.

I growl something wordless. I want to turn and stride away, leave him to his useless philosophical maunderings. But I can't, it's as if his words have cast some kind of dark spell over me. "How the hell can you know that?" I demand after a moment.

Once more he gestures around him, an all-encompassing sweep of his arm. "Where is everybody?" he asks simply.

A simple question, but one that sets me back on my heels almost like a physical slap. I've never thought of it; it's never occurred to me. But I can see his point at once. Where the hell *is* everybody? All the dead; all the people who've died since the beginning of the human race. I read once there are about as many stars in the sky as there are humans who've ever been alive — from the brightest star to the faintest, visible only through the largest of telescopes. One star for every man, woman and child who's ever lived. If that's true...

Where *are* they? The Shadowlands should be crowded, overflowing with them. Souls packed as tightly as stars in the sky. Yet there seem fewer — far fewer — wraiths in the Shadowlands of San Francisco than there are Quick in the city.

"Where?" Battersby repeats.

I shrug uncomfortably. Then I speak slowly, voicing the thoughts as they pass through my mind. "Maybe... maybe when most people die, they die all the way," I suggest tentatively. "They're alive, then they're gone. Except for us."

He's smiling slightly. I know that smile, I know it means he's already explored the corridor of thought I'm exploring, and is waiting for me to find the same obstacles he's already picked out. I suddenly realize I hate that smile. "Why not us too?" he asks me. "Why were we spared from oblivion? Was it our moral, ethical, just actions while we were alive that earned us a reprieve?"

I don't dignify his sarcasm with any reaction. "Strength of personality, maybe," I shoot back at once. "We're the ones who're strong enough to remain."

That smile just broadens. "And so what's the purpose of this continued existence? The purpose, Jonathan."

The anger in my chest is morphing into something else, a more uncomfortable, less familiar sensation. I try to keep the discomfort from showing on my face as I snap, "You tell me."

He speaks a single word in response. "Transcendence," he tells me simply.

■

Nick Stein, his name was. In the five years before I died, I'd probably thought of him once, maybe twice. But when I first saw him striding out of one of the buildings in the Hierarchy Citadel, the memories came flooding back with piercing intensity.

We'd been at business school at the same time, going after our MBAs, and we'd been friends. Together, we'd founded the amorphous group of hard-drivers we'd laughingly named The Rat Pack. Nick, and me, and Roger and Stu and Amy. Hell, we'd stirred that place up. We'd all been good in school — damn good — and everyone else had known it, faculty and students. And that had meant the system had cut us a hell of a lot more slack than maybe it should have. Shit that would have gotten other students dragged up before a disciplinary board — "warming up" for an exam with a couple of hours at the pub, for example — had just been ignored, mainly because everyone had known that, even half-cut, the Rat Pack would be setting the grade curve.

Nick. Nick's family had been rich, but that hadn't held him back any. He hadn't shown that apathy that so often seems to come with old money. He'd been as hungry as the rest of us — a fucking barracuda when it came to the deal. We'd always joked that Nick didn't consider a negotiation to be successful until he'd torn out the other bastard's liver and eaten it.

Still, Nick *had* had the money, and he'd enjoyed its

trappings. It had been his boat — the *Pendragon*, a J-30 — that the Pack had taken out into the bay for our regular Sunday-afternoon booze-cruises. And it had been the *Pendragon* that had finally killed him — seven years before I'd gone out — when he'd ignored a small-craft warning, bet his skill against the winds beyond Point Bonita... and lost.

And now here he was, a dozen yards away, and the seven years since I'd last seen him were like a single moment of time. Fleeting, meaningless. He hadn't changed (well, why should he have?). Blond hair, trimmed short. Smoothly handsome face. And those eyes of pale, washed-out blue. The eyes of a hitman, the Rat Pack had always joked. I tried to call out to him.

I couldn't do it. For a long moment, I was frozen, immobilized. *Isn't that the definition of rigor mortis?* part of my mind yammered. *When a dead man's body won't move?* My vision tunneled down, as if I were looking down a roiling, spinning tube of blood-red. My heart was tight, as though a fist squeezed my heart. I couldn't speak, I couldn't even draw breath to call after my old friend.

Why? Relief, that's why. An overdose of emotion, the overwhelming rush of release from a tension I didn't even know I'd been feeling. There, across the courtyard, was someone who I knew. Someone who knew me. An anchor, a touchstone — a link between the present and the past, between the Shadowlands and my life. It was as if just knowing there was someone here in the Shadowlands who knew me validated my entire existence somehow. It was as if... how to explain this? As if I knew who I was, that I was John Cross, but having someone else who knew the same thing confirmed my knowledge, reinforced my existence. I hadn't known that the lack of this validation had been stressing me — I hadn't felt the tension deep in my gut — but now I felt it leave, a wild rush of piercing emotion that almost unlocked my knees and pitched me to the ground.

"Nick!"

Finally I managed to croak the word out. I saw him turn, saw those hitman's eyes widen as he recognized me.

It was all I could do not to sprint across the intervening distance, to — yet another indication of how hard this unexpected emotion was hitting me — wrap my arms around him in a fierce bearhug. Somehow I managed to control that atypical reaction. I kept my step steady, controlled, as I strode toward him. When I extended a hand, I was reassured to see it wasn't shaking.

For a moment, Nick just stared at me, stunned. Then he was pumping my hand. "John. Johnny." He shook his head, a complex welter of expressions flickering across his face. "I didn't know, I hadn't heard…" He gripped my biceps, held me at arm's length as he looked me up and down, almost as if he was making sure it was really me. "It's shitty that you're here," he said. "I thought you had another good thirty, forty years in you." His face split in a broad grin, the wild, slightly manic smile that had fired so many of the Rat Pack's activities. "But damn, Johnny, it's good to see you." Finally he released me and stepped back, For an instant I saw the embarrassment in his eyes — that was just a little too much real emotion he'd shown — but it didn't last.

"Am I the first?" I asked him quietly.

"Hm?" He blinked, puzzled. Then I saw understanding dawn. "The first person I know here?" He paused, and his expression changed, became more guarded, the look of Nicholas Stein the professional financial consultant, rather than Nick the Rat-Packer. "No, you're not the first," he said slowly.

When he didn't continue, "Who, then?" I prompted.

"Geoffrey," he said quietly. "Geoffrey Battersby."

I think I must have gaped. "Battersby? He's here?"

Nick nodded. He was still wearing that guarded expression, but for the moment I didn't really care. Battersby — another name out of the past, another welcome motherlode of memories that had been misplaced or suppressed. From the same era as the Rat Pack, and including many of the same *dramatis personae*, but very different in tenor.

Other than my father — the intimidating, unapproachable bastard — Battersby was by far the most significant person in my life: mentor, role model, even sometime friend. A real kick-ass businessman, Battersby was a merger and acquisitions expert — a barracuda — who'd decided it was time to "give something back" to the business world by teaching for a couple of semesters at business school.

Man, did Battersby open my eyes to what the real business world was about. Most of the faculty were either ivory-tower academics — cloistered losers who'd studied the business world but never actually participated in it — or refugees from the hard world of reality, who'd decided that teaching about business was less threatening than actually doing it. Battersby was my first professor who'd actually taken on the real world of business... and conquered it. He could tell us personal anecdotes pointing out the weaknesses and foibles of the business luminaries the rest of the faculty knew only from textbooks and scholarly journals. And that made all the difference. Who would *you* choose to emulate: a professor who learned about negotiation techniques from psychology texts, or someone who personally cut Donald Trump out of a lucrative deal because "The Donald" couldn't get his board of directors to fall in line before the deadline? (And thinking of "The Donald," I remember laughing with Nick over Battersby's reaction when Trump's book *The Art of the Deal* came out in 1987. "Pretender," Geoffrey had snapped. "If Trump were as hot as he claims, he wouldn't be taking time out to write any book.")

"Battersby," I echoed again. "Where is he?" I laughed aloud. Suddenly I felt better than I had in... well, for as long as I could remember. "Knowing Geoffrey, he's probably running this fucking place by now. Huh?"

And Nick's face became even more of an expressionless mask. "Not exactly," he said quietly.

"What, then?"

"He's not involved with the Hierarchy at all. The way I hear it, he refused to join even when some of the higher-ups specifically approached him."

I shrugged. "He's got something else going on, then," I said surely, "something outside the Hierarchy."

Nick flinched, as if I'd slapped him across the face. He looked around him, hunching his shoulders slightly. "Don't say that kind of thing," he said, his voice low but sharp. "Don't even think it. Okay? *Okay?*"

His intensity set me back on my heels. "Okay, Nick," I placated him. "Just a slip, all right? I didn't mean it."

My old friend nodded, a little mollified. "There's just some things you don't talk about," he mumbled. "It's easy to get yourself in deep water if you're not careful."

"I said okay, Nick," I shot back sharply, maybe a little more sharply than I intended. "Point taken." I took a cleansing breath, slipped back into my calm business "mask." "So tell me about Battersby," I prompted. "What the hell is he doing, then?"

"Nothing," Nick responded at once. "Nothing."

I snorted. "He's got nothing going?" I repeated skeptically. "I find that hard to believe."

Nick shrugged again. "I didn't believe it at first either," he admitted. "But it's true. He's out of the loop, John. On the beach."

Out of the loop. On the beach. Those phrases brought back memories from business school days. We — the Rat Pack — had used them as the ultimate condemnation of someone who'd lost it, who'd lost his guts or his timing or his judgment, and was off the business fast-track. The saddest thing — the image most worthy of scorn, we thought — was the one-time "comer" who'd slipped out of the loop, but wouldn't admit it, either to himself or to anyone else, clinging pathetically to past glories while his fortune and his reputation leaked away. Like happened to The Donald, come to think of it. It was all too common a scenario, but, "Battersby?" I demanded. "That's one man who's never going to lose it."

"I didn't say he lost it," Nick corrected, a hint of impatience in his voice. "He didn't fuck up."

"He took himself out of the loop," my old colleague said bleakly. "He's not in the game, he won't get in the game… and from what people say, he never would from the first day he got here."

I shook my head in total incomprehension. "What the fuck does he do, then?"

"I don't know. Hangs around in Golden Gate Park, that's what I hear. Talks philosophy to anyone who'll stand still long enough to listen. Navel-gazes. That's what I hear."

I paused as a new memory, a new thought, tingled in the back of my mind. "You haven't gone to see him, then?" I asked, keeping my voice casual.

Nick dropped his gaze, and shook his head.

"Yeah, I know," I told him in commiseration. "I don't think I could handle it either." And all the while, I struggled to keep the knowing smile off my face.

■

I stare down at the diminutive man, wrapped in his garishly colored cloth. I try to reconcile that image with the mental picture my memory holds of my old mentor. I can't do it.

"And what the hell is *Transcendence?*" I ask, etching the word with an ironic echo of the emphasis he used.

"Our purpose here," he responds at once. He sits down on the stone step of the museum entrance, gestures for me to join him. I can't. I can't turn my back and walk away, no matter how much I want to. But neither can I sit still and pretend this isn't churning me up inside. He's watching me with a faint smile, his head swinging back and forth to follow me. I realize I'm pacing like a caged animal.

"Explain that, Geoffrey," I demand. "So I can understand it."

"It's simple," he tells me calmly. "So simple that few people here seem to grasp it. They seem to want something," he searches for the right word, "grander," he continues at last. "Something more self-aggrandizing, perhaps. Something that gives import, gives meaning, to their actions here."

I shift uncomfortably. The echo of my own thoughts just a few days before is disturbing. "And you've got the answer?"

He doesn't react to my acerbity. "Of course," he says quietly. "Anyone with the courage to actually think could have it, too. I know what the Shadowlands are."

"What, then?" I want to know.

Battersby smiles, almost beatifically.

"A way station," he says.

■

Could Nick Stein have forgotten? It certainly seemed he had. I chuckled quietly to myself.

Well, I guess I had been closer to Battersby than the other Rat Packers. It only made sense that I'd remember more of his personal anecdotes.

I sat in my "office" — more like a monk's cell, really, or a set out of the movie *Brazil* — in the Citadel, and grinned at the bare wall. The Cross luck was running true to form, it seemed. Finding Nick Stein had been the best thing that could have happened to me. Nick had always been a killer in business — a better negotiator than I was. (Suddenly I wondered if that had changed in the years since Nick had died? Maybe I'd closed the gap.) Yet he'd always envied me my instincts, my ability to read the dynamics. Nick was a master at closing a deal when it was on the table, extracting the maximum concessions, the maximum profit. But my strength was in sniffing out the potential deals — spotting businesses in weak positions, feeling out the trends, the way the wind was blowing — in bringing those deals to the table in the first place. We made a hot team in b-school, and if Nick hadn't drowned himself I wouldn't have been surprised if we'd eventually gravitated to each other and set up a real ass-kicking acquisition/development outfit.

And that's why he'd "recruited" me into the Hierarchy, why he'd taken me into his own "department" within the monolithic organization, reporting directly to him. My official brief was "staff work": more-or-less research, and keeping Nick up to date on changes elsewhere throughout the organization. Unofficially, but more practically, I was to look out for opportunities the two of us could capitalize on within the Hierarchy.

Hell, I'd been right all along about the Hierarchy, I realized quickly. Just like any big organization, no matter what business it was officially in, there was a kind of "secondary business" within it: the business of internal politics, of corporate climbing, of where-necessary back-stabbing. And it was that secondary business which interested Nick. I was to pick out the "seams" in the organization, the weaknesses, the power vacuums. And I was to provide Nick with the "staff work" he needed — the support, the information, the tactics — to exploit those opportunities. He'd climb through the organization, and he'd carry me along with him on his coattails. That was the deal as he'd laid it out to me, and it was that deal I'd accepted.

I think he'd been a little surprised that I'd bought in quite so easily. He'd been brusque, almost cold, when he'd put his proposal on the table — a dead giveaway, I remembered from the old days, that he was expecting hard negotiations. I'd pushed back, of course — he'd expected me to, and would have asked embarrassing questions if I hadn't — and had squeezed out a few additional concessions. But I hadn't ground him anywhere near as hard as I might have done otherwise.

When we finally shook on the agreement, Nick's smile wasn't quite as broad as it might have been. He had to be asking himself why I hadn't held out any longer, whether I had some kind of hidden agenda in mind. But I just talked about how good it was to be working shoulder-to-shoulder again — the heart and brain of the Rat Pack back together once more — and that set him at ease. It wasn't too unreasonable to assume I'd gone along with the deal out of some personal need, was it? While I was settling into my position as Nick Stein's staff officer, and getting a feel for how things ran at this level of the Hierarchy, I was going over in my mind what Nick had said about Battersby.

So the old shark had dropped out of the loop, huh? So far out of the loop that he rejected a personal invitation from the local higher-ups to get into the game? Yeah, right. I remembered the "war story," even if Nick didn't. How Battersby had upped his total compensation package with a Fortune 500 company by a cool million dollars.

The outfit — I honestly can't remember the name at the moment; Komatsu, maybe? — had given its last CEO the chop, and was looking for an interim, "bridge" replacement until they found someone for the long haul. The Board of Directors wanted Geoffrey Battersby, and approached the old barracuda with a tasty compensation package; something like $1.3 million lump-sum for a maximum 12-month stint. If they found a long-term CEO in less time than that, Battersby kept the money anyway; if they didn't find someone in time, the deal could be renegotiated for another year.

Battersby turned the deal down flat. Not interested, he told them, so sorry. He was 50 at the time, and 50 was the age he'd decided on for retirement. He'd made an oath to himself that he was going to get out of the rat-race when he finished his fifth decade, come hell or high water. Much as he'd like to help out the outfit, he just couldn't do it. Sorry.

Cut to the chase: The company bumped up the compensation package to $2.3 million for a year... and Battersby let himself be persuaded to stay in the rat-race for another year.

Did he finally retire when the one-year "bridge" appointment was up? He did not! He'd never had any intention of retiring, and he considered the Komatsu stewardship to be the perfect next step along his career path. He just didn't consider $1.3 mil to be worthy compensation. Negotiation via retirement, in other words. We'd laughed about it over a cognac, me and Battersby... and Nick too, even though he seemed to have forgotten it.

Because this was exactly the same move again, wasn't it? It had worked once when he was alive. Why not a second time, here in the Shadowlands? My old mentor wasn't out of the loop, "on the beach." He was playing a deeper game, that's all. If Nick had remembered that old war story, he'd have been able to cut himself in long before I came onto the scene. But since he hadn't done so — hell, all's fair in love and war, and business is just war by other means, isn't it?

I made a mental note to visit Golden Gate Park.

■

"A way station," I echo flatly. "Between what and what?"

"Between where we were, and where we should be."

"Circular logic, Geoffrey," I snap. He just smiles. "So why are we in this 'way station' of yours, then?"

"To learn." The simplicity of his answer sets me back. I open my mouth, and he answers my unspoken question. "To learn what we didn't learn before," he elaborates. "To find the meaning. Our meaning."

"And if we do? Then what?"

"Transcendence." And again the word seems to hang in the air between us, an almost-tangible presence fraught with complex emotional resonances. I feel compelled — repelled — by it.

With a hiss of frustration — only partially feigned — I shake my head once more. "Which is…?" I demand.

"An ending. And a beginning. A transition. An end to the striving. A growth from 'self' to 'not-self.'"

"'Not-self' is a growth?" There's something almost obscene about the thought.

"When it's the next logical step in our progression, yes," he confirms.

"So *you* say." I pause. The compulsion/repulsion feeling is still there. The next question is out of my lips almost before I'm aware of the thought. "And how do we find this meaning of yours, anyway?"

"Through self-examination," he responds at once. "By examining the life we've lived: the choices we've made, the paths we've taken, the paths we've avoided."

I close my eyes for a moment. There's a sound in my ears — a sibilance. The cold wind of oblivion as it keens through my soul. I want to clutch my hands to my ears, to keep out that sound, even though I know it's not coming from any source outside me. I force my eyes open, fix my gaze as firmly as I can on Battersby's face — strive to conceal the emotions that are whipsawing me.

He's watching me and that sad, knowing, *wise* half-smile is playing about his lips.

"A man makes a lot of choices in a lifetime," I temporize.

He nods. "Of course. But some are infinitely more important than others."

"Sometimes it's hard to tell." Again, I feel as though I'm speaking just to fill the silence, so he can't fill it with something I desperately don't want to hear.

"There are ways. Even now — even here — we carry

traces of our lives as we've lived them." His smile shifts, becomes faintly self-conscious. "'Deathmarks,' I've come to call them, analogous to 'birthmarks.' Here." He raises a hand, gestures at his own face. "Look," he suggests. "Can you see the deathmarks on my skin?"

I blink in surprise. He's got to be talking about the weal — the brand, almost — on his forehead, hasn't he? How could I not see that?

He shakes his head suddenly, as though he can hear my thoughts. "No, no, not this." He touches the weal with a slender forefinger. "*Here*, around the eyes, around the mouth..."

I don't really want to — in case I do see something — but I look anyway, leaning in closer. His eyes are bracketed by a network of lines, hair-fine wrinkles. I remember them as being much deeper. Surely *they* can't be what he means. I shrug.

"Look closer."

I try, even going so far as to squint my eyes. Still nothing but the lines. Again I shrug, and I see the disappointment shade his expression. "Sorry, Geoffrey." The apology is out before I can stop it.

He shrugs in turn, a sad gesture. "Perhaps you don't have the gift to see them," he suggested quietly. "If it is a gift."

I don't want to ask, but I can't help myself. "And you can see my... my deathmarks?"

A faint chuckle. "As clear as day," he confirms. "Dark traces beneath your eyes."

Inexplicably uncomfortable, I snort. "Bags under my eyes, you mean," I correct him scornfully. I try to laugh, but the bitter sound that comes out is chilling. "Next time I'll have to remember to get a good night's sleep before I drop dead."

Battersby doesn't so much as acknowledge the attempt at humor. "There's information in the deathmarks, I'm sure of it," he says firmly. "Things to learn. The course of one's life, and one's path to Transcendence." His eyes narrow as he scrutinizes my face. I think I know what's coming, and I'm afraid of it, but I can't pull myself away. His gaze holds me like a fly in amber.

"I see denial, Jonathan," he tells me, his voice seeming suddenly hollow, as the whispering of the witch-wind in my soul increases its volume.

I shake my head categorically no. "You know me, Geoffrey," I say, trying to keep my voice strong and hearty. "I've never turned away from a challenge." I chuckle again, and this time it sounds almost normal. "And you know I was never much good at denying myself anything I wanted…"

"That's not what I mean, and you know it." His voice is soft, melancholy, but the reprimand stings like a slap to the face. "You denied something that was part of your soul — that's what your deathmarks imply — and through that denial, you lost it. Forever. Your path to Transcendence is to atone for that loss."

The witch-wind in my soul howls, now, a storm, buffeting me from within. Imminence. Immanence… memory, right on the verge of returning. A dark pit in my soul, an emptiness never to be filled. A void I *could* have filled, if only I had…

No! The word rings in my mind, and then I scream it into Battersby's face. "No!" I turn, and now I *do* run from him. Out across the deserted parking lot, toward the road that loops through the park. I run, harder than I've ever run before, driving myself ever faster. As though, if I ran fast enough, I could leave behind the memory of Battersby's face, of his look of pity…

■

Nick Stein was standing in the doorway of my office/cell, watching me silently, as I looked up from my work. "How long have you been there?" I asked him a little sharply. There was something complex, some strange mix of emotions, in his eyes. (Had he found out about my visit to Battersby? I suddenly wondered. For a brief moment, embarrassment burned in my chest. Then it was gone. He'd had the same opportunity to approach Battersby as I did — not that it had worked out worth shit — and it was his problem if he hadn't followed up on it, right?) "Well?"

He walked in slowly, the curtain falling back into place to cover the portal as he did so. "Well?" I said again.

"An announcement from the bosses." His voice was flat as he spoke, but I could feel the effort it took to keep his emotions hidden.

Intrigued, I leaned forward. "What is it now?" I wanted to know.

"It's another Prohibition."

I chuckled. I didn't know if this was the way it worked throughout the entire Hierarchy — or even within the whole San Francisco "Necropolis" — but the senior wraiths (the Gaunts, they called themselves) in this division of the organization were always coming up with some new Prohibition. Every second day, it seemed, there was one more thing forbidden to the wraiths of the Necropolis. (It depended entirely on the Gaunts' mood as to whether those Prohibitions also applied to loyal members of the Hierarchy bureaucracy like me. Come to think of it, judging by Nick's expression, it seemed likely that this one would apply to us. Damn.)

"Another one?" I chuckled again. "Pretty soon, anything that's not obligatory is going to be forbidden." I shook my head. "So what now?" I asked again, grinning. "A Prohibition against haunting out of season?"

Nick didn't laugh in response, didn't even smile. He just watched me silently, until my own smile faded. "A Prohibition against reading deathmarks," he finally said, his voice cold and thin like a witch-wind. "Against claiming — falsely, and counter to the interests of the Hierarchy —

that deathmarks have any importance or significance." His eyes were half-shut as he recited the formal wording of the proclamation. "Against promoting the heresy that the standard classification of wraiths — based on manner of death — is invalid, or that a better system exists. Against disseminating the *obvious* falsehood that study of deathmarks may be invoked as a way of achieving Transcendence.

"It has been declared," he continued bleakly, "that such heretical falsehoods serve to distract wraiths from what is truly important — loyalty and obedience to the Hierarchy — and thus do directly court Oblivion, to the detriment of all."

With an effort, I managed to keep my deeper emotions off my face, leaving curiosity, nothing more. "Really?" I asked casually. "Doesn't affect us, does it? The Gaunts aren't expecting us to go out and enforce the declaration, are they?" I shrugged. "So what's the problem?"

"Battersby," Nick said quietly. "They know about him, John. The Gaunts. They know about Battersby."

I felt a sudden, cold chill deep in my gut. But I think I managed to hide my reaction as I asked guilelessly, "What about Battersby?"

"Fuck!" Nick spat. "No games, okay, John?"

So Nick *did* know. I examined his expression carefully, looking for anger or bitterness toward me. For a wonder, I didn't see traces of either.

"They know, John," Nick repeated. He hissed in frustration. "Shit, it's not as if he was making much of a secret of it. Anybody who'd stand still long enough, he'd read their deathmarks and start telling them what they meant. What he *thought* they meant," he corrected quickly, with a guilty twitch.

"So they know." I shrugged.

Nick stared at me, outrage mixed with desperation. "They're going to pick him up, John. They're going to send a fucking patrol looking for him. When they find him,

they're going to put him on trial — a fucking show trial —
and they're going to convict him of treason against the
fucking Anacreon. Okay? That's the way it works around
here, okay? Imprisonment, show trial, conviction — all to
'send a message.'"

With an effort, I fought down the disturbing, confused
churning in my stomach. "Convict him," I repeated. And
unwillingly I asked, "Then what? Treason." I snorted. "It's
not like they can execute him, right?" I added wryly.

Nick answered darkly, "You'd be surprised." He paused.
"For show trials, no, no execution. SOP is to ship the
convicted criminal," he etched the phrase with stinging irony,
"in chains to Stygia. Slavery, John. Eternal slavery." He
stared at me, his gray hitman's eyes wide, desperate.

I couldn't hold that gaze; I had to glance away. What
the fuck did he want from me? I didn't understand it. Hell,
it wasn't my fault that Battersby had gotten into deep shit
with the Hierarchy, was it? (That strange, confused churning
in my gut was back — stronger, more piercing than before.
It took even more effort to force it back this time.)

"Too bad," I said flatly.

"Goddamn it, John!" Those assassin's eyes flashed. "It's
Battersby, for fuck's sake. Battersby." Nick twitched, shifted
from foot to foot, almost as if the floor were hot as a griddle.

Again, I had to glance away. "So it's Battersby," I
mumbled. "He's a big boy, he's responsible for his own
actions."

"But..." Nick was starting to look as though he had St.
Vitus' dance. "We can't just..." He stopped himself with an
effort, shooting another one of those paranoid looks over
his shoulder. *Like a dog who's used to being kicked*, I thought
suddenly. He dropped his voice to a sharp whisper. "We can't
just let it happen, John. It's *Battersby*. Eternal *slavery*, for
Christ's good sake!"

I spun, turning my back to him. The muscles of my jaw
hurt, I was grinding my teeth so hard. Then I spun back,

spat out, "So why aren't you…" And then I stopped myself.

So why aren't you doing anything about it, for fuck's sake? That's what I'd started to ask him. But suddenly I knew the answer.

He didn't have the fucking guts. He wanted to do something — anything — but he didn't have the jam, didn't have the balls to do it. So of course he came to me. *Just like he always did,* I realized suddenly. All the way back to b-school it had been this way. Nick Stein, the hard-assed negotiator, the competent businessman — as long as someone else broke track for him. A great closer, that was Nick, a great tactician. A great follower. He'd always needed a leader, though, hadn't he? Someone to set the strategy, to tell him what negotiations to pursue, which to bypass. I felt my lips twist into a scornful half-smile.

It was almost as if he could read my thoughts. His cheeks flushed, then went bone-pale. And it was his turn to look away, unable to meet my gaze. "It's Battersby," he said again, a real edge of desperation to his voice now. "We can't hang him out to dry like this, John. We can't." In a startling, spasmodic movement, he reached out, grabbed my hand in a viselike grip. "We can't turn away from him. We can't just pretend he doesn't matter.

"We can't just deny him!"

I twitched. Nick's word jolted me like a charge from a cattle-prod. *Deny.* I tore my hand from his and I staggered back, my shoulders slamming against the wall of my office/cell. The word echoed in my mind like a gunshot in a canyon. *Deny.*

Denial. That was what Battersby had said he'd read in my face — in my deathmarks — wasn't it? *You denied something that was part of your soul…* That's what he'd told me. *And through that denial, you lost it.*

Forever.

A flash of memory transfixed me like a spear driven through the center of my soul. Hair like a waterfall of gold.

Gentle eyes — their color could be gray, or blue, or even green, depending on the light. A soft smile. Tears. Emptiness. A void, never to be filled...

No! I can't — I *won't* — remember.

Denial.

With a choked cry, I flung myself at the curtained door, knocking Nick Stein aside as I sprinted for the open air.

■

What in the name of God am I doing back here? Ever since I charged out of my office in the Citadel, it's as if my mind's been in a fog. I can't remember how I traveled across the city; I don't know if I met anyone, if anyone followed me, if anyone tried to stop me. But here I am, back in Golden Gate Park, hurrying across the parking lot toward the entrance of the M.H. de Young Memorial Museum.

Another flash of memory strikes, making me gasp with its intensity. *An eagle, a brass eagle, with empty eyes.* I hear a whimper. Only after a moment do I realize it's my own voice.

Where the hell *is* he? By God, after I've come all the way down here — at who knows what risk to myself — he'd better fucking be here. The museum doors will be locked — it's after hours, after all — so if he's in there there's little I can do about it. But maybe he's not inside. With a silent curse, I sprint around the right side of the building, through the foliage.

And there he is. Battersby. Standing in the middle of a small, well-tended lawn. Looking at me calmly, as though he somehow expected to see me.

"Jonathan," my old mentor — my old friend — says calmly.

I stop in my tracks. Part of me wants to grab him by the arm, drag him along with me — I don't know where; *any*where, just away from here. But another part wants to keep my distance. Self-preservation? I don't know.

"You look troubled," Battersby remarks.

I laugh at that. *Troubled*? I probably look fucking traumatized, the perfect archetype of the soul in torment.

"Get out of here," I gasp at him. "Geoffrey, they're coming for you."

He smiles gently. "Are they, now?" He gives a sigh. "Honestly, I'm surprised it's taken them this long."

I stare at him. "Don't you get it?" I demand. "They're coming for you, Geoffrey. The Legion. They're coming to arrest you, for treason against the Anacreon." In my own ears, my voice is rising in pitch, in intensity. "Do you understand what I'm telling you?" I almost shriek.

"I understand." His voice is soft, untroubled. "What would you have me do?"

I think my mouth gapes open for a moment, like that of a gaffed fish. "What would I…" I echo dumbly. Then, "*Run*, for fuck's sake!" I scream at him. "Get the fuck out of here."

"Where would I go?"

"I don't care! It doesn't matter where you go. Just go! Get away from here. Find a place to hide. Keep your head down until this settles down." I'm pleading with him, as desperate as Nick was an hour ago. "Geoffrey, *please*."

He's looking at me, a strange expression on his face. His eyes are fixed on mine, but they're not the eyes I remember. No longer the eyes of a raptor, now they're filled with sadness, with compassion. For himself? For me? I suddenly don't want to know.

Battersby's voice is little more than a whisper as he tells me simply, "No."

"Why not?" I yell. "Why not?" I force myself to stop, to lower my voice, to inject at least a hint of reason into it. "Why, Geoffrey? Because of this deathmark shit? It doesn't matter."

His jaw sets — an expression I remember from the olden days. "Oh, but it *does* matter." His voice is still quiet, but now there's a hint of steel underlying the words.

"Okay," I concede, quickly changing tack. "Okay, it does matter. And if it does matter, then you've got to keep doing it, right? And you can't keep doing it if you're in fucking chains!"

My old mentor chuckles softly. "Well argued, Jonathan," he commends me. "Succinct, cogent. But I can't accept it, don't you see?" An open-palmed gesture seems to encompass me, to invite me to join him. *In what? In heresy? In chains?*

"I can't run," he continues, his calmness almost preternatural. "I can't turn away." He chuckles. "I can't set aside this cup. Do you see?"

I can't force the words from my suddenly tight throat. All I can do is shake my head.

He smiles sadly. "I can't run from this," he repeats. "Oh, I grant that you're right. From a position of expediency, I *should* run. I *should* hide. But I can't, not any more.

"Do you understand that, Jonathan?" It's his turn to plead with me. "I've spent my entire life turning away from what really mattered for the sake of expediency." His voice turns the word into something ugly. "Don't you see? It was too difficult, too disturbing, to pursue the answers to the great questions about my life, to pursue the meaning. It was more expedient to pursue distractions — wealth, power, prestige — all the things that helped me forget about those unanswered questions. Do you understand me?

"I spent my life doing that. I will *not* spend my death in the same denial."

Denial. Again the word strikes like a weapon. Another flash of memory — a name... *Juli* — drives me to my knees. It's all I can do to force the memory back where it belongs, into the unseen recesses of my mind, where it can't harm me.

I look up at him, at my old friend. I can't bring myself to speak. But he seems to read my unspoken questions from my eyes.

"We each have our own course to follow, Jonathan," he

says. Then, gently, he adds, "Go. It wouldn't serve you to be found here with me." And he turns away.

Before I know what's happening, I'm on my feet and running. Not after him. Away. I sprint through the foliage, out toward the parking lot...

And skid to a stop a dozen yards short of a group of wraiths. An even dozen of them, a phalanx of looming shapes. The dim light of the Shadowlands glints off soul-forged spearheads, off polished breastplates and helmets. The leader of the phalanx steps toward me, hand on the hilt of a black iron sword hanging at his hip. His chains of office chime softly, discordantly.

"Centurion." I nod to him, a sign of respect.

Meanwhile my mind is racing, my thoughts a tempest of confusion. What the hell am I going to do now? This has to be the Legion patrol sent to arrest Battersby. I know their quarry is no more than twenty yards from where I stand right now. There's no way they're not going to find him, drag him off in manacles.

"Centurion," I repeat, trying to keep my voice calm. "Is there anything I can do for you?"

The armored wraith stares at me, his eyes cold and sharp as flint. The silence stretches. Then, "We seek a Renegade," he says at last. "A traitor. He who was known in life as Geoffrey Battersby. Have you seen this Renegade?"

And there it is, laid at last before me. The big question. Have I seen Battersby? How simple to say "Yes, over by the Arboretum," and send the Centurion and his patrol off on a wild goose chase, while I get Battersby to a place of safety, even if I have to drag him. There'd be paybacks, I know that. When the patrol found no trace of Battersby, there'd be questions asked of the wraith who sent them in that direction. But I could bluff, there's no question in my mind about that. It'd be difficult, it'd cripple my chances of advancing in the Hierarchy. But I could do it.

I *can* do it, and Battersby will be free.

Or will he? Will the stiff-necked old bastard keep his head down after this close escape? Will he hide out and stop his disturbing ramblings about deathmarks and Transcendence? Will he?

"Geoffrey Battersby," I temporize.

And if he doesn't, what then? Won't I have put my career — my existence, perhaps — at risk? Acting as an accomplice to treason... for no purpose? He *won't* have the sense to keep his fucking yap shut, will he? Even if this patrol doesn't get him, another will, and we'll both suffer for it.

Hell, it's not as if it means anything, anyway, his rambling. If it were something important, then it might be different. But all his talk about questions, and meaning, and... no.

It just doesn't make fucking sense. No sense at all, to put myself on the line, to risk... no, it's not even a risk, it's a fucking certainty. To dive on down the tube, to sacrifice everything for a fool who's lost touch with the truth. Of *course* not.

"Geoffrey Battersby?" I let my lips curl into a sardonic smile. "I was wondering if you'd get here in time, before he slipped away. I can only hold him so long, keep him distracted." I point in the direction of the well-manicured lawn. "He's through there... if your tardiness hasn't let him slip away."

The Centurion gestures. Half the patrol advances into the foliage, out of my sight. The Centurion remains behind, watching me emotionlessly. Less than half a minute later, from the bushes behind me I hear a barked order. I keep my face expressionless, even as I hear the clatter of soul-forged manacles slamming shut.

"And you are...?" the Centurion asks. There's a hint of doubt in his voice... but there's also respect.

Clearly, I state my position in the bureaucracy of the Hierarchy, carefully not mentioning Nick Stein's name, of course. "In life," I conclude, "I was known as John Cross.

"Remember that name."

■

My new office was in another part of the Citadel; still like a cell, but at least it was a *larger* cell. The wraiths who worked under me were all drones, incapable of anything but obedience, without even the slightest trace of initiative. Like Nick Stein, now that I thought about it.

For a moment, I wondered about Nick. Where *had* he ended up anyway? In a way, it was too bad; he'd have made a good addition to my department over here. But it hadn't been in the cards. There was no way I could have extracted the maximum advantage out of the situation without dragging him down. After all, if you want the most impressive-looking high-jump, it certainly helps to drag the bar down a notch...

I sighed. He was probably pissed, I realized. He was probably hating me about now, blaming me for the downturn in his fortunes. Second-raters *always* blame, don't they?

I glanced over at the hourglass. Battersby's trial should be starting. Any time now, the old man would be dragged out onto the floor of the rotunda, in front of the cold eyes of the Hierarchy magistrate, while the crowd of spectators howled their derision at the traitor. Politically, it would probably be expedient if I were there... and were seen to be there by my superiors.

But — I rubbed at my eyes, which suddenly seemed to be watering; strain, no doubt — I'd just have to give it a miss.

I had too much work to do.

RUINS

JIM MOORE

I.

I think there must be a fine line between love and hatred, because what I feel for Donna Cambridge certainly has a little of both running through it. It was Wednesday night and I stared at the couple walking along the path from the Alexandria Club toward the limousine that waited for them. Donna Cambridge and Vannevar Thomas. They made a stunning couple, and even people who didn't know them paused in conversation or at the very least watched them intently as they walked past. Vannevar was smiling, whispering in Donna's ear. Donna was laughing in response, a musical sound that sent wires of pain through my entire being. At that moment I hated them both for their beauty and for the love they so obviously shared. Even more, I loved her with all my being.

Once, long ago, I had held Donna in my arms, had kissed her skin and made love to her. She'd been engaged to marry me, and we would have lived happily ever after, just like in the fairy tales. I cursed myself for ever losing her, for ever letting her slip away. Mostly, I cursed myself for not realizing what I'd had in Donna until it was too late. I stayed where I was long after the limo had moved on, still thinking about her and wishing I could go into the past and make everything right.

The air was humid and the fog was building again; another night in the city by the bay. I'd come back to San Francisco almost a month earlier, compelled by a desperate need to remember when my life had been worth living. So far the only thing that had gone well was bartering my right to stay in town with the prince of the city, Vannevar Thomas — the man who held all the cards and even held the hand of my Donna. Much as I wanted to, I couldn't bring myself to blame Vannevar for anything that had gone wrong. I couldn't even be mad at him for exiling me from the city in the first place. Everything else in my life was a pale joke and not even a very funny one.

Fifteen years had mellowed my anger substantially, taken the burning hatred for Joe and turned it into a cold, bitter resentment of the cruel thing he'd done to me when he gave me the "gift" of eternal life. Life as a warped reflection from a fun house mirror. I still held a grudge, don't misunderstand me, but I understood his reasons better in hindsight. All his life — human and vampiric alike — Joe had been the outsider, so ugly that most only felt repulsion for him, and so frustrated that even his own family had trouble handling his violent temper. All except for Donna, his sister and my one-time fiancée.

Fifteen years had done nothing to calm down Joe's hatred for me. He hated me even more now than he had back then, a thought that had boggled my mind when we met at Vannevar's offices a month earlier. Thinking back on the occasion, I could feel the anger grow in my chest, swelling beside the fear that was always there. I won't lie about that; whenever I reflect on the tortures Joseph Cambridge put me through when he Embraced me — tortures both physical and mental — I can feel the fear bloom in the back of my throat. The fear always makes me hungry for blood, the only food my system can tolerate and certainly a better taste than the acrid flavor of my remembered tortures.

The fog grew thicker still, and I felt the first fat droplets of rain slide off the battered Stetson on my brow. I was preparing for the hunt, trying to think of a suitable place to find a new victim, when I felt the hand press down on my shoulder. I stared at the massive blue claw for a long second, eyes wide and knees weak, before I hastily stepped away from the shadows.

Joe Cambridge followed only a few seconds later. As was almost always the case, I noticed the sheer size of my enemy first. Joe towered above me, his toady face looming broad and malevolent against the shadowed trees and dark gray sky. Joe stepped forward another pace, and the expression he wore changed from a scowl to a sneer. "Well, well, well. Look what I found."

"Don't touch me, Cambridge. Just get the hell away from me. I don't want any trouble." Despite my best efforts, the fear still trembled deep inside, shaking my voice just enough for both of us to notice. "Vannevar Thomas made his ruling, and you'd do well to abide by it."

Joe just smiled, the false face he wore hiding the fangs he bared with the action, and chuckled deeply in the back of his throat. "I wouldn't dream of hurting you, Jeremy. I don't need to. I always abide by the letter of the law. Besides, just watching you squirm while Donna walks on the arm of Vannevar Thomas is all I need to see to let me know that you're already hurting."

I flared at the barb, stepping forward before I even realized what I was doing. Joseph just smiled, nodding his encouragement. "That's right, pretty boy, why don't you show me what a man you are. Take your best shot." The words were barely above a whisper, loaded with menace. Realizing that I'd stopped myself before it was too late, Joe continued. "Hmm. I rather thought you'd back down. You're not quite that stupid."

Joe moved closer, leaning within inches of my face and grinning evilly. "What if I gave you one free shot? Would you take it? Do you think you could hurt me?"

"I—"

"Hell, Cambridge, I'd take you up on it." The voice was casual, familiar. I felt myself relax slightly. "'Course, Jerry always was kind of a wuss when it came to you." Dawson winked at me and grinned amiably, letting his facial expressions take some of the sting from his words. He was leaning against the tree beside which I had watched my lost love walking with another man only a few minutes earlier, his hands resting against his belt. Dawson never seemed nervous about anything, a quality that I've grown to respect as time has passed. He was dressed the same as always, in a set of clothes that looked like it belonged on an extra from *Urban Cowboy*, right down to the lump of chewing tobacco in his mouth.

"Who the hell are you?" Joseph took the interruption with less grace than I did. His thick lips pulled away from jagged teeth, and his voice sounded much less serene than moments before.

"My name's Dawson," his strong Texas accent and jovial smile lent him an aura of confidence that I've always envied. "I'm an old friend of Jerry's, and I figured I'd track him down so's we could chew the fat for a while." Dawson's eyes ran the length of Joe's frame as he spoke, and his grin grew even wider. "Looks like you had the same idea, Joe. Want to join us?" Dawson winked at me again. "I think it'd be real interesting."

Joe Cambridge smiled broadly, exposing row after row of

razor sharp teeth as the Mask dropped away from his face. "No, I'm sure I can find Jeremy and finish our discussion later." The giant started walking away, then turned back to Dawson with another quick smile that didn't quite reach his eyes. "It's nice to know Jeremy's made new friends. Life can be so hard without them."

Dawson flashed a small smirk, paused and spit a wad of brown juice from his mouth. The spit missed Joe's foot by mere inches. "Hell, Joe. Ya'll keep practicin' how to play nice and you might even make a few friends of your own."

Cambridge stared at the glob of spent tobacco juice next to his foot, looked back at the man leaning against the tree, and then he threw his head back and laughed out loud. "You're a funny man, Mr. Dawson. Very funny. Rest assured, I have plenty of friends. You'd be amazed how many friends I have."

"Naw, shit always gathers a mess of flies." Dawson stepped away from the tree and sauntered over to where I stood watching the banter between the two other Kindred like a man watching a tennis match. "Back home, when the shit gets too thick we just scrape it up and toss it in the mulch pile. Nothing better as fertilizer."

"A good night to you, Mr. Dawson." He turned and looked at me as he finished, reweaving the illusion that he was only human in the process. "We'll talk later, Jeremy."

"Hey, listen. I sure didn't mean to break up the party. But I'm real good at keeping secrets if there was something you needed to say to Jerry. Hell, with me here you even have a witness, someone to prove you didn't defy the prince's orders." Dawson's eyes were sparkling, filled with good humor.

Cambridge stepped back into the shadows, his massive form fading from view. "I don't need to break Vannevar's rules. No direct harm will come to your little friend. I've already arranged to make certain of that." There was a great deal of gloating in the sound of Joseph's voice as he continued. "Jean-Claude sends his regards, Jeremy."

Ice filled my veins at his last words. Silence reigned for several moments as Dawson and I listened for sounds around us. Finally Dawson gestured toward the truck in front of the Alexandria Club, and started walking that way, never bothering to see if I was following him. As always, I did.

When we were safely in the truck, Dawson started the engine, cranked the stereo to near full volume and pulled out into the light traffic. I looked out the front window and watched the street move slowly past, picking up speed as we went. "Thanks, Dawson. That's another one I owe you."

"Shit, Jeremy. It ain't like I'm ever gonna collect. Stop trying to keep tabs on favors owed. It just ain't worth the time it takes." He paused for a minute, listening to the radio and thumping the steering wheel to the beat of a country-western song. Then he sighed mightily and placed a friendly hand on my shoulder. "You might want to watch out for Cambridge. Word on the street says he's got a bullet or twenty with your name on 'em."

I snorted at that. "No shit. He's got every Nosferatu in town giving me the cold shoulder. It's a sad world when even the other sewer rats won't talk to you."

"Yeah, you guys ain't normally picky about who you talk with, unless it's business. Old Joe's got more connections in this town than just about anyone 'cept the prince." Dawson rolled his window down part of the way and spit the wad of tobacco out of his mouth. "Damn, that stuff tastes foul after a few hours. Wish I could give that habit up. But it ain't like it's gonna give me cancer or anything, is it?"

"Not in this lifetime. How the hell can you put that crap in your mouth? The very thought of anything but blood and I'm ready to gag."

"That's just 'cause yer a pussy, Jerry," he said with a laugh. "It took about five months of practice. These days I can even eat a five course meal and never flinch, but it still doesn't do anything for me. Great for meeting with the kine in public though." He paused for a few seconds, and then looked at me from the corner of his eye as he eased the truck around another corner. "You can tell me to shut up if you want, Jerr, but I think you need to stop pining away for that little blond girl." There was a long silence while he waited for my answer, but none was coming his way. I knew he was right. I just didn't care. "Comes a time when you have to realize it's over and get on with your life. She's with another man for fifteen years now, and like as not she's Blood Bound to him. She ain't gonna come running back to you."

"Let's not talk about that, okay?"

"Not a problem." Dawson shook his head, failing in his attempt to hide his disgust over the situation. "So, other than Cambridge and his blue cronies wanting to stake you in the sunlight, how's life been treating you?"

I looked at my friend and laughed. The sound was bitter, even to my own ears.

II

I spent the rest of the night just hanging around with Dawson. We'd been in town for over a month, and whatever Dawson's business in San Francisco was, he'd been too busy to visit. Counting my friend's intervention earlier in the evening, this was twice we'd been together since we first arrived. I had too much time on my hands, Dawson had too little.

The first shades of false dawn were making themselves known when I finally made it back to my family home on Nob Hill. The lights were still burning in the living room windows, and I sighed, fully expecting another confrontation with my mother. At least once a week she felt obligated to explain how much she worried about me, and every time she did, the night ended with her in tears. I love my mother; she is a kind, giving woman, and she took me back in after fifteen years of not seeing me — she even accepted me after finding out about what I am. But, damn, that woman can really get on my nerves when she starts harping about my lifestyle, or rather, the lack thereof.

I slid my key into the lock and opened the door, closing and locking the front entrance behind me. Despite the brilliant light from the living room, there was no sign of my mother anywhere. Nor was Alicia awake, but that didn't surprise me. I set about turning off all the lights and was wending my way toward the basement and my haven. I felt the first pull of exhaustion seeping into me as the sun started to rise. There was no danger yet, as the brilliance from outside would not actually enter the house for a while yet, but I could still feel the demands of my body as it called for the deathlike trance that passed for sleep these days. I could resist the call if I wanted to, but the cost was always high: a feverish twitching in my body and soul that demanded payment in full for my insolence. Sort of like a hangover without the benefit of getting good and drunk in advance. At least with Daylight Saving Time in effect I had longer spans of time to enjoy consciousness.

Just as I was opening the door leading to the basement, the phone gave out a shrill cry, the sound loud enough in the silence to startle me. Without even thinking about it, I grabbed for the phone in the hallway and answered, my primary concern being the sound sleep of everyone else in the house. "Hello?"

"Jeremy?" The voice on the phone sent chills through me automatically. Joe Cambridge. Joe should not have had my unlisted number, but he did. "I just wanted to express my condolences, I know that your father's death was hard on you, but to have your mother so grievously injured... Well, I am truly sorry." The voice made a lie of his words, but I didn't even ponder the facts as I reacted.

"What are you talking about, Cambridge? What have you done?"

"Why, nothing at all, Jeremy. You offend me. I was talking to you when the accident occurred. Besides, I don't even drive."

"What are you talking about?"

"You mean you don't know?" The gloating voice was maddening. "Your dear mother has had a very bad accident. I'm afraid she's in critical condition." Silence then for several eternal seconds. "Well. I'm sorry to be the bearer of bad news, and I wish I could tell you more, but I only just heard about it myself. Besides, the sun is coming up. Sweet dreams, Jeremy."

The dial tone hummed in my ear a few seconds later, and finally I moved, crawling into my basement and hiding in a small supply closet as the sun finally reached the windows of the house. I was cold and numb, and sleep came upon me slowly, pulling me deep into its freezing embrace.

III

I awoke to the fading screams from my nightmares, feeling the dream recede even as I shook the sleep from my body. The room was cold, not that it mattered; everything around me was as cold and lifeless as I felt. After a few seconds, the thoughts finally came back, blowing the remaining fragments of my nightmares into so much dust. I remembered Joe's smirking voice on the phone and what had prompted the call in the first place. My stomach tried doing a few back flips as the memory grew. Pulling myself from my cubbyhole in the storage closet, I adjusted my clothes and climbed up the stairs, preparing for whatever might wait beyond the cellar door.

There was nothing, only silence and more darkness. It only took a few minutes to click on the lights in the living room and ascertain that no one but me was in the house. I felt a cold lump of dread ice over my insides. No one was home, and I'd looked and found no message on the premises. I finally checked the garage on the side of the house and discovered that there was no car parked behind the closed door, only more darkness.

I checked the answering machine: Three messages asking that my mother, Anita, call this friend or that one, nothing else. No message from my mother or from Alicia. I started calling hospitals.

After over an hour of playing phone-tag between different receptionists at several locations, I found out that my mother was in the Intensive Care Unit at San Francisco General. Visiting hours ended at 9 P.M. sharp, but I could still see her for a few minutes if I hurried. I called a cab; sometimes the extra expense is necessary.

Throughout the journey, I replayed the events of the previous night again and again. One sentence from Joseph Cambridge kept creeping back into my mind: "Jean-Claude sends his regards." I had literally purchased the right to stay in town at Jean-Claude's expense: I'd bought immunity for all past crimes by delivering the Settite's heart, along with the heart of Darrius Stone, to Vannevar Thomas, the prince of San Francisco. With the heart in his possession, Thomas could literally destroy Jean-Claude at any time with little more than a gesture.

In all honesty, I would have been a little upset if I'd been the bargaining tool in such a situation. Small wonder that the leader of the Children of Set would take offense. I had no idea where I could find the leader of the Settites, but I suspected the Sand Snake would find me when he was ready.

I thought about the exact words that Vannevar Thomas had used in regards to Joe Cambridge leaving me alone. The man had said that no direct action on Joe's part against me would be tolerated. Simply letting Jean-Claude know who had bartered his heart into the prince's hands could not be called a direct action. But the end result would be the same either way...

I was pulled out of my reverie by the voice of the cab driver. "Hey, mister. We're here." The man promptly lifted the flag and turned to smile at me with a deep concern on his face. "I hope everything's okay, mister." The thick Middle-Eastern accent made the words sound almost musical. "Me? I hate hospitals. Nothing but pain and suffering in these places. The total's $15.08, please." I handed the driver a twenty and slipped from the back seat before he could start counting change. He called out his thanks and pulled away from the curb. I noticed the cab-driver's name on his license, not that it much mattered to me. The name Amir Shubandabbi meant nothing to me. As I found out later, it meant a great deal to others. Amir was one of Jean-Claude's most faithful informants.

The interior of the hospital was busy, surprisingly so until I realized that it was Thanksgiving night. Plenty of people coming in later than usual and staying later as well to share the holiday with a friend or family member who had ended up in the cold, sterile environment. With my ability to make others ignore me, I had almost no trouble slipping past everyone in the hallways. The only exception was a dark-haired boy sitting with his mother. I heard the whispered words of the child: "Mommy, that man's got blue skin..."

I turned around just in time to see the woman grab her son's hand and squeeze gently. The boy stared at me with one bloodshot eye and then looked to his mother as she spoke absently to him. "What have I told you about lying, Christopher? He looks just as normal as you or me." The woman turned and smiled apologetically at me, only to look back at her son as he spoke again.

"But Mommy..."

"But nothing. You hush now, you might hurt the nice

man's feelings." She looked at me again and looked back to her child. "You apologize, right now."

"But—"

"Now, young man, or I'll tell your father about this nonsense." Her voice grew stern.

"I'm sorry, mister."

I smiled back, grateful for the illusions that hid my true appearance from the living. Just the same, the child recoiled from the sight of my bared teeth. "No harm done, Christopher. You be a good boy for your mother."

Christopher, on the verge of crying, nodded quickly. His eyes were threatening tears, and I suspected the infection in his left eye was bad enough without the waterworks. I turned away before I caused the boy any more trouble. I was upset that the child apparently saw past my Mask, but not very upset. No one would believe him, not even his own mother, and I had more pressing matters to attend. Like as not, in later years the ability to see past illusions would fade. I'd run across other toddlers who could still see with more than five senses, but had yet to encounter an adult who could.

When I reached my mother's room I only stayed for a few moments. She was broken and battered, and the tubes running down her throat, forcing air into her lungs, were more than I could stand. The woman I had been raised by was always healthy, always cheerful and vital. What lay in the hospital bed in front of me looked hollow and pale by comparison. She was deathly pale and her veins showed through her skin as if it were nothing more than tissue paper. The bed beside hers held Alicia, the family maid for as long as I could remember. She was asleep, but apparently in better shape than my mother. Both had broken bones and carefully bandaged wounds. The scent of blood was even stronger than the overwhelming stench of the disinfectant, and I was reminded that the time to feed was fast approaching. I walked to my mother's side and leaned over to kiss her forehead gently, but the need for sustenance was almost overwhelming and I stepped back, barely under control.

I grabbed a pen from the clipboard and scribbled a quick note to Alice and my mother. The note said: 'I had to leave. Will be back as soon as I can. All of my love, Jeremy.'

I almost ran from the hospital, cursing myself for my weakness and cursing Joe Cambridge for what he'd made me. Sometimes I almost forgot what I'd become, and when the memory came rushing back, it was twice as bad. When I finally found a place where I felt safe hunting, I located a target and assaulted the man brutally. He was a handsome man, in his mid-thirties, with clothes that spoke of money. I needed the release of tension almost as much as I needed the blood. I stopped myself in time and left the man alive, though just barely. I licked the wounds shut and ran from the area, teeth clenched together and hands balling into fists.

I was moving so fast that I didn't notice Mark Anderson until I literally ran into him. I grabbed his arms and held him up, starting to apologize automatically for almost knocking him down. Then I heard his voice, and the memories soared back. "Jeremy Wyzchovsky? Wix? Damn, I haven't seen you since high school!"

Mark looked me up and down and I returned the favor, trying to reconcile the differences twenty years had made in the captain of the football team. Where there had been nothing but solid muscle years before, Mark now carried a spare thirty pounds of flab, and he carried each pound poorly. I almost didn't recognize him until he smiled. The expression took years away from him and brought back a hint of the man I'd known so long ago. For a few years we'd been inseparable, then he went to school in New York and I'd never heard from him again. "Shit, Jeremy, you look great!"

"Jesus Christ. Mark? How the hell are you?" There was no awkwardness as we reached out and gave each other ferocious bear-hugs. The years faded away for a second, and we were good friends again, just like old times. Human contact can be a glorious thing; just the simple act of touching another person with affection. You never miss it until you realize that you haven't held a person in friendship or love for a long time. Maybe that's why so many vampires are bitter, and why so many of us refer to ourselves as the Damned. Loneliness must surely be an important aspect of hell. "God, it's great to see you, guy."

"Jeremy. You're crushing me." I hastily stepped back, releasing him from the unintentional death-grip I'd had on his ribs. I tend to forget the benefits of my condition as well, like the ability to crush a man to death without even breaking a sweat. He stepped back also, a smile still on his face and mild shock in his eyes. "Still as strong as you ever were, my man. Where do you work out?" His laughter was music to my ears, and my mind flashed on a hundred other times I'd heard the same sort of laughter from him. In fifteen years I'd almost never thought about Mark Anderson. I was surprised by the intensity of my feelings for him.

We talked for a few minutes, trying to catch up on twenty years in that time. He told me lies about how well he was doing, how much he loved his wife and how much she loved him, and how much he loved his job as the assistant manager at his bank; and I returned the favor by telling him that I was thrilled by my work as a stockbroker. They were good lies, the kind that cause no one pain and make everyone feel better about the failures they've had in life. I think Mark was almost as lonely and depressed as I was.

Finally, Mark looked at his watch and sighed. "Listen, Jeremy, I've gotta get out of here. I've got to meet my wife and her folks for a dinner date in half an hour. But why don't you give me a call later tonight and we can get together tomorrow?" He passed me a card with his business number and his home number, and I promised I'd do just that. I walked away from the meeting with a spring in my step and a stupid smile plastered to my face. I didn't think about Donna or my mother at all. I was happy for the first time in a long, long while.

I left myself open for a world and a half of hurt.

I'd fed, and I was ready to see my mother again despite the knowledge that visiting hours were long since past. I really meant to see her, but I just couldn't bring myself to face the grievous injuries she'd experienced, or the almost-certain knowledge that the wounds were caused by my very presence and my past actions.

Yeah, I know I'm scum, but at least I'm honest about it.

I spent the rest of the night wandering the streets and spiraling back into a self-pitying fugue. Thanksgiving night, and the only company I could manage to find was myself. The only time I paused in my solitary wanderings was when I called Mark and arranged to see him the next night. He wanted to meet for lunch, but I managed to convince him that later was better. With my particular condition, sunlight tends to leave nasty burns — if you manage to survive.

Around 5:30, I finally headed toward the house on Nob Hill where I'd spent as little time as possible while growing up. I guess some things never change, because I still hated being around the place when it was occupied.

I got there after the fire engines had left. The heat was still intense and the blackened, skeletal remains of my family home smoldered and steamed in the pre-dawn morning. I probably would have noticed the burnt-out shell earlier if I'd bothered to look past the shadows chasing my feet, or even remembered to breathe and sniff around for trouble. I stopped dead in my tracks less than a hundred yards from where the front door used to be.

Several people from the neighborhood stared at the carnage, mumbling to themselves and shaking their heads sadly. They were glad it wasn't one of their homes, and some were even saddened that it was the Wyzchovsky place that

burned, but most were just there to look on the ruins of
another person's world. What had been my mother's world,
and mine too, I suppose. What little was left of my human
life had been in that building: the trophies I'd won in tennis
matches, the photographs from simpler times when the world
still had color for me. Gone, lost to a fire that I knew in my
heart had been set. I had no proof, nor did I need it. Joseph
Cambridge was keeping his word — he was doing me no
direct harm. He just made me suffer for ever having met his
sister, and made me loathe the fact that he was alive at all.
I don't think I've ever hated anyone as much as I hated him
right then.

There were two other vampires there, both Nosferatu.
They were deep in the shadows, but not really trying to hide
from me. I'd seen them in passing, been snubbed by them
during my first week in town. The one on the right, dressed
in filthy rags and carrying a heavy bag on her shoulder, I
recognized as Vika. The other one I could put no name to.
Who knows, maybe they were planted by Cambridge, maybe
they even started the fire, or maybe they just came to see
the action and gather news for the highest bidder — that is
what the Nosferatu do best, barter information.

If they'd noticed me, they were very careful not to let
me know it. They were talking in subdued whispers, and I
decided to listen to what they had to say. There are very
few advantages to being a Nosferatu, but one of them comes
in the form of acute hearing. My ears are huge, pointy things
these days, and I guess that helps. The Mask is a mind trick,
and one I'm good at, but it has other applications as well.
There was no real effort involved, I just arranged my
thoughts and moved carefully through the darkness. They
never heard me or saw me as I moved closer to them. I
caught a part of their conversation: Vika was talking. "I don't
know where they're coming from, but I've seen them
everywhere. Every time I turn around, there's another human

running around with a bloodshot eye. And it's only one eye, never both of them. Let me tell you something else, Scabby, they can see us for what we are."

"I don't think they're human at all. I was over in China Town last night, doin' a little of the old song and dance for the Dowager, and she tells me they came from under the city. From the ruins beneath us in old San Fran."

"Yeah, I've heard the same. Whoever breaks this baby can write their own check with his lordship, Vannevar. I aim to be the one. Put the word out — I want to know what's what with the bloodshot humans. And tell Cambridge his little prize never showed up at the hospital a second time." The one she addressed as Scabby nodded vigorously and scuttled out of the shadows, hiding behind his own Mask as he went.

I waited for Vika to move, but she stayed where she was, her eyes closed for a few seconds. Then she looked straight at me and smiled. "Hello, Wix." I was a bit shocked, but only a little bit. There are enough vampires out there who can see past the illusions I create that I seldom grow unsettled when they manage to see me. "You're good. I didn't even notice you until a few seconds ago." She turned away from me, heading toward the lawn of the house next door. I was preparing to follow her when she looked over her shoulder and stared at me intently for a few seconds. She pointed to where the conversation had taken place between her and Scabby, and then she spoke. "I know what you must be thinking, what with the accident your mother had and all. But it wasn't me, and it wasn't any of the other sewer rats. We just came to see what was going down." She waited long enough to see me nod, and then she vanished into the darkness.

Where she had been pointing, a small sheaf of papers lay folded into quarters and half buried in the soil; she'd been standing on top of them, and she hadn't moved until Scabby had left the area. I took the papers and unfolded them. The

writing was immediately recognizable to me. It was mine. I
stared at a photocopy of the pages I'd given to my mother
the night I came back into town. The letter was a long,
abbreviated history of the events that led to my Embrace,
my exile from the city, and the life I'd been living for fifteen
years. It told of the Camarilla, the Kindred, the world of
vampires. And it mentioned Vannevar Thomas, Donna
Cambridge and Joseph Cambridge by name. I grew numb
while I stared at the lines of writing — if anyone else had
seen these pages, I was in deeper trouble than I wanted to
think about.

There was a note scrawled on the back of the pages that
was almost equally familiar. It was written in the tight, close
letters I recognized as coming from Dawson's pen. *I took this
off a corpse on the way to the morgue. Three other copies have
been found and reported to the prince by Emily Grange. She's
the night shift M.E. and a Ventrue. Rumor has it that Cambridge
has been calling for a Blood Hunt. Watch your ass, Jeremy.*
There was no signature, but if I'd been in the same position
I wouldn't have implicated myself either.

Someone had taken the papers I'd written away from my
mother and had been making copies. Cambridge, maybe, but
I doubted it. More likely it was one of the Settites, maybe
even Jean-Claude himself. Either way I was fucked. Thomas
knew about the papers, and I knew for certain he'd be
unhappy about them. Cambridge was probably in seventh
heaven by now, ready to strike me down the second that
Vannevar Thomas agreed to the hunt. I had to give him
credit where it was due; the last time he'd completely
shattered my life it took him a month. This time he'd
managed the feat in less than two days.

The sun was on the rise by the time I left the remains of
my family home. For the first time in over ten years I slept
in the sewers.

IV

As soon as the sun set, I was on my way. I slipped out of a manhole near the Tenderloin and called Mark Anderson. A man picked up after the third ring, but his voice was unfamiliar. My skin crawled for no reason I could think of when I heard the official sounding voice. "Anderson residence, who may I say is calling?"

"Jeremy Wyzchovsky. I'm calling for Mark Anderson."

"I'm sorry, sir. Could you spell that last name for me?"

"Just tell him it's Wix, he'll know who you mean."

"Please, if you could just spell the last name for me."

"Who am I speaking with?" He paused, and I repeated the question.

"This is Lieutenant John Coleson, San Francisco Police. What is the nature of your call, Mr. Wizlowski?"

I opted not to correct him on the mispronunciation of my last name. "I'm supposed to meet Mark later on tonight. Is everything okay over there?"

"Are you a friend of the family, Mr. Wizlowski?"

"Uh, yeah. Well, I know Mark, we ran across each other last night, and we were going to meet for dinner..."

"I'm sorry to be the one to tell you sir, but I'm afraid Mark Anderson won't be able to meet with you." Oh, I wanted to ask him why, I really did, but I was afraid I already knew the answer to the question. He proved me right when he continued after a few seconds of silence. "I'm afraid Mr. Anderson is dead." He kept right on talking, at least until I'd slammed the phone back into its cradle. I even wiped the phone clean before I left. Not that what passes for my skin these days has any recognizable fingerprints, mind you. I guess I just watch too much television for my own good.

It didn't take too much math to figure out what the hell was going on. Dawson's note said four bodies had been found with my letter to my mother. Mark told me last night that he was going for dinner with his wife and his in-laws. I'd have bet money that all four bodies came from one location, the same one I'd just called on the phone. I'd like to say that I mourned for Mark and his family, but in truth I was just too damned scared to care about them. Everywhere I turned, there was something going wrong. Every person I knew in town seemed destined for pain, simply because they knew me. I'd gotten sloppy after a month with no conflicts, and I never realized just how much trouble I was in when I crossed paths with Joe Cambridge. God damn him for being right. He didn't even have to lift a finger and already my life was falling to pieces.

I hid myself in the shadows until I found another pay phone a few blocks away. Then I called San Francisco General and asked to speak with Alicia White. I spent five minutes waiting on the line, listening to premature Christmas music, before I got a connection to her room. "Hello?"

"Alicia? Hi, it's Jeremy."

"Jeremy? Where are you? You've had your mother worried sick." Her voice was strong, and that was good, but the words she'd just said were even better.

"Mom's awake?"

"Well of course she is. She's in the next bed. Do you want to talk to her?"

"Yeah, please."

There was a few seconds of fumbling, and then my mother's voice came on the phone. "Jeremy? Are you all right? The police told me about the fire. They didn't find anyone in the ruins, but I was worried half to death about you."

"Yeah, Mom. I'm fine. How are you? You didn't look so hot last time I saw you."

"Well, I'm fine, Jeremy. Alicia's doing even better than me. She'll be out of the hospital in the morning, and if my recovery continues like it is right now, I'll be out before Monday."

And there they went again, a dozen little alarm bells ringing in my head, screaming that they didn't let people out of the hospital less than a week after they'd been forced to shove a hose or two down the patient's throat. I forced false levity into my voice. "Heck, sounds like you're doing worlds better. I thought for sure you'd be there at least a couple of weeks with the injuries you sustained."

"Seems everyone here thought that. But I guess there must have been some sort of confusion when they took my x-rays, because they thought there were a lot of broken bones in this old body, but when they checked again, everything was fine except a broken ankle." In her usual way, she deflected any further questions about herself and redirected the conversation back to me. "Are you sure you're okay, Jeremy? Where are you staying? Is there anything I can get you?"

"I'm fine, honest." But I wasn't fine, not at all. I'd seen the way she looked, I'd smelled the blood from what had to be internal bleeding in her body, and here she was sounding like the most damage she'd suffered was to her pride. Either my mother was more robust than I'd ever realized, or something was very, very wrong.

There are humans that serve the Kindred, called ghouls by most of us because they feed on the dead in their own way. They feed on the blood of vampires, and it keeps them young and in fine shape. It can even heal their wounds, the same way that vampires can force their wounds to heal if they have sufficient blood in their systems. What better place than a hospital to slip vampiric blood into the body of a wounded person and speed the healing process? Simple fact #703: If you can get another vampire, or a human, and convince them to drink from your blood three times, you can literally force them to like you, to want to please you and to serve you. It's called the Blood Bond, and I know it works, because that's how vampires ensure the loyalty of their ghouls. My mother had been in the hospital for three nights, and during that time, someone had been feeding her blood. Vampiric blood. I had no solid proof, but again, I didn't need it. Like I said, I saw her on her second night in the hospital, and she looked like death warmed over then. Now, only one night later, she was sounding healthy and cheerful.

I spoke without really paying attention for a few more minutes, and then I said my good nights. I'd called the hospital in the hopes that my mother was recovering, maybe coming out of her coma. Right then I wished that she had never pulled out. Someone had bound my mother to himself through the blood of a vampire, and I was a vampire without many friends in the Kindred community. The thought of seeing my mother again was one I'd have to repress, because I had no way of knowing who she now served, and no way to find out. Vannevar Thomas or Donna Cambridge? Not likely, they had little or nothing to gain except for money, and they had that in spades. Joseph Cambridge or Jean-Claude? One of the two vampires who almost certainly wanted me dead? Distinctly possible. I knew it wasn't Dawson; he'd have no idea where to look, and no reason for doing the deed.

I called information and got the number I needed from the operator. I slipped my quarter into the slot and punched the buttons carefully, as it was the last of my spare change. After seven rings I got an answer. When the person on the line announced where he worked, I asked to speak to his supervisor, Doctor Emily Grange. Less than a minute later, I heard her cool, cultured voice pick up the receiver. "This is Doctor Grange, how can I help you?"

"Doctor, my name is Jeremy Wix. I think we need to talk."

The night went downhill from there. The woman was sharp and definitely knew her business when it came to forensics. She carefully explained to me that the bodies had all been killed in violation of the Masquerade, the most important law of the Camarilla. She detailed the unique patterns of teeth used on the necks of the four people killed and pointed out that all four had been left with a decent amount of blood in their bodies, but not enough to hide that they'd been drained. She went on to discuss the importance of licking wounds, and how breaking the necks of the victims didn't necessarily kill them, but that I'd been fortunate this time. She let me know that Vannevar Thomas had agreed with Joseph Cambridge when my Sire suggested a Blood Hunt. She then heartily recommended that I turn myself in before it was too late, because apparently half the Kindred in the city were perfectly willing to make me their personal mission, especially in light of the substantial reward for my capture. A reward offered by none other than Joe Cambridge.

I hung up the phone when she started in on my lack of forethought for the third time. I remembered Vika's comments to Scabby earlier, the talk about how the strange people with the bloodshot eyes had come from the ruins beneath the city. Ruins largely unexplored, and certainly safer than any haven I might find in the surface world.

It took the rest of the night to find an entrance, but I did find one. I can't leave San Francisco, tempting as the idea is. There's too much unresolved, too much that isn't settled between me and my Sire, me and Vannevar Thomas. There was the situation between myself and the Settites in town, especially Jean-Claude and Darrius Stone. And then there's Donna Cambridge.

I love her, with all of my heart I love Donna Cambridge. And I guess a part of me hates her, too. I keep thinking that with just a gesture or two and a few words, she could probably clean this entire mess up. She could let the prince know that I've never been that stupid, that I'd never leave so obvious a trail. She could make him understand that her brother hates me more than anything he's ever seen. She could even resolve my worst problem, the Settites, just by convincing Vannevar Thomas that they are the likeliest choice for everything that's gone down in the last few days.

I keep seeing Donna laughing with Vannevar Thomas, the sophisticated, handsome man who rules over the Kindred in San Francisco. I see her laughing and smiling, holding his hand when once upon a time she held mine. I thought that maybe she'd found it in her heart to forgive me, but now I know better.

I think about the ruins my life have become, and I think about the differences between love and hate. I see Donna laughing at Thomas' little whispered joke. I hope the leftovers that rest beneath the city are empty and dark, with nothing moving, nothing to disturb me. Maybe if it's dark enough, I won't see her anymore, I won't think of what it was like before my life was destroyed by her brother the first time, and I won't keep hearing her laughter echoing in my mind. When she's gone from there, from the bitter memories in my heart and soul, perhaps I'll know peace again. I'll know only the darkness.

SPARROW'S SONG

JAMES S. DORR

He should have been thinking about
Ann, his girlfriend. He should have been,
yes, even though he realized now that it
had already been over between them. Still,
what had happened just five days before,
her body crushed in a cable car crash the
evening after the Friday night earthquake
— the one he had slept through — ought
to have filled his mind with horror. Or, if
not that, then he might do well thinking
about his own problems, as his apartment
building had been destroyed in an
aftershock just hours before Ann's death,
and the only possessions he'd managed to
save were the clothes on his back and the
coronet he held now.

He should have been thinking about
the concert he and his band had still
managed to play in Washington Square
that Saturday night, after so much had
happened. San Francisco half in ruins, yet,

somehow, people had crowded to hear them. He should have been thinking about his drug habit, how it had come back, and how he had kicked it all over again.

He should have been thinking of all these things as he stood on the bandstand, his sidemen around him, the lights turned down and the last patrons gone from the now-closed nightclub. Except Eddie Marsdon was a jazzman.

And he was composing.

The song had come to him on Sunday morning — the theme of it anyway — after the concert. One vision more out of so many visions, possibly in a dream. But all day Sunday it raced through his head. Then Monday he'd gotten back with his bandsmen — Ken Genovese on piano, Cruse on the drums and Carl Santiago playing guitar, Buddy Ferrin his trombone player and Bill Taylor on clarinet — and called up a jazz club owner he knew to arrange to use his place for rehearsals.

But it wasn't working. Tuesday's session had been a wash, Wednesday the same. The others, to be sure, were getting their parts down, were even starting into the embroidering that would make the music they played jazz, but his own cornet break just wasn't meshing.

He should have been thinking about all these things, weaving them somehow into the music. The jazz club's owner promising that, if the song came together, he and his band could open that weekend.

But something was missing.

He held up his hand, then nodded to Cruse. "Let's try it again," he said as the drummer answered with a cadenced rhythm. He nodded again and the trombone growled, paving the way for Ken and Carl to augment the rhythm while Bill raised his clarinet to his lips, then laid a descant part over the trombone. So far, so good, he thought as he counted the beats to his own entrance, lifting his cornet, then crashing in with a flurry of grace notes, then sliding back down to what Buddy was playing to reestablish the melody line —

one verse, one chorus — then arcing up high even over the clarinet, echoing both wind instruments now, yet striking his own path.

So far, so good, as the others dropped out now, one by one, leaving just him and the drums and piano, then just him and drums. A solo half chorus — brief, but soaring. Then back with the clarinet and guitar to help take all three down to where Buddy Ferrin's trombone was waiting. But…

"You Eddie Marsdon?" a voice broke in on them. Low, like the trombone.

He looked up. "What?"

He signaled the band to stop. He still wasn't getting it right, he thought. Technically, sure, it would probably pass. Most of the notes were there, even if some of the high ones were missing — enough to fake anyway. But it still lacked the *feeling* he knew his part had to have before he himself would be satisfied with it.

He thought about Sparrow…

The voice broke in again. "You Eddie Marsdon?" He squinted out onto the unlit dance floor and saw the policeman, the one he and Sparrow, the street punk, had argued with Saturday afternoon after the earthquake. He thought about Sparrow, how she had sold him the heroin Friday that had carried him through the main quake, then how that next afternoon she had helped him rescue his cornet after he'd fled his apartment without it.

He anticipated it — it *was* the same cop. The officer had let himself in surprisingly silently, but now he saw the cop was followed by other policemen. Out of the corner of his eye he saw Cruse start to stand up.

He signaled the drummer to sit back down. "Yeah, I'm Eddie Marsdon," he said. He almost smiled as he spoke the cliché. "Is anything the matter, officer?"

The cop shook his head. "We want you to come with us. Just an identification, that's all. We got someone we think is maybe a friend of yours."

■

He thought about Sparrow as the police car sped downtown, and about how the cops were in such a hurry, stopping him when he started to pack his things away and having him just take his cornet with him. He thought about how she had seemed so waiflike despite her cropped hair and her black leather jacket. Just a kid scarcely more than fifteen. He barely noticed the Pyramid Tower with its two-hundred-foot glowing spike looming leprous above them as they screeched past it, the dim, fitful street lamps that struggled to light the financial district, the rest of the city still mostly in darkness. He just followed silently when they halted, finally, in front of a darkened building and led him inside through a booking room where a fat police sergeant was taking a statement from a red-eyed vagrant.

But then when they started upstairs, the policeman he'd known before spoke. "You see that sign, Marsdon?" He pointed to a half-unfurled banner above the desk sergeant. "We're going to have TV people here later — I'm telling you now because we don't want to have any disturbances. Whole city's uptight, so we're going to calm them by giving out medals on tomorrow's news to policemen who showed bravery during the earthquake. And others, like now, who're bringing in looters. But then I guess you know all about TV."

Eddie shrugged. He didn't watch TV, especially now that he didn't even have an apartment. Ken Genovese had taken him in, but Ken and his wife didn't watch TV either.

But then the cop went on. "The mayor wants people to stay in their homes, to know they'll be safe there. Not like last Saturday when that TV crew filming the city's emergency workers came across you and that band of yours and put *you* on the news instead. Making people come out and listen. But anyway, Marsdon…"

The officer stopped when his partner unlocked the door to a second-floor room and led them both inside. Marsdon's eyes widened — yes, it *was* Sparrow, still in her street clothes, but held on the other side of the glass of an interview room, the kind of room used for inmate visits, with only a speaker hole open between them. He strode to the glass and tapped it gently, sensing its thickness from the dull thump it made.

Sparrow looked up. "Eddie?" she said.

Eddie nodded, about to speak, when the first policeman interrupted. "Your new girlfriend here's in some serious trouble, Marsdon," he said. "You know Ann Paxley — who you *used* to go with? Fine, upright woman. But she was killed last Saturday evening and, the way we see it, it was murder."

"Now wait a minute," Eddie said. "You're saying she had something to do with it? It was an accident — a stupid, freak, runaway cable car accident — I saw it all myself. Sparrow was clear across the street…."

The second policeman smiled and winked. "We got witnesses though, Marsdon, who're willing to swear they saw this 'Sparrow' at the controls of that cable car. Who're willing to say she released the brake, then jumped off just before it crashed. Good *police* witnesses, who people'll believe. Not like the word of some musician."

Eddie glared at him, then at the first cop. "So what do you want from me?" he asked. "Collaboration? You seem to know already who Sparrow is, and if, as you say, she's supposed to be my new girlfriend, it's not very likely you'll get it from me."

The first policeman smiled as well now. "Like I said before on the stairs, we just don't want any trouble, Marsdon. That's why we're willing to make a deal with you. Our captain drops all charges against her," he gestured with his thumb through the glass, "while all you do is give us your cornet."

"Huh?" Eddie said. Then it occurred to him. "You mean you want me to stop playing. Is that it, officer? So people won't come out to listen? I suppose maybe I could for a while,

I mean if it's still some kind of earthquake emergency thing and..."

The cop shook his head. "Music's a form of free expression, even that degenerate slop *you* play. We're not after your civil rights, Marsdon. Get a trumpet for all we care. Like you said once, a trumpet's different, a different sound from what a cornet makes. But that'd be okay."

He hesitated. He *could* play a trumpet, except the cornet was special to him. He'd been found as a baby in 1968 in Haight-Ashbury, or so he'd been told, and raised in a series of foster homes, but always he'd had that cornet with him, the one thing they said he'd been left by his father. It, like his music, was part of his life. But still...

"Eddie, no!" Sparrow shouted. "They're not saying everything. I overheard their captain talking. They think your cornet has some kind of power, something they want to keep away from people like you and me. But you've already started to use it. You're famous Eddie, because of Saturday night and the TV. That's why they couldn't just arrest *you* and take it themselves, because people would find out. And, you know, with looters and all on the streets already, they don't want to risk any more disorder."

Eddie turned back to the policeman. "Is that true?" he asked. "I can just say 'no' and I'm free to walk out?"

The two policemen looked at each other. "Yeah, for now," the first one said. "But if you walk out, you'll walk out alone. And murder's a capital crime in this state. Is an instrument worth your friend's life, Marsdon?"

Eddie shrugged. No. He started to hand the instrument over when Sparrow interrupted again.

"Then do me a favor, would you, Eddie? Play something for me first? You know, that new song you've been working on. I heard about it, and it's for *me*, Eddie. That's why you're writing it. Let me hear it?"

He saw the policeman grudgingly nod okay, and he raised the cornet to his lips. This time he had to play it perfectly, this one time only, because it was true. Cornets *were* different. Cornets were a kind of horn, like the rams' horns Joshua's priests played in the Bible, despite some translations calling them "trumpets." Trumpets had straight bores, while cornets were conical, giving them a fuller sound.

He started playing. He played for Sparrow, and this time the music soared like it was meant to, rich and full like a bird free in flight. He heard, in his mind's ear, the trombone, the clarinet, ending their phrases while his horn wailed upward, alone with only the drums behind it. Reaching higher and higher still, a full octave higher, he saw, in a glimpse, Sparrow suddenly look up, when—

He heard a *crack!* In front of him the glass wall shattered and Sparrow dived through, bowling over the nearest policeman. She wrestled the gun from the officer's holster and clubbed him with it while Eddie, unthinking, slugged the other. Then they were in the hallway outside and Sparrow locked the door behind them, then led him downstairs.

Halfway down the stairs they saw that the booking room was filled with vagrants — street people, many with bloodshot left eyes — while a TV crew was filming policemen, their chests filled with medals, bringing yet more in.

Sparrow began to laugh. She waved the gun she'd captured upstairs and then pointed it at Eddie's head. "Listen!" she shouted.

The TV camera, its own red eye glowing, turned to them and to Eddie's cornet as Sparrow continued.

"Listen: I've got Eddie Marsdon, the jazz player. He's my hostage. Now everyone stand back!"

Everyone did stand back, clearing a path to the station house door — except the street people. They began to stream outside too, carrying Eddie and Sparrow with them, blocking the police who tried to chase them.

Eddie held Sparrow to him, afraid they'd be separated as

the vagrants swirled off in every direction, when, just in front of them, he saw a van with its door partly open. He hustled her inside, then hot-wired the motor. He headed down Front Street against the one-way signs, then turned west on Sutter out toward the Haight — he didn't know why except, he supposed, he still had some roots there — while Sparrow climbed into the back of the van, rummaging through whatever she found there. "You've got an alibi, Eddie," she said. "The hostage thing, you know. It'll be on TV in the morning and people will see it. Still, though, the cops are going to be mad. They won't dare touch you, but still — at least when you're not on a gig — you might want to kind of keep out of their sight."

"Yeah," Eddie said. Behind them he thought he heard distant sirens coming closer.

"Me," Sparrow went on, "I'm kind of used to disappearing when I have to. I'll be okay, but…"

Her voice trailed off, and then she giggled. "You know what's in the back of this truck, Eddie? TV equipment. Now we're sure to get on the news — we stole the TV truck!"

Eddie laughed too. But then he stopped suddenly. He was *sure* now that the sirens were closer. "Sparrow," he said, "it just occurred to me. If what we've got is the TV van, we're not exactly inconspicuous. But if we leave it and double back toward downtown, maybe when the cops find it, they'll think we're still headed west."

"Sure, Eddie," Sparrow said, climbing out with him when he stopped the van. Hand in hand, they walked down the still-dark streets, jogging north first to obscure their trail further, then turning back east on Pine. Then Sparrow spoke again.

"Eddie," she said. "I've got an idea. About how we both can maybe disappear. I've got a place in Chinatown — and you know what they say about Chinatown, how not even the cops know their way around there. And I know how you need a new apartment.…"

"You mean stay with you?" Eddie asked. He hesitated. It made sense, sort of. Ken and his wife didn't have much room. He had to move somewhere. Still, he was practically twenty-seven, nearly twice Sparrow's age, and, even with Saturday and, now, tonight, they scarcely knew each other.

"Sure," Sparrow answered. She turned and looked up at him. "Eddie," she said, her voice serious now, "there are things going on — important things — and I need to talk to you about them. Except I don't understand all of them myself. You know, with the cops? Your cornet and stuff? Even your girlfriend getting killed that way. And as for me, I'm in and out all the time. It's not as though I'd be in your way."

Eddie still hesitated. He wanted to say yes — he knew that he did by the way he had missed her. That she had been right, that the song *had* been for her. That somehow, for some reason, things had been happening to bring them together. And yet, with all that, he still wasn't sure.

But then Sparrow smiled. "There is one problem, though," she said. "The place that I live in, it's kind of noisy — the neighborhood, that is. People up all night. Punkers. Tourists. Lots of traffic. You won't get much sleep there." She paused for a moment, then continued. But there's a good side to it too, Eddie."

Now Eddie smiled with her. He knew what it was, but he still asked her anyway, wanting to give her the chance to convince him.

She shrugged, then answered. "It's not a bad place to practice the cornet."

DEAD BEAT

DON BASSINGTHWAITE

"More blue," said Abra thoughtfully. Squatting in an unlit corner, Dan Barr tried to ignore him. "The darker shade."

Andrew, the one Abra was really speaking to, nodded and reached for another can of spray paint. Or rather the body that Andrew occupied, a young woman with a shaved head, reached for another can of spray paint. Andrew controlled her movements as though she were a suit that he wore. A can picked up. The sweep of an arm. The addition of a streak of midnight blue paint to the graffiti mural that was growing in the dark of the abandoned building.

The young woman's eyes were feverish. She knew that these motions were not her own. She knew that the horrific scene taking shape on the wall was nothing she had intended to paint. She also knew that the central image was not something she had imagined, because the model for that image stood in the shadows at the end of the room. Every so often, Andrew would turn her head so that he could look at it.

Another young woman was burning in the darkness. Fire licked at the long, blue turn-of-the-century dress that she wore. Her pale hair gave off ribbons of smoke. She wailed, a thin, reedy sound like rising wind, and thrashed about. The motion caused her skin, blackened by the flames, to crack and the glowing red of hot embers to show through. The reek of her burning hung in the air, but the odor was cold. The fire that had killed the woman in blue had burned out decades ago. Helpless, horrified, the living woman painted the dead woman's agony.

"Red," Abra pronounced.

"Would you shut up and let Andrew work?" snapped Jeremy. Dan tried to ignore him as well. Both Jeremy and Abra were seated on a moldering old sofa midway between the possessed woman and her ghostly model. The young woman's gaze passed right through them, but then she was the only living person in a room full of wraiths. "Who's the artist here?"

"I beg your pardon?" Abra gestured toward the burning wraith. "What is that, then? Charity hasn't looked so good since she died."

Dan knew the histories of some of the wraiths around him. In appearance, at least, they were all teenagers, though most were far older than they seemed. Charity had died in the fires that raged across San Francisco after the earthquake of 1906. She felt no pain from her present "burning." It was all just an act to terrify the young graffiti artist. Normally, she was quite pretty. Abra had shaped and molded the plasm of her immaterial body to make her appearance more frightening. Abra himself — tall, thin, blond, and still dressed in a pea jacket — had been a young Russian sailor in life. His body had been one of the last buried in the cemetery that gave Russian Hill its name. Andrew had died in the '50s in a construction-site accident — a budding artist frustrated by the lack of time to create. Now he had all the time in the world. Jeremy... Dan knew too well how Jeremy had died. Sixteen years ago, a car crash had claimed his life and that of his mother — Dan's wife. Jeremy was his son.

It had been a little more than a month since Dan himself had died. Ironically, he had killed himself in an effort to protect his other son, Josh, from a wraith. Except that the wraith had turned out to be Josh, and his living son, Jeremy. The brothers, twins, were periodically able to switch places with each other. One would be a wraith while the other occupied their living body. Josh had only "attacked" his brother in an effort to make that switch. Now Josh was alive, and Jeremy was dead, and so, needlessly, was Dan.

I know what dying is like, Josh had told his father when Dan had first become a wraith. *Things don't have to change much. San Francisco is full of wraiths. It's not like being alive, but it could be worse.*

Sammy, another wraith, walked through the wall and directly into the path of Andrew's spray paint. The paint didn't really hurt her, but it left her startled. "Hey!" she shrieked.

"Watch where you're going!" spat Andrew through the graffitiartist's mouth. "I'm creating!" He sprayed another streak of paint through Sammy.

"Bastard!" Sammy frowned. Where the blue paint passed through the indignant wraith, it suddenly turned blood-red and spattered against the wall in thick, half-clotted globs. The graffiti artist's skin paled to a ghastly shade and her arm shook in spite of Andrew's control. Her eyes rolled back in her head. Abruptly, her body went slack, held up only by the wraith's will.

"Oh, great!" Abra complained. "See what you've done now? She's passed out!"

Sammy stuck her ghostly tongue out at him.

It's not much like being alive, but it could be worse. Dan just wasn't sure how. Andrew, Sammy, Abra, and Charity were all friends of Jeremy's. They had taken Dan in at his urging. Somehow, though, an afterlife spent with teenagers was not something Dan had ever really imagined.

Andrew let the body of the graffiti artist fall to the floor like a living person might carelessly let clothing drop. Something about the way the young woman fell depressed the valve on the spray can in her hand — blue paint shot up in a mist, settling back down to cover her hand and arm and filling the air with fumes. Disgusted, Dan rose and walked over to her prostrate form. Reaching through the Shroud that separated the Shadowlands, the world of the dead, from the world of the living, he flicked at the valve with his finger. The spray of paint ceased.

He scowled at Andrew. "That could have asphyxiated her."

Andrew put his hand under his chin and turned his head from side to side. "Barr," he asked sarcastically, "is this the face of someone who gives a damn?"

It was too much. "Fuck you." Dan turned on his heel and stalked toward the door. Someone caught his arm before he could reach it.

"Dad..." Jeremy looked up at him. Dan's sons had both inherited their father's ginger hair and strong build, as well as their mother's pale-blue eyes. In the world of the living, that ginger hair had always been their most striking feature. In the Shadowlands, Jeremy's hair seemed faded and wan. His clear, pale eyes were what really stood out.

Dan refused to meet his gaze. "I'm going out," he said shortly.

"You know Andrew didn't mean it."

"Do I? Do I really know that any of you wouldn't have let her die? Jeremy, you were *terrifying* that poor girl."

Jeremy shrugged. "She was the one who pushed her way into our Haunt."

"And I needed a hand anyway," Andrew added. "I want

to create a death mural for each of us."

"She was looking for somewhere out of the rain!" Dan threw up his hands. "All she wanted was shelter and you turned her into a toy!"

"You don't understand how things work, Dad. Give it time..."

"It's been a month, Jeremy. I've been dead for a month. I know that might not sound like much to you, but I think that I have pretty much figured out how things work." Dan raked the room with a glare. "It's all just a game for you, isn't it? You're dead. The world is your playground. You bunch do whatever you want and to hell with the living people you hurt. You don't answer to anybody... no, you *refuse* to answer to anybody." He brought his gaze back to Jeremy. "I thought I raised you better than that."

Jeremy flushed. Dan turned away again. "I'll see you later."

"Are you going to go hang out with Sykes again?" Jeremy asked. Dan, already partway through the door, paused.

"What if I am?"

"Dad, he's Hierarchy! It's like hanging out with an occupying army!" hissed Jeremy, "It's like doing lunch with Mussolini or making small talk with Joe McCarthy!"

"It's like smoking a joint with a cop," commented Andrew thinly.

Dan whirled to spit at him. "I was a cop, you little shit. Remember it. There's nothing wrong with the Hierarchy. They're just trying their best to keep peace and stability when everything is falling apart and wraiths like you are turning against them because their laws interfere with your fun!" He glanced back at Jeremy. "Besides which, he's someone I can talk to. You're sixteen, Jeremy! I'm forty-one!" He stabbed his finger into the air, pointing at the other wraiths in the room. "Charity is sixteen, too. Abra is seventeen. Sammy is fifteen. Andrew's the oldest of you and he's only nineteen! You all died young! Sykes knows what it's like to get old — to have a career, to have kids. To have some responsibilities, for God's sake!"

"Dad..."

"Don't wait up." Dan spun around and walked out.

■

Ten years ago, Anthony's Spa really had been a spa — of sorts. Anthony's had been one of San Francisco's many gay bathhouses, not the best, or the largest, but certainly one of the sleaziest and one of the oldest. Then the city had closed the bathhouses down as health risks in the face of AIDS. Where other bathhouses had been sold and renovated or simply demolished, Anthony's had just been abandoned. Somewhere, in some forgotten corner of an obscure real-estate agent's office, there might still be a listing for it. No one would ever buy it, though. When the living had left the bathhouse behind, the wraiths had taken it over. And they defended their territory.

There was something about the cramped, dim halls and cool, vaguely damp walls that appealed to the restless dead of both sexes. A feeling of desperation pervaded the place, a feeling of needs fulfilled with cold, empty, impersonal detachment. Wraiths came to soak in the atmosphere. A thousand little deaths had been died here. Deaths of pride, of hope, of self. The place had come to be referred to as "the Dark Hole" or simply "the Hole." The empty bathhouse could have been some wraith's private Haunt, but instead it had become common ground as if by unspoken consent. The Haunt belonged to no one. It was a gathering place, a private, neutral space to meet and talk. It would almost have been like a bar for wraiths — if there had been anything to drink. Any wraith could come here and be treated as anonymously as living men had ten years ago. The Dark Hole was a haven in a city of conflicting factions.

Sykes was a regular at the Hole. Dan found him sitting

on a bench in the blackness of an old sauna and dropped
down next to him with a sigh. Sykes glanced over at him.
"Child problems again?"

"Sort of."

"What are the young terrors up to now?"

Without hesitating, Dan told him. It felt good to have
someone he could complain to. What Jeremy and his friends
had been doing to the graffiti artist was prohibited under
the laws of the Hierarchy and was punishable... well, not
exactly by death, since it was hard to kill a wraith a second
time, but the Hierarchy did reserve some harsh penalties for
those who abused the living. Jeremy would have been in
serious trouble had Sykes caught him personally. The
anonymity of the Hole, however, made it possible for Dan
to talk freely without fear. What was said in confidence
inside the Dark Hole remained in confidence. Even when
it was said to an officer of the Hierarchy.

When Dan had finished, Sykes leaned back against the
wall and sighed. He had been about Dan's age when he died,
although he seemed older. His hair was already gray and his
face creased and weathered. In life, Sykes had been a
commodore in the British Navy of the early nineteenth
century. "Little pricks. No respect for order. Those laws were
put in place for a reason!"

"Exactly." Dan shook his head. "You can't even blame it
on *kids today* because most of them have been kids for years."

"They're never going to grow up now, Barr. Besides, we
complained about irresponsible youths in my day as well."

Dan stood and paced around the narrow confines of the
sauna. "It was bad enough when I was alive, and at least
then I could do something about it! As a cop you were
speaking as an authority figure, whether people wanted to
recognize that authority or not. Now, I'm dependent on the
punks. You can't argue from that kind of position."

"Leave," suggested Sykes.

"For where? For what?" Dan sat down again and sighed.

"Sykes, ever since I died, I feel like I've been..." He groped for an appropriate word. "Drifting. Groundless." He grasped at the air with insubstantial fingers. "I miss the challenge of being a cop. I don't have anything to do. I don't have a purpose. I feel like a deadbeat!"

Sykes raised an eyebrow. "Have you thought about joining the Hierarchy Legions?"

Dan hesitated before replying. The thought had actually crossed his mind more than once. Dan couldn't fool himself — serving in the Legions wouldn't be exactly like being a cop again, but it couldn't be too much different. But the Hierarchy would give him something to do, a purpose in the afterlife. More importantly than giving him something to do, it would give him the opportunity to do something that mattered. Just as he had told Jeremy, the Hierarchy seemed to be fighting an uphill battle in San Francisco. They were perpetually under attack by rebellious Renegades and religion-inspired Heretics, as well as individual lawbreakers. The forces of law and order were barely holding their own against those attacks. "I've considered it," he admitted finally, "But Jeremy..."

"No." Sykes shook his head. "Barr, I know the reputation we have among Renegades and lawless wraiths like your son's gang. But you said it yourself — the Hierarchy laws are in place for a reason. And we need good wraiths to enforce those laws. You were, what, a lieutenant before you died? You could start out as an officer."

Dan sat down again. "I realize that Jeremy's views aren't quite in line with the reality of the situation. I meant that he's important to me. I wouldn't want to join the Hierarchy if it would mean alienating him."

"I'm sure he would get used to it."

It was tempting. Jeremy would get used to it. Dan knew he would. Joining the Legions would give him a chance to set an example for Jeremy and his friends. He could show them that the Hierarchy was a positive force, that it was important and necessary. Jeremy might not understand at first — in fact, he probably wouldn't — but Dan knew that he would eventually.

He looked up at Sykes. "It's a big decision."

"You have as much time as you need to make your choice, Barr." Sykes smiled. "I could arrange for you to go out with a patrol if you like. To see how things really work."

"That sounds good." A smile spread across Dan's face in return. "When could I go?"

"Anytime you like. I can set it up on a moment's notice — most Centurions would be glad to have an extra, experienced wraith with them."

"How about tonight? Right now?"

Sykes laughed. "Eager, Barr? All right. There should be a patrol going out of the Hierarchy Citadel in a couple of hours. I think I can get you into it." He stood up, ready to leave.

"Thanks, Sykes."

"Thank you." Sykes reached out to shake Dan's hand. "I think you're going to enjoy this."

"So do I." Dan felt better already, as though blood were once again pumping through his veins. He returned Sykes' handshake vigorously, and when he rose, he thought he stood a little straighter. "I'm looking forward to it."

■

The Hierarchy patrol that Sykes arranged for Dan to accompany was composed of five wraiths. Fox, Brandon, and Lucas were all legionnaires, the lowest rank of the Hierarchy. Walsh, a dark-haired woman with strong features, was the Centurion, their commander. The fifth wraith, Messina, stood somewhere between the two ranks. The legionnaires treated him with deference, the Centurion with uncommon respect. Messina was the handler of the patrol's barghests.

Dan couldn't help but stare at the monstrous creatures

from the moment Walsh ordered her patrol out onto the dark, midnight streets. Dan had heard of barghests, of course. They were the hounds of the Hierarchy, their trackers and attack dogs. Except, Jeremy had told him, they weren't dogs at all. They were wraiths, their forms twisted and shaped in the same way that Abra had sculpted Charity's ghostly body. The transformation from wraith to barghest was completed by the grafting of a cruel muzzle of Stygian steel, the metal of the Shadowlands, to the wraith's distorted face. Even when Dan had heard the peculiar, almost-human howling of a barghest in the distance, though, he had never quite believed his son's stories.

Now, looking at the two barghests straining at the chain leashes Messina held, he did. The creatures' jaws and exposed teeth were dull, gray, and metallic. Their forelimbs resembled human arms more than they did the forelimbs of an animal. Their bodies were frighteningly powerful, like muscular rottweilers, yet their spines protruded in unnatural, bony spikes. On their paws (hands?), what would have been a human's thumb seemed almost, but not quite, opposable. And when one of them met Dan's gaze, the eyes behind the iron muzzle were a human blue, but hazy with a rabid madness.

"Impressive, aren't they?" asked Messina with a laugh as the patrol lingered under the awning of a darkened storefront on Van Ness Avenue just north of Sutter Street. A cold rain was falling again and even wraiths felt more comfortable out of the worst of the wet. "I made them myself." He plucked at the hindquarters of one of the barghests, grabbing a handful of the plasm that made up the creature's body and stretching it out until it became a hairless, ratlike tail. The barghest whimpered in pain, but it didn't dare to turn against its handler. Dan could guess why: There were scars across the barghest's back that matched the steel-wire whip Messina carried. Stygian steel was one of the few things that could permanently scar a wraith.

Messina himself was tall, very muscular, and as attractive in an aggressive, dangerous way as his barghests were hideous. He had obviously used his abilities to shape plasm to enhance his own appearance.

Dan had taken an instant dislike to him. Messina reminded him too much of the people who wanted desperately to be police officers, but couldn't quite make the cut and instead went on to become security guards or bouncers — anything that put them in positions of power and authority above others. If those people did get onto the police force, they made the worst kind of officers. But the Legions of the Hierarchy were apparently a little more desperate for recruits than the living police — none of the other legionnaires were exactly elite troops, either. They were restless. They quarreled or joked among themselves. They seemed undisciplined. They were dirty, unkempt, and slovenly. At least Messina took some pride in his appearance, even if that pride was narcissistic and his appearance somewhat exaggerated.

Of all of the wraiths in the patrol, only Walsh seemed competent. The Centurion had bright, sharp eyes, and she peered into intently into the darkness, ignoring the mutterings of her legionnaires. "What are we looking for?" Dan asked her quietly.

"What any army or police patrol looks for, mostly," she replied with a shrug. "Criminals. Troublemakers. Renegades, if they show their faces."

"Souls for the Hierarchy," added Messina. His smile, white teeth against tanned skin that seemed utterly unreal on a wraith, was hungry.

Walsh nodded, distaste clear on her face. "Souls for the Hierarchy if we can find them." She sighed. "Let's get going."

"Wait a second," asked Dan hastily as they stepped back out into the rain. "What do you mean souls for the Hierarchy?"

"Our number-one assignment, Barr." Messina walked a

little bit apart from the others. His barghests had a tendency to snap at things. "The Shadowlands run on souls. The Hierarchy will buy up souls or captured wraiths, but it's much cheaper if we can collect them ourselves. That's what my boys are for." He stroked one of his barghests fondly. The beast almost cringed. "They track stray souls and run them to ground, and then we come along and pick them up."

"Messina!" Walsh spat harshly. She looked sideways at Dan. "It doesn't work quite like that."

Dan had heard about the trade in souls, weak and helpless wraiths sold to the highest bidder. It was something else that Jeremy had explained to him about the Shadowlands — although now that Dan thought about it, it had been Charity who had explained it to him with a certain ghoulish delight. Everything that existed in the Shadowlands was made of the same plasm. And that plasm was interchangeable. In the same way that a wraith could be turned into a barghest, she could as easily be turned into some useful, inanimate object. Dan had always pictured the soul trade as an activity of unscrupulous Renegades. He had never considered that the Hierarchy might be part of it as well. "How does it work, then?"

"We're under orders to gather any indigent or transient wraiths and take them back to the Citadel with us. The Hierarchy... has uses for them." She didn't elaborate on what she meant, but she didn't have to. Dan had heard stories of wraiths captured and enslaved or worse. Stygian steel, like the barghest muzzles or Messina's whip, was forged from souls. Walsh must have seen the revulsion in his eyes. "Think of us as an army patrol foraging for supplies as it moves, Barr. I don't like it, but it's necessary."

"Does foraging leave much time for keeping the peace and upholding the law?"

Walsh stared straight ahead again. She was silent for a moment, then muttered, "The commanding officers of the Hierarchy have conflicting priorities."

A pair of young lovers came hurrying along the sidewalk in the living world, laughing and giggling under the newspaper they used to shield themselves from the rain. They had blundered into the middle of the patrol before any of the legionnaires could move aside. Their giggling stopped almost instantly. Dan found himself staring into the girl's face. There was a nameless fear in her eyes, and she grabbed at her boyfriend. Living humans might not be able to see wraiths, but they were made uncomfortable by their ghostly presence. Dan stepped back hastily, giving the humans some space. The wraiths in the patrol did not seem as concerned. They simply ignored the humans. One of the legionnaires (Lucas, Dan thought) walked right through them, prompting the boy to give a startled gasp of fright and rush his girlfriend off down the street.

Dan caught up with Walsh and Messina at the head of the patrol. "Tell me about the last time you made an arrest. What was the charge?"

Walsh frowned. "We have a pretty quiet beat. I don't think we've had to take somebody in for breaking the law in... oh, three weeks. Minor offense."

"You have a pretty big area to patrol. Surely..."

"We have a *quiet* beat," Walsh said pointedly. There was frustration in her voice. "*Nothing* happens around here."

Suddenly, Dan knew why they were patrolling along busy Van Ness and not one of the smaller, darker side streets in the region. He recognized the frustration, too. How many times had he known that a crime was being committed, but hadn't been able to do a thing about it because of lack of support from his superiors? The Hierarchy didn't care what was happening on the back streets of Walsh's beat as long as they didn't have to deal with it. "I see. And the last time you... collected a wraith for the Hierarchy?"

"Four days ago." Messina licked his lips. "It's been dry lately." Dan glanced away. The patrol would go wherever the wraith's barghests led them.

"Shut up, Messina," said Walsh tiredly.

There was a flurry of car horns up ahead. Messina's barghests lifted their heads exactly like bloodhounds catching a scent, and bayed as if answering the horns. One of the legionnaires grumbled, "Looks like it won't be dry for very much longer."

Dan could almost hear Messina's smile grow broader. He looked up.

There was someone walking down the middle of Van Ness Avenue, staggering slightly as if drunk or in a daze, heedless of the cars that were speeding past just a foot or two away. One of the cars honked its horn just as it passed — the figure, shocked, reeled sideways, almost into another lane. And Dan recognized the figure.

It was the graffiti artist who his son's gang of wraiths had been tormenting earlier. They must have tired of her — maybe Andrew had finished his death mural of Charity — and let her go. Their Haunt wasn't far away. In shock, the young woman may have tried to cross Van Ness, only to find herself caught in the middle of it. Dan hoped that Andrew hadn't deliberately walked her into the middle of the street before leaving her body. The street would be a sea of light and noise to her: deafening horns and roaring engines, headlights coming from all directions, reflected in the wet pavement and falling rain. After the scare that Jeremy and his friends had given her, the young graffiti artist could only be further confused and frightened by her situation.

She staggered again. The path that she was walking was barely a yard wide. She could fall into the traffic at any moment. A car could weave out of formation and into the young woman's precarious space in an instant.

She was going to die. An air of death had already gathered around her and there was phantom blood streaming down her face, a sign of her impending doom.

She deserved better. There was a bitter taste in Dan's mouth. This wasn't her fault. He had to repay her for what

Andrew and Jeremy had done. Dan glanced at Walsh. "What can we do?"

The Centurion turned to Messina. "Set the barghests loose," she said flatly. Messina nodded happily and reached for the barghests' collars.

Dan's jaw dropped. "You're going to send the barghests after her? But she's not dead yet! We can save her!"

Messina leered at him, his hand paused on the catch that would release his unnatural dogs. "Uh-uh, Barr. Interfering with the living is against the law. Besides, what good is she to us if she *lives*?" His smile was as hungry as those of the barghests.

"Shut your fucking trap, Messina!" Walsh snapped. She met Dan's accusing gaze reluctantly. "He's right. It's against the law. Wraiths aren't supposed to interfere with the course of human lives. There's nothing we can do." She shrugged. "It's her fate, Barr."

"And the Hierarchy gets another soul." Dan hissed his words between clenched teeth.

"Barr, we're not mortal cops. Saving the living is not our job." She put a hand on his shoulder. "Do you want to support the law or break it?"

"It doesn't sound like a particularly good law at the moment." Dan looked sadly at the girl stumbling along between the columns of traffic. "There must be exceptions."

"No. I'm sorry." She gave Messina the tiniest of nods. His fingers fumbled with the catch. "You'll get used to it, Barr."

You'll get used to it, Barr. Give it time, Jeremy had said. The Hierarchy was as bad as his son's friends. Worse — they claimed the authority of law for their cruelties. Maybe once the Hierarchy had fought an uphill battle, but now they were sliding downward just like any other wraiths. "No," Dan breathed, "I don't think I will get used to it." He leapt forward, toward the street, just as Messina released the barghests. He whirled to face them.

"Barr!" yelled Walsh. "What are you doing?"

"Taking the law into my own hands." Dan crouched, his eyes on the barghests. They were hesitant, unsure of what to make of this obstacle that had placed itself between them and their target.

Messina seemed just as frustrated. His eyes grew wide with fury. "Kill!" he screamed. "Kill!"

The barghests charged, one leaping up and ahead of its partner, lunging toward Dan's head. The other barghest came in low, a little bit behind, trying to rip at Dan's legs.

Dan ducked down, dodged forward, and thrust upward with his arms, catching the leaping barghest from beneath and sending it sailing into the busy street. A wraith had to be aware of a threat in order for it to pass through him without damage. The startled barghest was hardly aware of the traffic. The speeding cars bowled it over, rushing through it and shredding its substance. The barghest howled in agony. It would re-form without permanent harm in a little while, but that was a little while in which Dan wouldn't have to worry about it.

The second barghest, however, knocked him down before he had a chance to prepare himself. Dan barely managed to get a hand underneath the creature's jaw and force its metal teeth away from his throat. He was fortunate that Messina was so obsessed with endowing his beasts with powerful forms — the barghest's chest was too broad for it be able to use its claws effectively in this position. Dan got his legs up under its belly and shoved up as hard as he could. The barghest flipped forward. Dan yanked down on its head with his free hand. The barghest slammed back-first into the wet pavement of the gutter. Dan scrambled to his feet.

The barghest was just a little faster. It had its legs under it before Dan was on his knees. It coiled, ready to spring at him.

It never saw the van that was traveling just a little bit out of line with the rest of the traffic, driving about half-a-car's-width closer to the sidewalk. It plowed straight through the beast's hindquarters. The barghest's howl was very much like a scream. Messina's cries of rage sounded like an animal's.

Dan didn't pause. He ran straight into the traffic, carefully watching each approaching vehicle and letting it pass through him. He had tried something like this once before, running between moving cars as a rookie on his first beat, watching and running at the same time. That time he had been chasing a purse-snatcher, and the street had been a lot quieter. Afterward, he had been surprised that he hadn't died. This time, of course, he was already dead.

The cars that whizzed through his insubstantial form threw him off-balance and slowed him down, but Dan kept going, praying that the graffiti artist wouldn't get hit before he reached her. He was lucky. Suddenly, he was standing beside the woman as she stumbled down the narrow path of safety at the center of the road. A sense of triumph soared through him. He reached out to steady her. And abruptly became aware of just how powerless he really was to save her. He couldn't touch the young woman.

It took skill and knowledge for a wraith to influence the living world, and Dan had not been a wraith long enough to learn those skills. Andrew's ability to possess living bodies, Charity's ability to appear in a material form, even Sammy's ability to invoke grotesque and frightening effects like blood dripping from walls — these had been learned over the course of years. All Dan had learned to do in a month of death was exert the tiniest fraction of his touch against material objects. He could move a penny, or shut off a light switch, or flick the valve on a spray-paint can, but there was no way he could carry the graffiti artist across two lanes of traffic to safety.

Maybe... He glanced back the way he had come. Messina was arguing with Walsh. The other legionnaires stood waiting for Walsh to give them an order. Dan had a little time. Maybe he could give the graffiti artist a push in the right direction. He focused his will and gave her a hard shove, the hardest he could manage, toward the far side of Van Ness, trying to propel her across the street as a gap in the traffic appeared.

The young woman shrieked and fell, scrambling to her feet and whirling around in search of her assailant. She was standing right in the middle of a lane with the traffic bearing down on her.

"No!" Dan screamed. He wouldn't let her die! He couldn't! He pushed at her, angry at Andrew and Jeremy and the other young wraiths, angry at Messina and Walsh and the Hierarchy for refusing to help, for *wanting* her to die. Angry at himself for giving her the push that had put her into the traffic and terrified now that he would be the ultimate cause of her death. "No!" He pushed at her again, frightening her into motion and bullying her across the street. She was shrieking constantly, but he wouldn't let her stop. "No! Move! Move!"

Across one lane. Into the next. Ten feet from safety. Six. Then the young woman looked up and saw the truck bearing down on her. She froze in its headlights like a wild animal.

Without thinking, Dan wrapped his ghostly arms around her waist and leapt toward the sidewalk. His anger gave him the strength to pull her with him.

The truck's horn blared as the graffiti artist rolled into the gutter. She was unconscious. Dan pushed her up over the curb. The sense of doom around her was fading — she would live. He looked back toward the Hierarchy patrol, victory in his eyes.

On the far side of Van Ness, Walsh was finally urging her patrol forward. Messina was leering happily, one of the barghests slowly re-forming at his side. Much nearer to Dan, however, was the other barghest. It was still limping from its encounter with the van, but it had recovered much more quickly than he expected. It was only about twelve feet away, stalking forward through the traffic.

Dan climbed desperately to his feet and fell back as the barghest drew closer. He wouldn't be able to trick it into the traffic again. It would be expecting that. And he had no other weapons. A normal dog he might have tried to choke, but a barghest didn't breathe. He and the barghest circled each other, each wary. Its neck? Perhaps he could somehow break its neck... no, he wasn't even sure that would work...

The barghest lunged.

Dan spun around almost on instinct and kicked out with all of the force and momentum he could gather. With luck, he could daze the monster and escape.

His foot slammed straight into the barghest's teeth. The Stygian steel muzzle was tougher than the skull behind it. Dan's kick drove the muzzle back into the barghest's head. The creature collapsed instantly, then vanished altogether, leaving only the muzzle and a collar behind.

For a moment, silence seemed to fall like a heavy blanket. Dan froze, his weight still shifted back on one foot. The patrol, halfway across Van Ness, seemed stunned. The barghest was dead — again.

Then Messina howled with insane rage and charged, his steel-wire whip held high in one hand, a gleaming dagger in the other.

Dan turned and ran, vanishing through a wall and out of sight.

■

The smell of spray paint was still hanging in the air as Dan stumbled through the back wall of the Haunt. Andrew had indeed completed his mural of Charity's death before releasing the graffiti artist. Jeremy and the other young wraiths were standing around looking at it. Jeremy glanced back at his father, then did a double-take as he saw the expression on Dan's face. "Jesus! What happened, Dad?"

"I think I may have made a mistake, Jeremy." Dan collapsed on the old couch and told them what had happened.

When he was finished, Andrew groaned. "Oh, God. This isn't just a mistake, this is a major disaster. You killed a barghest, you screwed around with a living person, and all in front of a Hierarchy patrol!"

"It was either the barghest or me!" snapped Dan. "And I wouldn't have had to do anything at all if you hadn't been fooling around with that graffiti artist!"

"Both of you be quiet!" Jeremy rubbed at his temples. "Shit. What do we do now?"

"Run?" suggested Charity, once more back in her normal form.

Jeremy shook his head. "I don't think the Hierarchy is going to let this one go. Barghest handlers tend to get really attached to their pets. And Dad broke the law in a big way, with major witnesses. I think they're going to make an example of him."

"They don't know I'm here," Dan pointed out.

"Wrong." Sammy dropped down through the ceiling. She had gone up onto the roof to keep watch. "There's a whole whack of legionnaires coming down the block. A big guy with a tan and one barghest is right at the front."

"Messina."

"They tracked you with the other barghest." Andrew was on his feet. "All in favor of running now and leaving the old man behind for them?"

"No!" shouted Jeremy, "Andrew..."

Dan put his hand on Jeremy's shoulder. "It's a good idea, Jeremy. It's me they're after."

"Dad, we can't just run away on you!"

"Yes, you can! What are you going to do? It sounds like you're outnumbered. If I surrender, they'll go away." Dan shoved his son away. "Get out of here."

"Come with us!"

"They'll track me down again." Out on the street, a barghest howled. "You don't have much time. Run! All of you!"

Andrew need no further encouragement. He sank down through the floor and vanished, probably into the sewers beneath the Haunt. Abra, Charity, and Sammy followed. Only Jeremy lingered. "Go, Jeremy!" Dan ordered.

"I'll come back, Dad." He disappeared between the floorboards. Dan walked toward the front door to meet the Hierarchy. One thought tugged at his mind, though. If the Hierarchy had tracked him using barghests, why had the legionnaires come to the front of the Haunt when Dan had entered through the back?

Messina's massive arm came through the door and seized Dan by the throat before he could think of an answer to that question. Dan didn't have time to will himself to phase through the door as Messina pulled him over to the other side. The passage was painful. It left Dan gasping. Messina threw him to the ground. Dan looked up to find the remaining barghest's steel muzzle in his face. It growled at him threateningly.

"Please," urged Messina, "feel free to move."

Past the barghest, Dan could see legionnaires swarming into the Haunt. After a few moments, some of them came back out. "Empty," one reported, "but there's a spray-paint mural on one wall. Looks like someone was painting a wraith."

"They got away." Walsh walked into Dan's field of vision and looked down at him. "Where are they, Barr?"

"Who?" If he had still had a heart, it would have skipped a beat. How did Walsh know about Jeremy?

"Your son. The other punk-wraiths. We're bringing you all in." Walsh knelt down. The barghest snarled and she glared at it. "Call off your puppy, Messina."

Messina grimaced, but whistled sharply. The barghest

turned its head to look at him, then slowly paced back to his side. Dan sat and looked around. He was surrounded by a wide circle of Hierarchy legionnaires. And Dan suddenly realized how Walsh had known about Jeremy, and why the Hierarchy had come to the front of the Haunt instead of the back.

Sykes was with them.

"You bastard!" Dan spat. "The Hole is supposed to be confidential!"

"A lot of wraiths would like to believe it is." The gray-haired wraith crossed his arms. "As long as they do — and as long as we don't abuse the resource, of course — the Hierarchy has easy access to information on every aspect of the Shadowlands. We would have brought your son and his gang in sooner or later anyway, Barr. What you've done tonight just forced our hand."

Dan lunged at Sykes, but Messina took two fast steps forward and grabbed him almost before he was on his feet. The barghest handler glared angrily at Sykes. "Try him now!" he demanded.

Sykes frowned. Quickly, Messina added, "Sir." Sykes nodded and glanced at Dan.

"Dan Barr," he began, "late and currently of San Francisco, you stand before this court..."

"Court?"

"The court of a magistrate of the Hierarchy is wherever he declares it to be," Sykes replied with a grim smile. He looked up toward the dark, cloudy sky, as if reciting a script from memory. "You stand before this court," he continued, "charged with breaking the Code of Charon and the Laws of the Hierarchy. You are charged with interfering in the life of a living human, with interfering in the duties of a Hierarchy patrol, with disobeying the order of a Hierarchy centurion, with resisting arrest by a Hierarchy centurion..."

The list of charges became a droning litany. Dan clenched his jaw in anger and tensed in Messina's iron grasp.

Most of the charges were nothing more than variations on
others. A few seemed almost tailored to twist Dan's actions,
twisting them and rendering them criminal. The Hierarchy's
"law" left a bitter taste in Dan's mouth.

Sykes recitation finally ended in "...and with the wanton
destruction of Hierarchy property — one barghest in the care
of Legionnaire Messina." He looked down again to fix Dan
with his gaze. "How do you respond to these charges?"

Dan held his head high. "Guilty," he declared with angry
pride.

Messina grabbed a handful of Dan's hair and lifted until
Dan was standing on his toes. He bent Dan's head back and
whispered, loudly enough for everyone around to hear,
"Guilty, your honor."

Dan had to roll his eyes down in order to see Sykes.
"Guilty, your honor." This time, his plea was considerably
less dignified.

"So be it." He smiled sadly. "I'm sorry, Barr. At one time,
I really did think you would make a fine Hierarchy officer."

There was a commotion toward the back of the crowd
of legionnaires. Someone yelled forward, "We have the
prisoner, sir!" Sykes glanced away from Dan and gestured
for the wraiths' captive to be brought forward. Dan felt ill
suddenly, certain that they had captured Jeremy.

Instead, the graffiti artist marched forward. She was still
alive, though clearly under the possession of a Hierarchy
wraith. Her eyes were dull — unlike Andrew, the wraith
possessing her now had robbed her of awareness and free will.
"What's she doing here?" Dan demanded.

Messina snickered unpleasantly. "You killed her tonight,
Barr. You should have let her die naturally."

"What?" Dan tried to pull away, but Messina just
tightened his grasp on him.

Sykes nodded. "She was fated to die tonight, Barr. The
entire patrol saw her death coming. You upset the balance
of fate, and you revealed your presence to her. In fact..." He

examined the smudges of paint on the graffiti artist's hands, then looked at the legionnaire who had discovered the mural inside the Haunt. The legionnaire nodded. The paint colors matched. Sykes straightened up. "In fact, I'd say that this young woman knows altogether far too much about our existence."

"But your own law says you can't interfere in the life of a living person!" Dan shouted.

"Mortal societies have had prohibitions against killing for millennia," Sykes replied, "but every one has also made provisions for executions in the name of the law." He pointed to the Haunt. The wraith possessing the graffiti artist marched her inside. "Make sure she's secured," he ordered a nearby legionnaire, "then start a fire. I want this haven for Renegades destroyed."

"You bastard!" Dan screamed. He kicked backward, trying to hit Messina's balls or shins or anything. Messina dodged his flailing legs easily. "You fucking bastard!"

Sykes' mouth twisted. "It's the law, Barr."

"His sentence!" Messina hissed eagerly.

"Shut up, Messina!" Sykes snapped. He glared at Dan. "Dan Barr, this court finds you guilty of all charges laid against you." His smile was sharp, and the first threads of smoke that drifted from the Haunt writhed around his head. He looked almost demonic. "You are hereby sentenced to replace the barghest that you destroyed. Sentence to be carried out immediately."

Dan felt Messina slide something cold around his neck. For a moment, he couldn't figure out what it was. Then he realized that it was a barghest's collar.

Messina thrust Dan's head and shoulders forward, bending Dan over as he forced his massive weight across his back. Excruciating pain bloomed suddenly throughout Dan's body. He couldn't stop himself from howling in agony. Messina was already beginning his reshaping. When the pain ebbed a bit, Dan could no longer stand upright. He was hunched forward, forced onto all fours like an animal. Messina squatted in front of him and pressed a steel barghest muzzle to his face.

∎

The barghest retained only a few memories of the moment in which Messina grafted the muzzle into place. It remembered Sykes (although it didn't think of him as "Sykes," just as it didn't really think of itself as a "barghest") turning his back disinterestedly. It remembered Messina grinning at it obscenely. It remembered Walsh looking away in disgust. It remembered screams and the crackle of burning wood, sounds that haunted its sleep. It didn't remember anything at all prior to the sharp agony of the cold muzzle becoming part of its body.

No other pain surpassed that agony. Messina's steel-wire whip was torture, but it was the lingering memory of that one moment that really made the barghest obey its handler. Memories of events after its transformation faded quickly as well. Time passed in a haze, cycles of rest and activity merging into a blur. A few things stayed with the barghest, although it couldn't really place them in any sequence or remember how long ago they had happened.

It sat with Messina and the other wraiths of the patrol as they waited for two old men to die on a doorstep. Messina had had the barghest chase off the other wraiths who would have fought with the patrol for the old men's souls. In the end, only one man died. The other, with a left eye so heavily bloodshot it appeared almost entirely red, seemed on the verge of death, but there was something about him that seemed to say he would not be dying anytime soon.

The barghest tracked a Renegade wraith through the city, leading the patrol to a living woman humming to herself as she made dinner in a middle-class home. The Renegade was hiding inside her. The patrol captured the wraith, though the woman suffered in the process. When they left, she was lying on the floor of the kitchen, shaking violently as dinner burned on the stove. The patrol didn't seem to care, though the barghest couldn't help looking at her sorrowfully over its shoulder. Messina saw that and punished the barghest later, his whip leaving harsh scars across its back.

Once Messina let the barghest off its chain. Together with the other barghest Messina controlled, it chased down two young wraiths. Something must have snapped inside the barghest, because by the time Messina and the patrol had caught up to it, the barghest had savagely mauled both wraiths. This time, Messina praised it. Strangely, the praise seemed odd. The barghest felt as though it really deserved to be punished.

Then the patrol was ambushed. It happened so quickly that the barghest wasn't really aware of it beginning. One moment they were alone on the street, and the next they were surrounded by a number of young wraiths, with two legionnaires lying helpless on the ground. The barghest strained at its chain, eager to attack the young wraiths. Messina reached down and released the chain from the collar. "Kill, boy!" the handler shouted. He had his whip out, cracking it through the air and forcing some of the wraiths back.

Released, the barghest surged forward like an angry storm, charging the nearest attacking wraith and knocking him to the ground. It was ridiculously easy, as if the wraith were offering himself up without resistance. The barghest almost had its metal teeth in the young wraith's throat when it paused for a moment and looked at the wraith's face. The wraith met the barghest's maddened gaze with frightened yet hopeful eyes.

Pale-blue eyes.

Messina's hand was suddenly on its head. A light push was all the signal the barghest would need to kill. "Freeze!"

the handler yelled at the attacking wraiths, "Any one of you moves so much as a finger and this boy's throat gets spread all over the sidewalk!"

The wraiths halted, looking toward the wraith on the ground. No — the barghest realized. They were looking at it. Why? *Why?* It growled, agitated by the attention. Messina stroked its head. "Drop your weapons!" he commanded.

The wraiths glanced at each other, then slowly, almost hesitantly, reached to set the knives and clubs that they carried on the ground. "No!" screamed the wraith under the barghest. "If he doesn't remember, there's nothing we can do! Don't trust..."

"Too late!" Messina hissed. He shoved the barghest's head down toward the wraith's throat.

Pale-blue eyes and washed-out ginger hair. A face a cop had once given his life for.

The barghest twisted its head around suddenly in an angry snarl. It would *not* kill this wraith! Messina was its enemy, not this young man! It hated Messina! The barghest's Stygian-steel teeth bit savagely into Messina's hand, ripping at the plasm. Messina shrieked in pain.

The young wraith was up from the ground instantly, grabbing Messina's other arm and tearing the terrible wire whip from his grasp. He kicked Messina's legs out from under him, then seized the barghest's collar and dragged it off the wounded legionnaire. The other wraiths snatched up their weapons — the rest of the patrol fell back before them. "Abra!" yelled the blue-eyed wraith, "Abra!"

One of the other attacking wraiths hurried over. Messina flailed at him with his good hand as he passed, but the wraith easily avoided his grasp. He knelt in front of the barghest and reached for its muzzle. The barghest snarled and tried to pull back.

"Easy," the wraith said soothingly. He put his hand over the muzzle. Pain shot through the barghest's head in a bright flash like lightning. The muzzle came away in the wraith's hand.

Dan collapsed with relief, almost weeping. His memory rushed back to him — all of it, including everything he had done during his time as a barghest. He felt sick. He tried to speak, but a barghest's throat was as altered as the rest of its body. Words were just a distorted howl. Abra touched his neck, though, and his voice was released. "Jeremy!" Dan choked.

"Easy, Dad!" Jeremy had his arms around his father.

"How long...?" Dan wished he could hold Jeremy back, but his arms weren't jointed that way anymore. "How long was I like that?"

"A week, Dad. Only a week." Jeremy looked up at Abra. "Can you put him back into his normal shape?"

"It will take time. I'll have to do it back at the Haunt."

"The Haunt?" Dan bit his lip. "But they burned it! And that girl...?"

"We got her out." Andrew, scowling a little bit, squatted down beside him. "After all she'd been through, we decided that we couldn't let her die. And we put the fire out after the Hierarchy left. The Haunt was gutted, but it's still standing."

"Wait... Messina!" Dan swung around, searching for his tormentor. All of Jeremy's friends — Abra, Andrew, Sammy, Charity, and even a few he didn't know — stood around him. But the defeated Hierarchy patrol was limping away, bearing their wounded. Messina was with them. An angry hunger for revenge burned in Dan's chest. "They're getting away!"

"No. We only wanted you, Dad. We had to let them go. It was part of the deal."

"Deal?" He looked at the fleeing patrol again.

Walsh glanced back at him.

Sykes was sitting in his usual place at the Dark Hole, talking to a wraith with long blond hair and a patch over her right eye. Dan caught the Hierarchy officer's gaze, then waited while he finished his discussion with the woman. Once she was gone, Sykes came over and sat down next to him. "When I heard about your escape, I wondered if you'd eventually wind up back here."

"Why not? The Hierarchy has been hunting for me everywhere else in San Francisco. The legionnaires you posted outside should be back in service in a couple of hours."

"So you did spot them."

Dan nodded. "Unfortunately, the one inside the Hole gave me a little more trouble. He won't be coming back."

"Too bad." Sykes looked down at his fingernails. He was afraid. Dan could feel it. "You know that Messina lost his hand?" the gray-haired wraith said casually. "The steel of the barghest muzzle... the wound was too serious to heal. He couldn't even shape himself a new hand."

"I'm all choked up about it."

They sat without talking for several minutes before Sykes finally broke the silence. His voice was tense. He was, Dan knew, expecting to die a second time. "What do you want, Barr? I can clear your name if you like — drop all of the charges against you. You wouldn't have to hide anymore."

"No."

"Revenge? Messina is yours if you want him."

"No." Dan sat back. "Last time we talked together here, you told me the Hierarchy could give me a purpose."

"Yes." Sykes sounded wary.

"I just wanted to tell you that it has." Dan turned to look at Sykes. Abra had managed to restore him almost entirely to his human form. Dan still carried a few physical traces of his experiences as a barghest. His voice was a little rougher. His chest was perhaps a little broader than it should have been. The scars from Messina's steel-wire whip still marked his back. Dan's eyes, however, had been changed the most. Not by Messina's hand so much as by what he had seen and, at the command of the Hierarchy, done. "I'm going to fight you, Sykes. I'm going to fight you and the Hierarchy."

Sykes snorted. "You can't be serious."

"I am."

"Without the laws of the Hierarchy, the Shadowlands would fall apart. All the wraiths in San Francisco would become unruly Renegades like your son and his friends."

"And me. I don't have a big problem with most of your laws, Sykes. I have a problem with the people who enforce them." He stood up. "The Hierarchy has lost sight of its purpose. Wraiths like you and Messina, you're too busy collecting souls to remember what you're supposed to be doing."

"You're making a mistake."

Dan's hand flashed out suddenly, grabbing Sykes' wrist and giving it a sharp twist. Sykes yelped. A shining knife fell from his grasp. Dan picked it up. "Tell your patrols that there's a new cop walking the beat in the Shadowlands, Sykes. Tell them to stay out of my way."

He walked away, into the darkness. "It's hopeless, you know!" Sykes called after him. "You can't win! We're the Hierarchy! We are the law!"

"No," Dan replied from the shadows, "You're only *a* law."

CAREER MOVE

EDO VAN BELKOM

The doctor flipped the pages attached to the clipboard in quick succession, his eyes stopping at the bottom of each page just long enough to scan the most recent information before continuing on to the next. Every once in a while he made a non-committal sound like a "Mmmmm," or a "Hummph!"

Romano Minardi sat propped up in his bed, impatiently waiting for the doctor to finish leafing through his medical records so he could get this charade over with and get himself checked out of the hospital.

It had been nearly a week since his last performance at the Pantages Theater, where the Technomancer in the dark suit had made things go so wrong. That night the Technomancer had tampered with his final death-defying escape, causing the world-renowned escapologist to be impaled by seven silver daggers. The mishap would have been fatal for Romano if the daggers hadn't just happened to miss all of his vital organs.

Had it been luck or just a coincidence?

He'd never admit it, but Romano knew it had been a little bit of both. Either way, it wasn't important now. All that mattered now was checking out of the hospital and getting his career back on track.

The doctor hesitated over the final few pages, then doubled back to the beginning of the file. Romano looked over at Roxanne May, the faithful acolyte who'd been at his side throughout the whole ordeal, and rolled his eyes. Roxanne smiled at him and raised her hands in a gesture that begged him to be patient.

"Well, doctor," said Romano, no longer content to wait for the man to finish studying the charts. "How am I?"

Doctor Vlasschaert, Northwestern General's resident internalist, put down the clipboard, ran a hand through his long brown hair and shook his head. "You seem to be doing *very* well."

Romano nodded, knowing the diagnosis was inevitable. As a mage whose sphere of magick was time, he had spent nearly a month in his bed healing while less than a week had passed in the real world. Of course he was doing well. "Time heals all wounds," Romano said, scissoring his legs over the side of the bed.

"Hey, whoa!" said the doctor. "Where do you think you're going?" He rushed over to Romano's bedside and helped ease his head back down onto the pillows.

"But you just said I was fine."

"I said you *seemed* to be doing fine."

"Well then?"

"I can't let you out of the hospital yet. It's still too soon. Your insides have healed enough for you to sit up in bed, but walking around is a completely different story. If you ruptured part of your insides and began bleeding internally it would end up being my fault for releasing you too early."

Romano opened his mouth to speak, but the doctor cut him off with a wave of his hand.

"I can appreciate that these four walls can begin to look like a prison after a while — especially for someone like you, Mr. Minardi — but let me assure you that I'm not in the habit of letting my malpractice insurance premiums double. I'll release you when I'm absolutely certain you've made a full and complete recovery." The doctor crossed his arms over his chest, a gesture that could only mean the matter was no longer up for discussion. "We'll see how you're doing tomorrow. If everything's fine, I'll sign the release forms then. Okay?"

Romano looked away from the doctor, saying nothing.

"Thank you, doctor," said Roxanne, moving closer to Romano's side. "See you tomorrow."

The doctor nodded awkwardly at the couple and left the room.

When Romano was sure the man was out of earshot, he turned to Roxanne. "How is it that handcuffs and torture cells can't hold me, but a little piece of paper and a man's signature can?"

"He's your doctor, Roman," Roxanne whispered, running her fingers through his thick, black hair. "He just wants to make sure you're okay."

"But I *am* okay," he said, his voice level rapidly rising toward a shout. "Just look at me!" He slapped his hands against his chest. "I'm fine."

"Not everyone's job entails putting their life on the line, Roman." She looked at him then, her head titled slightly to one side. "Besides, it's just another day."

Romano let out a long sigh, as if he were releasing the wind that had previously been billowing in his sails, and lay back on the bed. "I suppose so. It's just that Artie's set up an appointment with some television big-shot for later today and I didn't want to put the guy off."

"Why don't you meet with him here?"

Romano thought about it, then said, "Not exactly the kind of place to instill confidence in my abilities, now, is it?"

Roxanne just looked at him.

"All right," he said, his voice tinged with a tone of surrender. "Why the hell not?"

"Good," said Roxanne. "I'll give Artie a call." She walked over to the phone and picked up the receiver.

Romano stared up at the ceiling, watching the morning's light and shadows slowly creep across the room.

■

The orderly held the handles of the wheelchair steady as Romano eased himself into the seat. He could just as easily have walked to where he was going, but he wasn't allowed to go anywhere in the hospital without having an orderly accompany him — doctor's orders.

When Romano was comfortable, the orderly set the wheelchair into motion, gliding Romano through the door and on down the hall toward the elevators. "Mind if we take a little detour?" asked Romano.

"Where to?" said the orderly.

"To the lobby, outside."

"Need a smoke?"

"I'm dying for one."

"All right," said the orderly. "I might even join you."

They got on the elevator and went down three floors to ground level. The hospital was more than sixty years old and the lobby had an attractive mix of the building's original art deco decor and a host of functional upgrades, such as overhead fluorescent lights and automatic sliding doors. The orderly wheeled Romano down the ramp leading to the front door and then on out into the courtyard in front of the hospital. After setting the chair in the shade and locking its wheels, the orderly sat down on the bench next to Romano.

The mage slid a cigarette into his mouth, then offered one to the orderly. When the orderly accepted, Romano noticed for the first time that the man's left eye was almost completely bloodshot. He was tempted to ask the man about the eye, but figured it really wasn't any of his business.

"Thanks," said the orderly.

"Don't mention it." Romano began patting at the pockets of his bathrobe in search of his lighter and realized he'd left it up in his room. "You wouldn't happen to have a light on you, would ya?"

The orderly flashed a nervous smile and said, "No, I'm sorry. But I can go get us one."

"Don't worry, sit down," said Romano, holding the man back with his arm. "Am I a magician, or am I a magician?" He flicked his right thumb into the air and a flame suddenly shot up from his thumbtip.

"Hey, neat," said the orderly, quickly leaning forward to light the end of his smoke. A moment later, Romano lit his own cigarette, then closed his fist over the burning patch of skin.

Although he had been on his way to putting on a little magic show for the kids in the hospital, he hadn't prepared his thumb for that particular trick. Romano didn't like using vulgar magick so frivolously, but this had been such an innocuous little trick he couldn't see the harm in it. Besides, the orderly didn't seem to care about where the flame had come from, he was just happy for the chance to have a smoke on the job.

Romano sat back in his chair, inhaled deeply and watched the birds populating the courtyard flutter from bush to branch.

Maybe another day in this place might not be so bad after all, he thought.

■

"Now," said Romano. "What was your card?"

The blond-haired boy couldn't have been more than five years old. His eyes were full of awe and wonder as Romano shuffled and fanned the cards through his nimble fingers.

"Um..." said the boy, a little bit shy about being in front of a crowd.

"Can anyone help him?" Romano asked the group, making sure that the show kept flowing right along.

"The seven of hearts," eight voices shouted out.

"The seven of hearts?" said Romano, his face contorted in surprise. "You mean like this one?" He produced the seven of hearts. "And this one?" And another seven of hearts. "And this one?" And another and another until he'd shown the children that every card in the deck was now the seven of hearts.

The children giggled and squealed in delight.

Just then, Roxanne appeared in the doorway. "Sorry children, but the show's over for today."

"Awwww," the kids groaned in unison, including the blond-haired child.

"I know, I know," she said, her tone of voice genuinely apologetic, "but Mr. Minardi has some very important visitors." She turned to the orderly and nodded toward the door.

"Sorry, kids," said Romano, "but I have to see a man about a TV show."

"You're gonna be on TV?" asked the blond-haired boy.

"You bet."

"All r-right!"

The orderly pointed the chair in the direction of the door and began pushing him toward it. "Bye, everybody," he said.

"Bye-bye, Mr. Minardi."

He left the room waving.

"You just can't take it easy, can you?" Roxanne said as she walked briskly beside him, headed for the elevator.

"Hey, I'm a performer. It's in my blood. Besides, what better audience could you ask for than a group of kids like that. Did you see their faces?"

"Yes, I did," said Roxanne sternly. "I also saw Bill Butler's face when he walked into your hospital room and didn't find you there."

The orderly pushed the "UP" button. The illuminated number above the elevator doors read "8."

"Oh, shit," said Romano, noticing how far the elevator was from the ground floor. "Was he pissed?" he asked Roxanne.

"A little."

"Maybe he'll lighten up when he finds out I was putting on a show for the kids. You know, good PR and all that."

"Maybe," said Roxanne. "But I wouldn't count on it. From the way he was looking me over, he didn't exactly strike me as the kid-loving type."

Romano let out a sigh, cast a rote, and leaned forward to push the elevator button again. A second later the doors opened up onto an empty car. "Then let's not keep the man waiting."

■

Roxanne took control of the wheelchair out in the hall and, after thanking the orderly, pushed Romano into the room.

Romano's manager Arthur "Artie" Gardner was there waiting for them, along with Bill Butler, the television executive. Butler was a short, squat man in an expensive gray suit and matching silk tie. He stood over by the hospital room window, scanning the parking lot below like a sniper in a bell tower looking for victims. When Roxanne parked the chair in the center of the room, he turned toward them, looking none too happy about having had to wait.

"Sorry," said Romano. "I was downstairs putting on a little show in the children's ward."

Butler nodded, his bottom lip protruding in such a way as to make him look cynical, not only about what Romano had just said, but of everything around him.

After a moment of awkward silence, Artie stepped forward in a feeble attempt at damage control. "What did I tell you, he's a showman, it's in his blood." He gave Romano a gentle slap on the back. "Romano Minardi, meet Bill Butler, vice-president in charge of special programming for WSPR, the number-four satellite superstation in the country."

"Number three," said Butler.

"Right, number three."

Romano extended his right hand. "It's a pleasure to meet you, Mr. Butler."

Butler said nothing. His handshake was firm, but brief.

"Artie tells me you're interested in having me do a prime-time special for WSPR."

"That's not entirely true," said Butler matter-of-factly. "Whenever a special is dropped by one of the four big networks, we contact the show's producers as a matter of course. We've managed to sign on some excellent young comedians that way, and a couple of family entertainment shows."

"That's great," said Romano. "My show's perfect family entertainment."

"It *was*," Butler said, slipping his hands in his pockets.

Romano looked at Roxanne and then to his manager. Both of them looked as surprised as Romano. He looked at the television executive. "What do you mean *was*?"

"If we were having this conversation two weeks ago, I'd probably be waving a contract around and showing you where to sign right about now. But after that last show of yours at The Pantages, we're really not interested. I'm basically here as a favor to Artie."

Romano shook his head, realizing a crucial part of his Ascension was slipping through his fingers. "Look, you know I can generate the numbers, probably a higher share than you've ever had for a prime-time special. That's what it's about, isn't it? Big numbers? High ratings?"

Butler nodded. "That's what it's about, all right. But quite frankly, our marketing people don't think you can capture the same market share you were capable of a couple of weeks ago. People just aren't interested in escape artists who require medical attention to help them defy death."

The insult was thinly veiled, but sharp as a needle. Romano just looked at the man, his mind reeling with thoughts of that last show and the Technomancer who'd been sitting in the front row — sitting there, patiently waiting for an opportunity to kill him, then *trying* to kill him a half-dozen different ways. He *had* defied death, more so than anyone could ever know. As the memory sharpened, anger flared within Romano and he slowly rose from his wheelchair. "Listen, buddy—"

Roxanne's hands suddenly grasped Romano's shoulders, pushing him back down into his seat. At the same moment Artie stepped forward, cutting off Romano's words with a sideways flip of his hand. "What Romano was about to say was that he realizes his professional image has been somewhat tarnished by his recent and most unfortunate *accident*, but certainly he's been in the business long enough to put on a top-flight magic spectacular."

While Artie spoke, Roxanne slowly massaged Romano's shoulders, unknotting his muscles and easing his nerves into a state of relaxation. He took a deep breath, realizing that for all his cynicism and generally unfriendly demeanor, Butler did in fact hold all the cards. If Romano wanted his television special he was going to have to let the man win this hand.

"All right, Mr. Butler," said Romano coolly. "If you and your superstation don't think I merit a prime-time special as it is, what would it take to change your minds?"

Butler's face altered then, his eyes brightening and his lips turning up into a smile. Clearly, he was used to holding the balance of power and surrounding himself with people who knew their place.

"Well, if you were to go back out on the road for another few months, you know, build up some momentum through good press and word-of-mouth, we might reconsider. In fact, if you agree to bring your stage show to six or seven major cities where our station has a strong subscription base, I might be in a position to buy a six-month option to your next special right now."

Romano just nodded his head, marveling at how slimy a bastard the man was. After another few months on the road he'd probably be as popular as ever and could cut a deal with any one of the major networks. What he needed was for the special to air soon — this fall at the latest — or else its place in his Ascension would be lost and he might have to start all over again.

Romano looked over at Artie, who was passing a handkerchief over his sweat-dampened brow. When Artie realized Romano was looking his way, he began nodding as if to say, "Take it, take it."

He glanced at Roxanne, but there was no such look on her face. She was standing behind him, both literally and figuratively, and wouldn't bat an eye if he turned down Butler's somewhat-dubious offer.

"What if I managed to get some publicity?"

Butler took a deep breath, obviously disappointed.

"I mean some real publicity, the kind of thing that would have people talking about me for weeks."

Butler simply shook his head. "WSPR isn't interested in endorsing some half-baked publicity stunt. Disregarding the fact that you just might get yourself killed, these things never wind up helping anyone's career. If you recall what happened to Morton Downey Jr. after that 'Neo-Nazis in the Airport' stunt of his a few years back, I think you'll see my point."

"Never mind that bungling amateur crap," said Romano. "You seem to be forgetting that I'm one of the best escape artists in the world. What I have in mind is a top-rank mystery. The kind of thing the tabloids and prime-time freak shows would keep hot for weeks."

Butler looked interested. "Well, if you were somehow able to capture the public's imagination, that would change things considerably. If you were able to pull it off, then of course we'd be interested in a prime-time special."

Romano smiled, then laughed under his breath. "Good," he said. "That's all I needed to know. Sorry we couldn't strike a deal, but you have Artie's number, and you'll be able to reach him when you're ready to make him an offer."

"What?" said Butler.

"What?" said Artie.

"I'd like you to leave now, Mr. Butler. You've already wasted enough of my time."

Butler's face flushed red. Apparently he wasn't used to being told to take a hike by someone who was supposed to be licking his boots.

"Roxanne," said Romano. "Would you please show Mr. Butler the door?"

Roxanne walked over to the door and held it open for the stunned executive. Just before Butler left the room, he turned back around to face Romano. His eyes were squinted half-shut in anger and his lips were pressed together in a thin white line. "If you think I'll be in touch with you — if anyone will be in touch — you're crazier than I thought. After I get back to the office and make a few phone calls, you'll be lucky to get guest spots on local Saturday morning kids' shows."

"Yeah, right," said Romano, spinning around in his chair to show Butler the back of his head.

Artie put on his jacket and was about to rush out of the room after Butler when Romano called him back. "Forget it, Artie," he said. "In another week he'll be calling you, begging to sign me on."

Artie took a few steps, then slid into a chair, his head and shoulders hanging low and his elbows resting on his knees. "Is this a new thing with you?" asked Artie. "Booting someone out the door just when he's about to give you money?"

"After another few months on the road people would have all but forgotten about that accident and you'd be able to write my ticket, you know that."

"Maybe," Artie sighed. "But you seem to be forgetting something, Roman. *You're* the one who likes taking risks. I'm the guy with a home in Pleasant Valley, two-point-five kids, and a riding mower in my garage that starts every time on the first turn of the key."

"Well, you go to that home of yours and stay there," said Romano. "In a couple of days, your phone is going to be ringing off the hook."

Artie's face suddenly brightened. "Why? What do you have in mind?"

"Ar-tie." Romano's voice was dripping with mock disappointment. "When was the last time I let you in on one of my secrets?"

Artie thought about it a moment, then let out a sigh. "Never."

"That's right. And we're going to keep it that way. Just go home and wait. People will call."

"All right, but if I don't hear from you in a couple of days I'll... I'll—"

"You'll what?" asked Romano.

"I'll be worried about you," he said with a little laugh. Then he waved his hand, gave Roxanne a wink and left the room.

When Artie was gone, Roxanne moved around beside the wheelchair and knelt down to look Romano in the eye. Although she wasn't saying it, Romano could see she was thinking it.

"Don't worry. Everything's going to be fine," said Romano.

"I know."

"Good. Now, this is what we're going to do."

■

Romano began casting rotes shortly after the sun came up the next morning and was ready by eight. Still, he lay quiet on his bed, waiting for the hospital to fill up with people... and potential witnesses.

Doctor Vlasschaert made his usual visit around half-past ten, the spring in his step disappearing shortly after he entered the room. "Oh my God," he whispered under his breath.

Romano's body was covered by a oily sheen of sweat, and there was a definite pallor to his skin. His eyes had sunken deep into their sockets, and his breath was shallow and irregular.

The doctor placed a flat hand across his forehead, then took hold of his wrist, feeling for a pulse. "Nurse!" he shouted in the direction of the hallway.

Without waiting for an answer, the doctor tore the blood pressure cuff from its spot on the wall near the bed and wrapped it around Romano's limp right arm. In seconds he'd inflated the cuff, had the stethoscope in his ears and had begun measuring Romano's blood pressure.

While his actual blood pressure was normal, a crack in

the instrument's mercury-filled tube caused it to give the doctor a reading of 80 over 40.

"Way too low," he muttered.

He unstrapped the cuff and measured Romano's body temperature by clipping his aural thermometer to Romano's left ear lobe, the one which had been warmed by the bright beams of morning sunlight blazing through the window. The instrument's LCD showed Romano's temperature to be over 104 degrees Fahrenheit.

The doctor shook his head and began applying pressure to the areas surrounding his freshly healed wounds. Mostly Romano lay still, but every time the doctor pressed down on the upper chest area he'd flinch and moan as if he were in the throes of great agony.

"Nurse!" the doctor shouted again.

The doctor went to the end of the bed and checked the most recent set of x-rays. As he held a picture of the chest cavity to the light, the cause of the problem was obvious — a jagged white mark in the upper right-hand corner of the x-ray.

At last a nurse appeared in the doorway, a young man in his early twenties. "Find Doctor Katz and tell him to start prepping for surgery. Then contact emergency and tell them to clear OR 3. Apparently Mr. Minardi still has a piece of metal lodged in his chest. We're going to have to remove it."

"Yes, doctor," the nurse said, running out of the room.

Romano could hear the shouts and confusion starting to mount in the hall. In another few minutes everyone in the building would know of Romano Minardi's precarious hold on life.

He had to remind himself not to smile.

Fifteen minutes later the orderly with the bloodshot eye entered the room, followed by two nurses. Together the three of them eased Romano onto a gurney, then the nurses left the room, leaving Romano alone with the orderly.

If his plan was to succeed he'd have to make use of some vulgar magick. Usually that wouldn't be a problem, except this magick had to be performed in plain sight of the orderly and as a result risked a potentially dangerous Paradox situation.

But there was something curious about this orderly, something that led Romano to believe the man could not be a witness to vulgar magick. Yesterday, when he'd lit their cigarettes with his flaming thumb, the man hadn't questioned it; in fact he'd hardly reacted at all. Still, for the plan to work, Romano had to be sure. He decided on a little test.

As the orderly wheeled him toward the door, Romano cast a rote slowing time around him to a virtual standstill. Then he climbed off the gurney and turned his body around so that when real-time continued the orderly would see Romano instantaneously change position — one second he'd be leaving the room feet first, the next second he'd be traveling headlong.

When he was back in real-time, Romano looked up at the orderly. The man simply looked farther down the gurney — searching for the head he'd been looking at the second before — and said, "Don't worry. The doctors here are first rate. Everything's going to be all right."

Romano breathed a deep sigh of relief. Yes, he thought, everything is going to work out fine.

A few seconds later he was being loaded onto the elevator which would take him to the ground-level operating room. A crowd of people had gathered to watch the hospital's celebrity patient being taken into surgery.

As the doors began to close, Romano — ever the showman — took his right hand from under the covers and gave everyone watching a weak "thumbs up."

When the doors clanked shut, Romano cast another rote over time, again slowing real-time down to a crawl. Then he rose up from the gurney and stood on it, reaching up to push an overhead ceiling tile out of the way. The escape door was just a few inches above the false ceiling and opened with little struggle. After a couple of failed attempts, Romano managed to jump off the gurney and haul himself through the small opening onto the top of the car. He took his time getting into the operating hat, gown and mask Roxanne had left there for him, then replaced the ceiling tile, closed the hatch and exited through the second-floor doors which were just above him at waist level. After closing the second-floor doors behind him, he ran past the almost stationary bodies lining the hallway and hurried down the stairs to the first floor where the elevator car he'd just been on would soon be stopping. As he'd suspected, there was already a group of people surrounding the doors, some awaiting his arrival, others just happening by.

After he was sure he was in an inconspicuous spot and people wouldn't see him suddenly appear out of thin air, he brought real-time back up to speed. With everything back in motion, he stepped into the hallway and hurried for the elevator doors.

A moment later the doors rolled open.

The orderly stood there with an empty gurney and a dumbstruck look on his face.

"Where'd he go?" asked a nurse who was already prepped for surgery.

"Where is he?" asked another woman, most likely a clerk whose job it would have been to make sure Romano's insurance was up to date.

The orderly just shook his head, staring blankly at the crowd before him. "Gone," he said.

"What do you mean *gone?*"

"He's gone," repeated the orderly. "He was there one minute, the next minute he wasn't."

Romano stood just on the edge of the crowd, smiling broadly under the cover of his operating mask. "Wait till the papers hear about this," he said loud and clear, planting the idea of contacting the press into the minds of everyone present.

As the murmur of stunned voices began to rise, Romano turned and walked away from the scene, continuing on through the lobby and out the hospital's front door to where Roxanne was waiting for him in her car, the engine running.

"How'd it go?" asked Roxanne.

Romano pulled down the operating mask, then widened his eyes and dropped his jaw in a parody of the dumbstruck orderly who'd been left holding the empty gurney, and said, "Gone."

A PLACE TO STAY

DAVID CHART

I stalked through the blasted landscape, the shards of rock tearing at my pads. The air was heavy with the acrid scent of complete desolation, sharp and oppressive. Even the sickly odor of decay would have been welcome, evidence that something had once lived here. I sniffed cautiously at the air, searching for the biting sting that was the signature of the Enemy. I had wounded it badly last time, and our next battle, I was sure, would be its last.

The smell brought water to my eyes, but I was glad to find it. Silently, I turned to pad toward its source. As I advanced, other scents were overlayed on the cutting miasma of destruction: scents of fresh vegetation, living trees, and pure water. I suppressed the rising snarl, and vented my frustration to Oigimi.

"It's done it again. It always chooses to

fight in the uncorrupted parts of the Realm. Why can't it fight its battles on its own territory?"

An old rotting corpse
Is not hunted down and slain
By hungry lions.

"Yes, it suits its nature to destroy as much as possible. This time, though, I'm going to stop it, while there's still something left to save." Silently, I moved behind a rise of bare and shattered rock, peering around the edge at the glade. It looked peaceful, with several healthy trees dotted around an open area of grass while a clear stream flowed along one edge, but I could smell the burning reek of the Enemy, and I knew that it was here. Cautiously, I advanced, scanning the area for the signs of its presence.

The whistling in the air gave me just enough warning, and I dodged out of the way as one of the trees whipped down, burying its branches in the ground beside me. Snarling, I twisted and sprang into the midst of the foliage, thrusting my jaws toward the writhing that I could see in the trunk. I got a mouthful of splinters, and then the tree reared upright again, pulling me with it. The branches flailed at me, and I could feel myriad tiny wounds opening and closing as the squirming presence shifted among the boughs. Twigs snapped and I spat leaves out of my mouth, but so far I had not struck the Enemy. In its wake, the tree was becoming rigid and brittle, snapping under my paws as I kept my precarious station in the treetop.

The bitter, rotten taste and vile, slimy writhing filled my mouth as I finally struck home. Desperately, I tried to close my jaws, get a firm grip on the disgusting thing, but, my heart sinking, I felt it slipping out, and then there was merely a shimmering flying through the air to another tree. Growling my rage, I leapt after it. I had wounded it now, and it appeared to be scared, as the battle developed into a chase around the glade, the Enemy barely bothering to attack, but managing to stay just ahead of me. Instead of ripping its foul body, I found myself with a mouthful of grass and dirt, or plowing up the rocky bed of the stream. It leapt from tree to tree, and through the grass and undergrowth. Twice I tasted it, felt its putrescent writhings in my mouth, but each time it evaded me again, fleeing to another part of the glade. Now almost everything I touched was crumbling under my paws, burning them with cold, all the life drained from them to feed the Enemy's insatiable lust. The once-beautiful area was becoming as much a wasteland as the rest of the Realm. Fury at the destruction rose in my chest, and with a final leap I feigned to the left, and got my jaws firmly about the thing as it tried to flee to the right.

It was like biting a thousand worms, each one covered with slime that burned the mouth. Ignoring the pain, I brought my paws down, holding it still while I ripped at it. It struggled and writhed, and it felt as if the soil were boiling under me. Snarling, I tore at it again, determined not to be distracted by its last tricks. The Enemy would die this time, and the Realm be liberated. The smell of the Realm became more tenuous, less real, as I ripped at the thing, and, at the edge of vision, lines seemed to rip across the ground and sky. The worms were almost still, and I plunged my jaws down for one final attack. As I ripped the things apart, the earth shuddered, and the sky seemed to be torn apart. The scent of the Realm vanished in a moment, and for the merest instant I felt as though I were falling for ever.

I was in the Umbra, standing beside a pool, and Zeno was waiting, sitting on a rock a short distance away.

"So, Kaoru, what have you learned?" I was silent, gathering my wits. I sniffed cautiously, and it was certainly Zeno's scent. I could feel my Rage straining to break free, and I forced it down with an effort.

"Learned? This was another test?" I asked, my tone clearly begging for a negative answer.

"All of life is a test, and a lesson. What have you learned?" Zeno was calm, but I was far from being able to match his poise.

"Are you saying that the only purpose of that Realm was to teach me something?" Zeno shifted slightly, his posture expressing the merest sliver of impatience.

"Of course. One must teach in an ethical fashion, as well as an effective one. But teaching can do nothing if the pupil will not learn."

"Learn? I suffered agony fighting that thing: It destroyed the Realm before it was defeated. The Realm was lost, Zeno. That thing you introduced there destroyed it. Is it worth that just to teach me something?"

"If you have truly learned the lesson, yes."

"What lesson can be worth such a loss? What lesson could be worth hunting me for weeks? What kind of teacher are you, Zeno?"

"Knowledge is valuable, wisdom more so. How else can you learn wisdom?"

"Wisdom? That I am a hunter? I am lupus, Zeno, I grew up hunting deer for my food. There was no need to hunt me for that. And I know that the Wyrm's corruption is laced through everything: I can feel it. You would do this to teach me such things as that?"

"Ah, you have not learned, not yet."

"No? Then I don't want any more lessons. I want no part of those who think that such a price is worth paying. I want no part of you, the tribe, or the Garou. Do you hear? I will not be toyed with this way!" Afraid that my Rage would drive me to attack my Mentor, my former Mentor, I turned my gaze on the pool and willed myself through the Gauntlet so that I stood alone, out in the wilderness. The wilderness, the home of the Garou. I sniffed the air, and starting running, following the scent of the scab. It would be somewhere to recover.

The scent of the apes got stronger on the air as I ran

into a headwind which seemed to blow nothing except me. Oigimi, trying to make me go back. I ignored the wind and ran on; it soon dropped, as she realized that I wasn't going to change my mind. I did not want to be among beings that would destroy a Realm merely to set a puzzle for a student. The wilderness was thinning out, and soon the first signs of the apes' presence began to appear: their trash, lying amidst Gaia's beauty, completely unaware.

I ran on, into the scab, over the false stone that imprisoned the ground, into the stench of corruption and decay that hung over the place, away from the Garou, the tribes and the packs. The buildings got denser and higher, the cold of their shadows biting more cruelly than ever the shadows of rocks, and the streets were full of cars that spewed Wyrm-ridden vapor, and apes who shied away in a cloud of fear and unnatural scent, and there were garish lights that hurt my eyes, even in the light of day.

The unnatural place sapped my strength and long before darkness fell I was padding wearily through crowds of apes, throngs where there was barely room to pass, where the smell even of ape was drowned out in a clashing swirl of false rose, corrupt pine, cloying spices; where apes kicked me as I got in their way, or offered me food rank with the scent of the Wyrm, trying to enslave my spirit, as the crowd carried me along, sweeping me through cold canyons of the Weaver, denying me the chance to find a home.

Summoning my strength, I pushed out of the crowds, into a narrow cleft between buildings, where the darkness and the stench were worse yet, where the ground was puddled with foul things, things that released stronger odors of corruption as I touched them, which seeped into my fur, clinging as I tried to shake them off, while shapes moved in the shadows, shapes that seemed not even to belong to apes, shapes that moved forward, revealing themselves as mangy dogs, stinking of the place, their fur rubbed away in sores, snarling at me, driving me back, pushing me away.

I bolted, and ran from the alley, pushing aside the apes, whose noises almost deafened me as I broke through them, running across a miraculously clear area of false stone that an instant later wasn't clear, was filled with the roar of cars, with loud cries, with screeches and the smell of burnt rubber, with apes milling about, chasing me, yes, chasing me, as I ran for the cover of another alley, let the darkness swallow me, running along it, hearing the sounds of pursuit die behind me while the shapes in the shadows shifted and stirred, alarmed by the intrusion, sending things skittering across my path, forcing me to shy away.

The alley ended in blind walls, walls that surrounded a tiny area of green. A stunted tree, two small bushes, a carpet of grass, and a sense of rightness and belonging drowned out even the strong smells of urine and alcohol. I padded cautiously onto the grass, looking around. An ape, wrapped in rags, was shuffling back, away from me. I snarled at it, and it stood and ran down the alley. Another one, hidden below a large coat, lay asleep and oblivious as I growled at it, and didn't move until I bit its arm, when it rolled over, its eyes wide in terror and its breath stinking of the poor spirits it had been drinking. I let go of its arm and growled, my muzzle practically touching its face. It struggled to its feet remarkably quickly, and ran down the alley, the only exit from the garden, weaving from side to side and pushing off the walls. The few animals in the place all bore the corrupting marks of the scab, so I drove them out, not even the dogs daring to challenge me.

When the last of them had left, I paced the confined limits of my domain, and marked it with my scent. My territory claimed, I settled down under one of the bushes to talk to Oigimi. Breathing deeply, I almost choked on the odor of the scab. Steeling myself against its foul effluence, I let my breathing become calmer, more regular, as I formed the image in my mind. The scent of grass pollen, overlaid with hints of pine and fir, getting stronger. A clearing in forested hills, an area of grass crowning a rise from which I could see the woodland flowing away in all directions. A clear sky, in which hawks circled and called. The sound of small animals moving through the undergrowth. And then a wind blowing through the trees, strong enough to shake them, so that the forest bowed in waves as if it were but grass.

Rainstorm in the hills.
The pilgrim rejects the inn
With garish lanterns.

"It was a lot more serious than that, Oigimi. You know what he did. You were there."

A fish swimming down
A meandering river
Sees no reason there.

"Oh yes, I should meekly accept it because my elders are so much wiser than I. I did that, Oigimi. I did that, and they put a fetish in my Rite of Passage that summoned the Hunters, and then left me in a corrupted Realm, to see what I would learn. Why should I trust them?"

The eagle's offspring
Are cast, afraid, from the nest
And learn how to fly.

"I thought you would be on my side. I don't think Zeno really does have anything that he wants me to learn: He's just putting me in dangerous situations to see what happens. He's using me, that's all."

The wolf leaves the pack
As another is alpha.

The wolf dies alone.

"Oh, thank you very much, Oigimi. I didn't leave because I wasn't in charge. If I'd stayed with Zeno's teaching, I'd have been dead soon anyway. And now, because of him, I've had to flee to the scab, where there are apes everywhere. Come on, it's hardly my fault."

Apes murder Gaia
Because the Weaver drives them:
Should Garou not fight?

"What? Of course we should. What has that got to do with me? I'm stuck in the midst of millions of apes, in case you'd forgotten."

The wind whistles, howls,
Moans in the trees, scatters leaves,
Speaks if you can hear.

"You're no comfort, Oigimi. I'm alone in the scab, having fled from a dangerous teacher, and all you can do is dither on about how I should have stayed with him and been fed to the Wyrm. I'm going to get some sleep. If I can." I broke the trance, letting the image of the tiny, confined park slash across that of the boundless forest. I stood up and paced around my meager territory once again, making sure that nothing was there without my permission, before settling down to sleep in the shelter of a bush. The leaves and twigs shook briefly in a transient wind as I relaxed, and I let myself fall into dreams.

I awoke just after dawn the next day. The nearly full moon had already sunk behind the buildings, but its glow was still visible in the west. I couldn't howl, it just wouldn't have been right in that place, so I settled for growling my recognition of Phoebe. I paced around the park in the slowly growing light, reluctant to start out into the scab before I could see clearly, and while there were still too many shadows for things to hide in.

Finally, it was bright enough, and I walked out of my territory, past the apes and pathetic strays that were still congregated in the alley. I snarled at them as I passed, hoping to drive them away, but they just cowered back farther into the shadows that seemed deeper than they ought to have been and waited for me to leave. I left them for the moment and headed on into the scab, into the surge of apes that tried to sweep me down the streets, amid the begriming fumes of cars, the smell of gasoline, of faked natural scents, of the poisons of the Wyrm, and the shouting of the apes and the roar of their vehicles. My senses overwhelmed, I could only wander in my search for clean water, for something to hunt, passing by the pools that had collected on the false stone, with their Wyrm-betraying sheen and evil scent, passing by the sickly, corrupted birds and rodents that fluttered in the air or scurried into shadows, startled by the apes, not by their rightful predator.

The city was confusing, and I began to fear that I would be lost in its regular labyrinth of streets that suffocated the land like the Weaver's web, between the towering walls that hid the sky from view so that nothing of Gaia might intrude on this haven of the apes, of the Weaver, of the Wyrm, where there was no clean water, nothing to eat, where a Garou might die and never be missed. By midday, my wanderings led me to a larger park, where the press of apes thinned out a bit, and I could hear the splash of flowing water, a cleaner sound which I headed toward. The water flowed into a confining basin of false stone, formed by the apes to regiment and control Gaia's natural energy, and the water tasted foul, with hints of the Wyrm, hints of long, underground rivers filled with unmentionable things. I started back from the water, growling.

And then moved forward to drink again, cautiously this

time, testing the taste, the degree of corruption, and realizing
that it was only a little thing, that the water was cleaner
than any other source I had seen, and I needed to drink.
With my thirst barely slaked, I felt no desire to drink further,
and turned to look for food, for surely in a park there would
be creatures I could hunt. I prowled around, keeping out of
the way of the apes, for if I disturbed them, they would hunt
me, and this was their territory, and they were too many by
far for me to face. Stalking the pitiful animals of the park
was easy, the noise of the apes covering any sound I might
make, and the rank smells of their creations covering my
predator's scent, so that I caught squirrels as my prey with
hardly any effort.

When polluted water and tainted meat had taken the
edge off my hunger and thirst, I threaded my way back
through the heaving masses to my home, to the only place
I had found in this scab that felt at all right, more welcoming
than the cold, unyielding surface of the ground. Dogs snarled
from the shadows, and still the screech of the cars and the
shrill call of their horns disturbed me, but I had learnt that
if I kept to the crowds of apes, the cars would not bother
me, that the apes avoided their own creations. The sky was
darkening as I turned into the alley and made for my home,
and the pus of the scab that resided there got out of my way
as I hurried toward the small park, hurrying to get past the
corruption and back to somewhere I could rest.

The park was occupied. The stray dogs, fighting over a
bone in one corner, ran as soon as I approached them,
dropping the bone in their haste. An ape remained, leaning
against one of the walls, wrapped in a filthy covering and
clutching a bag which stank of poisoned alcohol. It was
asleep, and failed to wake when I growled at it. I butted it
with my muzzle, recoiling from the foul, slimy feel of its coat,
and it groggily opened its eyes and looked at me. Its left eye
was so bloodshot as to be completely red, and its startled
exclamation wreathed me in a cloud of stinking vapor. I

growled at it, and began herding it toward the exit. The decrepit thing struggled to its feet and staggered off, muttering as it groped its way through the park. I growled from behind it, and it broke into a lumbering run that took it careening into a pile of trash, stirring up a cloud of papers and other garbage.

I paced around my territory once more, marking the boundaries and standing at the entrance to the alley to snarl at the creatures gathered there. Those nearest the park shuffled further down, and I growled again, provoking one dog to leave completely, running down the alley whining. I settled down, ignoring the wind that stirred the grass around me: I didn't want to talk to Oigimi tonight, not after what she had said.

The next couple of days passed in much the same way. I left my territory in the morning to drink and hunt, snarling at the inhabitants of the alley as I went by, and made my way through the throngs of apes and the miasma of their scab to the park. I drank, and hunted, and then made my way back to the haven for the night. Little happened in those days: The city was as oppressive as ever, the shadows of the buildings as cold, and the outcasts of this outcast society still congregated in my home. I drove them out, biting one ape who seemed reluctant to leave and waved a tiny knife at me. This overcame its desire to stay, and it fled with the rest. Two blue-uniformed apes in a car surmounted by flashing lights visited the alley on the first evening, and I slunk out of sight behind the bushes: I knew that the Wyrm was served by such as those, and I didn't want a fight I could avoid, not here. The next night, I passed a well-dressed ape, searching for something near my alley. It stared at me as I passed, but it did not follow, as I had half expected.

The next evening, I returned to my haven, and found it as cold and empty as the rest of the scab, the walls that so recently had seemed to provide protection now seeming more of a prison, while the taint of the apes who had lived here seemed heavier and more oppressive in the air. I searched the area, snarling at shadows, but it was empty: no one had come here in my absence. I paced down the alley, sniffing at those apes and other strays that I found there, growling involuntarily at the scent of corruption and decay on most of them, but finding nothing that could have caused the emptiness I felt. Dejected, I returned to the small park and decided to talk to Oigimi, to find out if a spirit had noticed something I couldn't.

I settled down and held the scents of the sea in my mind, the salt spray and the cleanness of the air. I saw the water spread out around me and heard the quiet sounds of the small waves moving over its surface. A wind blew up, building bigger waves, and covering the surface of the sea with white foam.

Wind cries in the night
For a response from the flute
Which lies silently.

I felt a surge of guilt for ignoring Oigimi: I had forgotten that she would find the scab disturbing as well. "I'm sorry. I was annoyed that you didn't understand why I had to come here."

Son tells his father
"Don't cut the cherry tree."
But still he will help.

"Thank you. I'm glad you're staying with me. I had to come here; you do understand that?"

Hawk sees the rain fall.
He knows not the why or how,
But knows it must fall.

"All right, I don't want to fight about that again. I wanted to ask whether this place seemed different to you, more empty somehow?"

A house left empty
The wind wails within: it howls
In one abandoned.

"You do feel it! Do you have any idea why it feels different?"

A wolf sleeps, is still.
No change, everything changes
And the wolf is dead.

"So, this place has died, in a sense. I will leave tomorrow, then, and try to find somewhere else to go."

The lone wolf wanders
And finds no place to call home
Unless with a pack.

"Oigimi, I said I didn't want to discuss that. Will you keep watch tonight?"

Wind blows unceasing
In all places the wind blows
Wind blows here tonight.

"Thank you." I came out of the trance and settled to sleep in the park.

When I woke the next morning, I was wet from the rain that still poured from the sky. I shook myself, and sniffed around my territory. The rain was washing the smell of the homeless away, leaving a clean, wholesome scent in its place. It wouldn't last, but it was pleasant for now. And then it hit me: The place felt right again, the emptiness had gone. I yipped my pleasure, and ran quickly around the edge of the park. The wind swirled around me, making the rain dance in strange patterns, as Oigimi expressed her pleasure. I caught as much rain as I could in my open jaws, savoring the relative purity of the water, and then set off to hunt in the Wyld-cleaned city.

The rain stopped during the day, and I returned to a cleaner park, one that no longer smelled of the apes, or the dogs corrupted by the scab, or of the rodents that scurried around it. Even the alley was largely empty, as the inhabitants of the shadows sought safer lodging. The feeling of rightness remained, and I settled down for another night, rather more confident that I had found a place to stay.

The next day was uneventful, although I passed a searching ape close to my home. I caught its scent and realized that it was the same one I had seen before, and moved away cautiously. This time, however, it ignored me, and went on with its intense hunt for something no doubt trivial. The following day I padded up an empty alley to a park that felt empty, in the same way as before. This time, though, I could detect a new scent on the air, an ape scent, but somehow richer, more alive. I sniffed around, but there was no obvious source, and whoever had been here was clearly long gone. I settled down to talk to Oigimi, scenting the cold, neutral odor of snow, letting a calm silence enfold me as a white snowfield formed in my mind's eye, the drifts extending to the horizon. Small white clouds sprang up from the top of the heaps and drifted to earth, more and more, until the air was full of dancing whiteness.

"Do you think that the person I can smell has taken something?"

Paw marks in the mud,
Blood, claw marks on the hen house.
How to doubt the fox?

"Okay, okay, it is fairly obvious. I just wondered if you could scent evidence I couldn't that suggested something different. Well, I think I should wait, and intercept whoever it is who is despoiling my home."

Now the predator
Speaks as he ought and defends
His territory.

"I'm glad you approve. I don't suppose it'll come back tomorrow, but I may as well wait to be sure. Will you watch me?"

One must watch at night,
The other guard the daylight,
Lest the foe prevail.

"Thank you." I slipped out of the trance and paced around my territory a couple of times to reassure myself before I went to sleep.

I waited in my home for the whole of the next day, but no ape even approached the alley. Even the drunks seemed to have abandoned the area. The following day was equally quiet until about noon, when an ape cautiously approached up the alley. I sniffed at the air, but it wasn't the rich scent that had been left here, it was the scent of the ape who had been searching. I stood in the entrance to the park, facing it down. It stopped, looking at me, but not moving. I snarled, then, and took a step forward, and the creature turned tail and ran down the alley. Nothing further happened that day or the next, apart from apes going to and fro past the end of the alley, and I began to be hungry. The water standing in puddles was just drinkable now that the apes polluted the passage less, but the rats and pigeons had been scared off as well as the dogs, so there was nothing to eat. I decided to wait one more day and then go hunting.

Phoebe smiled on my decision to wait a little longer, because on the following day the ape responsible returned. It was a child, and it came confidently up the alley, the same, rich scent spreading around it. Its hair was long and black, reaching almost to its waist. It wore a black jacket made of leather, which added a subtle undercurrent to the scent, and it was humming a tune as it approached. I stepped out into the center of the alley, facing it and snarling. It stopped immediately on seeing me, its feet scuffing on the ground, and stood there for a long moment, staring straight at me, its deep brown eyes fixed on mine. And then it turned and fled down the alley, moving faster than I would have thought possible for an ape its size, its hair streaming out and its red shoes splashing in the puddles.

I returned to my sanctuary and settled down to talk to Oigimi. I tried to compose my mind to meditation, but I could see nothing in my mind's eye but the ape, its hair moving gently in a breeze. I tried to bring an image of a grassland to mind, with the scent of dust and pollen, but the rich scent of the ape overlaid it, and I could form no image that did not include the ape. Disgusted, I stood and paced around my haven for a while, as darkness fell.

By dawn I was ravenous, and I left my park as soon as it was bright enough to see, heading for my hunting grounds. There was a tune running through my head, and I snarled with irritation when I realized that it was the melody the ape had been humming the previous day. I drank from the fountain, and the splashing reminded me of the sound that its feet had made in the puddles. I hunted squirrels down, and was reminded of the leather jacket that it had worn. The apes that crowded the park reminded me of it by a detail of their walk, or the sound of their voice, or a hint of the abundant life in its scent. No longer hungry, but increasingly irritated by my lack of control over my memories, I returned to my home, and I thought at first that the scent was merely another memory. But it wasn't: The ape was there, waiting for me, sitting in my territory.

"Gaia be with you and Luna watch you, noble wolf. I am Aspasia, and we must talk about this place." She spoke the tongue of the Garou, albeit with a strong homid accent, and I felt my hackles rise as I padded forward cautiously.

"Gaia be with you, Aspasia. I am Kaoru Clouds-Turn-Back. This place is my home, and you were not invited here. By all the laws of the Garou, you should leave and ask my permission before returning." The homid was silent for a moment, and I sat down, watching her carefully. She had hardly moved since I arrived, but I could smell her tension.

"I did not know that those were laws of the Garou: I am not of that breed." I snarled, an involuntary expression of surprise, and she started back. "I only came because we need to talk. I would not want to cast you out of your home, but this place was mine before ever you came here. I have a claim on it also, and I would see our claims reconciled." I considered for a moment before responding.

"Where did you learn our tongue, if you are not Garou?" She seemed unperturbed by the question.

"All things that have been known can be known by those who know how to look. I know the secret of such knowledge, and so I can learn your tongue should I need it. But I did not come here to discuss the mysteries; I came to discuss this place, and our claims on it."

"If you are not Garou, I do not see how you can have a claim that I should recognize. If you are not Garou, you are just one of the despoilers of Gaia. Why should I make an agreement with you?" I felt the wind blow my fur back, ruffling it uncomfortably. Oigimi was not pleased with what I was saying. The ape was silent for a moment, obviously weighing her words carefully.

"The Garou," she said, "are not the only ones who fight for Gaia, and not all those who are not Garou fight against."

She paused for a moment, her eyes searching for my reaction. "This place," she continued, "is a place of magick, and I need the Quintessence it provides to support my magick. I need only gather the Tass that it produces and meditate here to refresh myself; I need not live here."

"So, you wish to take Gaia's gifts from this caern, without the proper respect. And you think that the fact that you have been doing so gives you a claim on it! Apes, you are all the same." The wind blew dust in my face, and when I had cleared my eyes and nose I could see and smell her nervousness.

"This is no caern; this is merely a Node…" she began, but I cut her off.

"This is a caern: I can feel it in the air. And I can feel the desolation that remains when you have raped it." She winced visibly at that, but I almost lost my balance to the strong gust of wind that buffeted my side.

"I do not rape the Node; I merely take the Tass it provides and allow the strong flow of Quintessence in this place to refresh my pattern. It need not interfere with your stay here; indeed, maybe an ally in the city would be useful to you." I opened my jaws to reply, but the gust of wind that struck me was so strong that I could do nothing for a moment. Oigimi was clearly unhappy with this conversation, and I realized that I would have to find out why.

"I cannot decide now. Come back tomorrow, and I shall tell you what I have decided." The ape rose to leave.

"May Phoebe light your path until we next meet." It was an odd farewell, but not impolite.

"May the wind be at your face and the forest screen your passage." She bowed slightly in response, and then left, walking slowly down the alley. I watched her leave, finding myself unable to look away until she had turned the corner at the end and disappeared from sight.

Although she had left, her scent still filled my nostrils as I settled down to meditate and talk to Oigimi. I scented for the dry smell of a desert, of windblown dust, and let the glare of a bright sun fill my eyes for a moment, so that when it cleared I could see the endless dunes, and hear the slithering of sand grains as they fell. Light plumes of dust rose from the tops of the dunes, and then heavier particles. The hot scent got stronger as the wind picked up, driving the sand into the air so that the vista disappeared in a wild swirl of windborne particles.

The bush scrapes the wolf.
In fury he rips it apart,
And destroys his shade.

"Why don't you want me to drive that ape away? She admitted that she rapes Gaia here, and I must preserve the caern."

Water from the spring
May drown a careless wolf-cub,
And bring life to Earth.

"Are you suggesting she's like a spring? She's an ape, Oigimi. She was responsible for emptying this caern. I don't understand."

As water flows out
From a spring, so life flows out
From Aspasia.

"Oh, I see. Well, I didn't, but I suppose you would know. So, maybe we could be allies if she agreed to leave the caern alone. It would be useful to know someone who understands the city."

Pluck the ripe cherries
And the tree is cold and bare.

Next year it bears more.

"What? Oigimi, I can't let her continue to gather her quinassens from this place. You know what it felt like when she had."

Gather dew in bowls
And leave the ground dry and sere.
More will fall with dawn.

"Yes, OK, it was all right again by the morning, but I still don't think it's right. She shouldn't empty the place even for that length of time."

By day the hawk hunts.
By night he berates the owl,
But catches nothing.

"What? Why should an ape know better what I should do with this caern? Oigimi, you aren't talking sense."

It is just a rock.
It leaps, flies, sings the Record.
Is it just a rock?

"Hmm. No, she isn't just an ape, that is true, but still..."

Lone wolf with no pack
May be guided by the fox,
Through perilous swamps.

"OK, you win. I will talk to her nicely tomorrow, and we will arrange something. I hope you're right, though."

The hawk dives for prey
And rises empty-taloned,

Still a good hunter.

"Yes, I know. You've convinced me to take the risk. So you can watch while I sleep. Good night." I pulled myself out of the trance and felt a gentle breeze play around me as I settled down to rest.

I went to hunt the next day, so as not to be hungry and distracted when Aspasia returned, and then waited in my caern until she approached up the alley, her hair tied back today. I took the initiative.

"Gaia and Phoebe be with you, Aspasia. Please be seated, we have much to discuss." She looked a little surprised, but she sat down.

"Gaia and Phoebe be with you also, Kaoru. I hope that we can come to some agreement." As she spoke, I started back in some surprise. Today, she spoke with a clear Black Fury accent, something she had not had the day before. She continued. "I have no desire to drive you from your home, and if you will allow me to gather Tass and Quintessence here, I shall attempt to bring you clean water and good food, for these cannot be easy to find in the city." A breeze blew around me as she spoke: Oigimi reminding me of our conversation.

"I have considered what you said," I replied, "and it seems to me that you probably understand the city, and this caern, better than I do." A cold gust of wind struck my side just then, briefly, but I had no intention of mentioning Oigimi at this stage. "So, I will accept your offer. You bring me food and water, which are hard to find in this scab, and I will let you gather your quinassy." Aspasia smiled at that.

"Quintessence. Thank you, Kaoru. I am pleased that we were able to reach an agreement. I am afraid that I must leave now; I must return home before my parents become worried. I shall come again tomorrow, with the food and water. May the wind be at your face, and the forest screen your passage."

"And may fine game be in your path." She stood and bowed slightly again before leaving, and once again I found myself watching her until she was out of sight. I settled down without talking to Oigimi; I wanted to wait and see how this risk turned out before I talked to her about it. I didn't want another pointless round of what-ifs and maybes.

On the following day I didn't leave my home, but paced around impatiently, waiting for Aspasia. She came in the evening, as the sun was setting, her hair loose over her jacket and a pair of low leather boots on her feet. She was carrying a large bag, and I caught a hint of the smell of meat through the almost overpowering life that flowed from her.

"Gaia and Phoebe be with you, Kaoru." Her accent was that of the Shadow Lords, although it was not pronounced. "I have brought the food and water, as I promised." She reached into the bag and pulled out two large bottles, a wooden bowl, and a piece of meat wrapped up in brown paper. She poured some of the water into the bowl, and I came forward to sniff at it.

I recoiled immediately. It smelt the same as the water in the fountain in the park.

"This is not clean water, Aspasia. This water is Wyrm-tainted." She looked shocked at my reaction.

"But I got it from the tap. It must be clean…" Her voice tailed off, and her face furrowed into a frown as she thought about the consequences. "I can try to find some proper clean water, but I do not know if there will be any such available. Do you want to try the meat?" I sniffed at it, but that was enough. At least the squirrels were fresh prey. I backed away.

"No, the meat is also tainted." Aspasia sighed.

"It seems that I am going to find it harder than I thought to keep my side of the bargain." She began to gather her things together. "I will return tomorrow with some more food and water, and to gather the Tass. I hope that you will not prevent me from doing that because I have been unable to find acceptable water?"

"No, you are trying to keep the agreement, so I must also try." She smiled and stood, hefting her bag again.

"Thank you. I will see you tomorrow then. May the wind be at your face, and the forest screen your passage."

"And may fine game be in your path." I watched her leave with a strong sense of disappointment, only realizing then how much I had been looking forward to a drink of truly pure water and some good meat.

She did return the next day, but the meat and water were again tainted. I watched her curiously as she gathered her Quintessence. First, she meditated, sitting in the middle of the park. I could feel the atmosphere changing as the power left it, and found myself unable to stay still. I paced the perimeter of the park, trying not to whine as I felt the security in the place drain away. When she had finished meditating, she wandered around the area for a little while, as if searching, and then dug into the ground, unearthing a small crystal, which she clasped tightly in her hand. As she did so, I felt the last dregs of comfort drain from the place, and I crept into one of the corners and lay down, watching her. Far from sharing my discomfort, she seemed extremely happy, and she bid me farewell cheerfully.

It took her three more days to find a good supply of water, and two after that for the meat, but it was worth the wait. The clean taste of the water seemed to wash the dirt of the scab from my soul, and the fresh meat reminded me how poor the fare I had been living on really was. We arranged a time to meet, in the evenings, and I began exploring the area around my home. I was starting to get uncomfortable with moving about during the day, but I wanted to know the area better before I went out into it at night. The alleys and shadows were no longer as threatening as when I first arrived, but they could still hide many things.

The dregs of the city had now abandoned my park and, for the most part, the alley. I would still sometimes return to find an ape curled up at the entrance to the passage, but a single snarl was enough to send it scurrying away. But none of them ever got as far as the park itself, not anymore. I was thus surprised, and worried, when I returned one evening to find a strange scent on the air in the park itself. I searched around, but I could find nothing except a couple of places where the earth had been slightly disturbed. Still, the scent nagged at me; there was something familiar about it. I didn't mention my observations to Aspasia, as this was my home, not hers, and indeed I largely forgot about it until I was settling down to sleep. Then, when my mind was wandering between reality and dreams, I realized that it was the scent of the ape who had been prowling around my home before.

I was woken by a sudden blast of cold wind, Oigimi's warning. I opened my eyes and sniffed the air; there were strange, ape scents on it, and the searcher was there as well. I stood and slunk to the end of the alley, looking along it. Three apes were approaching, walking cautiously. I could smell nervousness and excitement, and they were very obviously coming to my territory. I stepped out into the center of the alley and snarled, facing them down. They stopped, and one pointed something at me. There was a loud crack, and I felt a stabbing pain in my side, knocking me briefly to the ground. The apes continued to advance, and I struggled back to my feet, snarling at them and moving to block their path. There was another report, but this time I heard something strike the ground behind me. There was a strange, acrid scent on the air, and the apes were not backing down. Indeed, two of them were now pointing at me.

I summoned my Rage, and let it flow into my body. I felt the additional mass, the power and strength, flow onto my frame, as the pain in my side began to fade rapidly, sinking to nothing more than a minor irritation as I rose up on my hind legs, my paws developing into hands, and my jaws raised to the sky as I roared my challenge and defiance in defense of my home.

The apes had paused now, two shots having missed me

as I changed. They even took a couple of steps back, but I didn't smell real fear, only surprise. They raised their weapons again, and I leapt forward to the attack. As the explosions rang out, and I felt something strike me hard on my right, I lashed out with my left claws, striking hard at one of the apes, who just barely twisted back so that I only raked lightly across its chest. I twisted sideways to bite at another ape, but my jaws clamped on nothing, the ape having moved out of the way with lightning speed.

Another stabbing pain erupted in my leg as I reached out to claw at another of the apes. This time I made solid contact, and the creature screamed as it pulled away from me, leaving its blood dripping from my claws. There was a whistling from above me, and I dodged sideways as a sparking cable fell toward me, the fire leaping from the end singeing my back and sending spasms through my limbs. Impossibly, one of the apes was behind me, and I felt a blade nick my skin as I spun around, swinging a claw that caught the dodging ape a glancing blow, enough to send it staggering against the wall.

I roared again, in pain as well as anger, and sprang again for the ape I had just struck. Pain dulled my reactions, however, and my claws plunged into the earth, the ape having rolled out of the way. Another report, and something nicked my shoulder. I turned, and found myself staring into a light so bright, so dazzling that it actually hurt my eyes, and I staggered back, blinking and then closing them, relying on scent and sound as I slashed forward. I was rewarded by contact, and the feel and smell of blood running over my claws. I opened my eyes again, and the ape was raising its gun, pointing straight at my chest.

The sound, the flash, and the explosion of pain were simultaneous, and I staggered backward and fell, unable for a moment to keep my feet. I heard the shuffling steps of one of the apes moving behind me, and a scrabbling as another one seemed to be using the wall to pull itself up. In front of me I could see only the ape I had attacked, holding a wound in its side with one hand, and deliberately pointing the gun at me with the other. I tried to stand, but although I felt the wound knitting together, it wasn't healing fast enough, and I couldn't quite stand. I stared at the ape's finger on the trigger of the gun, searching for any sign of movement, and readied myself for a quick change.

The alley exploded with a screaming as if all the denizens of Malfeas were loosed upon it. The ape in front of me glanced over his shoulder, letting the gun droop, and, for a moment, I could do nothing except follow his gaze. At first I thought that we were under attack by the Wyrm's minions, as a garish pink, clashing with a revolting blue, came barreling toward me, screaming horribly. Recognition came swiftly: Aspasia, dressed in blue, mounted on a pink bicycle, the screaming coming from some sort of siren on the front of the bike.

With recognition came action. The delay had let the wound in my chest heal so that I could move, and I launched myself at the fallen ape, ripping its hand apart as I pulled the gun from it. It collapsed, blood pumping from the shattered remains of his forearm, and I threw the gun across the alley, turning to face the other enemies. One was clawing at the air, desperately gasping for breath, while the other had sunk to its knees, its hands clamped over his ears. As I watched, the one that Oigimi was suffocating stopped struggling, a look of intense concentration on its face. I tried to leap toward it, but my wounds slowed me, and by the time I reached it, it had vanished.

I spun around, but it was nowhere to be seen, and its companions had disappeared as well. Their blood was still scattered about the alley, and I caught a glimpse of the gun lying against the wall, but of the attackers themselves, there was no sign. Aspasia was leaning her bike against a wall, away from the blood, and shivering slightly as she came over to me. I noticed that her feet were bare, and that her clothes were covered in distorted pictures of rabbits, all in the revolting blue. She crouched down beside me, and carefully ran her hands over my wounds. I could feel life - force flowing out of her, and for the first time I really understood what Oigimi had meant. I could feel my wounds closing even faster than normal, and soon I felt fully recovered, and well enough to let the Rage slip away, as the mass melted from my body and I reverted to the form of a wolf. Aspasia was the first to speak, but she seemed to be only musing aloud.

"They will remember, and they will tell, and then…" She broke off, and visibly took control of herself before continuing, clearly talking to me this time. "Now *they* really would have raped the Node." She hugged herself, shivering in the chill night air. "I must go home, or my parents might notice I'm gone. Are you all right now?"

"Yes. Who were they?" She glanced around, as if nervous of being overheard.

"Quintessence-thieves. Mages who gather their Tass from other mages' Nodes, even from your caerns, and who don't care what damage they cause. After all, they need never use the Node again."

"Do you think that they'll come back?" She shook her head.

"Node-raiders like them prefer easy pickings. I don't think they'll be over-eager to go up against a Garou again. If they do come, though, you can always send Oigimi for me." I started up.

"Send Oigimi?" She looked a bit surprised, and then smiled.

"Oh. I think you will probably want to talk to your familiar, then. I'll see you tomorrow." She got on her bike, and sped down the alley impossibly fast, swerving around the pools of blood with total control. I padded back into a park which was suspiciously free of wind and settled down into a trance.

"Oigimi…"

RECONCILIATION

MATT FORBECK

Paul was drinking again, but it wasn't doing him a damned bit of good. He stared at the glass of Glenlivet in his hand and contemplated its golden color, its biting aroma. He brought it to his lips again. It tasted like fire.

He swallowed it carefully, savoring the slow burn. He'd almost sucked half the bottle dry, and it hadn't had the slightest effect. He threw his glass away in anger. It narrowly missed the deejay's head and shattered against the wall behind her, showering the area with sparkling shards of glass and scotch.

The drone of conversation in the Black Hole screeched to a halt. For a long moment, Paul felt the eyes of the last few late-night stragglers upon him. The only sound in the nightclub was the pulsating music pounding out of the speakers near the deejay's booth. Then someone laughed, and the others joined in. Situation normal, all fucked up.

The deejay stared hard at Paul, who met her gaze solidly. Then Paul bared his fangs, and she flinched and looked away. Paul returned to his scotch, and realizing he had thrown away his glass, raised the bottle to his lips.

When he brought it down, Sebastian Melmoth was sliding into the seat across from him in the low booth. Sebastian was smiling broadly at him, but Paul declined to return the gesture. Sebastian's look turned to one of concern.

"My dear chap," Sebastian began, "what is it that's eating at your soul?"

Paul snorted and stayed silent. After a moment, he said, "I can't get drunk."

"Not on alcohol," Sebastian answered, his smile returning. "You're dead. Your heart beats no longer, so the blood cannot carry the booze to your brain. I admit to missing the sensations of a good glass of sherry myself from time to time, but after all, it still tastes the same. It's a small price to pay — don't you think? — for immortality."

Paul grimaced. This man before him — this creature — was the closest thing to a friend he had in this city. Father Steve Singer, his old roommate at Marquette University, was the only person he was closer to. Sebastian had been good to Paul, far kinder than custom demanded, and the very sight of him made Paul sick.

"That's just it, Sebastian. This whole life — no, this... existence. I can sense everything just like I could before, sometimes so sharply it cuts deep. This scotch, I can see it, I can smell it, and I can even taste it, but it has absolutely no effect upon me. It's like this every day. I walk around the city. I see people out there running around, racing against time to do what they can with themselves."

"Yes. Isn't it grand to be free of such constraints? To be able to ignore things like poverty and disease or the ravages

of time? To have eternity as the canvas upon which to paint
your accomplishments?"

Paul growled. "That's just it. Those 'constraints' are what
I considered inspiration. Now I feel like a shadow, unable
to affect those around me and, worse yet, to be affected by
them."

"But when you feed…" Sebastian began, but when he
saw the look of disgust on Paul's face, he stopped. "I see. I
forget that you were a man of the cloth before your
transformation. Of course these things would be troublesome
to someone of your moral standing."

Paul grunted. He was not eager to have Sebastian move
too far in this direction. Paul had vowed never to feed on
any of God's creatures, and that only left vampires. To drink
the blood of another vampire was to be controlled by that
creature, unless of course, the creature was dead. Killing a
vampire by sucking it dry was the worst crime a vampire
could commit, and Paul had done it often. Although he was
sure someone as sharp as Sebastian would have suspicions
about it, Paul was hardly about to admit to being a diabolist.

"That's part of the problem," Paul said, eager to change
the subject. "But what's really bothering me is that I feel so
lost."

Sebastian nodded. "Of course. As a priest, your life was
defined by your relationship with your God. Now, like the
rest of us," Sebastian waved broadly at the few other
occupants of the Vampire Club, all of whom were as undead
as they, "you are not in God's good graces."

A pained look crossed Paul's face. "How could I be? I've
become an abomination, the opposite of what I once was. I
feel like staking myself out in the middle of Golden Gate
Park and waiting for the sun. At least I'd get to see daylight
again one last time."

"Perhaps you're suffering from the bane of vampires
everywhere: seasonal affective disorder." Sebastian chuckled
at his little joke. "Truly, it can be depressing to always be

surrounded by darkness, to never feel the warmth of the sun. But then that should go to show you that we Kindred aren't so different from the kine we once were. If you prick us, do we not bleed?"

Sebastian's demeanor shifted once again to concern. "Many initiates into our little club suffer through their first few months. You've been unceremoniously served divorce papers by the human race, and like most such splits, it was emotionally messy. But just because you're dead, don't think that you have to give up the things of life. In your particular case, something a wise man once wrote leaps to mind: 'How else but through a broken heart may Lord Christ enter in?' It seems to me that now, more than ever, you're in need of that which got you through your living days."

Paul regarded Sebastian solemnly for a moment before bringing the bottle of scotch to his lips once again. This time when he lowered it, he had another visitor.

It was Tex R. Cainen, the manager of the secretive Vampire Club and its upstairs neighbor, the exclusive Alexandrian Club. Paul could normally hear Tex's boots clanging on the Black Hole's metallic floor from a mile away, but he'd been too caught up in his conversation with Sebastian to pay attention to anything else.

"Howdy, y'all," Tex began in his drawn-out drawl. "Pardon me, Paul, but Sebastian here is needed upstairs. There's some 'administrative duties' he needs to attend to." He flashed a wink at the two of them and turned to go.

"Smashing," said Sebastian. He got up to follow Tex and then turned to make his good-byes to Paul. After one look at the ex-priest's face, Sebastian called after Tex and asked him to return to the table.

As he ushered Tex into the seat he'd just vacated, he said, "My good man, our friend here is struggling with some inner demons, and I thought that perhaps he might benefit from your eloquent perspective on the matter of our mutual condition."

Tex looked up at Sebastian uncertainly. Then he noticed the bottle in Paul's hand. He flashed Sebastian a knowing smile. "Why, sure thing there, Sebastian. You just head on upstairs quick-like, though. I've got everything well in hand right here."

With a quick smile, Sebastian turned and left. Tex turned to Paul and started in. "Well there, Paul, lemme guess. You just figured out you can't get drunk no more, and unfortunately, that's what you want to do most. Tell me, was this a problem for you when you were breathing? Believe it or not, I think we've got some former AA members around here somewhere. If you like, I can see if I can scare one up for you."

Paul raised a hand to stop Tex's verbal barrage. "No, Tex, thank you. I wasn't an alcoholic before, and apparently there's no longer any chance of me starting down that road."

"What is it, then?" Tex rubbed his lantern jaw with a rough mitt. "A girl?" He raised his eyebrows. "That's it, isn't it? It's always some lady."

"Tex, I'm a priest."

"Well, no you ain't. Not anymore. You're dead, son. The old rules don't apply no more." Tex snapped his fingers. "That's what it is. You know, when you've been cold as long as I have, you tend to forget these things. You're like one of those plant-eaters they got so many of in this city."

"A vegetarian?"

Tex nodded emphatically. "Yep. Your problem, son, is that you're still thinking like a breather. You ain't part of the herd anymore, kid. You're a higher order of being. You shouldn't feel bad about feeding on the herd." His tone became conspiratorial. "That's what this is all about, isn't it?"

Paul was in too much shock to reply. Tex was comparing human beings to cattle, creatures to be slaughtered as the need arose.

"I'll take your silence as a yes. Look here, son, there's

nothing to be ashamed of. It kind of turned my stomach at first, too. Hell, most of you tenderfeet actually vomit on your first few times out. Don't worry. You'll get used to it."

Paul picked his jaw up off the table long enough to say, "How?"

Tex shook his head at him knowingly. "Come on, son, didn't you feed on your fellow creatures back when you kept banker's hours? You never had a nice thick steak? Or a barbecued chicken? Almost makes my mouth water just thinking about those things again. It's been a long time since I actually ate any regular *food*. You know what I mean?"

Paul nodded. He didn't know what else to do.

"Look, son, most of us don't feed on the warm ones because we want to. It's because we have to. My point is that you shouldn't feel bad about it. Did you cry over every hamburger you ever chowed on? This isn't a matter of conscience. It's about survival.

"The way I see it, our kind have been around since the beginning. We're not the monsters people think of us as. We're part of the natural order of things, just another step up on the food chain.

"Of course we've got into people's nightmares. Don't the predators always cause fear in the prey? But that shouldn't stop us from being what we are or from doing what we got to in order to survive. Hell, it *can't*."

Tex paused for a moment. "Is any of this sinking in?"

Paul nodded slowly, sadly.

"Well, then, kid, let me give you a little advice." Tex leaned forward across the table. "Make the most of your rookie years. I'm telling you, the hardest thing about being immortal is watching other people grow old and die." He sat back in his seat. "But if you tell anyone I said that, I'll deny it. All right?"

Paul nodded again. He didn't know what to say. He didn't think he knew much of anything right then.

Tex stretched his neck and looked around. The place was

empty except for them. "My, it's gotten late so quick. About how far away from here is your place?" Paul started to speak, but Tex pointed a finger to shut him up. "Don't tell me *where* it is, son. I don't want to know. Besides," he pointed at his ear, "the walls, you know."

"What time is it?"

"Fifteen minutes to dawn."

Paul cursed softly. "I'll never make it in time."

Tex grimaced. "Well, I'm sure we can set something up for you. Just wait here, and I'll be right back."

In just a few minutes, Sebastian entered the nightclub, stifling a yawn, and walked up to Paul's booth. "Well, Tex tells me you two were 'shooting the shit' and lost track of time. I suppose I should have mentioned it after we finished talking. After all, it was getting early even then.

"Tex asked me to make his good-byes to you on his behalf, since he's in a bit of a hurry to get home himself. As you know, you're welcome to spend the night here. We have no other guests tonight, so you'd have the aft hold all to yourself."

Paul stood up, leaving the bottle on the table. "I don't really have much of a choice, do I?"

"No," Sebastian smiled crookedly, "not really."

Sebastian led Paul to a door in the back of the club. It opened onto a dark chamber lit only by the dimness filtering in behind Sebastian and Paul. The floor of the hold was covered with futons and pillows. A metal stairway led up into the darkness.

"You'll have to pardon there not being any lights in here, but most of us are used to the darkness by now. Make yourself as comfortable as you can," Sebastian suggested. "Perhaps we'll continue our conversation in the morning."

Paul threw himself down on the cushions and was asleep before the door shut behind him, sealing him into the darkness.

He woke up early the next evening as he always did. He

was amazed that he had slept so soundly. If Sebastian or Tex had wanted to, they could have had someone come down and dispose of him during the day. It wasn't that Paul didn't trust them, but they were vampires. Then again, so was he.

Paul got to his feet and stumbled forward, feeling for the door. Eventually he found it, and he stepped back into the Black Hole. He knew that it must be barely twilight outside, even though the portholes in the grounded pleasure yacht that housed the Vampire Club had been painted over too thickly for any light to pass. Paul had always been an early riser, and vampirehood hadn't changed that fact, just the hour at which he rose. Likely Sebastian was still asleep.

Paul walked through the dark, empty nightclub and exited through the front door. He found himself in a room known as the Eternal Pageant. It was lit with red spots, and paintings of the 13 vampire clans were displayed on one wall, while a mural depicting a vampire's path to Golconda, a kind of vampirical heaven, filled the other.

Along the wall with the mural, a stairway led to the upper deck. There were two other doors in the room. One led to the library, and the other to Sebastian's sanctum. Paul strode up to the second door and listened at it. He heard nothing. He tried the door but it was locked.

For a long moment, Paul considered breaking down the door and killing Sebastian while he slept. Paul had sworn to help humanity by destroying the creatures that would feed upon them. The death of the owner of the Vampire Club would be a horrible blow to the creatures of San Francisco. It would put them on notice that they were no longer the predators but the prey.

But Sebastian had been a friend to Paul. And Paul had never seen him kill anybody or, for that matter, do anyone any sort of harm. Who was Paul to judge him? Didn't he have murderous cravings of his own?

Paul was tired of the slaughter. He'd killed several vampires since he'd been fanged, but there were only so many of the creatures he could destroy before drawing attention to himself and getting caught up in a war for his life with every other vampire in San Francisco.

The only other alternative was to leave town, but he had come to enjoy the city. He had made some friends here, including some vampires — like Sebastian — and he was reluctant to simply throw them away. Anyhow, running would do no good. He'd run out of Milwaukee — he understood that now — and if he didn't stop soon, he might never put an end to it. Also, what good was he doing with his life, simply killing a few vampires and then moving on? How was that helping anyone, really? More vampires simply sprang up in their place. It was impossible to stop them.

He was being swallowed up by death, and if something didn't give soon, he was afraid for what he might do — or become.

Cursing himself for a fool, Paul silently turned and left.

Upstairs in the Alexandrian Club, Paul stepped into a phone booth. First he phoned for a cab. Then he dialed up Marty Chin. Chin was another friend — a breather — an information trader who had realized that having Paul in his debt could only work to his favor. It was only with Chin's help that Paul had been able to purchase a place of his own in which to live. Most real-estate agents wouldn't meet with anyone after dark, so Chin had acted as Paul's proxy in the matter. And Chin had done him other favors as well. Paul trusted him as much as anyone else in this city.

"This is Marty Chin. May I help you?" Chin's voice came over the phone, slightly tinted by his Chinese accent.

"Hi, Marty."

"Father!" Chin seemed genuinely glad to hear from him. "What is it I can do for you?"

Paul told him.

When the cab arrived, Paul got in hurriedly and gave the cabby the address that Marty had supplied. He knew he was failing to hide his agitation. The cabby kept one bloodshot eye on him the entire trip, but Paul ignored him.

St. Jude's was in a run-down part of town. According to Chin, it had been scheduled to be closed several years ago due to lack of attendance, but apparently the bishop had never gotten around to actually giving the order.

When he walked in through the front door, Paul was surprised for a moment that he hadn't instantly been struck down. The power of God, he remembered, only worked against a creature like himself if directed by the will of a believer. Since no one had actively opposed his entry, he had been able to stride freely into the church.

The church was old and in poor repair, but it was free of dust and cobwebs. Some of the lights had burned out, and those that were working were dim. Votives burned softly in a niche off to the left. It seemed as if no one else was there.

Keeping his head down, Paul crept slowly down the center aisle like the prodigal son returning home, trying not to make too much noise on the creaking floorboards. After stepping on a particularly loud one, Paul looked up. His eyes darted straight to the crucifix hanging over the altar.

Like Christ, Paul had died and been resurrected, but what good had come to the world? He was a creature of evil. He caught his breath and lowered his head in shame. He made his way into a pew and got down on his knees.

He reached into the breast pocket of his brown bomber jacket and pulled out a large wooden cross. The lower end of it had been sharpened to a point so it could be used as a stake.

It was an instrument of both good and evil. The fact that it could keep other vampires at bay had reinforced his faith in God — that was his salvation. But he also used it to kill those creatures — people not too different from those they once lived among. That was his damnation.

Sebastian had been right. Vampires weren't so different

from the living. Some of them fed on animals, just like most people did, often without even killing the creatures. And some of them were horrible, cruel bastards that did their best to scare the hell out of their victims before killing them, getting high on the adrenaline coursing through their hot blood. As a priest, Paul had heard many confessions. He knew that the Kindred weren't the only ones who harbored such darkness in their souls.

Paul was sick with himself. When his life had been torn from him, he'd been enraged. He'd turned that wrath upon those who shared his fate, thinking that by destroying them, he could cleanse the horrible stains on his own soul. But doing evil to evil was still evil.

But he wasn't entirely irredeemable, was he? Was anyone — even a vampire? In his short time in San Francisco, both Sebastian and Tex had shown him friendliness, even kindness. But in this world of darkness, such acts were precious and few.

If Paul thought he was worthy of it, he might try to bring the word of God to the Kindred. He had read Sebastian's "History of the Camarilla" in the Vampire Club's library, and he knew that no one had ever tried such a thing before. Who would be strong enough to be a missionary to the Kindred? If you were a human and knew so much about them, they would most likely kill you. And all vampires, by definition, would have difficulty condemning sinners for the same sins they were committing.

No. Too much had happened. There was too much blood on his hands for him to ever forgive himself.

Paul suddenly realized that he was crying. Crimson tears dripped slowly down his cheeks, contrasting sharply with his pale skin. He wiped his face carefully with his fingers and then cleaned the blood off on his pants.

Then there was a hand on his shoulder. "Are you all right, my son?"

Paul nearly jumped out of his skin. He spun around on

his knees and looked up to see an elderly nun gazing down at him. He had been so engrossed with his own thoughts, he hadn't heard her come up behind him. She seemed nearly as startled as he was, but she had barely even flinched. He could see the concern etched on her wrinkled face, although it was mostly in shadows from the light framing her from overhead.

"You seem troubled, my son. Is something wrong?" She gestured at the stains on his shirt where some of his tears had fallen unnoticed. "Have you been hurt?"

Paul stared at the vibrant red marring his white shirt. "Yes, sister," he managed to get out. "I have." He looked up into her eyes and saw only a person's desire to help a stranger. Perhaps there was still hope after all.

"God forgives all my son, as long as you are truly repentant. It seems to me that you are ready for such a blessing."

"Are you sure, sister?"

"I could call for the priest. Would you like to make your reconciliation?"

Paul stood up and took the nun's hand in his own. "Yes, sister, that's exactly what I want." And with that, he stepped out of the pew and strode out of the church, back into the cold November night.

Paul walked down the deserted street until he reached a basketball court. There was a pay phone there under a street light, and he picked up the receiver and dialed a number he knew by heart. It had once been his own.

It was two hours later in Milwaukee, but Father Steve Singer had not yet gone to bed. He was reading by himself when the phone rang. He picked it up, and on the other end of the line, there was a voice he had given up hope of ever hearing again.

"Paul," he said, "is that really you?"

"Yes, Steve, it's me. And I need your help."

Paul told Steve about his night and about the epiphany

he'd had in the church. He was going to bring light into the darkness and become God's first messenger to the vampires. "But first I need you to do something for me, Steve."

"Yes? Anything."

Paul took a deep breath before he began.

"Bless me, Father, for I have sinned. My last confession was... a lifetime ago."

SHADOWPLAY

J. G. BANKS

Iaisha Monroe realized she should be running, screaming, like everyone else fleeing the small auditorium, but her body was responding more like she was seeing her first man after years on a deserted island, and that man being Denzel Washington. It was an odd reaction to have on seeing a real, live, honest-to-god werewolf.

She had watched him come in, another straggler to the emergency city council meeting called on account of last night's earthquake, a tall, attractive man with silver hair falling softly over his shoulders. At over six feet herself, Monroe noticed tall men, and the hair was striking all on its own. He'd said something about shoring up the businesses damaged in the 'quake, then let it drop as he stared at her. *Into* her. Something happened then, something passed between them like a shared secret. And he'd turned into a silver-furred wolfman.

Panic had ripped through the crowd then, like the concussion front of an explosion. The other councilpersons sitting with her had toppled the table off the stage in their rush to get away; one of the plainclothes police officers had drawn a bead on it then just ran away instead; a woman with hair a shade of comic-book blue just leaned back in her seat, rolled her eyes up into her head, and passed quietly into unconsciousness while another person pitched forward in the same state amidst a clatter of collapsing folding chairs.

And yet so far, all the werewolf had done was become one. Monroe stood, facing it. For a moment she wondered it this was some sort of elaborate Halloween trick — but she knew it wasn't as strongly as she knew the two other people in the auditorium were out cold, not dead. There was a *realness* to the werewolf no makeup, mirror or movie trick could duplicate.

"What — whadda you want?" she asked.

"When will you rage?" the werewolf asked. It sounded like it didn't expect an answer. Well, she hadn't, either. "I need your time," it continued

Monroe looked around them. "Looks like the meeting's been canceled."

"What I have to say isn't for the cameras." He flicked a pointed ear toward the abandoned KRON video camera set up along one wall, then tipped his chin to one of the security cameras bolted to the ceiling, sweeping lazily toward him. "I'll meet you in the garage."

And he left, eight feet tall and all silver fur; and while part of her felt she should be running for security, some other part, deeper and less civilized, followed him with a want so intense it was frightening — all the more so because she didn't know what it was she wanted from him. She felt as if she were starving but had no concept of eating; and the silver werewolf had just shown her a picture of the world's juiciest prime rib.

She followed him as surely as if she were on a leash.

■

Peter Rivard loped out of City Hall into the sprawling underground parking garage that underlaid the entire Civic Center complex, shifting from the wolfman Crinos to the human Homid form even as the door shut behind him. Naked but human-seeming, he launched into song and began sauntering toward his car. In San Francisco, he wouldn't get a second look. Well, not until the gendarmerie showed up, anyway. But if the scene kept playing out as well as it had been, he'd be long dressed by then. Gone, too — with a newfound lost cub. All right, she was marked by the Wyrm. Other Garou had been marked by the Wyrm. Admittedly, he didn't *know* any, except possibly young Calley — the sept's reaction to Aunt-to-Strays returning home with him made it seem likely; and neither did he know of any recently — say within the last generation or two — who'd successfully freed themselves of the taint of the Wyrm. Also admittedly, it seemed she might be of the Shadow Lord tribe, and if he know Nikos Ripthroat, their leader here in San Francisco, they'd just as soon cull as cure her.... Well, any idea had its drawbacks.

With a screech of tires, a car rounded the corner in front of him far too fast. Rivard jumped to the side, but in his human form he was hardly fast enough. A fender caught his foot and he went sprawling. The car stopped abruptly, the tires protesting once more, and the driver poked her head out.

Rivard recognized her by her bloodshot left eye. She'd been in the meeting, in the row behind him. It had been months since he'd seen this much fear in a human face.

"Oh my god! Sir, are you all right?"

"I'm fine," Rivard answered, standing. "I'm glad you weren't in more of a hurry."

She was too panic-stricken to save face by lying. "I gotta get outta here! I just saw a *werewolf*! It was…"

Rivard watched her eyes grow wide as she finally took in his nudity and his silver hair and the obvious conclusion rose to the top. "Third floor, ladies lingerie," he said, and as he went "Ding!" the woman screeched, pulled her head back inside her car and floored it. She fishtailed around another corner and was gone. Rivard shook his head. "Oops."

He found his car and crawled in through the sunroof because he felt like it. He dug into the glove box, pulled out a small tape recorder, thumbed it on and set it on the dashboard, then climbed into the back seat where a spare change of clothing lay. As he dressed he dictated:

"Umm — 'Feral Heart,' Peter Rivard, first draft, 24 November. Fade in. Flashback. Establishing, abandoned mansion, night. Stormy, but no rain. The storm is *not natural*. Cut to interior mansion, a bedroom. The room is swathed in shadow. A woman lies on the four-poster that dominates the room, obviously giving birth. Through a window we can see an ancient tree and flashes of lightning. The woman is Garou, and with each flash of lightning, she shapeshifts toward the wolfman. In the last lightning flare before we cut, she is fully Crinos.

"Cut to exterior mansion. We can see a window, obviously the birthing Garou's bedroom. Indistinct but clearly menacing figures move against the house, then seem to vanish. In the foreground, blocked from view of the bedroom by the tree, is a huge, misshapen Wolf-form Garou, tearing the throat out of another. The misshapen Garou is a Black Spiral Dancer.

"Cut to interior bedroom. This is the moment! The Crinos Garou delivers her child — it looks fully human. As the birth concludes, a tree limb comes crashing through the window! The Garou turns, startled. As she does, figures materialize out of the shadows and attack her! These are fomori, twisted servants of the Wyrm. Against so many she doesn't have a chance, and soon her blood runs down the walls. At the conclusion of the battle, the Dancer walks in, shifting from Lupus to Crinos as he does. He takes the child in his arms and speaks.

"Black Spiral Dancer: 'The Wyrm claims this Shadow Lord. It places its Mark upon her!' The Dancer raises the baby over his head and the fomori gesture, together weaving some type of spell. The Dancer continues: 'It is done. When the time is right, this Shadow Lord shall lead her packmates and her tribe into the Wyrm. Then together, the Shadow Lords and the Black Spiral Dancers will bring down the remaining 12 tribes of the Garou! Without her defenders, Gaia shall die in the embrace of the Wyrm!'

"Well, that will do. Work on the Dancer's exposition. And find a name for him."

Rivard slipped into a black sweater vest, then clambered back into the front seat. A moment later he was pulling in front of the door he'd left the Civic Center through, and Iaisha Monroe was just coming through it.

◼

Monroe knew who was driving the Ford Tempo before it stopped in front of her. Leaning across the passenger seat, he unlocked the door and pushed it open. She peered in. "Why should I go anywhere with you?"

"Because you laugh in the face of danger?" he asked back. "Because I'm irresistibly charming? Because I know what happened inside and you don't have a clue? Maybe your feet are tired and this is the closest place to sit down? Or maybe you have a thing for silver Tempos? I don't know: Why should you go anywhere with me?"

"Fine," Monroe said tightly. "You just go on and have a good time wherever it is you're going. I'm history." She turned and began to move back to the door.

"It really happened," the werewolf chanted through the window. Then he asked, "How long can you go on not knowing just what happened or why?"

She turned and glared at him. "Till they plant me in the ground, mister!"

"Or you can have all the gory details in a ten-minute ride. I guarantee it'll change your life!" He crooked a finger at her. "Come with me to the Casbah."

"You are some kind of lunatic—"

That's the nicest thing you've said to me so far. That's the sort of thing that makes us werewolves feel all warm and fuzzy. You can feel that way too, you know."

"Mister, you are some kind of *fool*!"

Suddenly his tone was all seriousness. "Iaisha. Get in the car. You know you want to; you know you're going to. Otherwise you wouldn't be standing there babbling at me. So get in!"

She shuddered, angry and fearful. He was right. She went back to the car, leaned in through the still-open door. "Look, if this is some kind of black/white thing and you've got something to prove…"

"You'll have to find another soapbox to stand on. This is a Garou thing."

"What's a 'Garou'?"

"In the car."

She rolled her eyes, then turned to sit, and the car jumped forward a foot. She barely caught herself on the door. "Yo!"

"What? Get in!"

She tried and the car zipped forward again. "Stop, dammit!"

"Oh," the werewolf said accusingly. "That's how it works, is it? Now that you know you can shapeshift into a werewolf just by wanting it you're looking for an excuse, and I get to be it! Huh, is that it?" He managed to stop the car short enough to actually make the tires squeal, then stormed out of it like an angry cabby. "Well, Miss Iaisha Monroe, Miss I'm-On-The-City-Council-So-You'd-Better-Kiss-Up-To-Me, old Peter Rivard can show you a thing or two about *that*!"

And he reached out and swatted her. But the hand that hit her, and the arm and shoulder it was connected to, were suddenly huge and covered in silver fur. She slammed back into a car, and its alarm began shrieking. The arm he'd hit was tingling. She ducked between cars.

"Don't cower!" Rivard yelled. His face was twisted in fury. Monroe wondered what she'd done to deserve this, to be ripped apart by a monster; she hadn't gotten into the car, all she'd done was *talk*. It was something out of a nightmare.

Yet at the same time she felt her anger growing, hot and pure.

"Don't cower!" Rivard roared again. "Fight back! *Change!*" And he rushed her, his huge paw swinging up and over as if he intended to smash her into the pavement.

Monroe scrabbled backward and caught up against the bumper of the Ford behind her. She scrambled up onto its hood as Rivard's paw came down. He gouged furrows into the concrete where she'd been moments before. She crabbed backward, hit the edge of the hood, and fell off.

Her head slammed into the fender of the car next to the Ford. Her shoulder took the rest of he weight of the fall, and she cried out as pain rayed out from it. Her teeth snapped together so hard she wasn't sure if she'd heard the shoulder break or not. She tasted salty wetness in her mouth, thought she was bleeding, finally recognized it was tears.

Who the hell was he that he could do this to her? Who the *hell* was he!

He appeared like the revenge of the Lord over the hood of the Ford, and she realized that, with the way she'd fallen, he could look straight down her skirt.

Her Rage erupted. She roared out, a melange of pain, anger, frustration and humiliation. She reached out for a weapon, found the side mirror on the car she'd hit, tore it off and threw it at him.

It caught him full in the face; but when it dropped away, leaving a deep, bloody gash along his left cheek and eye, he was grinning.

That *bastard*!

She heard herself growl low in her throat. Almost before she knew she'd moved she had pounced, and then they were both falling backward onto the car with the shrieking alarm, her jaws snapping for his throat while she tried to pin his arms down. She relished the look of surprise on his face as he fell underneath her and the look of sudden pain that soon followed it as she raked he claws across his chest.

"Iaisha! That's enough!"

She found herself bounding away from him at his snapped command, feeling for a moment like a child who had disobeyed a parent's command. Still, she felt the victory was hers. He'd think twice about treating her like that again.

Yet he was still grinning at her. "You haven't even noticed, have you?" he asked. "Look at yourself."

She did.

All she really noticed that first glance was the fur, thick and black, and the claws, tapered and wicked. She screamed; or it would have been a scream had her throat still been human. Still, her howl reverberated through the parking garage with fear, anger — and delight.

"Iaisha," Rivard said gently, "it's all right. You're Garou. A werewolf, just as I told you." He sat up and reached out.

"*Don't touch me!* What did you *do* to me?!"

"I didn't do anything. You were born this way. You've been Garou all along — you just didn't know it. All I did was bring you through first Change—"

"You fucking *bastard*!" Monroe snarled. "I have a job, a life — I'm on the fucking city council! I'm not some kind of *monster*! I don't have *time* for this kind of shit! What, now every month I have PMS and I howl at the moon?" She crossed her arms and sat down heavily on the hood of the alarmed car. It buckled beneath her. She stood and turned to see the damage she'd done. "Jesus!"

"Gaia. You're in Crinos form right now, the traditional wolfman, and uh — you weigh probably four times what you used to. There are four other forms, from full wolf to full human. Crinos is the middle one, and the one in which you can do the most damage. It's the purest physical expression of a Garou's Rage, that quality which allows us to change form at will, perform extraordinary feats and be unwelcome guests at dinner parties and china shops. Probably the thing you'll spend most of your time doing is learning how to control and use your Rage. Can you take Homid form now?"

"You don't give up, do you?"

"Never."

"Yeah. Well, I don't forget — ever. Okay, Rivard: how?"

"Just think about it. It's not that easy and it's not that complicated all at the same time, but you have to do it a few times before you know what I'm talking about."

"Like sex. All right." She closed her eyes, and in a moment was human-appearing once more. It didn't take her any time at all to realize she was naked. "Jesus fucking Christ! Where the hell are my clothes?!"

Rivard pointed behind her. "Back there where you tore out of them. You'll get used to being naked. It's another part of being Garou. I generally keep a spare set in my car for the benefit of humans. And if you're worried about it, there aren't very many Garou who get excited at the sight of nudity. It would be like getting aroused by a tree, or embarrassed by seeing a cat without any clothes on."

She resisted the temptation to cover up. Obviously the man got off on seeing her embarrassed. "I'm a woman, not a cat, and I'm naked in a public parking garage on a weeknight. You're a psycho, a woman-hater and a pervert who gets off on humiliating women in public places. How'm I supposed to get out of here?"

"I told you I'd give you a lift."

"That didn't work too well last time."

"It worked just fine. You know you're Garou now and you're ready to start training. That's what I wanted."

"You just wanna stay on my shit list, don't you?"

"Not particularly, but if that's what it takes to make sure you're ready, then I'm willing."

Monroe looked at Rivard's car. It was two cars and a traffic lane away: call it twenty feet. The door to the Civic Center was just beyond; she'd have to go around the car and in front of it to get in.... The hell with it, she decided. It was only the difference between ending her career and only ruining it. "Let's go." She made a point of walking at a normal pace, when every part of her was screaming "Hurry! Run!" She hadn't let this much all hang out even at college, and her body seemed to bounce and jiggle far more than she remembered from this morning's shower. But they reached his car without anyone seeing her and he got in, and the car didn't move at all when she paused before getting in; then they were on their way.

■

Rivard was pleased that Monroe let him do most of the talking. She stiffened a moment when he turned away from the Civic Center, then asked where they were headed. He honestly answered his apartment building. She mostly stared out the window after that, looking at him only for clarifications or a question. He told her of the Garou and their position as Gaia's defenders, which led into an explanation of Gaia that ended up an explanation of the Weaver, the Wyld and the Wyrm, which segued nicely into an explanation of just what the Garou were defending against. And he felt her resistance grow with each word he said.

He was dumbfounded, bordering on frustrated. He'd never been rebuffed this soundly. She obviously understood what he was saying, her questions showed that. Either she didn't understand the import of what he was telling her, or she just didn't want to hear it from him. Well, maybe one of the others could get through to her. A Garou on the city council could be vitally important.

He pulled to a stop in front of his apartment building. "I'd like you to meet some friends of mine, if you don't mind."

"Without clothes, I most certainly do."

"Umm — just a moment. Don't go anywhere." He was already moving out of the car as she grimaced, and in a few steps he was walking into the foyer.

"Peter!" cried Jana Polokowski, the building's manager and one of Rivard's packmates. "You're all right! The news has been saying there was a gunman at the council meeting tonight!"

"Oh, that was me. You haven't got any extra—" He stopped himself. Polokowski was five and a half feet tall at best. In heels, Monroe had been taller than he was — at 6'2" that wasn't a common occurrence. "No, I guess not," he finished. Polokowski just shook her head.

Zakiya, his other female packmate, was certainly tall enough but was far too slender. Ah well. He moved to his apartment door and started to enter, then paused. "Jana, are you free this evening? I've got a lost cub with me, and I'm beginning to think I may not be her best teacher."

"Sure. But I don't know what you'd want me to teach her."

"About being Garou, defending against the Wyrm, that sort of thing. She seems a little reluctant."

"Okay," Polokowski replied half-heartedly.

Rivard nodded and entered his rooms. He pulled a pair of sweatpants and a matching sweatshirt from a bureau drawer and went back to the car with them. He didn't realize until he saw her still waiting that he'd half-expected her to leave.

"You've got a neighbor who'll probably complain to you 'cause I cussed him out. He wanted a free show. He didn't get one."

"I'm sorry. I hurried."

"Hey." She struggled awkwardly into the clothing, then followed Rivard inside.

Polokowski was waiting. She saw Monroe, looked at Rivard and said, "Oh, Jesus, Pete. You aren't serious — of course you are. Ms. Monroe, I'm so sorry. I'm Jana Polokowski, the manager. You might want to call somebody; the news is saying your whereabouts are unknown. You can use the phone in my apartment." She pointed to the open door.

"Thank you very much, Miss Polokowski," Monroe said, and went to call her office.

"Pete, what is she doing here?!"

"I told you: She's Garou."

"She's a member of the city council!"

"That's just a job. Being Garou is her life. She needs to learn it before it's too late."

"And who made that decision? You? No, don't even answer: I already know. Sometimes I can't *believe* how cocky you are! You just — do what you want, then wait for the world to fall in behind you and pronounce it good! The really amazing part is that that *happens*! A *lot*! I mean, this place is turning into 'Peter Rivard's Home for Wayward Souls and Center for the Redemption of the World As We Know It,' apparently with the blessing of all involved!"

Rivard shrugged. "Not hers. I brought her through her first Change. She doesn't want to know more. She's a Shadow Lord; she's got to be ready. If nothing else, she needs to be able to defend herself when Nikos Ripthroat gets wind of her. Shadow Lords play for keeps, and Iaisha's Wyrm-tainted. That's not generally a good risk. They'll probably just kill her to be sure."

Polokowski was shocked. "Does she know that?"

"No. I didn't want to scare her."

"Pete, does the word 'incentive' mean anything to you? Why don't you go… write something. Stay out of our hair, okay?"

"Fine. We won't have very long. I'll have to call the Western Eye tonight and let them know. I don't know how long or how willing Celeste will be to keep this quiet, but as soon as he gets word, Ripthroat will be here."

■

"No, that's the right address," Monroe said into Polokowski's phone. "I was reading it off the manager's mail. His apartment is 102. Find me anything you can, Trina — back taxes, late fees, whatever. I want this white boy to know who he's messing with. Oh, and Trina, I need some clothes and underwear when you come, okay? No, I told you I'm fine. Let's just say I fell in something rank, okay? Thanks, Trina. See you when you get here." Monroe hung up the phone and put the electric bill back where she had found it, then slowly browsed Polokowski's apartment. She was just nudging the sofa cushions back into place when Polokowski came in.

"Hi," the manager said. "Can I get you something to drink or something?" Monroe shook her head. "Pete's a good guy, I just want you to know that. He's just a little… dedicated."

"That's not the word I would've used."

"Well, there are those who wouldn't argue with you." She sat on an arm of the sofa. "Are you really Garou?"

"There's something wrong with me. I don't know what. And — I imagine that I turn into a werewolf, yes."

"You don't 'turn into' a werewolf, you *are* one. Lots of people are."

"Not people like me. I can hold down a job, I'm important in this city."

Polokowski frowned. "Roderick Harrington in Silicon Valley. Nikos What's-his-face downtown. They're both Garou, they're both important, they both *live* their jobs. You don't believe me? Ask them. You can get away with it, now. You're a member of the club. You won the birthright lottery."

"You don't sound real pleased. Are you a werewolf, too?"

"No. I'm Kinfolk. That means I'm related by blood to someone who's a werewolf; in my case, my grandfather. He was a Bone Gnawer. That's a tribe of werewolves." She smiled. "Being a Bone Gnawer is a lot like owning a Yugo. But it beats the hell out of walking."

"Have you ever met Nikos?"

"Not personally, no."

"You will. Soon." She began playing with the corner of one of the sofa throw pillows. "He's the leader of the Shadow Lords here. Pete says you're a Shadow Lord. The twelve tribes are kind of cliquish and he'll want you. The only problem with that is that you're marked by the Wyrm. The Wyrm is the Bad Guy. Are you religious at all? Think the Beast, and you've got 666 tattooed on your forehead. A lot of Garou would rather not take the chance on you, and would just kill you—" Monroe leapt up in alarm, trying to find the door and watch Polokowski simultaneously. "Sit down, councilwoman; Pete's not like that and neither am I. In fact, Pete's kinda notorious for taking misfits under his wing. You'll be okay with him as long as he can prove to himself he hasn't screwed up. But to do that you're going to have to *try*. It won't be fun for him to stand up to Nikos — his name among the Garou is Ripthroat — but to him you're worth it."

Monroe raised an eyebrow. "Why?"

Polokowski laughed. "*That's* the $64,000 question. I can't answer it. I don't think *he* really can. Pete's... a creature of impulse. He does things on a whim, on a hunch, because it seems like a good idea at the time; and it usually works out okay. It's like he's been — well, never mind what it's like he's been. But it's hard on those around him. Like you. Like me. We don't get the security of knowing there's a 'why' for anything he does. He never gets to the stage where he considers how you might feel about what he's done. He just does a thing, and you and I have to deal with it."

"So I'm supposed to do what he says just because he says it. Abraham Lincoln freed the slaves, remember?"

"Goddammit! Councilwoman, you can be as proud as you want to be, or as proud as you need to be — just don't let it get in the way of people who want to help you!

"This isn't about race. It's not about gender, or age, or whether or not there'll be Social Security money when I'm sixty-five. It's about saving a planet, or trying to, and about having some pride and place whether you do or not! You don't need to be black or white for that; you don't even have to be Garou. What you do have to do is look, and listen, and learn! And if you can't do those, then maybe we should just let Ripthroat do to you what he does best!"

Monroe looked incredulous. "Well, fuck you!"

■

Peter Rivard lay on his side in the darkness of the apartment building's cool cement basement floor, curled around and staring into what resembled an old firepit. It was a caern, older than San Francisco, older than California, nearly older than humanity. Most who knew of it regarded it as a shell, a husk, the slough of a great power; but to Rivard it was more than that. It had been a Visions caern when it was active, and he was convinced in some way that it would be again, still was.

And in the meantime, it was the place he went to gather himself, when thought was too fast or too slow, too confused or too rigid, when his writing wasn't enough and Rage wasn't useful. This caern's light shone inside. He'd needed light after his call to the Sept of the Western Eye.

A figure lay down on the floor across the caern from him. "This is not very much like days past," said Zakiya.

"Which days?"

"You. Me. Colson. Trust."

"Not very much. We were all… driven… then."

"What would you have her do, Peter?"

"Just let me help!"

"Echoes…" Zakiya breathed. "He may be your best friend. You are certainly his. You are mine. Yet we should all be enemies. Perhaps we have not tried enough?"

"All the effort was twenty-five years ago, so we wouldn't slaughter each other."

"Mmm, yes, it begins to come back to me now. Tell me again how Colson saved your life, and forever revised your opinion of vampires. It's such a thrilling story."

Rivard looked at her in the darkness, puzzled, expectant. "He never saved my life. You know that."

"Then tell me of the terrible atrocity from which you saved the lady werespider, thus learning the value of trust and allies."

"You know as well as I do that never happened."

"Then a union forged in despair and tempered through hardship? Or perhaps a mutual love of fine things?"

"You're reaching, Zakiya."

"Then what created such a strong bond between Garou, Ananasi and vampire? The Garou believe the Ananasi and vampires servants of the Wyrm; vampires regard Garou as an excellent entree and fear the Ananasi, the Ananasi regard the Wyrm as evil but not vampires and regard Garou as a mortal enemy. Perhaps they are only my perceptions, but I see there several stumbling blocks for friendship. Yet that friendship is fact."

"Time. Shared experience. Trust. We don't have the benefit of the first two, and Iaisha won't give me the last."

"The first can be bought, even from Ripthroat. Perhaps *especially* from Ripthroat. The second can't occur as long as you're hiding, but with Ripthroat's visit pending, I'd certainly say there was potential for it. As to the last, the first two are its coin."

"Why are you telling me all this, Zakiya? I usually have to drag answers out of you."

"Sympathy? For what you will have to drag from Ms. Monroe?

"Besides, if you don't win on occasion, you won't continue to play. And it is time to play."

■

Monroe was pacing the hallway, waiting impatiently for Trina to show up. She kept her face professionally neutral when she saw Rivard and an exotic-looking black woman come through a door that obviously led to the building's basement. They moved too close together to have just been switching laundry.

They always went after the pretty ones.

"Ms. Monroe," Rivard began, "I owe you an apology for my behavior. I'm very sorry I've put us all in this position. I can't undo the knowledge I've given you, and you'll still have to integrate your being a Garou into your life, but I can at least treat you like a human being instead of a pup or a chess piece to move across some board. Can we start again that much?"

"Now see, there you go! Every time you try to make us move, it doesn't work so you come on with the nice. I've heard it before, Rivard. If you want to be nice to me, I don't want you to talk to me anymore. My administrative assistant will be here in a couple of minutes, and I'm gonna change into my own clothes, and I'll be outta here. *That's* what kind of nice I want from you. Can you do that for me? I didn't think so."

"Well, actually, I *can* give you that, with qualifications. The first is that, like it or not, you're Garou. You're susceptible to Rage now, which means you can find yourself changing when you don't expect or want it. You'll have to be on guard for that. If you know when you were born, be careful on nights that match the phase of the moon then — you'll be more susceptible to Raging. Another is you can't tell anybody what happened to you, including your assistant. We like to keep a low profile, in general. There's a protective mechanism called the Delirium that'll help: Basically, any humans who see you as a werewolf will come up with some explanation — any explanation — to rationalize what they've seen. But it's not one hundred percent. The other is that I'd like you to come back, on your own, soon, to learn more. Will that do? Your convenience, your pace?"

The door buzzer sounded from Rivard's apartment. "That's my assistant," Monroe said. "Tell you what, Rivard: I'll think about it. If I like it, I'll give you a call." She moved to the door and pulled it open.

A man stood there, big, hulking in fact, seeming shaggy and unkempt despite his good clothing and the stylish leather trenchcoat he wore. His hands were shoved far down into the coat's pockets, and the bulges there were far too large for hands. Monroe thought she would be gunned down right there. He smiled, and it was the look that serial killers aspired to. "Avon," he sang. "Are you the lady werewolf of the house?"

Rivard gently moved her aside. "It's all right, Iaisha. I was expecting someone like him."

Monroe let herself be moved. She felt an odd sort of fear

in her chest, of a kind that made her want to hide in a closet or under a bed; and that, in turn, made her angry, the same kind of anger she'd felt in the parking garage under the Civic Center. She knew what would happen if she gave in to that anger. And suddenly she realized this man was a werewolf, and nowhere near as good-natured as Rivard.

"I don't know you," Rivard told the man.

"Well, I know you, Wyrmtempter. And after your stunt last month, I don't think there's a Garou in southern California who doesn't know of you." He pointed at Zakiya with his chin. "That must be the Spiderlady. There's three missing: the humans and the metis. Where are they?"

They all heard the sound of a shotgun round being chambered, at nearly the same time Polokowski's door opened. "Go ahead and talk," Polokowski said.

"My, we've got all those happy homemaker skills down pat, haven't we? Don't worry about it. I'm not here to tussle; if I were we'd be doing it by now, on my terms. I'm just here to make sure the cub's really a cub, which is obvious, and a Shadow Lord, which seems pretty damn likely from her human form, and to tell her that Nikos Ripthroat would like to see her at his home at her earliest convenience. He does add that he expects to be out of town for a few weeks come the weekend, so sooner is better. Here's a card. It's in my pocket, ma'am," he called out to Polokowski's door, "so don't shoot me." He slowly pulled his hand from his pocket, and it was perfectly Crinos.

Monroe remembered Rivard doing the same thing when he had attacked her in the garage. She panicked, and Rage took over. In a moment she was fully Crinos and was racing toward the man in blind fury. He calmly stepped back and tapped her on the shoulder as she came close. Monroe went sprawling as though he'd clubbed her. Zakiya moved toward her, transforming as she moved into the gaunt, black, four-armed shape that was her Lilian form, the Ananasi equivalent of Crinos, and began spraying a thick fluid from her arms over the frenzied Garou. In a moment she was pinned to the floor in oversized spiderwebs.

"Definitely Shadow Lord," the man said as he handed the now slightly crumpled card to Rivard. "Make sure she gets there in one piece, eh, Wyrmtempter?"

"Only if she wants to be there," said Rivard. "We're doing this her way, her speed. You'd best go. I don't want to have to sit on her all night."

"Hey," he said, "I'm just the messenger boy. Nice piece of work, by the way. Simple, sweet. G'night." He left and pulled the door closed behind him.

"Well," Rivard commented to no one in particular, "that was nowhere near as traumatic as I'd expected it would be. Zakiya, can you let her up?"

"Easily. She is already coming to herself."

The more human she became the more embarrassed Monroe looked. Fully human and fully freed, but still sitting on the floor, she asked, "I lost it, didn't I?" Rivard nodded. "Why? I mean, I know why, but *why?*"

"It's called frenzy, and it can hit you just as suddenly as that. You'll find yourself checking it all the time: when things are going badly at a council meeting, when someone cuts in front of you on the freeway, when the person in front of you in the express checkout has sixteen items and not fifteen. What we call the Beast is awake within you now. Controlling it will require constant work, and even at your best everyone will know it's there. We can try to teach you how to accommodate it so that it doesn't rule you, but it may be the hardest thing you've done yet."

"Yeah. Well." She was silent for a moment. "I guess I don't need to maul people in their cars.

"Can I get a little help?"

ALL ROOTLESS
ANGELS FALLING

A. G. MARTIN

November 3: My name is Andrew Malone, and this is my journal. I'm writing this to serve as something for the world to remember me by when I'm gone, because I think my time's going fast. After all these years of going through death more than half-asleep, I finally feel that I'm awake, and I need to write quicker to catch up while there's time.

Suddenly, it's something I care about. Being dead means I've already missed most of my chances to leave some traces behind. I didn't build any lasting legacies or make any timeless impressions on the world. If I disappeared, I'd like for there to be something left behind to testify that I was here. This book isn't much, but it'll speak for me when I'm gone. Even if no one but the fascist Establishment bullies ever read this, that's better than nothing.

Here's why I need to write fast: They

took my house today. When I resigned my slave-chaining contracts with the Establishment, I don't know what I was thinking. I was too busy seeing the sky and remembering what the stars looked like or something; I don't know, maybe I was almost pretending to be alive for awhile. I should have realized that the world goes on no matter how many personal revelations you have. No matter what kind of glorious visions the shadows on the inner walls of your house give you, you should always remember that the ground can crush your house at any time. And the Establishment is the ground, for the dead.

I don't know what I thought. That they'd actually let me go? Too damn busy seeing the sky and thinking I remembered the world, I suppose. I never thought they could turn it all on me. But they did. Growing up in earthquake country, I should have remembered that the ground gets hungry for sacrifices.

I never really thought about what we did in the Establishment, what we did to people. There's part of your brain that needs to keep some kind of balance, that says that sort of thing just shouldn't happen, so you try not to see it. All those years, it was only something that we did, like an assembly line or a hobby or even an art form. And we did some pretty awful things in the name of that hobby. Really, it's only fair that I should finally be on the other end, so I can say I'm sorry.

Anyway, they gave me two and a half days before they came to accept my resignation. They came in through the windows and they came in through the doors and they came in through the walls, two elite cohorts in full mask. One moment, I was alone like always in my empty rooms. The next, they were full of jungle animals let loose with human shapes and shadows, snarling at me.

Then the chief of the jungle animals came up through the floor, James Lick. Even in living days back in the old century, he was a famous miser and hermit, someone for fathers to use for threatening wayward boys with. Dead, he looks like a walking stick — all bony, hateful forehead, elbows and shins — and he still serves the same purpose: When someone is naughty, the Establishment threatens to send Lick to get them, and he usually does.

Once upon a time, before I'd resigned, we'd been equals in crime, although we were never friends. That mantis has no friends, and I suppose the recluse spider who I was didn't either. He was the talent scout, the catcher of dogs, the finder of lost slaves. Then, when he'd caught you, the Establishment sent you to me, and I made sure the chains held tight to keep you property of the Establishment till hell froze over. We're not equals any more. We're even less friends.

He never wastes anything; every word, every gesture he makes is so economical, so necessary that it can be horrifying to watch him apparently doing nothing. I knew he was happy to be punishing me when he didn't waste any time getting to it. As soon as he arrived, the first thing he did was order the legionnaires to restrain me. My arms were pulled up behind me as my chest was pushed to the floor, almost tearing me. My face was thoughtfully yanked upward by my hair, apparently so I could enjoy the situation to its fullest.

Lick himself was doing something extraordinary that I'd only seen him do once before, on the day the Spaniard stopped talking. He was smiling. It was not a cheerful sight, especially because he was smiling at me.

He turned to look behind me at my Angel, which was still lying propped-up against the corner of the room, half-repaired from the last earthquake. The Angel is a statue I made of a girl I once knew. For a long time, she — it — had meant everything to me, but I finally pulled away from it at about the same time I finally quit the Establishment. I suppose you could say I was obsessed with it. That statue gave my life weight and stability. It had anchored me, kept me from falling.

Lick smacked his tight lips. "Your friend, Renegade?"

I said I wasn't a Renegade. That would be stupid.

One of the guys behind me holding my arms gave me a kick in the small of my back. Lick shook his head and brought his finger to his lips, mouthing it as though lost in thought. As he did so, my Angel hissed and rocked slightly, and the light flickered. It looked like she was charring, then smoldering as her bark skin and woven substance began to catch inner fire. The only fire of death. In almost no time, the charred, twisted, popping statue fell, and in falling she disintegrated, blowing away in a billow of soot and stray leafy wingfeathers.

I felt like fainting. If I'd had time, I probably would've screamed or maybe vomited, but Lick took advantage of the moment to hit me across the face hard enough to knock me down. It took a moment or two, but I actually felt my face hurt when I realized what had happened. I'd forgotten what pain feels like. Before, in all those years I was sleepwalking through death, locked up safe in my slaver's house, there was part of me that thought it missed pain the way it missed everything else in the world. I thought pain was something noble because I only remembered meeting it at a distance.

Whatever Lick does, hurts. I suppose that's the cold world's way of reminding you that it's still going on outside whatever safe places you can make. The world has no meaning but hurt. They punished me for trying to find something else.

When I raised my head, the Presidio crowd was all there, Brannan and the Spaniard and the Finn and all the others, with their bodyguards and hangers-on. I think I saw Brannan's harbinger, the one who delivered their last message to me, but he turned his head and muttered to the ghost standing next to him when I caught his eye. Brannan was laughing. I think the Spaniard was laughing too, but his silence makes it hard to tell. I must've cut my face on something when that rat Lick hit me, because my insides were leaking out of my eyebrow.

Brennan stopped laughing long enough to look at me and then at Lick. He wiped a hand across his dry, shopkeeper's face.

"To think I considered you a son, Malone, a possible replacement for me when I get my promotion. You're a disappointment and a waste."

I looked at him, wondering whether they were just going to kill me or whether they had something else in mind.

He looked around, nodding his whiskery chin approvingly, like he was knocked out by his own lecturing style. "We've got ourselves a problem, pardon-boy. Too many souls, not enough chains. Never enough chains. Takes money and too much time to bring 'em up from the Dark Place, but you had the gifts and the know-how we needed to make them locally."

Lick frowned and turned to Brennan, mouthing something. Greenback put him in his place by ignoring him. Instead, he looked straight at me. "Because I consider you a son, I've decided to treat you fair. I'm giving you thirty days to rejoin the business, prodigal son. Same contracts, same terms. You get Richmond and you get your house back, everything forgiven. It will have meant nothing."

The Spaniard raised his hand and the legion boys let go of me. The sudden release from them made me stagger forward a step and it didn't hit me until afterward what he said next.

"Thirty days. It'll take that long to get a set of custom chains sent up from the Home Office. After that, well, you'll be working for us for free."

Then they started pulling the faded yellow wallpaper off my walls to feed to the hounds. I lay there for a moment, but Brennan or the Spaniard must've given them a signal because they all did their dirty work like I wasn't there and ignored me when I got up. Obviously a way to bring it home to me that I was no longer Hierarchy, no longer part of the in-crowd, the Establishment. Fine.

I lingered cautiously for a while, but it was too depressing to watch them feeding my home to their pets. Since no one else seemed to care about where I was (or how I spent my thirty days of freedom), I went to the pile of ashes and jagged sticks which now constituted my Angel and scooped up a handful of her substance. Then I turned and left my house by the front door, my hand clenching the ashes.

When I got out, I made this book, using pressed memory for the pages and the dead Angel's ashes clotted with spit and the other fluids that seeped from the cut in my forehead for ink. There are some tears in it, I have to admit. I'm writing in it now not so much for anyone who'll come after me, but, well, I don't know why I'm writing. I'll stop now.

Farewell, farewell to you, my Angel. I may only have loved you because I thought you were someone else, but that isn't a good enough reason to have hated you. I hope you find whatever heaven that beloved toys can get to.

My head still hurts.

November 4: Woke up in the middle of the night missing Ceille. Not the Angel, just my old dear friend. I want to talk to Ceille, but I'm not strong enough to use a phone, and I wouldn't know where to find one if I tried. I'm in an alley somewhere close to downtown. I don't know the streets any more and I get lost easily. It's dirty and I'm very cold and it's almost impossible to sleep because things are always moving out here.

I don't know what I'm going to do. It would be easy to go back and ask for my house back and pick up my back contracts as if nothing had happened. Go back to building cages inside people so they can go anywhere and still stay in prison. Go back to finding the cords behind every face to knot together.

I don't want to, but if I don't do it freely, they'll wait until one last set of prison bars gets vomited up from Stygia and they'll find me and put them behind my face. Then they'll get what they want just the same, only I won't.

And I know now that the world we're part of only tolerates you until you ignore it. I've learned to see that much. Once you've tried to escape, it'll never let you out of its sight again, never give you a moment's rest. In more ways than one, trying to resign from my contracts reminds me of killing yourself. If you try and fail, you rarely get another chance so easily.

Nothing is ever as if nothing had happened. Everything is a sin that can never be erased. And I've sinned against everyone, even the bad guys. I deserve whatever hell I've made, and this city is definitely hell. I deserve not to find Ceille.

November 9: I've been out here for days, but these streets full of quick are one of the things I can't get used to. I've never liked crowds, and now it's harder to avoid them. I wish they'd all slow down or even stop. I always thought that once you die, the world blinks out for you and everything stops. I thought you'd be alone forever.

If I had ever dreamed it would be like this, I never would have done it. No matter how bad life gets, at least there you can be alone sometimes.

It's the quiet moments on these streets that keep me going. No constant interruptions, no staring-eyed men in threadbare coats looking through you, no screaming children when you're trying to think. Just you and the dead, silent streets and alleyways, with the gusts of ash falling from the heavens like dirty snow.

Why couldn't just one person in those constant crowds be Ceille? I feel like the entire living world has passed by me but her. Every day so far, I've looked for her, but it wasn't until today that I realized that I have no idea what she looks like as an old lady.

November 11: It's the empty places in this book that scare me the most. Time goes by so fast when it's all empty. The years that I have been dead now outnumber the years that I lived, but I can hardly remember a handful of days since dying.

I'm going to have to fight this, find something to remember every day, to fill this book with. The streets might be filled with people, but I need to find something to fill my streets with.

November 12: Only trivia. The month is going by so quickly and I still don't know what I'm going to do.

November 16: I think I've found a lead on one of the halfway haunts where the other tattered, homeless ghosts stay. It's supposed to be down south of Mission Street, in an old boarded-up derelict house covered with graffiti old enough to've been there when I was alive. I've heard that it's one of Lo Ma Cameron's Salvation Army outposts, and that all the dead are welcome there. I looked for it all day today, but couldn't find it. Maybe tomorrow.

November 19: Found the halfway haunt today. At first, I was so happy to finally be there. There was a little sign in the window with a skull and bones and the words "Little Maudlin. Public House" written on it, so I knew I was in the right place.

It was a bit ratty. but I'm used to my own place. It was crowded, too. I had no idea there were so many dead people, or that so many of us were so tattered. Most of the people there were dressed in very little but their shrouds, and I think there were one or two in the shadows who didn't even have that. Likewise, they weren't dressed in very much body; they probably couldn't afford things like hair or fingers or both eyes or opacity. Maybe they'd had those things once, but had had to sell them. Maybe we in the Establishment had taken them. I don't know.

At first, everything went very well. I sat down on a crooked stool and the old man with the red armband came and gave me a bowl of warm memory to drink. It tasted like boredom, but it was warm. A wild-eyed man in the corner kept staring at me, so I said hello.

He must've recognized me then because he leaned over and told something to the fat, faceless woman sitting next to him. She leaned over to the next person, and so on. A boy got up and ran back into the kitchen or wherever and then the man in the corner cleared his throat.

"Richmond boy, aren't you? Got any pardons to sell me, or are they all reserved for the gutters your Hierarch friends call souls?"

Another one, a very pale woman who never blinked when I was there, joined in. "Hey, it's the Soul Carver. Turn me into a wineglass, Soul Carver Richmond boy."

That started them all going. They kept calling me obscene names like "Soul Carver" or "Crossmaker" or "Facelicker" and spitting at me. Finally I had to take my face off and run away, or they probably would've ripped me apart. It took me forever to calm down enough to see where I was going. I really don't want to write about it anymore. All the dead are welcome there.

November 20: I've been thinking about the people in the halfway haunt again. What would they rather I have done? I'm not a monster like the others anymore. I'm just a person like anyone else. It was the only thing I could've done.

I also just remembered something. When I was running out, there was a woman there, dressed in fine clothes, staring at me. I don't remember much else about her; there seemed to be a haze around her, but the whole place was sort of hazy. I bring her up here because she kept staring at me, but didn't say anything like the others. She just kept staring.

November 22: Still hungry.

November 25: Desperate enough to barter for a bag of soul cakes from one of the street vendors. At first, I was going to offer him my memories of mother, but when he saw the pardon marks on my hands he asked instead for me to hear his life for a half hour's time. I of course agreed, even though I hadn't done any real shriving for years, since I stopped to do fulltime facework for the Establishment.

He lived a nice, quiet life. No real triumphs but no real tragedies either. I don't really want to talk about it, and really shouldn't because of the Pardoner's Code, but it was nice. Balanced.

Afterward, I ate half the cakes myself and then walked along the street until it got dark. When the dead children started to come out to light the beacons, I gave them what was left of my food. Having learned my lesson from Little Maudlin, I made sure to leave my face off, and they took the cakes. They were a bit cautious, but at least they didn't run away or scream at the slavemaster from suburbia. Watching them eat with my face off, I felt jealous of the street vendor and his nice, quiet memories. There were no crimes on his face to pay for.

November 26: Having nowhere better to go, I was out on the beach looking at the oceanbreak that previous Pardoners built to keep the water out. They made it out of tombstones and used tombstone dust in the mortar, and so the wall mumbles to itself when the waves hit it, whispering faded dates and epitaphs from stone to stone as if desperately trying to remember what it once was. For some reason, this whispering was immensely comforting for me, and I stayed there for a long time, working on this journal and just thinking miserable thoughts.

There's a tree on the edge of the beach where the sand stops and the pavement starts. I don't know why the city planted it. Maybe they meant well, but just didn't realize how hard it is to keep a tree alive so close to the ocean. Anyway, my parents used to take me on picnics under the tree when we first moved here, back when I was young and alive. They were happier then.

Anyway, the tree's still there, but somewhere along the

way it got burned, and now it's nothing but black, tightly packed charcoal. Maybe it was lightning, or a bonfire back when they used to have them, or just someone with a cigarette lighter, but it's dead. I don't suppose living people even know it's there anymore.

After a while, I came to the tree again. It's strange to see the things you knew as a child a lifetime later, especially when they've turned dark and jagged. I wanted to see if there was any part of the tree still alive, so I bent down in the dirt to check the roots. Dead. All its roots are dust now, and the trunk teetered a bit in the shallow soil when I touched it. Underneath the charcoal there was nothing but sand.

When I stepped back again, that burned dead tree, up against the night sky, looked like it was trying to reach for something with numb, stubbed branches. Somehow it reminded me of something, but it's not important. Nothing seemed important then. The soul cake man had roots. I didn't; no establishment, no rebellion, no religion, and I kept thinking about how that was going to lead me to become nothing but firewood for the people who did. Underneath the charcoal was nothing but sand.

I closed my eyes. You wish you could die, but the closest you get is closing your eyes and killing the world for a while. You forget what being dead is like, and there's part of you that remembers what you wished it would be like, all quiet, all dark and silent and sleepy, the way you feel when you're first dead. It makes you think of heaven, but it never seems to last. No rest for the dead.

When I finally had to open my eyes, there was a young, dark woman standing beside me. She was wearing a dark dress that came to below her knees and a pillbox hat, and she was smoking. By that, I mean she was surrounded by a cloud of vapor and ash that made it difficult to see her clearly. She looked a bit like Ceille, but more like the Angel, and mostly just like herself. Looking straight back at me, she raised a prim, smoky finger to her lips and smiled, and then I recognized her from Little Maudlin. She was the woman who had watched me as I left.

"Not that easy after all, is it?" she asked in a soft voice. "Takes quite an effort, staying dead for any real length of time."

I just looked back at her. "Are you dead too?" I asked. "You must be."

She must've thought it was funny, because she laughed. I don't remember the last time I'd heard someone laugh, so it made me uncomfortable when she did it. "Maybe I am, maybe I'm not," she said when she was done puffing out her smoky laughter. "Maybe I don't believe in ghosts, Ghost."

She took a few steps toward the water, then said, "If you people really wanted to be left alone, you'd refuse to stay dead. You'd walk into the ocean or fall into an open grave or just let go of yourself one day and unravel like smoke and cinders, but you'd do it."

She didn't look at me, but at the waves that flowed all the way to the horizon. "I think you're afraid, Ghost."

I glanced down and away. In the sand, she had left a trail of footprints on the beach, little crescent toes and pinpoint star heels like magic writing to show where her shoes had been.

"It's different for you," I told her. "You're alive. You're still part of the world, so you can talk about that stuff all you want."

"Am I?"

I nodded. "Look at your feet. You leave marks in the world. I don't." I took a step toward her. The sand where my foot had been remained undisturbed, almost as if it was personally ignoring me. "See? There aren't any footprints left for me. You are alive and I am dead. That's not a metaphor, or any kind of symbol, it's just the way things are."

She kicked sand at me and ran across the beach, trailing her smoke behind like a formal train.

Not having anything else to do, I followed. She still felt

so familiar, like someone I'd known all my life. We left a single row of footprints behind us to mark two people running.

Suddenly, she stopped short and turned to face me. "You leave no footprints because you're afraid to get your shoes dirty. Same reason you don't cast a shadow. Why don't you want to *impose* on the world, Ghost? Even the other ghosts wallow in the dirt as best they can.

"I've watched them, Ghost. I've watched them all. They do good and they do evil, but you do neither. They are brave enough to cast a shadow. You, you walk on the air, afraid to come down on either side. No wonder you don't touch the ground."

We walked together for a bit, making a slow circuit back to the tree while we talked and watched the angels fall from the sky in the form of cinders. What she was saying reminded me of how when I was a child, I hated walking on anything clean or fresh like the floors after mother had just waxed them, or fresh-mowed grass. It always made me feel a terrible need to balance myself and walk a sort of careful tightrope because I was terrified of being the one to come along and mess it up. Does that make sense? Somehow, it's important, to me at least.

I told her all of this and she nodded. "Doesn't sound like a happy way to go through life," she said, and I agreed. When we got back to the charcoal tree, she pulled a yellow, folded newspaper page out of her handbag and covered her smoking fingers with it. Having done this, she slowly traced her fingertips through the newspaper down the twisted black tree trunk, almost lovingly.

"This tree, this rootless thing," she said, almost to herself. "What a mystery. Look at it, Ghost. Why does it bother to keep existing? Look how fragile it looks, all alone out here in this poor soil, choked by the crowded city, leeched and stunted by the sea."

She continued inspecting the tree. "Look. Here's a place

where the ants in their swarming crowds built a shelter for themselves where they could huddle against the tides. I hate ants, don't you? They're almost unimaginably cruel when they're trying to protect their chosen haunts."

I could almost imagine the Establishment bosses there, like ants, bracing themselves, hiding themselves in boxes, anything to keep from being moved by the world of Oblivion around them. Kind of like me in my house, really. Even thinking about it now makes me feel a bit wistful for my old haunt, but it makes me feel horrified as well. Suddenly, I felt sorry for the terrified Hierarchs, even the nastiest ones.

She bent and turned her neck to look at the tree from all angles. "Looks like it's got the whole sky on its fallen boughs. That's a lot of responsibility for one tree," she said. I just shook my head while she unfolded the newspaper again to make room for her to put both hands together on the tree trunk.

Funny how I'd forgotten until now how her hands were covered with powdery, ash-colored stains, even though she'd made such a big deal out of using the newspaper to keep them clean. If I didn't know better, I'd say she was a Master Pardoner like I am.

"Want to help?" she asked, grinning and looking up at me.

"Help with what?"

"Making the tree fall. All the leaves of summer are fallen, so now we push the corpse. Tidy. Oh... but I'm the only one with leverage, aren't I? I apologize. I forget, you're *dead*." She kept grinning at me. "Don't look for meaning in this. There is none that you do not put there, and that is dangerous."

She lowered her head and made a small noise in her throat that reminded me of the last earthquake we'd had. Then, still making the noise, she pressed against the burned tree, which, being rootless in the sand, seemed to slip and fall to the ground effortlessly. Part of it cut into the beach where the oceanbreak was anchored to the shore, and a little trickle of sea began to drip through.

She reached down into the sand and found the smashed pieces of a conch shell that the falling tree had both uncovered and crushed. She looked at me as she took the pieces into her hand, where for a moment they got lost in her smoke. Then she let them fall, and then she picked them up again and gave them to me.

"These are for you, Ghost. Whenever you need gravity lessons, take them out and look at them. Look how they trust the ground. The ground will catch you quite perfectly."

I looked at her. She nodded.

I let my knees buckle and the next thing I knew, I was on the ground. It was easy, and you get used to the sudden pain. You get used to suddenly, finally having sand in your hair and clinging between your fingers.

She knelt down to kiss me on the forehead, the place where Lick had hit me and it had not quite healed. "The day after tomorrow, when the falling hurts, Ghost, don't hate me. Remember that when it hurts. I've been dead a long time, and it still hurts. Just like it does for the living." I closed my eyes. When I opened them again, there was no trace of her left but her footprints in the sand, filling slowly with the tide that seeped through the crack in the wall she'd made.

When I got up, I'd left a shallow print of my own in the sand. Not much, but it was a start. Best of all, it looked like one of those angels that children make in fresh, unspoiled snowfields.

I wandered the city streets until dawn in a weighted-down state that I seem to recall as joy. I feel so heavy. It's like I'm falling every moment, and in between every moment, but every single time I fall, the world comes up to meet me. I almost remember this as dancing. This might not make sense to you, but it is important to me.

November 27: Carried on until this morning, at which

time I went straight back to Little Maudlin. This time, I was expecting that they'd give me some trouble, so I reworked my face to keep anyone from recognizing me. I asked to see their leader and waited until she arrived. Then I showed her my real face and asked her if I could join the Renegades.

If you're reading this, you're probably dead, so you know about famous Lo Ma Cameron, the Salvation Army leader, and want to know what she's like. To be honest, she reminds me of my mother. She looks like a cross between a slightly prim schoolmarm and a French Resistance cell leader. Something like Che Guevara in a bustle, but she's not one I'd want to cross.

When we got to her room, she put her spectacles on and peered at me for a moment. That's the kind of Renegade she is. "To be frank, Mr. Malone," she said, "I don't know why we should trust you. You've done a great deal of damage to our people in the past."

I nodded with what I hoped looked like earnesty. "You have no reason. I've done horrible things. For no reason except that I was afraid. All the chains, all the erased faces, all the unmoldings. I'm sorry…"

She cut me off. "I'm quite aware of your crimes, Mr. Malone. We don't call you 'Crossmaker' as a compliment, you know."

I raised my hand. "That's why I'm doing this."

She pursed her lips. "Good. I suppose we shall find out over the next few days. Tell me, then, about how I can get my people out of the Winchester House. You've a long obligation to repay, so let's start with something impressive."

"Also," she almost smiled, "if those degenerates up in the Presidio really have lost you, perhaps now is the best moment for our side to press the advantage."

Then, finally, we really began to talk. In the end, she seemed to accept that I had fallen to her side, and let me stay.

November 30: This is the last entry in this journal, because it is no longer needed. I'm not afraid of falling now, so I don't need this book any more to prop me up and keep me from falling down. My footprints in the sand of this dead world will be all the memorial I need.

As I write this, I'm busy eating the other pages that have gone before, one by one. Tomorrow I am going on a raid with Lo Ma's people, and she suggested that I simplify my affairs in case I don't come back. She's given me a new name and a new face, not only to keep the Establishment away from me when my time is up, but also to keep her people from finding out that they're working with one of their chief demons. It seemed like a good idea, so I'm carrying it a bit further by taking all these memories back, all these traces of those days, that younger Andrew Malone. I'm taking my house and its loss back, and the names they called me the first time I came here, and the faces of the dead children when they ate the food I brought them.

It tastes good, this book, satisfying in a fugitive way that fills the old cravings for living food that I thought I'd forgotten, bitter, sweet, and salt. The memory tastes like that, like salt. I'm chewing slowly on the weightless pages, trying to make them last awhile. Just now, I realized that the reason they taste so good is because they are my life.

Now that I have finished this last page, I will eat it also, and then there will be nothing left but falling day by day until the falling stops.

SHADOW OF A REFLECTION OF A

CAT'S HEAD

JANE M. LINDSKOLD

"Tieh, what would you do if you learned that someone had tampered with your memory?" Lung Lei asked me.

"I'd kill whoever did it," I replied without a pause.

My bloodthirstiness surprised me considerably. Such concern with something of this world seemed undignified for a member of the Akashic Brotherhood. My teachers emphasized the Do — being everything and nothing — as the path to Ascension. I thought I had accepted their emphasis as my own. I thought again about what Lung Lei had told me.

"I'd kill whoever did it," I repeated.

Lung Lei and I had been strolling down Grant Avenue, window-shopping and enjoying the warm November sunshine. I paused in front of a tearoom window and pretended to study the menu while I fought for self-control.

Dim sum, oolong tea, noodles. For a moment I toyed with the idea of going in and purchasing a red bean bun and a cup of tea, but as quickly dismissed it.

In the few weeks since Lung Lei had become my nearly constant companion I had learned to live with the company of an increasingly talkative spirit. I had learned to control how I spoke — barely moving my lips or resorting to disciplines of the Mind so that I need not speak aloud at all. I had even taken to carrying a Buddhist rosary so that any muttering or distracted expression might be taken as the fervor of prayer, but those would be difficult to maintain in a crowded tearoom.

"Why do you think that someone has altered my memory?" I said, turning away from the window and continuing down Grant.

"You are too compassionate to care so little about murder," the spirit said serenely.

"Murder!" I blurted aloud, drawing stares from several passersby. "We had better go and discuss this in my room."

The fourth floor walk-up that I rented could politely be called a studio apartment. There was one large room with a small bathroom and a kitchen niche. Since, however, I got a discount on meals from Mama Wong's restaurant on the ground floor, I rarely cooked. My sleeping mat occupied one corner, bookshelves lined the walls, and — except for a low table — the rest of the room was given over to the polished hardwood floor, which was covered with bright, hand-knotted Chinese rugs. Normally, I found my room a comfortable refuge, but today even the sight of the various butterfly mobiles turning in the breeze from the partially open window could not soothe me.

After putting out water for tea and shaking a few leaves of dried jasmine into a smooth, white porcelain pot painted with an Indian Moon Moth, I sat cross-legged on the floor. Lung Lei waited in patient silence while I chanted the meditation on the Flow of the Cosmic All. Despite being Chinese, the spirit was not of my Tradition. His practices more closely resembled those of the Order of Hermes, although his knowledge and forms were shaped by Taoist alchemy rather than the European version.

When the water in the kettle whistled for my attention, I was balanced and calm. I poured the water over the dried jasmine, and when the tea was ready I poured two cups. One I set on my table, the other I placed, making proper obeisance, before the stark but elegant shrine I had built for Lung Lei atop one of the bookcases.

The spirit bowed his thanks, hands folded within the sleeves of his mandarin robe. Then he knelt on the floor across from me at the table. He waited until I had tasted my tea before beginning his account.

"You recall how I met you, Tieh," he said.

"Of course, Abraham the Dreamspeaker summoned you from the early years of San Francisco to accompany me on a journey into the city's past." I found a smile. "You found your own way back to me when that journey was ended and have yet to depart."

Lung Lei folded his hands and bowed again. "You continue to fascinate me, Butterfly. Perhaps one source of this fascination is your near indifference to the murder of those closest to you."

"Indifference to murder?" I asked, unable to comprehend what he could be talking about.

"What else could you call your reaction to the deaths of Master Shan, Yueh Ch'iu, and Hung Po?" Lung Lei said sternly.

"Oh," I said, my hand fluttering to cover my mouth. "That. Yes, of course. How could I be so foolish?"

"Not foolish," Lung Lei replied. "Ensorcelled."

"Ensorcelled!" I repeated, incongruously blushing, as ashamed as if I had fallen for some simple practical joke.

"So I believe," the spirit patted my hand, his touch, as

always, as solid as any living person's. "Tell me. What do you recall about the day of the murders?"

"It was last spring," I said promptly. "May. The weather was quite beautiful. There had been lots of rain earlier in the week, so a sunny day was an unasked-for gift. I took my staff out to a quiet portion of Golden Gate Park and practiced martial Do forms. Then I had tea and rice cookies in the Japanese Garden. After that, I came back and wandered around Chinatown until I realized that I was late to appear at Master Shan's sanctum. I hurried there and found the other three had been murdered by the Technocracy."

"How did you get back from the park?" Lung Lei asked.

"I was going to take the bus, but I met a friend in the Japanese Garden and she gave me a lift as far as Union Square. I walked the rest of the way home."

"And then you walked some more around Chinatown?" Lung Lei asked skeptically.

"That's right," I said impatiently. "I told you that the weather was beautiful."

"Beautiful enough that you would overlook an invitation to your Master's sanctum?" Lung Lei's voice was stern, "Such are not frequently given — especially within your Tradition. I would think that you would have been eager, even impatient to arrive."

"Such strong emotions are among the threads that bind us to this realm and keep us from Ascension," I said automatically. "But you are right. I remember now. I was excited. That's why I had gone out to practice. I felt that I needed some self-discipline."

"Yet, when you returned, you simply wandered around," Lung Lei said. "Where did you go?"

"Places. Looked in windows, like we did today," I said. "You know how it is."

"I do," Lung Lei said, "and so do you. Tell me, why are you so angry with me?"

"Angry? I'm not..." I stopped, looking at my reflection in the polished teak of the tabletop. My eyes were narrowed, the corners of my mouth turned down, my hair disarrayed, though I could not remember ruffling it.

"I am angry," I admitted in wonder. "Is this part of it? Part of the ensorcellment that you suspect?"

"I think so," my spirit said gently. "Anger. Embarrassment. All veneers to keep you from probing too deeply into your memories of that day. You Akashics have an almost Buddhist revulsion to strong emotion — it is a weakness."

"Let's leave discussion of Tradition philosophies for later," I begged. "This scares me. Why would someone alter my memory?"

"I don't know," Lung Lei replied, "but I suspect that if we are to learn anything, we must discover what has been taken from you."

We spent the rest of the afternoon and well into the evening methodically working through my memories. The job might have gone faster if I had called on another mage. However, I had never become close to the remaining Akashics in the region — not all that odd a thing, since we are a Tradition that cultivates individuality.

Despite not having other members of the Akashic Brotherhood to call on, I shied away from confiding in mages of other Traditions. Only a mage could have altered my memory in this fashion and I did not wish to send even unwitting notice to my enemy that I was on his — or her — trail.

Lung Lei, although Awakened, was only now rediscovering his power. Death had effectively severed him from what he had known in life. We both expected that we would need years, rather than months, to find what he could do.

After many hours and dead ends, Lung Lei sighed. "Your memory is sound right until Jessica D'or dropped you off in

Union Square. I propose that come daylight we retrace the route you took that day from that point. Perhaps something will spur your memory."

"Maybe," I said, allowing myself a touch of hope. "Maybe."

I awoke the next morning early enough to hear Mama Wong going out to shop for specialties for the day's menu. Rising, I put on water for tea, showered, and then dressed. My outfit was not greatly different than what I usually wore. My blouse was long-sleeved white cotton, my trousers loose and black, my footwear the flat, black slippers that Americans call kung fu shoes.

Around my waist I tied a black sash embroidered with minute, perfect butterflies. The black symbolized my rank in my many martial arts — kung fu, wing chun, karate, jujitsu, aikido, kenjitsu, and others. The butterflies each marked some past achievement. As I tied the sash, I tapped the Sri Lankan Blue Peacock that commemorated my recent trip through time into the Montgomery Block.

Once dressed, I poured tea and took out a dish of sticky rice balls from my tiny refrigerator. Lung Lei appeared as I rose from offering my respects at his shrine.

"Where do we begin?" he said.

"At the statue in Union Square," I replied. "Jessica dropped me off on the Geary Street side. We'll walk down Stockton to Sutter and then take Powell to Geary. That way, when we retrace my route, we'll see everything with fresh eyes."

Before we left, I pulled on the black leather jacket which a friend had painted with a Philippine Scarlet Swallowtail — the female, which has white on the lower pair of wings instead of only red and black. On an impulse, I pulled my long hair back with the wooden clip painted like a Monarch butterfly. Thus armored in icons and images, I set out to confront my memory and those who had stolen it.

Arriving at Union Square, I sat on the stairs on the

Geary Street side. It would be some hours before the expensive department stores that bordered the square opened. Lung Lei sat beside me, hitching his robes up and shooing an indifferent pigeon away.

"I thought that we were going to walk?" he said.

"We are, but I want to prepare myself," I said.

"Are you stalling?" he asked. "Do you still feel afraid?"

I bit back my negative retort. "Maybe so."

I was rising to my feet when I saw the man with the bloodshot left eye shuffling up the stairs toward me. He was tall — well over six feet — with dark brown skin and short hair that shone like steel wool in the morning light. The clothing he wore had seen better days, but I recognized a Brooks Brothers label on both the shirt and trousers. Either he had once had money or he'd gotten first pick from the Salvation Army bin.

I freed my staff for combat, but I wasn't really afraid of this derelict. Actually, I felt a little sorry for him and my own eye itched in sympathy. I wished I dared conjure him a bottle of eyedrops.

He paused in front of me and looked me up and down, his gaze resting on every butterfly and lingering on my staff. There was no sense that he was Awakened, yet I could have sworn that he understood the significance of each item. Frightened by his scrutiny, I reached out and gave him a mental nudge, a command to go away.

My command slid off something in his mind. I could have sworn that it didn't take hold, but after another searching stare, the man stepped to one side. I hurried by, aware of Lung Lei trailing me, glancing back over his shoulder.

"That," I said decisively, "was one creepy guy."

"I agree," Lung Lei said, "and as much as I dislike telling you this, I believe that he is now following you."

"Great." I crossed Geary at the corner of Stockton, stopping to look into the windows of Neiman-Marcus.

The plate glass showed off an array of gifts far too

expensive for anyone's kid for Christmas — no matter how special the kid was. It also revealed my tattered dandy shuffling across the street, just about where I had crossed.

"Let's keep walking, but faster," I suggested. "We should lose him. He's pretty slow."

"But will you be able to concentrate on remembering?" Lung Lei asked worriedly.

"I can only try," I replied.

At the corner of Geary and Grant, I paused, breathing the sharp, somewhat acrid odor of tanned leather that emanated from a shop's open door. My stalker was still tailing me, but he had barely passed Neiman-Marcus. I felt confident that I would lose him when I turned onto Grant.

"Have you remembered anything?" Lung Lei asked as we started walking.

"Yes," I said, pleased despite myself. "After Jess dropped me off, I realized that I still had a magazine she had given me in the car so I could read a review of a rock band she was following. She had said that she was going over to a café on Market Street to meet some friends, so I decided to walk the block or so out of my way and return the magazine."

"I wonder if the café will be open this early," Lung Lei said.

"I think so," I answered. "I haven't been there since — since I went by there to find Jessica, now that I think about it — but as I recall, it did mostly breakfast and lunch trade."

The café was open, and I ordered an espresso and a sticky bun before taking a table in a corner from which I could survey the room without being easily seen.

"Anything?" Lung Lei asked.

"Give me a moment," I whispered, covering the words with a sip from my espresso. Then I remembered.

Jessica's car had been parked out front when I'd arrived, but I hadn't seen her when I went in. The woman at the cash register had seen me come in and with a glance at my staff had spoken to me in a hushed voice.

"They're in the back room. Don't worry about knocking."

Slightly mystified as to how she could have known that I was looking for Jess, I bowed my thanks. The door she had indicated was ajar and I pushed it open without making any sound. As I stepped in and shut it behind me, I heard a discussion already in progress.

"We cannot get the mountain to go to Mohammed," said a resonant male voice with a clipped, Eton accent, "so we must allow Mohammed to go to the mountain."

"It could be more effective," said a woman with a flat, Midwestern accent. "Remember Pearl Harbor."

"Or the slaughter of the Jesus Indians by the American troops," said a second female voice.

"Or the Black Hole of Calcutta," said a man.

"Then we are agreed," said the first man. "Remember, no one must know of our part in this. Factionalism can be overcome by enlightened self-interest."

"Or fear," said Jess D'or.

I slipped out, certain that I had not been meant to overhear that conversation. Their words made me uneasy and I decided to report them to Master Shan to see what he could make of them.

"Shan!" Realization jerked me out of my memories so rapidly that I clung to the table edge.

"Tieh?" Lung Lei said.

"Come outside," I muttered. "I think I have something."

I quickly summarized what I had remembered as we walked down Market to Grant. Lung Lei nodded.

"And what you just now realized," he said, "is that 'Shan' means 'mountain.'"

"Right," I said, not bothering to subdue the anger I felt building in me, "and I was too stupid to know."

"Is this Jessica D'or who so conveniently appeared to give you a ride from the park perchance a Mage?" Lung Lei asked, clearly certain of the answer.

"Yes," I sighed. "She's what they call a 'Hollow One' —

a new Tradition, some say no Tradition at all. Even her name is a sort of joke — Jess D'or. She said it's a pun on Ties of Gold. I think her birth name was Door."

"That is portentous enough," Lung Lei said. "Tell me, what happened after you told Master Shan of this conversation?"

I stopped in the middle of the sidewalk. "Lung Lei, I don't remember ever telling him. I don't think that I ever did."

"That seems improbable," Lung Lei soothed me. "I suspect a second memory block. Try and remember what happened directly after you left the café."

"I walked down Grant, just like we are." I dropped my voice to a whisper, "Look across the street, up by Brooks Brothers."

"The man with the bloodshot eye," Lung Lei said. "He is looking for you. Something about him troubles me."

"Well, he is stalking me!" I said, a trifle indignantly. "Isn't that enough?"

"More than that," the spirit mandarin frowned. "Something I should remember from my training."

"Never mind that now," I insisted. "We'll turn here on Maiden Lane and lose him. We can cross back to Grant a block up."

"But what about your regaining your memory?" Lung Lei protested.

"My memory has waited since May," I said. "I want to keep my body and soul together without racking up a charge for battery. The courts aren't very sympathetic to martial artists."

"As you say, Butterfly," the spirit trailed me, "but I fear that you flee not the man with the bloodshot eye, but what you will learn when your memory returns."

I didn't dignify this with an answer, but concentrated on mingling with the growing throng on the street. This close to Chinatown, I felt nearly invisible. In a few blocks, I could practically vanish. At the edge of St. Mary's Square, I remembered how this tactic hadn't helped last time.

A voice had called my name from the shelter of Old Saint Mary's Church. Foolishly, I had stopped, and from that moment on I could remember nothing but aimless window-shopping and the horror of finding Master Shan and the others dead later that night. Without explanation, I brought Lung Lei to the church.

"This is where it happened," I said. "I remember, rather, I don't remember, but I'm certain that this is where my memory was altered."

"A rather public place for mage craft," Lung Lei said doubtfully.

"Mind magic is subtle," I said. "I've had that drummed into me often enough. They wouldn't have needed fireworks or earthquakes.

"And, in this city, who would have noticed if they had?" Lung Lei forced a laugh. "I suppose that your last lead is Jessica D'or."

"I agree. I haven't seen her since last May," I frowned, "but I know some of her usual hangouts. However, we will need to wait until evening for them to open."

I turned then to head home. As I did, I realized that my persistent stalker had caught up with me again.

I walked over to him. "Why are you following me?"

He smiled. He had good teeth, not like a street person's. His eyes seemed to focus independently.

"Why? I am curious, woman."

Then he turned and walked away. Only after he had vanished into the morning traffic on Kearny did I register that the last word had not been the English "woman" but the Chinese "nu." And his accent had been perfect.

That night I borrowed Mama Wong's car and drove out to Nightclimber, a club that I recalled Jessica mentioning during that long-ago conversation at the Japanese Tea Garden as one of her favorites. Even as I parked the car, I could tell that it was open. Despite the damp chill of the evening, a few windows were open and music heavy on metallics and beat but low on melody poured out. A small crowd clustered around the open front door where a doorman in a sleeveless T-shirt kept guard.

I paid the cover and, accompanied by my insubstantial escort, went in. The converted warehouse was dimly lit by erratically placed overhead lighting and long, glowing purple blacklight tubes. Strobe lights on the stage made the performers jerk like stop-action animation.

A faint hint of mystical energy eddied through the place. Glancing at Lung Lei, I could tell that he felt it, too. However, more of his attention seemed to be on the noise hammering from the huge tower speakers suspended from the ceiling and stacked along the walls. I was more worried about what the haze of tobacco and marijuana smoke was doing to my lungs and promised myself a three-day purification when this was over.

We took a small corner table and I bought an overpriced mineral water from a waitress in a white hot pants and halter outfit that glowed in the black light. Her pupils were pinpricks despite the dim light and I wondered what reality she was seeing. Many of the others I saw were equally strung out.

On a solely intellectual level, I could understand the attraction of such a place for Jess D'or and her kind — Paradox would be the only paradox in such a haven for surreal fantasy.

I let my gaze drift, scanning the crowd while appearing to see nothing. I found him first, the man with the bloodshot eye and the steel wool hair. He had added a torn Bob Marley T-shirt to his earlier ensemble. Given the costume of the average Nightclimber customer, his mismatched outfit wasn't at all noticeable.

Before I could decide whether I really wanted to speak with him, I saw Jessica. She was dancing, long-nailed hands waving languidly over her ice-white and green spiked hair.

She looked thinner than I remembered her, almost gaunt, and her loose-fitting, ragged flapper dress accentuated the effect. I waited out the band's set, but when she continued to dance through the recorded filler, I rose to confront her.

I swayed awkwardly through the thinning crowd until I was across from her. I'd been afraid that she was stoned, but her green eyes were clear and unforgivingly bright. They widened slightly when she saw me, but she didn't miss a beat.

"I want to talk to you about mountains and Mohammed," I shouted into her ear. "About Jesus Indians, Pearl Harbor, and the Black Hole of Calcutta."

She put a hand on my shoulder and I could feel her squeeze a warning through my leather jacket. Then she leaned forward and kissed me full on the lips. I could taste her lip gloss and smell her drugstore perfume.

"Tieh, darling," she enthused, "this is no place to talk. I have a room next door. We can talk there."

I followed. I knew that Lung Lei was still near, but, prudently, he had made himself as unnoticeable as possible. Jess took me to a building so close to the warehouse that the thudding music carried through the brick wall. In a small foyer that reeked of spilled beer and old vomit, Jessica pushed the "Up" button beside the elevator.

"I live on thirteen," she giggled. "They call it that here. Isn't that a laugh?"

The elevator was a converted freight model, so noisy that we couldn't talk until we reached her apartment, a one-bedroom, with several windows overlooking Nightclimber. Fractured bits from the strobe lights bounced off the walls, creating odd shadows, even up here.

"Want something to drink?" Jessica asked. "Like Japanese tea?"

"You remember," I said, "and so do I."

"You weren't supposed to," she said coolly, "and I'm not sure that it's so great for you that you have."

I studied her. She was gaunt. Ankhs, crucifixes,

pentagrams, and other occult garbage hung from a steel chain — the type banks use to anchor ballpoint pens — around her neck. One was probably her Focus. Her apartment was decorated in a similar pop-occult mishmash. Black velvet posters dominated the walls, a Ouija board sat on the scarred coffee table, a crystal ball collected dust on the cluttered bookshelf. I had no way of knowing what — if any of this — she believed in.

I decided to be direct. "I want to know who altered my memory. I owe them not only for that affront, but for preventing me from warning my Master about the Technocracy's planned assault."

Jess laughed, a dry sound. Hearing it, I could understand why her Tradition used the zero for its emblem. The sound was without humor, without passion, an empty form.

"You still don't get it, do you?" she said. "I'm getting a soda. You want anything? Last call."

I started to decline, then remembered that some cultures have a custom of respecting a guest. I needed whatever faint assurance I could get here in an enemy's base.

"I'll take some tea," I called. "If you have it."

"The tea bag type," she said. "Generic."

I heard her clattering pots and running water. She came out and leaned against the kitchen door frame and stared at me.

"Pearl Harbor. The Jesus Indians. The Black Hole of Calcutta," she intoned. "Don't you get it? Babe, the Technocracy didn't ace your mentor any more than F.D.R. bombed the U.S. Navy. F.D.R. was smart, though. He used all the patriotism that attack stirred up to get the U.S. into World War II. The other events aren't quite the same — F.D.R. probably knew that the attack on Pearl Harbor was coming, but he let those ships and men be blasted because he wanted an excuse to get into the war. Public opinion is always a powerful tool for getting your own way, especially when it's fueled by fear and righteous indignation."

"Are you saying that someone," I very carefully didn't accuse her, "used the Technocracy to kill Master Shan and the others because they wanted to stir up opinion against the Technocracy? That seems unlikely. The Technocracy is the enemy of every Tradition except its own."

"Sure, but the Traditions don't work together against their enemies. Sure, lots of chantries have mixed memberships, but most of them spend lots of energy bitching about who has the better path to Ascension."

Remembering how Lung Lei and I debated that very issue, I could only nod.

"The one thing that most Traditions agree on is that the Technocracy is a danger to us all, but then they take a head-in-the-sand, nose-to-the-navel position," she bragged, her tone like a preacher on speed. "So we decided to change this. Scare all of them by having the Technocracy knock off a bunch of the most peaceful, least-threatening mages around — and for gravy we dropped some hints that guaranteed that the hit would happen in the Master's sanctum!"

My gorge rose. I swear that the only thing that kept me from snapping her neck is that I needed to know more. Her pitifully arrogant "we" made quite clear that she wasn't the only player in this sick game and, almost certainly, she wasn't the most powerful.

"I didn't think that you Hollow Ones went for this group bonding stuff," I said more flippantly than was my wont. "Must be nice to have a club to plan activities with."

"You sanctimonious bitch!" she cried. "What do you know about what I've been through? Your Master was a family friend. Your Awakening was an extension of an art you have studied since you were a toddler. What I belong to isn't any support group, any mere chantry! We are a force for changing the world! We are the unseen…"

The shadow saved me, a peculiar double image, a two-headed cat. I twisted to see what had cast it and the knife blade meant for me went wide. The one meant for Jess caught her in the throat, slicing through her spine, pinning her to the wall.

I bounded across the room, putting the window at my back. I could feel the windowpane vibrating against my back in sympathy with the pounding music from the club. I readied my staff and faced my enemies.

They stood in the apartment's entryway, blocking my way out. There were seven of them, all robed, all cowled, their faces obscured both by shadow and by a pulsating blue-gray mist that disoriented me if I looked at it for too long. One was lowering its arms and I guessed that this was the thrower of knives. I didn't see the cat, but it must be there, probably one of these cowled creature's familiar.

I didn't spare a glance for Jessica. After that strike, she had to be dead. I resolved to be very careful.

"I don't suppose this is a chance visit?" I said, surprised at the steadiness in my own voice.

"No," said the tallest figure in a clipped male voice. "Jessica talked too much, proving herself unworthy to continue in our company."

"She really did envy you," said another female voice. "Envy of you and those like you drew her to us. She called herself a Hollow One, but she was an Orphan at heart."

A sleek black cat with a single star of white between its eyes emerged from behind her and rubbed against her robed legs. As I bowed a mental thanks to my inadvertent savior, the last piece of missing memory returned.

This cat had been there, this cat and three humans. One had been Jess, but I could remember nothing of the other two except that one was male and the other female. They had taken me inside Old St. Mary's and in an empty confessional had buried my memories beneath a veneer of false ones. Then they had laid on an emotional imperative meant to keep me from probing. The mind work had not needed to be particularly seamless because they didn't envision needing it to last.

"You meant me to die with the others!" I blurted out. "But you made the impulse to go window-shopping too strong. I never went back and—"

"Left us with an ugly loose end," the knife thrower said. "You had lived beyond your appointed time, but arranging your death separately would have been suspicious."

"Instead," continued another, "you became a poignant emblem of our cause, pathetically bumbling along without your chantry."

"Why are you telling me this?" I said, "You surely don't expect me to join you in this crusade of yours."

"Sadly, no, for you do have talent," said the woman with the cat. "The knife in the back would have served you as it did Jess, but anything else would arouse suspicions among those we seek to manipulate. But there are other ways for you to die."

"No one will question Jessica's death?" I asked, stalling while I sought a way out.

"No one," the knife thrower said. "She had dangerous friends and this is a bad neighborhood."

"I did bring backup with me," I bluffed. "He's going to notice if I don't come back to the Nightclimber."

"Then you will have to go down with us," said a voice that hadn't spoken before, but I knew was that of the man who had been at Old St. Mary's, "and tell your friend that your business is completed, but for safety's sake you had better take different routes home."

His words seemed eminently reasonable. I fought against compliance, realizing that he had probably hypnotized me last May so that he would find it easier to control me a second time. I thought about how stupid I had been to go after something like this with only a spirit for backup.

I wondered, too, if my stalker would follow me from here and what he would do when my captors slew me. Probably he would think it uninteresting.

A particularly jarring piece of music began down in the Nightclimber. I imagined the crowd, stoned or drunk, gyrating in the smoky haze. And I remembered the lesson of the nightclub.

Spinning my staff in my hands, I shook the other mage's compulsion from me. Then I shattered the window. The cowled mages inadvertently stepped back from the hail of glass. I bowed to them.

"Paradox is not Paradox when no one believes what they are seeing," I said as I leapt out of the window.

I plummeted down, faster than I had believed possible, but as I fell, I drew on the stillness at the heart of the Do. Out of that composure, I brought butterfly wings of red and black and white to life, unfolding them from the painting on the back of my leather jacket. They caught the air, slowing my fall so that I drifted to land in the alley below.

Lung Lei materialized as I landed.

"By Yu Huang Shang Ti, the Jade Emperor, and Lei Kung, the Thunder God, I have never, dead or alive, been so frightened!"

"We must get out of here," I said. "That little show won't hold them for long."

I spun as a shape blocked the end of the alley. My stalker shuffled up, his hair a halo in the streetlight, his bloodshot eye almost glowing.

"Interesting," he pointed up. "Butterfly."

I fled. Let these unseen mages find him in the alley. That would puzzle them. Much, much later, Lung Lei and I sat in a back corner of Mama Wong's kitchen. I set a portion of my lo mein aside for the spirit and bowed to him over my tea.

"I have my memory back," I said, "but I cannot say I much like what I've learned."

"Did you expect to like it?"

"No. I didn't even have the satisfaction of killing those who did it — even though their offense was worse than I had dreamed." I sighed. "Only Jessica D'or died and, despite what she did to me, I feel sorry for her."

"What are you going to do about her associates?" Lung Lei asked.

"I'm not certain," I admitted. "They are clearly from different Traditions. The black cat seemed to indicate a Verbena. The guy with the knives talked like a Euthanatos. That routine about Mohammed and the mountains makes me wonder if one might be of the Ahl-i-Batin. I don't think they're a large group, but I hardly dare go asking around. I might inadvertently jeopardize someone else. I'll just need to follow up what clues I do have — the church, the café, even the cat. I also need to figure out how my stalker fits into the picture."

"He doesn't," Lung Lei said. "At least I don't think that he does. I finally recalled why his inflamed eye seemed so familiar. There is an ancient Chinese ritual for possession that marks the possessed with a bloodshot eye."

"So someone trained in this form is apparently operating in San Francisco," I said, "and has set a servitor to watch me."

"I'm afraid so," Lung Lei said.

I finished the rest of my lo mein in silent meditation before glancing up at the spirit. His expression was worried and he looked easily as tired as I felt.

"I never understood why it was a curse before," I said.

"What?"

"May you live in interesting times."

Lung Lei didn't smile. "Now you see. I suspect that you are indeed doomed to live in interesting times."

"I only hope that I don't die in them," I said and picking up my staff, I adjusted my sash.

Tonight I would add a scarlet swallowtail to commemorate my experiences. Tomorrow might not be another day.

SOME   THERE   BE   THAT

SHADOWS KISS

JOHN H. STEELE

"Let the accused stand forward!" The magistrate's gavel thunders as it strikes the podium, and the very foundation of the court itself shudders under his fury. Shadows dance on the mask that covers his face above the mouth. The illumined portions of the mask glow red, reflecting the subdued light from the fiery coals in the pit in the center of the chamber. Even flames do not seem to give much light here. Light is whisked away by the oppressively heavy air, absorbed by the living stone of the court. The shape of scales, *iudicium* perhaps but not *iusticia*, is etched upon the surface of the magistrate's mask. His rotting wig of curls seethes with insect and reptilian life. No eyes are visible beneath the shadows of the mask, only hollow, smoldering rage.

The pathetic figure of the accused is pushed forward. Justin Parker is weak. He has always been weak, and although I have grown strong, I am forced to see through his eyes. The pit is before him. Beyond it, the magistrate towers above him. Behind the accused are his captors — those who have dragged him here in chains to be condemned, those who will bear witness against him, those who would use him for their own ends, those who would frustrate my plans. But time is with me, and I will be triumphant.

The gray and black-veined walls of the chamber are, as I have said, living stone, formed from a masonry of souls. Human essence smelted in the cursed forges of this hellish city and shaped into whatever substance is required. Faces are almost visible in the surface of the stone, but just as one begins to form, just when it is about to achieve a discernible pattern, it is distorted like a reflection in a pond when a rock is thrown in, and then scattered like smoke on the wind. The almost-image of the soul suffers, among other torments, the torture of eternal tantalization, never allowed, even for a moment, to regain its lost identity.

I refuse to submit to such a fate. I will not allow Justin to submit to such a fate, although there are many worse. The air here in Styli is constantly laced with the screams and anguished cries of the damned. The forges are always burning, and the flow of souls is constant.

Looming over the open court are the massive, stained towers and grimy spires that are Stygia. The Lords of Death may reside in some infernal splendor, but their *locus operandi* is a sprawling mass of filth and refuse, an almost endless array of dilapidated and deformed Stygian metal and stone saturated by the spirit of the atrocities committed within. Justin trembles, but I feel right at home, except that I should be handing out sentences, consuming souls to feed my own passions rather than trapped within this quivering vessel.

Overhead is the dark, dull red sky of this realm. The shade matches the flickering shadows within the pit before me, darkened but able to burst into fiery life at any moment. A smoky haze hangs in the dank air.

The magistrate raises a scroll, the edges of the parchment singed by heat and corruption. His hands, although covered with taut, leathery skin, verge on skeletal. There is constant movement beneath his robe, as if his form is composed of nothing but a squirming mass of snakes and other crawling creatures of the grave. "You stand accused, Justin Parker, of heinous crimes against the Hierarchy," he thunders once again. "Having partaken of *sibi mortem*, it is your lot, as enumerated in the *Dictum Mortem* of Charon, to pay homage to the Quiet Lord, master of those who have surrendered to despair. Your capitulation, freely chosen, assigns you to him."

Finally, the mouse speaks. "But I have to…"

"*Silence!*" the magistrate roars, and Justin cringes at the force of his bellow. Does he really think these beings care one wit for his pleas and excuses? "You have no voice here!" the magistrate rages. "Another such outburst and I shall wear your tongue on my belt," he hisses with a forked tongue of his own. His belt is indeed adorned with fragments of previous supplicants. "You are here to receive judgment. Let the proceedings begin."

∎

It was way too late for me to change my mind. I could've done that all my life but never did. Once I sliced open the veins and let my life run out into the steaming water, it was too late to turn back. I thought I was escaping. If I'd only known.

First there were the strange, blurry encounters with my past, truth and lies equally mixed. The memories returned slowly, bit by bit, just as painful, maybe more, in death as they were in life. My mother was there, and something that was but wasn't Uncle Vinny, and my father. He was the most real. He too walks these lands of the dead, and I ran from him. The last memory was the most torturous because it was still part of life — Randi. I watched her find my body, and for the first time, I felt the pain that I'd caused more than my own, now that it was too late to do anything about it. Worse still, I saw that she was pregnant. She didn't even know yet that she carried my child, my son. I could see the life growing within her. God help him. God help them both, because He abandoned me.

I thought I had it bad when I was alive. Now I was dead, but still with Randi in the apartment, still in the world that I had created, only it had changed. Shortly after I returned from the otherworldly journeys into my past, a withered ivy, its leaves brown and shriveled, grew across the walls. The ivy was soon joined by a dull green, rancid-smelling mold that spread down across the floor. The ceiling, which should have been high but in sight, vaulted into impenetrable shadows. Blood and water constantly dripped from the darkness and formed pools on the floor. Apparently none of this was visible or tangible to Randi, because she continued the day-to-day normality of her life; as normal as life can be in the apartment where your lover committed suicide. I often wondered how she stayed there, and what would happen if she moved. Would I go with her, or was I tied to this place?

Life, or unlife I suppose, was full of these gross distortions of what I'd known before, and tedium also abounded. I spent my weeks watching Randi, every detail of her body magnified in my mind. I wasn't able to touch her, but I could imagine; I could almost *feel* her silky, black hair as it fell in front of her face. I could smell her scent so vividly — even her sweat enticed me — that I would close my eyes and pretend that, once again, I was lying beside her. I watched her paint in the studio that had once been a combined living room and dining area. Not once did I see the result of a single brush stroke. Her canvases remained empty and dead to me. I watched the miniscule child continue to grow within her and wondered when she would become aware of its existence. I stood and watched her sleep, counting her breaths through the long night, seeing the rise and fall of her chest. The sound of her beating heart was music, a tantalizingly sweet rhythm. I wanted nothing more than to *feel* it, her chest pressed tightly against mine, but of course, that was not to be. The only indication I ever had that she was aware of my presence was when she would shiver and pull her sweater more tightly about her when I passed nearby. She would then stand and gaze around the room looking for something, for me perhaps, but I was separated from her life now. My days and nights were broken promises, wishes without hope of fulfillment.

Sometimes at night when I could tell that my death and other matters were weighing heavily on Randi's mind, a terrible transformation occurred. She would pour herself a glass of red wine, and instead of the beautifully petite woman that I loved, I saw before me a walking corpse enveloped by the stench of death, flesh falling away from her bones. Seeing her that way, gripped by the forces which had taken me, bereft of joy and life, was more horrible, by far, than all the other frustrations and agonies I'd undergone. The transformation didn't happen often, but when it did, I couldn't help but run to the opposite end of the apartment where I would huddle, full of fear and revulsion.

I was more or less a prisoner within the apartment. Although I couldn't manipulate physical objects in the real world — I was as insubstantial and invisible as the ghosts about which I'd always read — the walls contained me like a firefly in a jar, or a rat in a box. I had the worst of both worlds. I couldn't penetrate the walls or the door, and in a way my sentence was fitting. I had always hidden from life, and now I was shut away from it.

One day led to another, and that to another and another and another. If there was some purpose for my existence, some task I had to perform, I saw no sign of it. I didn't sleep.

I wandered from room to room. I watched Randi, or examined another square inch of my cell. Before long, I knew every step of the apartment more intimately than I had ever dreamed possible. Along with the regret and despair that were always with me, I was consumed by boredom.

Gradually, I came to the conclusion that I must get out and see more of this new world, however morose and decayed it might be. I knew I wouldn't leave Randi and my unborn son and the apartment permanently. I would always be drawn back by a longing beyond my control, but there had to be more to this life after death than the monotonous cycle of listless days and interminable nights through which I was wandering, filled only with emptiness and hollow desires.

As I've said, I couldn't get out on my own. I couldn't quite grasp the doorknob to turn it. I wasn't able to open the window to the fire escape. I didn't know how to affect the physical world and was constantly frustrated by the fact that, although I couldn't even turn the page of a book or pick up a penny from the floor, I was burned by the flame of a candle when I held my fingers in it, and I was most definitely impeded by the walls that entrapped me.

I could've left much sooner, but my obstinacy and my desire to control my own existence knew no bounds, and only after days of failure after failure did I resign myself to depending on Randi. One afternoon as she left the apartment (I'm not sure where she was going; I didn't really acknowledge her existence beyond my presence, as if she ceased to exist when she left my sight), I slipped through the open door with her. I was free, or so I thought. So caught up in the notion of my deliverance from containment was I that I didn't even notice where Randi went. She was gone. Maybe she *didn't* exist apart from me.

I stepped out of the building onto 16th Street, and whatever brief euphoria I'd experienced quickly faded away. The neighborhood I faintly remembered had been undergoing a gradual gentrification, spruced up by the arty types and social and political radicals with whom Randi fit so well. What I saw now as I walked in a daze was more reminiscent of a war zone. Entire blocks of buildings were gone. In their places were a mix of rubble, weeds, open graves, and partially buried remains of bodies. The almost-tangible, putrid stench of the area forced its way into my nose and mouth and lungs. I constantly fought back the urge to retch. The buildings that were standing barely did so. They were a collection of architectural despair from across the years; from primitive wooden huts to modern row houses, sharing only a sense of imminent collapse.

I recognized the Quick, the living, as they rushed here and there on their meaningless errands. They all shared in the hideous transformation I described that sometimes afflicted Randi. Those still connected to the world of the living were walking corpses, dangling flesh and deformed bones held together by some force of life which I no longer possessed.

There were others who were not among the Quick, shades more like myself. Ohlone Indians roamed aimlessly, their once-shimmering, fine hair chopped brutally short, their forms clothed in blood-stained white frocks of the Spanish Mission Delores. Long-dead prospectors and sailors gazed vacantly ahead as they shuffled through the streets. Was this the fate that awaited me, to continue on as an apathetic husk of a soul long after every semblance of passion and will had drained away?

I found no traces of hope beyond the walls that had contained me, only more despair, so I retreated toward the apartment which I wouldn't be able to enter until Randi returned. I actually looked forward to shutting myself away from this external misery once again and wallowing in my own.

■

"Let the first witness stand forward." The fire in the pit leaps higher as the magistrate pounds the podium with his gavel. Justin's father, my father, steps forward. I remember Leonard Parker from life. It was the memory of him, in fact, that helped me grow strong, that helped me lead Justin away from life. Leonard Parker is a tall, imposing figure in his expressionless black mask and the long black cape that covers him completely.

The magistrate glowers at the elder Parker. "By what right do you bear witness?"

"In life," states Parker, "I was father of the accused, in death, reaper. I also am marshal to He-Who-Is-Without-Words, the Quiet Lord, and his representative in this matter."

The magistrate is satisfied. "Present your evidence," he snarls.

Justin is lost in fear; he shivers uncontrollably. His father is unfazed by the palpable antipathy of the magistrate.

"I discovered the accused," begins Parker the elder, "while he was still an Enfant, his death Caul still fresh upon him. He was marked, as a soul given in to despair, for my master, and I attempted to perform my duties as Harvester for the Quiet Lord. I protected the accused from a less-reputable suitor," Parker glances over his shoulder at an indistinct figure held behind him in the shadows, "and then removed his Caul."

The magistrate glares silently, radiating impatience; he hovers on the precipice of action, his restrained intensity revealing his desire to be done with the matter.

"I explained to the accused his obligation to my lord," Parker lies, "but he discarded the ways of this realm, even though he knew next to nothing of them, and fled."

Parker's words are tainted by malignancy and deception. Their very utterance grates against truth with a resonance that none present can mistake. Parker explained nothing to Justin, but rather attempted to cajole, coerce, and threaten

him into submission. His words ring untrue, but the sound
is drowned out by the tortured screams of the nearby forges.
No one cares. Parker the elder is singularly treacherous, and
in this I feel my kinship to him. I see Justin's doom, the end
toward which I maneuver him, and it pleases me.

"Since then, I tracked down the accused, apprehended
him, and brought him here to receive judgment," concludes
Parker.

The magistrate nods gravely. He extends a robed arm and
his pale, outstretched finger points to the shadows behind
Justin and his father. "And what is this other creature you
have brought to my court?"

Parker the elder gestures to the figures in the shadows,
and two soldiers step forward dragging a pitiful being
between them. The soldiers wear black capes similar to
Parker's, except visible beneath theirs are breastplates, sword
belts, greaves, and other tarnished fragments of armor. Their
heads are covered with plumed helmets with guards that
extend downward to protect eyes and nose. The creature
they hold is a battered and bloody sight. Its upper body is a
facsimile of Justin's Uncle Vinny, Leonard Parker's brother
Vincent — approaching obesity, balding but otherwise
extraordinarily hairy. Tears run over the bruises and scabs,
making streaks across the grime and partially congealed
blood that are mixed with the stubble on not-Vinny's face.
Between its teeth is a metallic bridle bit which has worn
his mouth raw. The soldier on the right holds the reins. Not-
Vinny's lower portion is stunted and corpulent. Six wiry
appendages ending in claws protrude from its body; one of
the six, mangled, hangs limply. Its bottom two legs, barely
touching as the soldiers hold it aloft, scrape and clatter on
the stone floor.

"This creature," Parker points, "serves Aliman the
Decadent of Bali-Huran, a counterfeit demiurge of the Far
Shores. It attempted to deceive the accused into bondage,
and would thus have denied my master his rightful bounty

had I not intervened." Parker turns to the cowering prisoner. "Is this not true, groveler? *Speak.*" It cringes at his admonition.

The words come with difficulty until the soldiers remove the bit. Even then, its speech is clouded by sobs and gasps of lingering pain. "Yes, yes, yes. It is true. I am unworthy." Tears stream down its cheeks. "I wanted to trick him, to take him to my master." Parker the elder steps closer and the creature flinches. Not-Vinny's words tumble out of its bloody, gaping mouth. Its bloodshot, rheumy eyes look only at the floor. "To my foul master who has no claim to any soul. I am treasonous. I have betrayed the Hierarchy." Its words are lost in sobbing, its body wracked by convulsions.

Parker lifts not-Vinny's head by the chin. "And what of the accused?" he asks. His question, softly issued, is an unstated threat.

"He ran, yes, he ran," it complies. "Ran from his rightful reaper, ran away…" It can speak no more but trails off into incomprehensible mumbling and whining. Collapsing, it gives over completely to the flanking soldiers to support it.

Parker the elder, satisfied, faces the magistrate, who pounds his gavel once again. The reverberations quiet not-Vinny somewhat. Justin still stands transfixed by his fear.

"I will not allow this court to be further sullied by the presence of such vermin as this piteous creature," thunders the magistrate, pointing at not-Vinny. "First, I render judgment against you." The creature seems to have remembered its surroundings. It stares ahead fear-stricken. "To obstruct the duties of an official of the Hierarchy is grievous enough an offense, but additionally to profess subservience to a rebellious charlatan such as your so-called master is unconscionable. As one beyond redemption, the only possible worth you may yet achieve is to be found in the forges. Away with him."

At this pronouncement, not-Vinny screams a hideous and frantic defiance. It struggles briefly and then slumps again into the grip of its captors, all coherence lost in tears and barely audible protestations. Madness is the only response to such a sentence. The magistrate's gavel seals the fate of the unfortunate creature that is being dragged away through an arched doorway into darkness.

And now the magistrate's hellish glare locks upon Justin, upon me.

■

After my brief sojourn beyond the apartment into the Shadowlands, I had little desire for further explanation. I had more than enough guilt and despair of my own — I didn't need overwhelming doses heaped on me from that grim reality. Rather than feeling trapped by the walls against which I'd pressed so ardently before, I felt safe within my tiny enclosure. Not that the degeneration of this existence wasn't apparent, for the stench of death permeated everything, but I was comforted by my decision not to face the external world. While it could be better that what I now experienced — although my one excursion didn't suggest that — it could certainly be worse.

I continued to watch Randi. In fact, I became nearly obsessive about her. I followed her everywhere in the apartment, from room to room, like a dog waiting to be fed. I was her shadow. When she shivered as I passed, I was both reassured that my presence did have some effect on her, that I wasn't completely irrelevant, and conversely angered that she drew away, that we could never again share the warmth we once had.

When she left the apartment, I huddled in the corner near the door and trembled with fear and rage. How dare she leave me? Never mind that I'd abandoned and hurt her more absolutely than should be humanly possible. What if she didn't return from one of these errands, one of these exoduses? I could've tried to follow her, slipped out as I had that once but stuck with her closely, found out what she did, who she saw, but that would've required me to face once again that cruel outside world. So I was content to construct my elaborate self-justifications and blame her for leaving. The necessities of everyday human life — buying groceries, selling paintings, social interaction — were only vague memories to me now. No reason was valid if it took her away from me.

It was at those times that I noticed the slashes on my wrists, not always visible, and the occasional trickle of pus and blood that oozed from them. It was my action that had set all this in motion, yet I found reasons to blame her for our separation.

When Randi returned, I watched her even more closely. I sniffed at her and examined her every detail to determine where she'd been and what undertaking had taken her there. I was consumed by jealousy. Was she seeing another man? Had she finished grieving, forgotten me already? And then I was filled with anxiety that the next time she left, she might not return.

I took to following her into the bathroom, slipping in before she could close the door, even though it meant facing the room and the large, white, iron bathtub in which I'd ended my life. Strangely enough, the pain of letting her out of my sight was greater than my dread of the room. I was fascinated by biological necessities that were so distant to me now, and to watch her bathe was a torturous ecstasy beyond description.

One evening in particular I remember well for several reasons. Randi and I were in the bathroom. She'd been gone most of the day, so my separation anxiety, my fear and lust and anger, had all been stoked to a fever pitch. The tub was filling with hot water and bubbles, the mirror covered with warm fog. Randi laid her clothes on the floor. She stood naked before me, her small white breasts, nipples hardened from the cool air — or perhaps from my presence; I trembled at the thought. I wanted desperately to caress her smooth stomach and hips and thighs, to kiss them, to feel her skin against mine again. I stepped forward, for whatever good it might do me, but before I could even reach out to Randi, she was lowering herself into the soap and water, and my delusions discorporated. Just as her body was hidden from my view by the bubble-covered surface of the water, any intimacy for which I might hope was forever denied me, aversion being the only response I was capable of evoking, and that only mildly.

For a split second, I wanted to reach down with a razor blade and slit Randi's wrists just as I had my own. I felt an urge to violence, my thoughts bent only on destruction. And then the feeling was gone.

Suddenly, and just as inexplicably, I felt confined in the room. The intensity with which I'd wanted to get in reversed itself, and I felt the urgent need to escape this place that had already witnessed my undoing once. I didn't experience physiological terror — my heart wasn't pounding; I wasn't sweating or gasping for breath. The mental anguish that overwhelmed me was far worse. I knew with complete certainty that the room was shrinking, the walls closing in to crush out of existence my crude mockery of life, and while the walls closed in, the bathtub was growing larger. It expanded toward the walls and grew taller, filling whatever space was available, conspiring with the walls to grind my wretched corpus to dust.

I threw myself against the door, trying to find some avenue of escape. Even in my horror, however, I couldn't help but worry about Randi. Would she be destroyed with me? Had my reckless misery condemned us both? When I looked back at her, I was shocked to find that she was staring directly at me; not at the area that I happened to occupy, as usually happened, but directly at *me*. She didn't seem to mind the upheaval in the room. In fact, she began to laugh. She threw back her head and cackled maniacally. Then I noticed that the bathwater was no longer soapy. The tub was now a huge basin full of blood, in the middle of which sat Randi, rubbing it through her hair, leaning down and lapping it up.

She was not alone.

Swimming about in the bloody pool was our child, our *unborn* child. He dove under the surface and resurfaced with glee, taking in mouthfuls of blood and spitting it into the air like a fountain. I could see the umbilical cord that still attached him to his mother.

How was this happening? What kind of ghastly vision was I seeing?

I pounded on the door, frantic to get away from those I loved the most, and then, somehow, I was on the other side. Whether or how I was transported or passed through it, I don't know, but I was on the other side of the door.

I didn't have long to ponder the question, however, because at that moment, the front door to the apartment came crashing in. Storming into the room were several glaringly pale men — six, seven, I wasn't sure — dressed something like Roman legionnaires. They carried drawn swords, and one held chains that were attached to two great beasts — *barghests*, I would later learn they're called; large dog-like creatures but with faces and limbs that were grotesquely human.

The legionnaires moved with amazing speed. Before I could react, several had pounced and wrestled me roughly to the floor. Too late did I struggle, worried that they would attack Randi, but they made no move past me toward the bathroom. The attention of the four legionnaires who held me down and the two others standing nearby was directed, as mine was drawn, to the front door and the tall, dark figure that strode into the room. The barghests, which had been pulling at their leads and howling uncontrollably as their handler held them back, immediately quieted, and I, without realizing, ceased my struggle.

The new entrant was dressed completely in black — his robe, his long, flowing cape, his boots, and mask. Even before he reached up and removed the mask, I recognized my father, his air of vicious superiority. I shuddered involuntarily as he stood above me, his shadow covering me. He gestured to the legionnaires who raised me until I was only inches from his face. His features were sharper, more handsome than I remembered them, enhanced by whatever method he used to hide or repair the damage from the shotgun blast with which he'd taken his life.

"Run from me again, boy," he said, "and see where it gets you." His smile was a confident sneer. "Had to go out and explore, didn't you? The Restless of the Quiet Lord are everywhere, and word always comes back to me." He turned and headed toward the door. "Bring him," he said to the legionnaires without turning back.

They bound me, taking little care for my comfort, and dragged me out the front door, but instead of going down steps and out to 16th Street, I was aboard a ship, a nineteenth-century clipper from the looks of it, masts and rigging and sails towering above. I caught only a brief glimpse of the sails before I was thrown into the hold where I was left to lie with numerous other similarly bound wraiths. Many had been beaten into submission. They were pitiful creatures in various states of physical and mental degeneration, abused in both corpus and psyche, and I was no better.

My hands bound behind me and my ankles manacled and chained together, I slid on my face to a dark corner where I collapsed and kept to myself. The ship began to move. I heard the sounds, the voiceless screams, of the Tempest outside, but I couldn't concentrate on where I was or where I was being taken. I lapsed into and out of slumber, for how long I don't know. When I was conscious, I was often seized by dark moods beyond my control. I wished for my own destruction. I wished that the entire ship and all aboard would be sucked down into Oblivion. I wished for Randi's destruction and my son's. Mostly, however, over the course of the journey, I stumbled through nightmare after nightmare, one horrific image after another, until I was taken by rough hands from the ship, dragged through a monstrous city of death that was merely another nightmare to me, and into the court.

■

"Now for your sentence," proclaims the magistrate, "for your guilt is without question."

Justin's mouth opens. For the second time he speaks in this court. The spineless fool's mind is muddled; he is awash in some fearful stupor. I am rising; I am very close now. I feel that my time is almost at hand. "But I haven't... haven't had a chance...."

Somehow the magistrate's arms are long enough to reach Justin. Instead of the two being separated by the pit, the magistrate is clutching Justin in his bony hands, holding the accused by the shoulders several feet above the stone floor. The flame pit roars to life; bright sparks escape into the gloomy red sky, free for an instant, then extinguished.

You were warned, wormtongue. The magistrate shifts his grip. With one powerful claw, he holds Justin aloft by the neck, with the other he reaches into Justin's mouth and rips out the offending flesh.

Justin, released, falls to the ground. *I fall to the ground.* Justin is no longer present; he is banished from this horror, unable to comprehend any more. I was close to the surface. Now I surge to the fore. I writhe on the floor, moving my fingers, feeling muscles respond to my commands. I feel my body, my face. I touch the mangled stump in my mouth, feel the blood running down my throat, *and I rejoice.*

"Your sentence, wormtongue," thunders the magistrate, his new trophy already displayed upon his belt. "You belong to the Quiet Lord, as ordained by the *Dictum Mortem*. You will be taken to the forges, rendered into oboli, and awarded to the Quiet Lord as coinage."

The magistrate raises his gavel to punctuate the sentence but is stopped short by Parker the elder's call. "Your honor."

The magistrate, gavel suspended aloft, licks his sharp teeth with his forked tongue. "What now, Harvester?"

Parker approaches the bench, stepping over my still-twitching form. He hands the magistrate a twice-folded parchment. "I have here a writ from my master." The magistrate begins to read. Parker continues. "Anticipating the favorable outcome of this matter, my master requests that this criminal be released to my care, in lieu of being dealt with otherwise." Parker almost hides his self-satisfaction, not wanting to upset the magistrate unduly.

The magistrate's hidden eyes undoubtedly race back and forth across the parchment. The award is to the Quiet Lord. The magistrate has no choice but to honor the request of a Deathlord, regardless of his personal satisfaction at stoking the forges. He glares at Parker one last time. "Very well. Your master's request is granted," he snarls. "Remove this creature from my sight and begone."

■

I ride my father's ship, *The Harrowing*, across the Tempest, the Sea of Souls, away from Stygia. He is a dashing, dark figure at the helm. So lost in life, he has found his calling here among the tortured souls of death. Possibly, with time, I could destroy him, take his place, turn about the intended fate as Zeus did to Cronos. But I must enact my own plans, steer my own course. This wraith's corpus is resilient. The tattered remnant of my tongue has grown out, still raw and bloody but sufficient for speech.

Father relinquishes the helm to a lieutenant and approaches. His black mask hides his face. "Soon I may hand the wheel to you, my son," he says. "It's only fitting that a son follow his father, obey him."

"Worship him," I add. "Idolize him. Supersede him. Eat his soul. Destroy him." I can see his eyes wrinkle. He is smiling.

"I know you are there deep inside, Justin," says Father, "controlled by your darker side. Perhaps that is necessary for you to survive. For a time."

"Your son is weak and lost, Father," I explain. "I no longer tolerate him. I will serve you; I will learn from you, but first I must remove certain constraints."

"Oh?" His smile is gone, his voice emotionless.

"Take me back to the Shadowlands, to the place of my capture," I instruct him. "There is destruction to be wrought."

"But you are here in my control already, my son. What need have I to humor your dark fancies?"

"With the woman alive, I will always be called back. I will not be free to serve you as I could otherwise. With her, and the child she carries, removed from the living, I will rise to greatness beside you." I lie as smoothly as ever he did. "And you will have two more souls to present to your lord, to *our* lord."

He ponders behind his mask only a moment and then, without turning from me, calls to the helmsman, "Change course to the Shadowlands." His voice is quieter now, for me alone. "We will go," and he is back to the helm.

I wait in my cabin, for I am an officer on this ship now. I rub my young tongue along the roof of my mouth, savoring the taste of blood. I chase after Oblivion, and like a snake swallowing its tail, I will be consumed. In time. I long for such rapture. First, however, I must free myself of the entanglements of life which Justin so thoughtlessly constructed and cultivated, even beyond life, the pitiful wretch. Father, in his arrogance, will help me.

Time is inconstant upon the Tempest. Days, hours,

seconds are all interchangeable. They have little meaning here, but today time crawls. Eventually, I feel that we have slowed. I venture out of the cabin and can tell that we have not reached our destination. "Why have we stopped?" I ask.

My father points to the boiling sea. I see a small rowboat with two of our sailors. They pull onto their craft out of the waves a child. "A soul adrift," Father comments. "Perhaps fresh from life. No sense leaving him to the Spectres. There's always time to stop for cargo."

The rowboat returns and the sailors pull the child aboard. He is no older than four. His death Caul is in place, obscuring his vision. Too frightened for speech, he is an Enfant in more ways than one. Death by drowning for this little one. He does not technically belong to our lord, but such technicalities can be overlooked when convenient. I can smell life on the boy still. It attracts and repulses me.

"Do you hunger?" Father asks, and suddenly I know that I do.

This soul is still warm, still sparkling with the vestiges of life. I touch the child. I slide my hands over his face, through his short hair, down his chest, over his entire body. His soulful scent is at once both enraging and inviting. That life exists in any form is a crime, yet it draws me to it unavoidably. I press my face against the top of his head. I can feel the warmth fading already, drawn away by the wind of the surrounding Tempest. I am kissing his hair, wild passions in the lead, and then I am stretching my jaws wide like a serpent ingesting a large rat. My mouth is stretched around the top of his head. His aroma fills my nostrils. He does not cry or struggle as I lean over him, sliding down over his face and neck. I am lying on the deck of the ship now as I continue to draw him in. I do not care who sees the impossible contortions of my body. Torso, hips, thighs, knees. I consume that which is close to life; I have my own small victory over it. Soon I swoon like a contented drunkard, only my potable is the essence of life itself.

Lost in digestive exaltation, I am carried back to the cabin. My dreams of a small boy's brief life are mixed with the ghostly sounds of my father's laughter. I grow stronger.

I do not know how long my stupor continues, but now I hear knocking. I open my eyes and see I am still in the cabin. One never knows. Case in point: I open the cabin door, but instead of being on deck, I am in the apartment. Father stands before me. Randi paints on one of the several canvases in the room. Tinged with the residual life of the soul I have consumed, I can actually see what she paints — some tiresome neosentimentalist balderdash — but only for an instant, then it is gone, the canvas once again empty to me. The child in her belly, cursed by me as I am by my father, is larger. Randi still does not show, but she must be aware of it by now. I notice the telltale way her hand absentmindedly rests on her stomach while she examines her work.

"So it is destruction you crave, my son," says Father. He walks toward Randi. I knew he would complete the task for me. Affecting the physical world is difficult, and he is certainly more practiced in the art than I. Once the deed is done, I will be unfettered from the world of the living, and free to plunge into the Tempest and fall toward Oblivion. I can smell the end of this horrid journey that Justin began so badly.

Father stands next to Randi. He looks over her shoulder at her work. She is unaware of our presence. With the flick of a finger, he knocks the brush from her hand onto the floor. She grimaces and leans and picks it up. She resumes painting, but he knocks the brush from her grasp again.

"Dammit," she mutters.

This time when she goes to retrieve the brush, Father kicks it across the floor.

"I am not impressed by your parlor tricks, Father," I chide him. "I could do as well."

He does not respond, but when Randi stands up with the

brush, she sees that her easel and canvas are two feet off the floor. She only flinches slightly as, with a quick gesture, Father lets them fall to the floor. Blinking several times, she approaches cautiously. Almost more quickly than I can follow, he raises his hand and strikes her across the face. The force of the blow flings her body through the air. She lands jarringly on the hardwood floor and does not move immediately.

I feel Oblivion approaching. My plans will soon be fulfilled.

Father stands above her as she attempts to rise. He viciously kicks her in the stomach, jolting the unborn child violently. I revel in their agony. He strikes her again in the back of the head. She lies still, moaning intermittently. I am drawn by the speed and brutality of Father's actions, the power he wields over life now that he is apart from it. He turns and points to the canvas, and it bursts into flames. Then another canvas and another, until the room is filling with smoke and the curtains are igniting.

Thank you, Father.

He faces me and removes his mask. He is smiling again. "Is your scheme almost complete, my son?"

He is too satisfied. Why?

"You plan to leave me?" he asks.

"What are you talking about? I said I would serve you," I respond.

"We say many things, and we mean many others." His evil grin is maddening. "Destroy your fetters and you can be free of me. Is that it?" He laughs now. "Do you think me ignorant? Do you see how paper-thin are your plans?" He is suddenly, without moving, directly in front of me, no more than a step away.

The flames are spreading. The furniture, the walls, all ablaze. "You're wrong." Can he hear the panic in my voice as everything unravels?

"I helped you *for my own reasons*, son," he gloats. "There

are other fetters you don't know of, and those I control. These are not your only fetters."

These are not your only fetters.

I know it now. I feel it to be true. I am closer, perhaps, but still far, so far, from my dreams. He knew all along. I have failed. I am falling. It is all so very far away now.

■

First I saw the burning bodies of my lover and my child within her, and I knew unmistakably that I had brought this about. The inferno around me was the true Hell. *Let it consume me, God, so that this may end.* Then he hit me, my own father, flesh of my flesh, ravager of souls. But how different was I who had feasted upon a child?

He was standing over me, shouting at me. The words resounded in my mind. "You are too weak, Justin. Grow stronger or perish. I care not which. Come after me for your revenge if you can, and if you are strong enough, then I will bend you to my will. Otherwise, I do not care." He pointed at the smoldering bodies on the floor. "These souls I will harvest, for my trouble," and he was gone.

Flames and black smoke were everywhere. They threatened even this strange, unearthly corpus of mine. If I possessed courage, I would have let them consume me, but I was moved by anger and fear. I crawled out the open door and down the steps into the street where I lay for countless hours, the taste of a child on my lips, and my father's words echoing in the air.

NO TURNING
BACK

THOMAS M. KANE

The bed felt just a degree too warm, too soft, indeed too comfortable for Clifford Rafferty to endure. Cliff's body slid into a cozy hollow of the mattress, made half by him and half by his wife, Margaret, who lay asleep by his side. Still, Cliff's eyes moved about the room, pausing on the date, visible in red electronic digits upon the clock, pausing again upon the wispy curtains, which veiled the waning moon. The clock gave Rafferty three more hours to sleep, three more hours before going back to the office, three more hours before returning to his mundane life, which he had escaped once before, and which had risen again to consume him.

Two weeks had passed since Halloween, since the day when Cliff had learned that there were indeed werewolves — Garou — in the world. Cliff had seen the Garou sacrifice their lives. Cliff had also killed — he had shot three men with a high-powered rifle. After a lifetime of working his office job at Trans-Con, doing what people expected of him, the Garou had taught Cliff about Trans-Con's operations in cooperation with Developer Forestry Group Incorporated in the Amazon basin, where the two corporations were engaged in the manufacture of death. Rafferty had helped the Garou strike back against Trans-Con, blowing one of the company's shipments to kingdom come with the holy fire of Semtex plastic explosives.

After the Halloween raid, when Cliff had returned to his home as the sole survivor of the battle, he had assumed that it was only a matter of time before he received a knock on his door, either from the Garou come to spirit him away into their shadowy organization, or from Trans-Con investigators, there to arrest him. Instead, the fall sun had shone, and life had seemed eerily, oppressively normal. All the Garou Cliff knew were dead, and it seemed possible that their brethren did not know of his existence, or saw no reason to contact him. As for Trans-Con, Cliff had gone back to work there, making the decision after an hour of silent agony Halloween morning, reasoning that if Trans-Con security had not already identified him, it would be wise not to arouse their suspicions by suddenly quitting.

Now, Cliff found himself rolling over in bed, twisting sheets around himself. Memories of the past two weeks flowed around him, of sitting in his office cubicle, listening to the same droning hum of copiers, trading stories about sports and car trouble around the coffee machine, and always looking over his shoulder, always feeling his stomach quiver when he walked over the threshold of the Trans-Con building, always wondering if he would feel a hand on his shoulder as the Trans-Con company's security men seized him at last. Cliff whispered aloud, "I can't live in fear." He repeated it. "I cannot live my life in fear."

However, even as Cliff whispered, he knew that fear was

only an excuse. Each day, the fear grew a little less. The real danger, Cliff knew, was that he would sink back into the familiar contours of his life, just as, at that moment, his head was sinking into the softness of the pillow. Cliff jerked his head upward, making the springs of the bed groan. Aside from an itchy red scratch on his wrist, Cliff had nothing to remind him of the raid, and when the scar faded, he would be as if the raid had never occurred.

That was the thought which tormented Cliff. What if the raid and the Garou were simply an isolated moment, an aberration, which came without warning and vanished without a trace, leaving him stuck in his old life again? Cliff told himself that he would try to locate other Garou and rejoin the battle, but what if his resolve was not as strong as he thought, or what if there were simply no Garou to be found? What if, in the course of time, his own memories faded, and the very desire to fight for Gaia faded as well?

And so, Cliff found himself asking, *Did any of it really matter?*

For an instant, Cliff considered shaking Margaret awake, admitting that his story about a Halloween party with the boss had been a lie, and spilling out the whole story to her, gaining at once a historian and a confidant. Cliff reminded himself that he had shared everything with Margaret throughout a marriage which had lasted eleven years. Few of the people he knew at the office could say the same. However, as soon as Cliff considered waking his wife, he found a flood of reasons not to.

Cliff told himself, in a stern mental voice, that he was merely trying to shift responsibility from himself onto Margaret, and that he had no right to do this. He was the one who had met the Garou, and he was the one who would have to do what it took to rejoin their cause, whatever decisions that entailed.

Furthermore, as Cliff reflected upon the matter, he realized that he had no idea how Margaret would react to the tale. Cliff raised himself on an elbow, looking at his wife in the half-light, noting her pink, faded nightgown, noting how she slept with her palms together and her head pillowed on her hands like a mattress advertisement or a drawing of a sleeping woman made for a children's book. There were no werewolves in Margaret's world. Cliff told himself that Margaret would not want to hear the truth and added that she was safer not knowing.

Cliff sat upright, filled with the determination to find the Garou again. His motion pulled down the covers, causing the entire bed to shake. Even after the motion of the bed stopped, Margaret continued to move, her legs curling upward, her eyes blinking open and gazing up at her husband.

Margaret brushed Cliff's arm, her hand smelling of lotion. She opened her mouth, and croaked, obviously half-lost in sleep, "Bad dream?"

"No." Cliff spoke more harshly than he might have, feeling a sudden, intense and almost childlike burst of self-consciousness. "Not a dream!"

Margaret blinked slowly and settled into the covers again. Cliff lay down, but kept his eyes wide open until the alarm rang.

By the time Cliff reached his office, his thoughts had cooled, settled, changed from seething worry to a sense of purpose, and to the knowledge that if he did not want to live with them for the rest of his life, it was up to him to take fate into his own hands. Evening found Cliff driving toward the docks, where the smell of salt mixed with the fumes of factory smoke. It had not been hard, Cliff reflected, to get the information he needed. Cliff remembered how his heart had pounded when he thumbed the button for the sub-basement level, and the stainless-steel doors of the elevator sealed themselves shut. However, the file librarian in the Secure Data sector turned out to be a middle-aged lady in a turquoise dress, who had squinted at Cliff's I.D. badge through tortoiseshell granny glasses, given him a tired nod, and then authorized him for the records he wanted, her red fingernails flashing over the keyboard as she entered an access code which appeared on the computer screen as "########-###."

Cliff shot another glance at the slick laser printout which lay half-curled upon the dashboard. "*Moonbeam Expeditions: Summary Report*. This organization, purportedly a firm sponsoring marine mammal research and private tours off the California coastline serves as a front for the eco-terrorist organization 'True Green.' Group owns & operates a 34-foot converted fishing vessel registered as 'Beamer.' Surveillance indicates likelihood (prob. est. 76%) of direct Garou involvement..." Cliff couldn't help noting the line at the bottom of the document too, which bore the warning "HIGHLY CONFIDENTIAL (Security Intelligence Department)." However, the most important part of the report was the line which provided Moonbeam Expeditions' address. Cliff noted that he had found the right street, and with this thought, he felt a treacherous flash of apprehension.

Cliff drove from the bottom of the steep street to the top and back again, through a tunnel of aging brick buildings, all worn by the salt air. Only on the second pass did he see the Moonbeam Expeditions headquarters, lodged in an alley on the side of a vacant-looking old house, a house which had its front door chained shut and its top-story windows covered by plywood. A hand-painted sign identified the building, showing the pale slash of a moon against a background of blackness. The moon had eyes and a mouth, and if it had been a full moon, the face might have shown a beatific smile. However, the moon was crescent, and the darker side seemed to mask a feral snarl.

Cliff parked the car. A few steps took him up the street, as if he were climbing toward the darkening sky. Cliff felt as if his knock sounded pitifully faint against the timbers of the side door. However, a moment after the knock, a deep voice growled from within, "Come in." Finally, Cliff knew that there was no turning back. Cliff gripped the knob, found it unlocked, pushed the door open, and stepped in, discovering himself in a room lit by the rainbow colors of a cracked disco strobe.

People gazed at Cliff from all sides. In one corner, a lean man leaned back in a rocking chair, cradling a guitar in his lap, his mane of dark hair flowing behind his head. A blond woman sat on the bare floorboards beside him, her plump legs crossed, idly rocking the chair as she stared at Cliff, her blue eyes wide with undisguised curiosity. A pair of burly fellows sat on opposite sides of the room as if facing off for a duel, each clutching a can of beer, each grunting as he turned to view the open door. Cliff saw a pair of older men in the room as well, seated upon the stained cushions of a couch.

One of the men on the couch responded first, rising and drawing back his lips in a smile which revealed a mouthful of tiny, perfect teeth. The man's eyes glinted knowingly at Cliff and then flickered away as he glanced at the other people in the room. "Well, hello... my friend. My name is Blake." The voice was higher in pitch than Cliff expected from a man. "What... what may we do for you?"

The man with the guitar slashed his hand in a wave. His tone was suave, but his blue eyes carried a hint of menace. "Wildman Jack. C'mon in, and shut the door."

The first time Cliff opened his mouth, nothing came out. However, he reminded himself, the werewolves he had known seemed to value nothing more highly than courage. Therefore, Cliff closed the door behind him, planted his legs wide, and spoke a little louder than necessary. "My name is Clifford Rafferty. I was a friend of Garou named Yolanda and Odin — perhaps you knew them. I am looking for other Garou." Cliff trusted that, if he had made a mistake, and these people were not Garou, they might think he was crazy, but at least they would not know what he was talking about.

For a moment, nobody answered. Then the big man on Cliff's left slammed his beer can down on the glass top of a card table. "Odin died."

Cliff took a breath and released it. "Odin did die. Bravely—"

"You are not Garou, little man." The figure on Cliff's right rose with a stomp of his worn boots. "We can smell it. Where d'you come in with Odin? Huh?" The man bared his teeth, flaring the nostrils of a misshapen and oft-broken nose.

The woman on the floor began to rock Wildman Jack's chair a little faster. Blake turned his head, watching Cliff through narrow eyes. The man on Cliff's left rose too, and the two burly fellows approached Cliff from either side. Cliff glanced from one to the other, seeing only half-shaven faces and scowls. The man on Cliff's left began rumbling in his throat, and the others took up this growling as well.

Suddenly, the other man on the couch, a thin, elderly fellow with a bald head and a wisp of a beard, broke the growling with a cough. Having gotten the group's attention, the man shrugged slightly, raised his hands in the air, turned to Cliff, and then to the others. The man's gaze was steady, and Cliff sensed something kindly in the man, despite the burst vessel which ran across the white of his eye like the bloody taproot of a plant, sprouting a web of fine red capillaries. "Listen to me for a moment, listen to old Wilson. No need for all this haste and waste…"

The men who towered over Cliff visibly relaxed, and turned to Wilson. Blake ran a hand through his halo of graying hair, then lowered it to stroke his chin.

Wilson turned his gaze fully upon Cliff, his mouth forming a gentle smile. "Perhaps we find out what Mr. Rafferty wants before we decide not to let him have it. What is it, Mr. Rafferty? What want you with the Garou?"

"I want…" Cliff scrambled in his mind, trying to think

of an appropriate word. To offer them his help might be fatally presumptuous, but to request their sympathy would probably be futile. "I want nothing. I ask only that you give me a chance to do what must be done. Odin and Yolanda trusted me, and if we had not worked together, a shipment containing fifteen tons of nerve gas and silver nitrate would have reached the Amazon. I... I am still human, but my place is with the Garou."

"Do you really think it's that easy?" Wildman Jack let the guitar slide farther into his lap and folded his long arms.

Cliff kept his mouth firmly shut, suppressing his initial choke of indignation. Abandoning his life did not seem "easy." However, Cliff forced himself to remember how he must appear to the Garou — a mere human, and worse, a human who had spent thirty years of his life comfortably ensconced in the Establishment. Cliff could not blame the Garou for being reluctant to accept him into their circle.

For a moment, Cliff stared down at the polished shoes he had worn from work. Then he glanced around the room, but he saw no sympathy in the eyes of the big men on his left and right, nor in the deep brown eyes of the guitar player, who looked down the length of his sharp nose at Cliff. The blond woman on the floor smiled when Cliff met her eyes, but the smile did not seem to promise much. Blake merely raised an eyebrow at Cliff. Wilson, however, nodded encouragingly, and Cliff turned to him. "If you want me to prove myself, I will do whatever you ask."

"Rite of Truth!" The man on Cliff's left practically bellowed, his whiskers curling back to reveal a broken tooth. "You face me in the Rite of Truth."

"Bull!" The man on the right shouted with equal force. "This ain't your fight, Mike. Odin and I go back — way back. The human's ass is mine."

Cliff stood stock still, watching Wilson for more reassurance, not knowing what to say.

"What color," Mike puffed up his chest, "is the sky on *your* planet? Odin let you run in his pack because he felt sorry for you. I called the Rite. I fight the fight."

"Why don't you fight to see who gets to fight him?" The plump woman giggled and flicked the tab from a beer can at Mike. Both Mike and his opponent laughed.

"Ah." Wilson smiled fondly at the woman, then looked at the two big men. "Tonight it shall be Piper's turn to test, I think. Another time for Mike will be the Rite." Instantly, both Mike and Piper bowed their heads.

Wilson took Cliff by the shoulder, and although his hand was shrunken with age, the grip was firm. "Not weapons shall you use, but with your courage and your hands shall you prove yourself before us. However, in this Rite, you may take one possession with you, one token for your luck and your skill." Wilson glanced from Cliff to Piper and back. "What will you wish to be taking?"

Piper reached into the denim folds of his jacket and produced a crescent knife in a sheath of finely tanned buckskin. "I want my father's klaive."

Wilson turned to Cliff.

Cliff stuck his hands in his pockets, finding nothing but his Trans-Con I.D. badge and a wallet. Then he leveled his gaze upon Wilson. "Nothing. I bring nothing from my past into this battle."

Wilson only shrugged, his bloodshot eyes calm. "If that is what you wish."

Even as they talked, the blond woman began to clear the center of the room, with Mike helping her. The two of them brushed Blake aside as they picked up cans and wrappers. Wilson pulled the card table aside. Piper walked over to the wooden entertainment console, which held a television, VCR and stereo. With a flick of his hand, Piper got the systems unplugged and the speakers disconnected. Then he lifted the entire console without a grunt and lugged it through a curtained doorway into a back room.

Cliff stood in the center of the room watching the proceedings, wondering what came next. A chill of fear spread through Cliff's body, working from the body up. None of the Garou had mentioned whether the fight was to be to the death, or what the penalty for losing might be, and as Cliff looked around the room, he realized that his life might end in this shady, smoky room, under the poster of a cartoon chimpanzee wielding a monkey wrench. Cliff found his musings from the morning before coming back in a new, sour way, and although he raged at himself to quit being a coward, he found himself wondering whether death would be any less ignominious than living out his life as a middle manager.

A brown stain on the flood caught Cliff's eye, and in his mind, it became a pool of crimson blood. Cliff realized that, even if he did not face death there, he was almost certain to suffer horrible pain. Death was an abstract, almost philosophical fear, but Cliff could actually imagine his ribs cracking under Piper's blows, his flesh bludgeoned and torn. Cliff noticed Piper's muscles, grimly noting that the fight could have no other outcome, and his knees buckled with the thought.

Piper grinned at Cliff, his fists clenched, eyes flashing from beneath thick brows. Cliff caught his breath with the realization that, with no more ceremony, the Rite was about to begin. In that instant, Cliff's heart leapt, and suddenly, he saw the solution to the problems which had been vexing him. Cliff saw that if he could not face pain and death in the initiation, he could not possibly claim the courage to face them in the Garou's cause. Having had that thought, Cliff cast his brooding aside, tore off his jacket, and lunged at the werewolf who stood a head higher than himself.

Piper seized Cliff in a headlock, crushing Cliff's nose against the sweat-stained cloth of his jeans. Mucous flowed into Cliff's nose. However, Cliff pummeled the side of his opponent's thigh, pounding the nerves of the leg. As Cliff punched, he twisted, not to break free, but to keep the werewolf occupied. Piper lifted an arm, and brought down his elbow on Cliff's spine. Cliff twisted and bit. Just as Cliff felt his own teeth crack, Piper grunted, released him and pulled back.

Mike, on the sidelines, raised both hands and roared, "Get 'im." Mike turned to Cliff and shouted louder. "Kill him."

Cliff, shocked to receive encouragement from the Garou, attacked again, battering Piper chest-to-chest. Piper drew back and drove a kick at Cliff's kneecap. By bracing his leg, Cliff avoided a shattered leg, but the force of the blow knocked him over backward. Cliff howled as he went down, scrambling with all limbs. Hooking his leg behind Piper's ankle, Cliff managed to trip his opponent too. Both Piper and Cliff crashed to the floorboards.

A chord from the skinny Garou's guitar thrummed over the room. Piper's steely muscles relaxed. Cliff looked up into Wilson's red eye. The old Garou smiled with satisfaction. "With both fallen, the Trial has ended."

Cliff twisted from Piper's grip, Mike whooped, Blake ran his hand through his wisps of hair and grinned a skull-like grin, and the blond woman slung a can of beer to Cliff where he lay, then proceeded to hand out beers to the Garou, giving each can a hearty shake before releasing it.

"Thanks, Sadie." Piper popped the top of his can and pulled the tab right off, letting the suds burst out to spray Cliff and run down his neck into his white collared shirt. "Got me down, human. Not bad."

Cliff righted himself, and after an instant's hesitation, pulled the tab on his own beer with a lusty tug, letting the beverage foam up and spill over his hand.

The skinny Garou began playing a tune, a rapidly-changing melody which Cliff had never heard before.

"You have passed our test." Wilson spoke from just behind Cliff, in a soft tone of voice.

Cliff turned and, knowing nothing to say, raised the beer

in a gesture of triumph, then took a drink.

"Happy are you now?"

Cliff paused. For an instant, Cliff found himself feeling a little like an outsider, admiring the camaraderie of the Garou but unsure whether he would ever fit in. "I'm happy."

"Why?" Wilson raised the white tuft of his eyebrow. "What is important to you?"

"The cause." Cliff took a drink. "What... what else am I supposed to say?"

"Whatever is in your heart." Wilson nodded, waited a moment, and turned away.

Only as Cliff let himself through his front door at four in the morning did he wonder what he would tell Margaret. Margaret would have gone to bed without him, since both of them worked late more nights than they could count. Cliff told himself that his beer-soaked shirt could have come from another office party, but the time would come when Margaret would have to know more; unless, of course, he were simply to disappear from her.

Cliff wondered what Margaret would do and think if he vanished. Would she search for him? Cliff suddenly imagined his wife on tabloid TV, telling a reporter with a varnished toupee about her hunt for her vanished husband. Would she suspect him of running away with another woman, or of being a criminal, or would she take his innocence for granted and assume that he been in some sort of accident? All these thoughts made Cliff feel dark and traitorous.

Cliff flipped on the living-room light and instantly felt dazzled. The telephone jangled as if in unison with the light.

Cliff scooped up the receiver, still blinking, dizzy from the beer. "Hello."

"Hello Mr. Rafferty." The voice was clear, female and exacting, pronouncing each syllable with precision. "I am Ms. Anita Sivard of Trans-Con Incorporated. Come to the office." Anita paused briefly. "Now."

Rafferty licked his lips. At that moment, he heard the

grind of an engine outside and saw headlights play across the shadows of his lawn, coming to a stop on the picture window. The pair of yellow lamps glared from the darkness, invading his house.

Again, Ms. Sivard's clear voice sliced into Rafferty's ear. "You will see a company car outside. That is your transportation. We are watching the exits to your house, and we hope that you will come promptly."

With that, Rafferty's teeth came together. Rafferty felt the awful weight of realizing where all of his plans for the future had been blind. Rafferty realized that a seasoned Garou might contrive an escape, but he was not a warrior, he was a thirty-six-year-old office worker, and Margaret was asleep in the next room. Although Rafferty was more athletic than most, and had seen more than most, at that moment, he knew nothing to do but step out into the night's chill and climb into the back of the immaculate blue rental car. Rafferty did not say a word as the driver, a nondescript fellow in a gray suit, whisked him to Trans-Con headquarters and down to Sivard's office on the sub-basement level, only a few doors down from the Secure Data sector.

The driver stood aside as Rafferty entered Ms. Sivard's office. Rafferty found himself in a sparsely finished room, the off-white walls bright in the glare of fluorescent tubes. Ms. Sivard sat there waiting for him, a slight woman in middle-age, her straight hair falling to just above shoulder-height on either side, thick, square glasses on her knife-blade of a nose. "Please seat yourself."

Rafferty lowered himself into the metal folding chair before Ms. Sivard's desk.

"Trans-Con Security has an assignment for you, Mr. Rafferty." Ms. Sivard's blue eye glittered through her glasses. "I hear that you have made quite an impression upon the Moonbeam Expeditions Garou."

"I... don't know." Rafferty felt cold inside.

"Then perhaps you have less experience with their kind

than us." Ms. Sivard folded her long, dry hands upon the empty desk. "The one who calls himself Wilson is quite taken with your dedication. That is something which will prove useful to us."

Ms. Sivard tapped a nail upon the steel surface of her desk. "Thus far, you have met the front-line Garou, who are of little consequence. Forget them — you will not be dealing with those lesser Garou again. Wilson will introduce you to others, deeper within the Garou organization. When that happens, you will report to Trans-Con on the people you meet, their locations, plans and equipment."

"You don't want me!" Rafferty grunted out the words before he had a chance to change his mind.

"Oh, but you are mistaken."

Rafferty swallowed. Only a few hours ago, he had brooded on whether he had the strength to face torture and death, and now Rafferty guessed that he was about to face the test. Still, Rafferty knew that if the alternative was to betray the Garou, he had no choice. "You don't know everything I've done. You don't know about shipment—"

"Do not worry, Mr. Rafferty." Ms. Sivard's voice grew falsely reassuring as she spoke the word "worry." "We may know a great deal more than you give us credit for. In any event, Trans-Con does not throw away potential assets."

Ms. Sivard pulled her back, if possible, a little straighter. "You will work with Blake. Blake is one of the Garou who work on our side, what they call a Spiral Dancer. He is a remarkable fellow, from all I hear, and when it suits his purposes, he can call upon stranger powers than you or probably even I could imagine. I believe that you have met him?"

"I refuse." Rafferty lifted both of his empty hands, palms forward. "I refuse."

"No, you most certainly do not refuse." Ms. Sivard did not even seem upset. "You have Margaret to think about."

Those words caused Rafferty's arms to fall to his sides

again. Rafferty pushed back into his chair, as if he could fade back into the seat, telling himself that he had made a muddle of everything.

"Margaret is quite safe now. In fact, she is probably the safest woman in your neighborhood, because I have two security teams watching her at this very moment. So you do not need to worry." Ms. Sivard tapped her nail again. "As for you, you will spend the day here. Tonight I will give you instructions for finding Wilson a second time. After that, you will not come to me again. Blake will make contact with you at regular intervals. I know that you will do everything within your power to keep your connections with Blake discreet, because you must surely be aware of what the Garou will do to you once they know that you are working with us."

Rafferty nodded. Inwardly, he cursed himself. How could he have ever forgotten that she was in just as much danger as himself? How could he have left her ignorant of what he had done? However, Rafferty knew that there was no time left for pondering.

"...Do you wish to call Margaret now?" Ms. Sivard's eyes bored into Rafferty. "You might want to let her know that you will not be seeing her for some time. I am sure you can come up with a plausible explanation."

Rafferty shook his head.

"You do not wish to speak with Margaret?"

"I am not..." Rafferty's voice grew thick. "Very good at lying."

"Very well. You'll have plenty of time to practice." Ms. Sivard smiled and then raised her head to the door, where the driver still stood, motionless. "Odell, please escort Mr. Rafferty back up to his office. He is to remain there until Blake arrives."

Rafferty rose, not thinking now, all his options stripped away. Odell padded after him as he left the office and entered the elevator's chrome maw. The engines hummed as the elevator headed upward, and Rafferty inched around the tiny space, trying to look aimless, his eyes flickering once to the elevator controls as he positioned himself between Odell and the emergency button.

Odell stood, his shoulders slumped, watching Rafferty with bleary eyes. Rafferty stared back, and for just an instant, he felt the same weariness, reminding himself that it had been over twenty-four hours since he had slept. With a shuffle, Rafferty moved forward. Then Rafferty hooked his foot behind Odell's ankle, yanked his foot back and imitated his final move in the duel with Piper, jerking Odell off-balance. As Odell fell, Rafferty lunged forward and stiff-armed the man in the chest, accelerating his fall and smashing his head against the metal frame.

Odell wriggled. Rafferty dropped to his knees and punched his enemy once in the jaw, pounding his head against the frame a second time. Blood oozed from the man's scalp. Rafferty fished through the warm folds of Odell's jacket and found an automatic pistol. The digits above the elevator doors counted upward, approaching Rafferty's floor. Rafferty used the last moments remaining to him to slide the clip halfway from the gun and note that the bullets had silver tips, well-suited for hunting Garou.

When the doors opened, Rafferty left at a sprint, the gun inside his own jacket now. Rafferty loped down the corridor, not stopping to greet the janitor in his gray overalls. Trans-Con did not post guards in its offices. Rafferty made it to the stairs, the door and the street. For an instant, Rafferty wondered if he had acted too hastily, if he should have played along with Ms. Sivard for a while. However, that was the mistake he had made all along — he had let chances slip by.

Rafferty winced, thinking how Margaret might pay for what he had done. But he told himself that if he had not done it, the Garou would have paid for it. Either way, he had blood on his hands. By running away, by acting, Rafferty hoped that he could at least keep his honor clean.

Rafferty sprinted down the street and as his lungs filled with air he felt a burst of exultation, and he dared to hope that, by doing what he was doing, he and the Garou could cheat Ms. Sivard. If there were anyone in the world who could help him save Margaret, it was the Garou of Moonbeam Expeditions, and by showing himself to be a man of bravery, Rafferty hoped he might earn their assistance. However, as Rafferty's feet struck concrete, he knew that life was as hard as the pavement and that his hope was chancy.

The noon sun burned blurry in a hazy sky. Clifford glimpsed the glare of it upon the gray sea as he picked his way back to the Moonbeam Expeditions headquarters on foot. When Rafferty knocked on the door, he received no answer for a moment. Then Wilson's mild voice rolled outward. "Come in."

The door proved unlocked, and Clifford pushed into the room, which appeared far smaller, more cluttered and less mysterious in the light of day. Wilson reclined on the couch, his bare feet propped on one armrest, reading the *San Francisco Chronicle*, the paper folded for easy handling. Blake paced behind the couch, one hand behind his back, the other curled toward his chin in an unnatural position.

Clifford glanced around for other Garou, but his gaze met only the cold blue eyes of Blake.

Blake curled back his lip, which appeared black inside, like the lip of a wolf. "Why are you early, human?"

"Where… where is everyone?" Clifford tore his gaze away from Blake and turned plaintively to Wilson, who had swished his paper down and was now glancing quizzically from Cliff to Blake and back.

"At sea." Wilson gestured with his paper, pointing through the walls, west toward the harbor. "Blake dreamed of the sea—"

"The others are on board the *Beamer*." Blake's voice was low. "If you are interested in joining us, you might do well to, ah, learn more of sailing yourself. If you care to come with me, I will show you." Blake touched his tongue to his lip, and glanced down at Wilson. "I am sorry to disturb you."

"No trouble." Wilson smiled warmly, and looked back to Clifford. "Is all well?"

Clifford shook his head. Ms. Sivard's words echoed in his head. *Forget them — you will not be dealing with those lesser Garou again.* After a moment, Clifford raised his finger, pointing at Blake, and, ignoring the glitter in Blake's eye, repeated the words Ms. Sivard had used. "Spiral Dancer."

Instantly, Wilson went from the couch to his feet, and although his shoulders were skinny with age, he had a fighter's posture. Wilson did not appear angry, but Blake stepped back from his glance.

"That was stupid, human." Within an instant, Blake's voice became a hoarse growl, and he changed into Crinos form all at once, sable fur covering his body, yellow fangs snaggling from his maw, and his eyes turning the dead white of cue balls.

Clifford fumbled the gun with its silver bullets from his pocket, dropped to one knee and fired. However, even as Cliff squeezed the trigger, Blake stepped aside, and then the wolf seemed to fade before Cliff's eyes, his black fur melting into the shadows of the room, with the white eyes blinking out last. Wilson lunged for the door, but it flew open as he arrived, and swung in the wind as the elderly Garou gazed onto the street.

"The ones on the boat..." Clifford stuffed the gun back under his jacket. "It's a set-up. Blake wants them dead."

"Then to their aid we must go swiftly." Wilson did not seem upset, but the wrinkles of his face seemed to tighten a little.

"Can we get to them... on the water?" Cliff glanced back,

torn, thinking of the Garou, but thinking of Margaret too.

"I know not." Wilson lowered his white eyebrows. "But Blake will reach them, yes. If he has to grow gills and ride a fish, he will do it."

At another moment, Cliff might have laughed, but Wilson's expression was entirely serious. Cliff raised his voice one more time, opting for directness. "My wife. They threatened my wife."

"Four Garou upon the sea," Wilson muttered. Clifford could not deny that logic of simple numbers. Clifford followed as the elderly Garou walked through the door and proceeded, still barefoot, into the city.

A brief run took Clifford and Wilson to the harbor. Clifford rowed and Wilson gave directions in the wooden rowboat they had found on the pier. The exertion felt good to Clifford — straining against the oars, he felt only the energy of labor, with no time to worry. *Beamer* idled on the bay, a silvery vessel with the werewolves' moon on its hull, its engine humming over the surf, proceeding in a lazy circle, as if nobody was on board. Stroke, pull, stroke. Wilson pointed, and Clifford saw where to go, how to intercept the moving ship without colliding with it.

For the third time in his life, Clifford saw a werewolf change to Crinos. Wilson balanced on the prow of the boat, his toes curling around the wooden edge and hunched forward, his jaw popping outward, silky gray fur rippling from his arms and legs. The *Beamer* bore down toward their craft. Clifford paddled one oar, edging a bit farther away from the knife-like prow of the ship. The thing which was Wilson took the rowboat's line in its teeth and then vaulted, making the rowboat rock like a hobby-horse, flipping in the air to land upon the deck of the *Beamer*.

The oar flew from Clifford's hand. Immediately, Clifford grasped for his gun. However, no enemy rose from the deck to challenge the intruders, and Wilson dropped a rope ladder for Clifford to climb. As Clifford clambered up, inches from the wet steel of the ship, he could hear a rattle within, an endless crackle, but he could not guess the source of it. An inch of salt water flooded the deck itself, and Clifford thought he glimpsed flecks of pale scum floating upon it.

A half-wolven body lay on the deck, rent by dozens of slashes, trickles of blood turning pale as they diffused into the shallow water. Clifford recognized Piper's klaive in the dead thing's shaggy grip. The crackling sputtered on below. Wilson moved without hesitation to the hatch, and Clifford followed, the gun out and in his hands now, his grip tight.

As the hatch opened, Clifford glimpsed wreckage on the decks below. Ropes, ship's furniture, torn metal of internal walls lay scattered in the half-light of the lower deck, and as Clifford looked on, the debris shifted, stirred by a chain of bone-white links, like the vertebrae of a serpent. The howl of a wolf rose from the lower deck. With that, Wilson slung himself into the hatch, and Clifford followed.

The thing on the lower deck resembled a skeletal eel, its spine as long as a bus, nearly a foot and a half wide, with scraps of tan flesh tight upon its fanged skull. Shadows played within the thing's eye-sockets. As Clifford descended, the eel writhed in the middle of the ship, half-coiled, cornering three wolf-Crinos forms in the prow. A lean Garou and a female whom Cliff took for Wildman and Sadie had, apparently, torn a rack of bunks from the wall, and they wielded the metal frame to keep the eel's fangs at bay.

A howl rang in the steel walls, as if the ship itself was a speaker, and Clifford thought he heard words in the keening. Clifford could not mistake Blake's tone.

Wilson leapt toward the battle, planting a clawed foot on either side of the eel's spine. The elderly Garou seized a vertebra in both hands and wrenched it around like a wheel. With that, Wildman and Blake drove their barricade forward, and Mike sheared flesh from the eel's skull with his klaive. However, the eel did not flinch.

The eel twisted, sank its teeth into Sadie's shoulder, and

bit through with a snap of bone. Clifford saw blood flow, and knew that whatever the sacred immunities of Garou to harm, the eel's fangs had the power to overcome them. Then the eel's bony body buckled in the center, driving up into Wilson's groin, spilling him off. Bone squealed against metal, and the eel's body crackled as it moved.

With five Garou fighting the eel, Clifford moved toward the chanting. The sound seemed to come from another hatch, half-buried in the mess upon the floor. The odor of rust and oil rose from this portal, but Cliff did not hesitate to plunge in, descending into dank shadows.

Cliff guessed that he was in the bottom of the ship, in a space originally intended for carrying fish. Blake's voice rang from every corner in the darkness, and Cliff suspected that he heard laughter mingled with the howling chant. For a moment, Cliff glanced about, searching for Blake's black form in the darkness. Then icy pain raked down his back, followed by a warm trickle. Blake howled, and Cliff slumped downward, seeing the Spiral Dancer hovering over him. Dark fluid dripped from Blake's claw.

Cliff lay on the ground, fumbling in his jacket. Blake bent his knees, elegantly sinking to Cliff's level, raising a single claw over Cliff's eyes. As the Spiral Dancer's howl sank to a low mutter of triumph, Cliff pointed the pistol, still in his jacket, at Blake's foot and fired.

The report echoed in the hull. Blake toppled head over heels with a squeal. Cliff did not give the Spiral Dancer a moment to counterattack. First Cliff rose to one knee, then he took the pistol in both hands, fired three shots into Blake's torso, and moved closer to fire the last five point-blank into his enemy's head. As bullets pulverized Blake's lupine skull, Cliff heard a cascade of objects striking the deck above his head, and then the rattling of the skeletal eel come to an abrupt stop.

Cliff clambered back to the mid-deck again, to see the eel lying inanimate. Wilson lay groaning on the floor. Sadie lay on the ground too, with Mike bent over her, using both paws to apply pressure to her wound. Clifford, however, did not stop. He continued on up the next ladder, his breath coming quickly now. "Margaret." Wilson rose, and, with a limp, followed Cliff up, and Wildman came after him as well.

Evening shadows filled Cliff's house. Margaret's Saab stood in the driveway, next to Cliff's BMW, but Margaret was not inside. Cliff called her name twice to the empty house. Then Wilson, in human form again, took Cliff by the shoulder and led him back to the streets.

"They took her." Clifford put his hands in the pockets of his ruined clothes. "A week ago, maybe we could have planned something together. I guess... I guess I didn't think."

"You thought... of your own heroism, yes, and pathos." Despite the words, Wilson's voice did not contain a single trace of harshness. "Yourself only."

Cliff had expected sympathy, but he did not recoil from Wilson's answer. The two Garou and the human walked back into the city to rejoin their wounded friends.

WAITING FOR
GODDARD

PHILIP NUTMAN

The Grim Reaper was heading straight at us with Godzilla as his copilot as we fish-tailed around the bend onto the wrong side of the road.

Kara shouted a warning, but I was already jerking the wheel — partially fighting the sliding skid which was sending us toward the hard shoulder, and now, in the blink of an eye, to avoid a head-on collision with a Buick filled with death and destruction.

My conscious mind whirled in a high-speed centrifugal spin: The events of the last sixty seconds had thrown the gyroscopic equilibrium induced by the tranquility of the night drive for a loop, both figuratively and literally. One minute we were cruising along trading lines from the movie *Pulp Fiction* and discussing the merits of '60s surf music; the next, two limos stuffed to the gills with Men in

Black had tried to run us off the road and rip us apart with a blizzard of bullets from a pair of MAC 10s. But they were now just so much bruised flesh and ruptured organs by the side of the road three thousand yards back on the start of the bend.

And now, after that party crash, we were about to fuck fenders and kiss it all goodbye in a body slam with a skeleton in a cowl and a big rubber monster.

Life, as I'd discovered thirty-six hours ago when I'd Awakened, could be full of real surprises, and everything I'd been taught to believe in had as much value as a fake Van Gogh.

"*Look—*"

My instinctual mind, my Avatar, spun the wheel —

— and with inches to spare —

we shot past the dark blue Buick, the faces of the freaked-out kids in the back (a Karloff *Frankenstein* monster and a *Plan Nine* Tor Johnson) as clear as day in the strobe of the two cars' head lamps. Both their mouths formed perfect O's of terror, and in that instant I could hear their wails of fear in my mind.

"*—out!*"

The rear tires slid for a heartbeat, then I floored the accelerator of the Geo Metro and sped down the straight incline, not wanting to acknowledge the fact that I'd escaped an assassination attempt at the hands of the Technocracy's footsoldiers only to nearly kill myself, Kara, and a car filled with kids dressed in Halloween costumes.

They blasted their horn in fearful defiance, but the sound was nothing more than a fading whine against the scream of the Geo's engine as the revs touched the red line.

"*Slow down!!*"

"Okay, okay," I muttered, easing my foot back.

We're okay, I heard myself repeating as magickal instinct guided the car forward.

"James, *please*... slow down — oh, God!"

Kara dry-heaved with shock, struggling with the primal instinct to puke.

"We're okay. We're going to be fine," I replied as she stifled another retch.

She succeeded and I dared take my eyes off the road, looking at the woman I was falling in love with, whom I had met only the previous morning. To say Kara Turner looked like the character of Death from the *Sandman* comic book did her a disservice. Sure, the raven mane of hair was the same, as was the cute, oval face with the pale skin, but her beauty was more than Gothchick skin-deep; Kara's allure radiated from within, was transcendent, and, as I was to discover over the coming months, we were Avatar mates.

Within twenty-four hours of the earthquake which had rattled San Francisco, my life had transformed. One day an assistant manager in a hip video store, the next heralded a messiah by mages and hunted by dark forces undreamt of by horror movie hacks.

Which is why we were driving up alongside Interstate 5, about seventy miles from Frisco, heading toward Mount Shasta, near the Oregon border. After narrowly escaping the machinations of the insidious Technocracy and repulsive actions of the eldritch Nephandi, it was obvious we needed a place to hide, to reevaluate what was happening. Instinct — so many of my actions during that infinitesimal period of Awakening had come from a deeper, almost *a priori* understanding — told me we must head north, away from the city of darkness, a city I'd considered home for several years, to seek sanctuary. And somehow I knew Mount Shasta was it. A place renowned for strange phenomena and ravishing natural beauty, I knew now in my new state of consciousness that it was a Mother Node of Quintessence. It was perfect. Perhaps too perfect, too obvious, which was why the Technocracy had the route covered. Now we had to get off the road.

Kara shivered. "Stop... the ca—"

Too late. Before Kara could grab the window handle she heaved a third time and spewed all over the floor, splashing her boots.

I did as she said, braking as gently as possible, which is easier said than done when you're going eighty-five in a fifty-five zone. We passed a sign stating the town of Arbuckle was seven miles ahead before I was able to safely bring the vehicle to a halt on the hard shoulder.

"Sorry," Kara mumbled through her fingers.

I smiled. The British are so unfailingly polite, even in times of maximum stress.

"I think we need to change plans," I said, rubbing Kara's neck with my right hand. "If we try to think-transport away from here, we'll run the risk of a Paradox Backlash. That's too risky."

She half-nodded as she opened the door and stumbled over to a clump of bushes. Besides, we'd already done it once last night and I was still feeling weak from the incredible effort the working demanded. Still, it had been a better option than being consumed by a fomori.

While Kara tried to clean herself up, I sat there and thought things through. Going to Mount Shasta was now out of the question, but we still needed to find a Node to replenish our energies, and somewhere to lie low for a few days. The thought of returning to Frisco didn't thrill me, and I didn't like the idea of hiding in Sacramento. Maybe we should head for Mendocino and find a little town along the coast, I mused. Find a guest house and act like a honeymooning couple for a few days. Still, we had to find a Node. My sudden, rash, and exorbitant use of my newly discovered mage talents had taken its toll, and I was starting to feel achy and mildly feverish, like I was coming down with the flu.

Kara slid back into the car, her usually pale face almost translucent.

"There's a town called Arbuckle a few miles ahead. There

must be a diner or something off the Interstate somewhere. I think we need to chill out, get our heads together and figure this out," I said. "And I need some coffee."

My stomach growled, demanding attention. Since Awakening, I'd had an appetite big enough for two.

"Some food would be good."

"Ugh! Shut up, *please*..." Kara murmured, pressing her fingers to her lips.

I chuckled softly and put the car in gear.

If there's one thing you can always count on in this country, it's finding someplace to eat, and three miles down the road we saw a sign for Herb's Diner, a joint situated half a mile off the main route. Pulling into the parking lot I was relieved to see only two cars and a semi. Herb's was no Jack Rabbit Slim's, but it was an authentic piece of '50s roadside history, a squat, silver-and-neon-topped eatery.

The interior perfectly complemented the outside; as we walked through the door, I smelled the rich aroma of the old red leather seats nestling in the booths, each of which had its own mini jukebox. From across the room I heard the soft sounds of Gene Chandler singing "The Duke of Earl." Even the middle-aged waitress whose name tag proclaimed her as Marge had the right bouffant hairstyle, and the chubby old guy behind the counter sported a perfect grease-backed DA cut. If he lost forty years and dropped fifty pounds, you could imagine him riding with Marlon Brando in *The Wild One*. In fact, with his bloodshot left eye and the bandage on his right cheek, it looked like he'd been in a rumble. Maybe some trucker hadn't liked the cheeseburgers.

"I'm going to the loo," Kara said, tapping my elbow, dispelling my *American Graffiti* reverie.

"What?"

"You know, The Ladies — the restroom?"

I smiled. Kara's Briticisms were often confusing but always charming.

"Okay. You want me to order you something?"

"Just a glass of water."

I nodded and she disappeared through the pink door marked 'Gals' as I picked up a menu from the counter.

"You kids wanta take a booth?" inquired the counter guy — Herb, *the* Herb, according to his name tag. "Marge'll take care of ya'll."

"Thanks," I replied, surveying the room and smiling to myself at his deep Alabama accent.

A trucker seated nearest the door was the one playing Gene Chandler on his juke. Two booths to his right was a balding man in a rumpled brown suit, sipping coffee and smoking Winstons. Everything about him said "traveling salesman." To his right, over in the corner booth, sat a big guy wearing a well-worn denim jacket, a small backpack resting on the seat beside him.

If the diner was classic '50s, then this guy had stepped straight out of the Summer of Love. His thick black hair was long and framed his strong, bearded face. The flaps of his jacket breast pockets were festooned with old buttons: the peace sign, a smiley face, the Woodstock symbol, the Deadhead skull, and other classic counterculture icons. And beneath the jacket he wore a psychedelic tie-dyed shirt. A necklace of Native American beads completed the picture.

He looked up from the small traveler's chess set in front of him and stared at me with dark, deep-set eyes which spoke of things not seen by the light, of mysteries and strange wonders. He picked up his glass of water and sipped slowly, never once taking those black opal eyes off mine. I felt goosebumps creep up my arms and sensed...

Sensed what?

Power. Knowledge. Something ancient, earthly.

It wasn't a bad feeling, just—

"Honey, you gonna stand there like a tree an' put down roots, or you wanta take a seat and have me bring you somethin'?"

I turned to discover the speaker was waitress Marge, still feeling the big guy's eyes upon me.

"Er... um, sure," I replied, sliding over to the nearest booth, looking back at the '60s dude who, without breaking his gaze, lifted a black bishop from the board and captured a white knight. Then he blinked slowly, like a big cat, and dropped his gaze.

I gave an involuntary shudder and turned my attention to the jukebox. It held a good selection: Elvis, Jerry Lee, Danny and the Juniors — "Jailhouse Rock," "Great Balls of Fire," "The Hop." Every one a winner, and at three songs for a quarter, an unbeatable deal. I slipped a coin in the slot and made a selection, then looked over the menu as The Dixie Cups' "Iko, Iko" started to play.

"Garou," Kara whispered as she sat beside me, smelling of soap and scent instead of vomit.

"What?"

"The guy in the corner — he's a werewolf."

Before I could reply, Marge reappeared.

"Ya'll ready for somethin'?"

"Just a glass of water, please," Kara said.

"Mm... a stack of pancakes, french toast, a side order of sausage, and plenty of coffee," I replied.

"You got it," Marge said, cracking her gum before strolling to the counter.

"James... ugh, how can you eat after we almost died back there?" Kara blanched.

I shrugged, noticing the big guy was watching us intently.

"How can you tell our friend over there's a werewolf?" I whispered.

"I met some in Colorado when I was hitching west. Once you've come into contact with even one, you just know," she replied mysteriously and smiled serenely at the watcher.

He smiled back, a warm but commanding expression, and raised his right hand slightly, making a slow patting gesture over the seat.

"He wants us to join him."

Before I could reply, Kara stood and walked over to the corner booth.

In the brief time of my Awakened state, I'd learned many things, much of it from Kara's memories during the periods in which our minds had melded. I knew a little about the other races — that the vampiric Kindred were a constant threat and tended to align themselves with the forces of darkness, and wraiths, too, could be a problem — but other than their existence, I knew nothing about the Garou.

My curiosity aroused and my feelings of discomfort dispelled by Kara's obvious confidence we were in no danger, I slid out of the booth and went to join them.

"Dreamspeakers?" I heard the Garou ask Kara as I approached.

"Orphans," she replied as I sat down.

He grunted softly, clearly amused by her remark, then turned his attention toward me.

"Do you play?"

"I used to," I replied as he pushed the chess board in my direction.

I hadn't played chess since I was eleven. Carl, my best friend in grade school, had been an obsessive and we played together every day for a year. But he was also a whiz and always beat me, no matter how hard I tried, and eventually, humiliated by the constant defeat, I gave up. By the time we turned thirteen, Carl was playing in international tournaments, beating Russian prodigies. I, on the other hand, embraced rock 'n' roll and movies, and our friendship evaporated like water in the desert.

"You start," he insisted.

I hesitated, trying to remember what to do.

"Owen Flaxman," he suddenly announced, taking one of

Kara's hands in his. They were big, plate-sized, the fingers strong, but his touch was delicate and he bowed his head slightly.

I moved a pawn covering a bishop two squares forward.

"Ha!" he laughed softly as Kara introduced herself.

"Not the wisest move," he said, grasping my right hand in his, giving it a firm squeeze.

"James Labac," I informed him, relieved his shake hadn't fractured any bones; his grip was incredibly strong.

Flaxman the Garou moved a pawn from in front of a rook.

"Tell me, child," he said, directing his attention to Kara, "why weren't you afraid of me? Foolish courage or ignorance?"

"I'm sorry?"

"Most of my kind despise or distrust you wizardlings. You are either servants of the Wyrm or fools blindly violating Gaia's beauty — to say nothing of raping our caerns in your hunger for Quintessence."

"Now hold on—" I started to argue, but Marge appeared, announcing her presence by cracking her gum. Flaxman glared up at her, his lips pursed in either irritation or offense at her rudeness.

"There ya go, hon."

She placed my order before me and gave Kara her water.

"Anythin' else for you, handsome?" she asked Flaxman.

"No. Thank you."

"Was that burger rare enough for ya?"

"Yes. Perfect."

He handed her his empty plate, and Marge turned tail with the inevitable crack of her gum, seemingly oblivious to his curt manner.

Owen Flaxman glanced back at the tiny chess board and moved a bishop up into an offensive position, forcing me to move a pawn or lose it.

Kara looked a little hurt by his terse comments.

"I... I met a small pack in Colorado shortly after I Awakened, and... well, they were very nice. They invited me to stay with them, and—"

"That is good," he said, making another move and taking my pawn with a knight. I never saw it coming.

"The younger Garou are tending to communities founded on friendship and objectives rather than tribal bonds. Some say this is an unhealthy sign. I think it is for the best, and harmony between mages — those who cherish the Light — and Garou will become a necessity."

I didn't have a clue what he was talking about.

"Would you mind?" he asked me, then plucked a sausage from my side order and devoured it in a gulp.

"So, if you don't mind me asking, what are you?" Kara inquired in her most polite British way.

He smiled and licked his lips.

Was it my imagination, or did his face change for a second?

He smiled again, a sly lupine expression beneath that beard, and for a moment I saw the Big Bad Wolf about to eat Little Red Riding Hood.

"Don't think in clichés," he said softly as he continued to look at Kara.

She looked at me. I glanced at her. Owen Flaxman looked at both of us, then burst out laughing and slapped us both on the back.

"Oh, you kids," he said, suddenly warm and paternal.

"My dear," Owen Flaxman began, dropping his voice, "I was born Ahroun — under a full moon, which makes me a warrior — into a Sept of Silent Striders."

"Oh, yes, I've heard they tend to be mystics," Kara interjected.

"Correct. And we are prone to wandering. Other tribes consider lone wanders Ronin, but we Striders do not consider that to be an exception. Sometimes we travel in pairs, but many of our tribe prefer a solitary path."

"You mean Ronin, as in the Japanese concept of the masterless samurai?" I asked.

"Yes. An image I like."

"What do you do?" Kara worried her lower lip with her teeth.

He dropped his voice to an almost inaudible level and paused. Then:

"I kill people."

Kara gasped and I nearly choked on a mouthful of pancake.

He lowered his hands under the table and gently touched both of us.

"Fear not," he whispered. "Only those in the employ of the Wyrm. Those who feed off corruption and wound our beloved Gaia."

I swallowed uncomfortably and looked away. The trucker stood by the till, paying his bill. The sad-sack salesman was chainsmoking, lighting a fresh cigarette off a butt.

"And I'm here to kill someone tonight," he added.

As if emphasizing the point, he captured one of my rooks.

Suddenly, I had no desire to continue playing chess with the Garou, and my appetite vanished.

"Your move."

I looked at Kara instead of the board. At that instant the pieces were no longer pieces of carved wood; the board was the world and we were only pawns in the cosmic scheme of things. The black side was the Technocracy, the Nephandi; and Kara and I were the white king and queen. But who was Owen Flaxman?

As if reading my mind, he spoke again.

"We're on the same side, do not worry. And while you are with me, I'll not let anyone—" he looked across the room at the salesman, "—or *anything* harm you."

"But who are you goi—"

"Shh!" he whispered, seeing Kara start to turn her head toward the salesman, who was checking his watch again as he stubbed out a cigarette and signaled more coffee from Marge.

"Yes. He is one who doesn't have much longer to live, but he's not the main reason I'm here. He's just a stooge, a delivery boy. That briefcase contains half a million dollars — a payoff for a disgusting crime against the Earth Mother. No, the one I am waiting for is the perpetrator. A certain vile specimen of humanity called Drew Goddard. But he's a week late, and I worry he knows I am coming for him."

"How?"

He looked deep into my eyes and narrowed his until they were dark slits.

"Goddard murdered one of my brothers — Reynold, my youngest sibling — when he learned of Goddard's plans to pollute the South California coast."

"You mean—"

"Yes," he said firmly, turning his attention to Kara. "Last month's oil spill, that cancerous stain which now coats the coast from Big Sur to Morro Bay, was no accident. And Goddard was responsible."

Owen Flaxman explained it all. How Reynold had been watching Goddard for months and intercepted a top-secret order from one of the most powerful oil companies instructing him to rupture the hold of a rival company's tanker so public outcry would be misdirected. The reason for all this had to do with vast oil and mineral deposits located under the seabed five miles off the coast — deposits so large this company had decided to get its hands on the resources no matter what the cost to the environment. And that price would be great indeed. To mine and refine the earth's treasures efficiently (that meant as inexpensively as possible so they can maximize their greed, Flaxman sneered) would entail the construction of a huge complex between Morro Bay and San Simeon. The impact on the environment would be catastrophic, destroying the Los Padres National Forest in the process.

For some reason, Flaxman continued, Reynold decided to go after Goddard alone. Perhaps it was because time was short and Owen was returning from a trip to the Amazon rain forest. Either way, on arriving in San Diego, Flaxman heard the news about the spill and learned his brother was dead — his throat slit from ear to ear by a silver dagger.

He'd not wasted any time on grieving his brother's loss. There would be time enough for that in the months ahead. Barely containing his rage, Owen had aggressively pursued those responsible, and the apparent suicide of the CEO and the accidental death of the chairman were his handiwork. But before they died, Flaxman forced them to give up the name of the saboteur. Fortunately, he spared us the details of exactly how he'd obtained the information.

"Goddard was scheduled to collect his fee here last week but didn't show," Flaxman said. "I learned that in the event of a missed rendezvous, the bag man returns at the same time each week."

He looked at the clock above the counter. Herb had surrounded it with Halloween items: a large rubber spider sat stuck in the middle of a painted web as a silhouetted witch rode a broomstick beneath the cobweb-coated clock face.

It showed 11:30 P.M. Thirty minutes to the witching hour.

"And I don't think he's going to show," Owen added.

"Closing time, folks," Herb said, suddenly emerging from the kitchen. "Time to go. Better get home before the goblins come out to play."

The bag man looked at his watch, pocketed his cigarettes, and made for the till. He looked tired and pissed off.

"What are you going to do?" Kara asked.

"I am going to follow our friend here," Flaxman replied. He turned to me.

"Did you move?"

I nodded.

"Look at the board."

I saw my error as Flaxman moved his bishop and took my queen. The king was trapped. Checkmate.

"Work on your strategy, Labac. You will need every pound of cunning you can muster in the years to come."

With that, he closed the lid on the set and finished his water.

Marge smiled at us with a will-you-get-a-move-on expression, and we vacated the booth.

After Owen insisted on paying for my meal and Herb took the money, Marge gave us all little bags of chocolate Halloween candies.

"Treats for the road," she said, letting us out the door as Herb called out, "Happy Halloween."

Outside, Kara squeezed my hand. She didn't need to voice the question.

What were we going to do now? We had no plans, no destination anymore. As I turned to ask Owen if he knew of a place to stay, I saw the shape of a figure appear from behind our car, right arm extended, pointing directly at Flaxman. Some deep instinct moved me in front of him, shielding both Owen and Kara.

A soft, sibilant whoosh traveled across the parking lot as a light exploded from the figure's hand, and my chest took a punch from an invisible fist, sending me back into the other two. We fell like dominoes, my eyesight suddenly dimming. But in the instant before the darkness claimed me, I thought I saw Owen's face change....

■

akeup
jamespleaseowencan'tyoudosomething...
he'll ome ound soo...

I wanted to stay in the darkness. It was warm and safe

and snug there. Nothing mattered, just staying in the cocoon of comforting dark, but there were insect noises buzzing in my ears and they wouldn't go away, and for some reason a bull elephant was sitting on my chest and wouldn't get off. Then someone kissed my forehead and I smelled patchouli and it was Kara and I didn't want to be in the darkness anymore I wanted to be with her and—

I opened my eyes and groaned at the sunrise as I squeezed them shut against the glare.

Someone chuckled. A deep, wolfish sound. *Owen.*

I cracked open my eyes and tried to sit up, but the invisible bull elephant was still sitting on my chest.

"Don't move. Another hour and you'll be as good as new," Flaxman said, laying a firm but affectionate hand on my shoulder.

"What happened?"

"You saved my life, James Labac, and for that I will forever be in your debt."

"Huh?" The last thing I remembered was leaving the diner.

"It was a set-up," Kara explained, kissing my forehead again. "Goddard was waiting in the parking lot with a gun loaded with silver bullets."

"And if you hadn't thrown yourself in front of me, we would have all died.

"Do you know the word *giri*?" he continued.

"No."

"It is Japanese and means 'ultimate obligation.' You saved my life, my friend, and now you and I are bound together for eternity. Whatever help you ever need from me, I will be there."

"Well, okay, whatever you say."

I was having a hard time taking it all in.

"Lie there and rest. I will make some herbal tea to give you strength."

Owen stood up and I saw we were in a verdant hollow

somewhere on a hillside. As he walked off toward a copse of trees, Kara answered my next question.

"We're at a Secret Strider caern in Napa. I drove us here while Owen operated on you in the back seat," she explained, stroking my head.

"Now don't ask any more questions. Do as he says and rest."

"But—"

"No 'buts.' Garou are Shamen. And no, I don't know exactly what he did to save your life. It's a secret only the Striders know.

"And, yes, Goddard and the bag man are dead. Owen tore them apart. And I don't want to see anything like that ever again."

Kara kissed my lips to shut me up. I closed my eyes and dreamt of pumpkin orange goblins serving chocolate pancakes in a diner.

We stayed in the hollow for the remainder of the day, drinking a potent tea, the ingredients of which Owen refused to divulge, and watching gossamer clouds drift across an azure fall sky. No one said much; Owen was silent in memory of Reynold, and we were quiet in respect of his feelings. Finally, as night's curtain began to close around us, Owen gave us parting words of guidance. Kara had explained everything while she and our new friend nursed me through the night: my Awakening and the Technocracy's attempt at kidnapping and/or assassination; our narrow escape from the fomori the Nephandi had sent to Art Baisden's apartment. Art, my former friend who had triggered my Awakening and betrayed me, and who was now dead at the Technocracy's hands.

"Go south," Owen said. "Return to San Francisco. The Technocrats and their minions won't expect you back there so soon. This will help."

He handed me two thick envelopes.

"What's this?"

"$50,000. It will buy you anonymity, and that you will need in abundance. Hide your magickal talents, but learn all you can and grow strong. We will all need strength in the times ahead.

"And this, Kara, I entrust to you."

He fished under his tie-dyed shirt, producing a leather thong holding a wolf's tooth engraved with runic symbols, which he hung around her neck.

"If you need me, hold it up to the moon and say my name. I will find you."

Then Owen Flaxman turned away from the setting sun and walked into the deepening twilight to mourn alone.